This book belongs to

....

....

The Hound of the Baskervilles
and other stories

This volume contains two of the greatest Sherlock Holmes novels penned by Sir Arthur Conan Doyle, together with six of his other shorter classic tales.

The Hound of the Baskervilles is the classic detective chiller. The Baskerville family is haunted by a phantom beast which roams the mist-enshrouded wilds of Dartmoor. Now the hound seems to be stalking the young Sir Henry, new heir to the Baskerville estate. Is this devilish spectre the manifestation of the family curse? Or is Sir Henry the victim of a vile and scheming murderer? Only Sherlock Holmes can solve the mystery.

The Sign of the Four, the second Holmes novel, presents the detective with one of his greatest challenges – solving the theft of the great Agra treasure in India.

A Scandal in Bohemia was the first Holmes short story and introduces Irene Adler. It was published in June 1891.

The Red-Headed League, Doyle's second most favorite Holmes story, was published in August 1891.

The Five Orange Pips, one of only two short stories where Holmes' client dies, was published in November 1891.

The Man with the Twisted Lip, Doyle's sixteenth favorite Holmes story, was published in December 1891.

The Blue Carbuncle, a near priceless gem, was published in January 1892.

Silver Blaze, containing the phrase 'the curious incident of the dog in the night-time', is about a racehorse and was published in February 1892.

All the above short stories first appeared in *Strand Magazine*.

The Hound of the Baskervilles

and other stories

➤❋◄

ARTHUR CONAN DOYLE

WORTH
PRESS

SIGNATURE CLASSICS

First published in 2017 by Worth Press Ltd, Bath, England
Email: worthpress@btconnect.com

Concept, design, introduction, reset text and colored images of this edition
© Worth Press Ltd, 2017

British Library Cataloguing in Publication Data
A catalogue record for this book is available from the British Library

ISBN: 978-1-84931-138-0

10 9 8 7 6 5 4 3 2 1

Publisher's Note   Every effort has been made to ensure the accuracy of the information presented in this book. The publisher will not assume liability for damages caused by inaccuracies in the data and makes no warranty whatsoever expressed or implied. The publisher welcomes comments and corrections from readers, emailed to worthpress@btconnect.com, which will be considered for incorporation in future editions. Every effort has been made to trace copyright holders and seek permission to use illustrative and other material. The publisher wishes to apologize for any inadvertent errors or omissions and would be glad to rectify these in future editions.

The images used in this book come from either the public domain or from the public commons unless otherwise stated.

Page Resetting: John Button
Illustrations: Colored by Barbara Frith
Cover Design: Jess Moon

Printed and bound in China

Contents

Sherlock Holmes

Figures in a Landscape

David Sinclair

'Perhaps no fiction character ever created has become so charmingly real to his readers as Sherlock Holmes.' The words are those of Christopher Morley, founder in 1934 of America's premier Sherlock Holmes appreciation society, the Baker Street Irregulars – named after the group of street urchins referred to thus and employed by Holmes in *The Sign of the Four*. 'The whole Sherlock Holmes saga,' Morley continued, 'is a triumphant illustration of art's supremacy over life.' And yet that is not the whole story behind the extraordinary interest of successive generations of readers in the adventures of the world's most famous detective, an interest that shows no sign of waning with the passage of time. What Morley failed fully to appreciate was that Sherlock Holmes was not the result of mere artifice on the part of Arthur Conan Doyle. He and his chronicler Dr Watson were in many respects as real as so many of their followers have believed.

Conan Doyle himself commented, 'A man cannot spin a character out of his own inner consciousness and make it really lifelike unless he has the possibilities of that character within himself.' To which the author's son, Adrian, later added: 'More than the possibilities were here ... Sherlock Holmes *was* Sir Arthur Conan Doyle.'

Introducing a radio adaptation of one of Holmes's best-known cases, 'The Adventure of the Speckled Band', for the BBC Home Service in 1945, Adrian Conan Doyle revealed that his father had much in common with his great detective:

> Many cases that baffled the police were brought to him and I can re-call no single instance in which my father failed to solve the problem. He proved the innocence of a man convicted of murder – Holmes himself had no more difficult test. When a difficult case demanded the utmost from his powers of perception and deduction, he would,

like Holmes, retire into his curtained and silent study for two or three days on end. As for those powers, I have never known his equal.

Adrian recalled his father's habit in restaurants of quietly speculating 'as to the characters, professions and other idiosyncrasies of our fellow diners, all quite hidden from my eyes', and that 'the accuracy of the deductions proved to be absolutely startling.' Holmes's iconic curved pipe and the famous dressing gown came from Conan Doyle, too, and in his own work as a detective the author received death threats just as his finest character did – 'one from an outwardly respectable person, in the best Sherlock tradition, and the other from a man he had landed behind bars', according to Adrian.

Of course, it was not as simple as that. Conan Doyle knew that in order to capture the imagination of readers his creation had to be not only lifelike but also larger than life, and to that end he borrowed characteristics from other people he knew. The most famous of these, as the author acknowledged, was Dr Joseph Bell, professor of surgery at Edinburgh University, for whom Doyle worked as a medical student in the 1870s.

It was from Bell that Holmes's physical appearance was derived: lean and dark, with piercing grey eyes and a nose like the beak of a hawk. The doctor also provided the model for the detective's rather theatrical delivery of his observations and deductions. Bell enjoyed astonishing his colleagues and students by correctly diagnosing patients before they had described their symptoms, and by identifying their occupations and characteristics. As an example of the technique, Doyle remembered Bell announcing that a new patient was a non-commissioned officer recently discharged from a Scottish regiment stationed in Barbados. 'You see, gentlemen,' the professor explained to his students, 'the man was respectful but did not remove his hat. They do not in the army, but he would have learned civilian ways had he been long discharged. He has an air of authority and is obviously Scottish. As to Barbados, his complaint is elephantiasis, which is West Indian and not British.'

Holmes performs a similar demonstration at his very first appearance in *A Study in Scarlet* when, upon meeting Watson, he observes, 'You have been in Afghanistan, I perceive.' It is only later that he reveals, Bell-like, how he arrived at his conclusion: 'Here is a gentleman of a medical type, but with the air of a military man. Clearly an army doctor, then. He has just come from the tropics, for his face is dark, and that is not the natural tint of his skin, for his wrists are fair. He has undergone hardship and sickness, as his haggard face says clearly. His left arm has been injured. He holds it in a stiff and unnatural manner. Where in the tropics could and English army doctor have seen much hardship and got his arm wounded? Clearly in Afghanistan. The whole train of thought did not occupy a second. I then remarked that you came from Afghanistan and you were astonished.'

Such expositions were to become central to the legend of Sherlock Holmes, but of equal importance to his undying appeal are his eccentricities. These, too, were drawn from Doyle's own experience and observation of character. Holmes's mercurial moods and restless energy, his almost manic displays of physical strength and agility, his obsessive dedication to arcane experiment and interest in invention – these were all traits found in Doyle's university friend and sometime medical partner Dr George Budd, a man of alarming peculiarities.

A direct link to Budd is clearly indicated when Watson pictures Holmes 'in one of his queer humours', sitting in an armchair 'with his hair-trigger and a hundred Boxer cartridges', and proceeding to 'adorn the opposite wall with a patriotic V.R. done in bullet-pocks.' Years earlier, Doyle had watched George Budd firing Boxer bullets into the wall of a room in his house as he experimented with a magnetic defence system for warships.

In considering the lifelike qualities of Sherlock Holmes that have made him the most famous detective in the world, we should not overlook the same attributes in Dr John H. Watson MD, whose memoirs of his friend created such fame. Here it is evident that other aspects of Conan Doyle's personality were revealed when he sat down to write those 'memoirs'.

Watson has none of Holmes's idiosyncrasies and seems eminently well-balanced, subject only to mild bursts of irritation at his friend's displays of impatience or insensitivity, including on occasion Holmes's violin-playing. Kind, considerate towards others and generous, with an innate thirst for adventure, he is a thoroughly good chap, solid and dependable. Those are all traits we can see in his creator. As Graham Greene observed, 'It isn't easy for an author to remain a pleasant human being: both success and failure are usually of a crippling kind ... a human being has seldom stood up so well to such a test of freedom as Doyle did ... unlike most great writers, he remained so honest and pleasant a man.'

It goes without saying that it was necessary to portray Watson as less intelligent than Doyle himself in order to show off Holmes's powers to the full. Yet in the doctor's charming naivety and romantic leanings, in his willingness to believe what he sees, there is much of his inventor. Obviously it is no coincidence that both were medical men, and there is a suggestion that Watson might also have been Scottish by birth and English by adoption, as Doyle was. In *A Study in Scarlet* Watson notes that 'I had neither kith nor kin in England', while in the early part of *The Sign of the Four* he reveals that his elder brother has recently died. Can we not assume, then, that such kith and kin as he had were somewhere in the British Isles other than England? That the good doctor was anything but British is not worthy of consideration. In this context, it is interesting to note than in the 1945 radio play referred to earlier Watson was played by the noted Scottish actor Finlay Currie, with a light accent such as Doyle had.

'There was,' writes Doyle's biographer Hesketh Pearson, 'enough of Doyle in Watson for us to look no further for a model. He frequently and unconsciously pictured himself in the character.' As examples, Pearson quoted a number of the comments on Watson's character that Doyle put into the mouth of Holmes:

> 'Your fatal habit of looking at everything from the point of view of a story instead of a scientific exercise has ruined what might have been an instructive and even classical series of demonstrations' ... 'My dear Watson, your instinct is always to do something energetic' ... 'Watson, you are a British jury, and I never met a man who was more eminently fitted to represent one'. This was surely Doyle describing the side of his own character that was *not* Sherlock Holmes.

So I think we may take Christopher Morley's assessment a little farther and assert that Holmes – and, indeed, Watson – have become so charmingly real to their readers precisely because the reality with which Doyle imbued them was not solely that of the imagination, but a compilation of genuine human characteristics that the author found in himself and people around him.

Would two such distinctive and empathetic characters alone have been sufficient to provoke and sustain the cult of Sherlock Holmes, which crossed frontiers and cultures to become a worldwide phenomenon? I rather doubt it. There are arguably equally great characters in detective fiction – Poirot, Maigret, Marlowe – who have become famous for solving mysteries more complex than anything that confronted Holmes, yet none of their stories has either achieved the same legendary status or attracted such a variety of 'scholarship' and societies dedicated to their celebration. Arthur Conan Doyle must have done something more to place the Sherlock Holmes novels and short stories in a league of their own.

His unique skill was to apply the same skills he used in fashioning his heroes to describing the world in which they lived, so that it became as real to his readers as they are. I can think of only one writer of detective fiction who comes close to Conan Doyle in laying out the backgrounds of his cases so tersely and vividly, and that is Georges Simenon. The creator of Maigret places his audience firmly in the cities, suburbs and outer reaches of France in the 1930s and 1950s just as Doyle makes his readers walk the streets of Victorian London, or tramp across the wilderness of Dartmoor.

Doyle's method, as with his characters, was to draw his landscapes from life, and to rely as far as possible on his own experience and observation. He did it with a magnificent brevity which Graham Greene considered poetic, which heightens the sense of being there because the detail is often of the sort that a witness might absorb within a few moments. Sometimes he identified locations exactly as they really were; on other occasions he played little games by renaming streets and buildings but offering clues to their actual identities.

For example, in *The Hound of the Baskervilles*, Watson records Sir Henry Baskerville as staying at a real hotel behind Charing Cross station on his first visit to London. This was the relatively modest Northumberland Hotel, an odd choice for the wealthy baronet when there were more suitable establishments just a few yards away. Doyle emphasises this by having Holmes look at the guest list – 'One was Theophilus Johnson and family, of Newcastle; the other Mrs Oldmore and maid, of High Lodge, Alton', indicating the soul of ambitious provincial respectability rather than metropolitan luxury. He also has Watson describe the lunch they had at the Northumberland as 'pleasant', such faint praise putting it firmly in its place. All this serves to add to the realistic elements of the story, since the hotel had been booked not by Sir Henry himself or his travel agent, but by his impecunious doctor friend who had evidently known the place when working at Charing Cross Hospital.

Yet when describing the nearby hotel where the villain of the piece stayed as he followed Sir Henry, Doyle identified its location accurately as Craven Street, but chose not to use the names of any of the four private hotels in that street and instead made it the fictitious Mexborough, leaving the London readers of the *Strand Magazine* to speculate. While he was anxious to locate the establishment somewhere recognisable, he perhaps felt that the owners of real hotels, such as the Craven and Warner's, would be upset to be associated with criminally-minded guests. This mixture of fact and fiction gives the Holmes stories the irresistible aura of a real world that has added considerably to their longevity. Even today, our notions of what late-Victorian England was like are moderated by Doyle's masterly evocation, and this is likely to be the case far into the future.

It is not simply London that shines through the pages of the Sherlock Holmes novels and short stories. In *The Hound of the Baskervilles* Doyle allows us accompany him as the train glides out of the station *en route* for Devonshire: 'The journey was a swift and pleasant one ... In a very few hours the brown earth had become ruddy, the brick had changed to granite, and red cows grazed in well-hedged fields where the lush grasses and more luxuriant vegetation spoke of a richer, if damper climate.' When they arrived at their destination, 'Rolling pasture lands curved upward on either side of us, and old gabled houses peeped out from amid the thick green foliage, but behind the peaceful and sunlit countryside there rose ever, dark against the evening sky, the long, gloomy curve of the moor, broken by the jagged and sinister hills.'

We can see it, we can smell it and we can sense the nagging uneasiness which increases as 'The wagonette swung round into a side road, and we curved upward through deep lanes ... high banks on either side heavy with dripping moss and fleshy hart's-tongue ferns ... to me a tinge of melancholy lay upon the countryside ... yellow leaves carpeted the lanes ... The rattle of our wheels died away as we drove through drifts of rotting vegetation ... '

Such description is the result of keen observation. Doyle had been there, or somewhere very like it, and recreated the scene so neatly and so skilfully as to give the reader the impression of seeing it all for the first time, however often the story is read. Similarly, Doyle's picture of Baskerville Hall has the stamp of actuality. 'The whole front was draped in ivy, with a patch clipped bare here and there where a window or a coat of arms broke through the dark veil ... twin towers, ancient, crenellated, and pierced with many loopholes ... more modern wings of black granite ... heavy mullioned windows ... high chimneys.' It is the very model of Doyle's old school, Stonyhurst, which he attended before it was substantially extended and modernised, though for atmosphere the author had added elements of Cromer Hall in Norfolk, which he had visited.

Doyle's commitment to endowing the backgrounds of his Sherlock Holmes stories with unarguable verisimilitude was present from the start. In *A Study in Scarlet*, published in 1887, he takes us not only to Bart's Hospital but also to the well-known Holborn Restaurant and the even more famous Criterion Bar, which is still to be found at Piccadilly Circus. When Holmes and Watson agree to share rooms, they are in the instantly identifiable Baker Street, while Brixton, Kennington, Camberwell, Peckham and Euston also feature in the mystery. All would have become familiar to Doyle during a year he had spent wandering about London when unemployed and living with relatives in Maida Vale.

The American back-story, by contrast, must have been the result of detailed research. Although Doyle had travelled extensively as a ship's surgeon, he had at that time only read about America. The confidence and authority of his portrait is striking – his ambition, after all, was to be a serious historical novelist – but it does not bear comparison with the American section of *The Valley of Fear,* published in 1914, which he wrote on the basis of first-hand experience.

In the meantime, Doyle had honed his technique of topographical authenticity on the Holmes short stories, but for me his *tour de force* in this respect is the second of the novels, *The Sign of the Four*, published in 1890, before any of the tales upon which the legend of Sherlock Holmes was founded. Here is the Doyle method of drawing his readers into the scenes of the action in all its glory.

It starts with a drive along the Strand to the Lyceum Theatre: 'It was a September evening and not yet seven o'clock, but the day had been a dreary one, and a dense drizzly fog lay low upon the great city. Mud-coloured clouds drooped sadly over the muddy streets. Down the Strand the lamps were but misty splotches of diffused light which threw a feeble circular glimmer upon the slimy pavement. The yellow glare from the shop-windows streamed out into the steamy, vapourous air and threw a murky, shifting radiance across the crowded thoroughfare.' Those few short sentences served to bring the city alive to contemporary readers and to fix it indelibly in the imagination of generations to come.

From the rendezvous at the Lyceum, we embark on what must be one of the most remarkable and detailed journeys in fiction. 'Sherlock Holmes ... muttered the names as the cab rattled through squares and in and out by tortuous by-streets. "Rochester Row," said he. "Now Vincent Square. Now we come out on the Vauxhall Bridge Road. We are making for the Surrey side apparently ... Wordsworth Road. Priory Road. Lark Hall Lane. Stockwell Place. Robert Street. Cold Harbour Lane."' This is a real journey, much the same today as it would have been then, except that some printer must have misread Doyle's handwriting and put 'Wordsworth Road' where Wandsworth Road should have been. At the end of it we are in Camberwell and we know just what the 'questionable and forbidding neighbourhood' was like in those days: 'Long lines of dull brick houses were only relieved by the coarse glare and tawdry brilliance of public houses at the corner. Then came rows of two-storied villas, each with a fronting of miniature garden, and then again interminable lines of new, staring brick buildings – the monster tentacles which the giant city was throwing out into the country.'

That is only the beginning. From Camberwell, the story moves to suburban Norwood, where Conan Doyle would live himself for a time, then Holmes and Watson retrace the journey on foot all the way back to Kennington, with a diversion via the White Swan tavern (which Doyle calls the White Eagle) in Nine Elms, and on to the Thames in Lambeth – each turn of the route minutely described. It is almost like an A–Z guide to south London, and the reader cannot help but follow it breathlessly. Crossing the river, we move through Westminster and so back to Baker Street, where there is a brief rest for further investigation before we find ourselves noting landmarks along the river as we hurtle eastward aboard a police launch in the most exciting finale of any of Holmes's cases.

'Genius,' wrote another great Victorian, Thomas Carlyle, 'means transcendent capacity of taking trouble, first of all.' Arthur Conan Doyle, in the depiction of both his characters and the world they inhabited, took infinite trouble to observe, to note and to recreate what he had absorbed in the most convincing way possible. We are still happily reaping the fruits of his genius; still seduced into believing, if only for a moment, in the reality of his creation.

Nature and Spirit in *The Hound of the Baskervilles*

Caroline Dalzell

The Hound of the Baskervilles is one of the most famous Sherlock Holmes mysteries. A dark and gripping tale of a spectral hound that plagues the Baskerville family, *The Hound of the Baskervilles* is alive with drama, tension and surprises. Uncertainty abounds as we witness Holmes undertake his greatest challenge yet: his fight against the irrational and the unknown. Nature and spirit are two of the key themes in this novel as they enable Conan Doyle to address important issues including the place of science, nature, and the evolution, influences and rationality of the human mind. Nature and spirit take many guises in the book but ultimately focus on the rational and irrational: the scientific and the supernatural. The main themes are shown to be transient, influential and ultimately, inseparable.

The Hound of the Baskervilles has mystery at its heart. This is encapsulated by its very inception, being written eight years after the great sleuth had seemingly plunged to his 'death' in *The Final Problem* (1893). Conan Doyle had wanted to kill off his most famous creation. However, he was forced to revive Holmes in the wake of public and agent outcries, and does so in 1901 with this book. It could be argued that the fact that *The Hound of the Baskervilles* is set in 1889 – twelve years earlier than it was written and preceding both Holmes's death in *The Final Problem* and his coming 'back to life' in *The Adventure of the Empty House* (1903) – enhances the air of suspense and uncertainty which are trademarks of this great novel.

Even the document at the novel's centre, which details the terrible family legend, dated 1742 and written by a descendant of Sir Hugo Baskerville, is shrouded in obscurity. Although we know it heralds from the mid-seventeenth century because we are told it is from 'the time of the Great Rebellion', there is no preciseness to its origin. The only certainty is that the Baskerville family has been cursed because Sir Hugo Baskerville's wicked deed unleashed the 'hell-hound' of legend.

This constant battle between what is and what is not certain or rational, plays particularly in the ultimate fight between the power of nature and the power of spirit. This is demonstrated early on in the book, when Sir Henry Baskerville arrives in London soon after his uncle, Sir Charles's death. He has been living in Canada, away from the family legend and its melancholy setting. Upon hearing the dark legend, as read by Dr Mortimer, Sir Henry jokingly refers to the curse as 'the pet story of the family' and one that he'd never taken seriously before.

This jovial take on his dark family history emphasises that the spirit, the supernatural, only really penetrates when the setting, nature, is right. As the tale unfolds, it becomes clear that the moor has a great effect on people's perceptions and Sir Henry is soon saying to Watson one night in Devon, ' ... it was one thing to laugh about it in London, and it is another to stand out here in the darkness of the moor and to hear such a cry as that ... ' (Chapter 9). He talks about his uncle, Sir Charles's death and that it all begins to 'fit together'. The bleak and haunting nature of the moors penetrates his character and changes his opinion of what happened to his uncle from one of 'natural causes' to thinking the 'hell-hound' may be real after all. Watson also feels the force of nature. Although he would not be drawn to believe in any supernatural elements in London, he describes Baskerville Hall as glimmering 'like a ghost' when he first arrives there with Sir Henry. Perched on the edge of the treacherous moorland, the Hall takes on a ghostly appearance. Later on in his stay, Watson mentions the influence of bleak countryside more directly: 'The longer one stays here, the more does the spirit of the moor sink into one's soul, its vastness, and also its grim charm.' (Chapter 8).

The stark contrast between the sophistication of London and the wilderness of the Devon moors is emphasised even before Sir Henry and Watson travel to Baskerville Hall. For example, the warning letter Sir Henry receives upon first arriving in London contains words cut from a recent article in *The Times* – with the exception of the word 'moor'. This had been added by hand because it is so infrequently used in *The Times*, creating the impression that the worlds of London and Dartmoor very rarely collide and have little in common.

The moor is portrayed as having a character of its own. It is alive and dangerous; unlike anywhere else. Even nature is very specific to the moor. There are moor ponies which, despite their lengthy history in this environment, are still adapting to the harshness and are shown to 'wander' into the Grimpen Mire. The moor seems to pulse with danger, claiming victims both present and past. The Grimpen Mire 'means death to man or beast' if a false step is taken. There are 'great circular rings of stone' where prehistoric man used to live and it is this vast expanse which adds to the moor's intimidating presence. The naturalist, Stapleton describes the moor as having a frightening beauty: 'It is so vast, and so barren, and so mysterious.' (Chapter 7). Watson, however, is clearly overawed by the moor's 'undulating downs, long green rollers, with crests of jagged granite foaming up into fantastic surges'. The guttural 'uh', oh', 'eh' and 'ah' sounds extenuate the severity of the landscape and echo its terrible influence.

Natural elements on the moor appear to be alive too. This is dramatically conveyed by Watson in the moments before he, Holmes and Lestrade face the hell-hound in the book's climax: 'There was a thin, crisp, continuous patter from somewhere in the heart of that crawling bank. The cloud was within fifty yards of where we lay, and we glared at it, all three, uncertain what horror was about to break from the heart of it.' (Chapter 14). The word 'heart' is used twice in quick succession, emphasising both the pulsating nature of the moors and the undoubtedly quickened pace of Watson's own vital organ, pumping furiously in anticipation of the hound.

Against this backdrop of the natural world influencing and altering previously rational perceptions, the more scientific side of the hound legend plays against, with and for this concept. The early twentieth century, when this book was penned, was a time of radical change. Science was advancing quickly and the previously condemned works by Charles Darwin and his contemporaries were beginning to conquer the backlash from the Church and gain widely acclaimed respect. As a trained doctor of sharp intellect, it was only natural Conan Doyle would keenly follow scientific developments. As James Kissane and John M. Kissane wrote in their 1963 essay entitled *Sherlock Holmes and the Ritual of Reason*, ' ... what *The Hound of the Baskervilles* almost uniquely presents is the hero-detective acting specifically as the champion of empirical science, facing its crucial challenge, the challenge of the seemingly supernatural ... '

From the opening scene, we are presented with the theme of supernatural behaviour which turns out to have a perfectly rational explanation. As Dr Watson studies the stick the previous night's visitor had left behind, he is startled when Holmes asks him what he makes of it: 'How did you know what I was doing? I believe you have eyes in the back of your head.' Holmes's reply swiftly solves the mystery: 'I have, at least, a well-polished, silver-plated coffee-pot in front of me.' In this minor example, Holmes's ability to elucidate the situation is emphasised from the outset.

When Sir Henry receives the letter warning him to keep away from the moor, both he and Dr Mortimer are puzzled how it could be addressed to the Northumberland Hotel, London, as he only arrived in the city that morning. Holmes likens his ability to get to the root of the mystery so quickly, by drawing a parallel with Dr Mortimer's work, asking him: 'I presume, doctor, that you could tell the skull of a Negro from that of an Esquimaux?' (Chapter 4). He describes the art of spotting the different newspapers' leaders in a scientific manner, emphasising the practical benefits of logic. Before too long, Holmes has ascertained that Sir Henry and Dr Mortimer had been followed since their arrival in London, hence the hotel was known, and quickly establishes the words in the letter, bar 'moor', were cut from the previous day's copy of *The Times*.

Sir Henry's missing boots are further examples of when Holmes utilises his 'scientific imagination' to shed light on the matter. The new tan boot, which was taken after being placed outside the hotel door, is soon returned. As Holmes comments prior to its return, 'It seems a singularly useless thing to steal', and he is shown to be right. We soon realise the reason this new and never-worn boot is returned, and the old black boot is taken instead, is because Stapleton is using them to train the hound to track Sir Henry's scent. A brand new boot which Sir Henry has never worn is 'useless'.

Similarly, the mystery of how the escaped convict Selden is able to survive on the bleak and cruel moors for so long is cleared up by the rational explanation that he was receiving human help from his sister, Mrs Barrymore and her husband Mr Barrymore. They had been smuggling food out to him nightly, along with castoffs from Sir Henry – which also explains why the hound went after Selden on that fateful night, thinking it was the baronet, and frightened him into falling to his death. A recurring theme throughout *The Hound of the Baskervilles*, the hand of man is often shown to be behind the cause of a seemingly supernatural occurrence. It is also man – in the case of Selden's helpers being discovered, Watson and Sir Henry; and with Selden's fall to his death due to the castoffs he is wearing, Holmes and Watson – who uses the power of deduction to ascertain the human culprit.

This enlightenment of dark and uncertain events through the use of logic occurs time and again as the story unravels, and none more so than with the hound of the legend himself. Portrayed as a 'hell-hound', 'luminous', 'ghostly', 'dreadful' – and yet nothing prepares Dr Watson for what he eventually sees: 'Fire burst from its open mouth, its eyes glowed with a smouldering glare, its muzzle and hackles and dewlap were outlined in flickering flame. Never in the delirious dream of a disordered brain could anything more savage, more appalling, more hellish, be conceived ... '

(Chapter 14). Holmes and Watson have soon wielded science against the supernatural being and proven man is at the helm. The abomination of the creature is explained by Watson's announcement upon closer inspection of the 'glowing muzzle', of its being caused by 'phosphorous'. It is this substance which Stapleton added to the simple hound to give him his supernatural nature.

There are reminders throughout the book that this is one of the hardest cases Holmes has been presented with. For example, in Chapter 7, Watson comments: 'Holmes himself has said that no more complex case had come to him in all the long series of his sensational investigations.' The fact it is so baffling only serves to heighten the impressiveness of the swift solution Holmes is able to deliver and, in turn, the importance of science. Furthermore, Watson describes Holmes's actions in medical terms, always shown to be using scientific measures and procedures despite not being a scientist himself: ' … he weighed every particle of evidence, constructed alternative theories, balanced one against the other and made up his mind as to which points were essential and which immaterial.' (Chapter 3).

On the surface, science undoubtedly triumphs in *The Hound of the Baskervilles*. The 'hell-hound', the 'dreadful apparition', is revealed as being just a hound which has been abominated by man. There are definite nods that science cannot provide the answers to everything, however. James Kissane and John M. Kissane discuss Holmes's statement ' … to take on the Father of Evil himself would, perhaps, be too ambitious a task' (Chapter 3), in their 1963 essay entitled *Sherlock Holmes and the Ritual of Reason*. While they acknowledge Holmes is speaking facetiously, the remark and whole exchange with Dr Mortimer presents us with the possibility that 'there may be limits to the ways of reason.'

One of these 'limits' is human nature. Sherlock Holmes ponders issues beyond science and the supernatural in *The Hound of the Baskervilles*. In Lawrence Frank's 1999 essay entitled *The Hound of the Baskervilles, the Man on the Tor, and a Metaphor for the Mind*, he highlights that Holmes considers the implications of human origins. As the 'man upon the tor', Holmes is portrayed as being above the moors: 'He stood with his legs a little separated, his arms folded, his head bowed, as if he were brooding over that enormous wilderness of peat and granite which lay behind him. He might have been the very spirit of that place.' (Chapter 9). Holmes is master of all he surveys, working behind the scenes to solve the mysterious crime. As the 'spirit' of the moor, he is at once linked to the place and surveyor of it, overseeing its vast expanse of physicality and longevity. Frank (1999) calls this image the 'figurative rendering of a generalized evolutionary perspective'. The scene alludes to Darwin's *The Descent of Man* (1871): man is on top 'the very summit of the organic scale' but ultimately linked and with the 'indelible stamp of his lowly origin'.

We see the theme of evolution and the nature of human beings in particular in the two characters that are most at-one with the moor: Stapleton, the naturalist and mastermind criminal, and Selden, the escaped convict. As Holmes closes in on Stapleton, the language used is reminiscent of that used to describe Sir Hugo's crime. Animalistic imagery for Sir Hugo includes 'cage empty' and 'bird escaped', highlighting what a beast he was. Stapleton, as a naturalist, is akin with nature in a cruel way, catching butterflies and moths in a way that 'made him not unlike some huge moth himself'. (Chapter 7). Just as Stapleton views beings as his prey – the creatures of the natural world, his wife Beryl whom he bullies and torments to achieve his end goal, and of course Sir Henry himself – the hunter soon becomes the hunted. The natural world is cruel and it is not long before Holmes is talking about the 'nets' closing in on him, having used his cunning logic. The scene is then set for nature to reclaim him, and he is taken by the Grimpen Mire of 'his' moorland.

When Watson and Sir Henry go after Selden, after hearing that the escaped convict is actually Mrs Barrymore's brother, Watson paints him as having 'an evil yellow face, a terrible animal face, all seamed and scored with vile passions'. (Chapter 9). It is little wonder he can adapt so well to the brutal Devon moorland, which is also the death of him. These two characters are portrayed as the lowest forms of man, with undeveloped emotional capacity. It is fitting on both occasions that they meet a natural grave.

The inherent wickedness of Stapleton is implied by Holmes's observation of the Baskerville family portraits. Holmes deduces that the motive behind Stapleton's crime is natural – he is in fact Roger Baskerville's son and a claimant to the estate. Roger was the 'black sheep of the family' who 'came of the old masterful Baskerville strain, and was the very image ... of the family picture of old Hugo ... ' Roger inherited Hugo's wickedness, his bad genes, and so did his son Stapleton. That he inherited his nature and spirit are stated by Holmes's comment on the likeness of Sir Hugo's portrait to Stapleton: 'Yes, it is an interesting instance of a throwback, which appears to be both physical and spiritual.' (Chapter 13).

Through the link with evolution, we are shown it is not possible to escape human nature, which retains certain mysteries. Given the complexity of humans, it is little wonder that the characters are complex and inconsistent at times. Even Holmes, notorious for scientific precision and calculated reasoning, is shown to have foibles. He has a quasi-respect for Stapleton's 'profession'. Stapleton understands his victims perfectly. For example, he knew that nothing would draw Sir Charles out to the moors at night, except for Mrs Laura Lyons in distress, due to his belief in the family legend. This, combined with the knowledge gained from Dr Mortimer that he had a weak heart, resulted in a fatally effective plan. Similarly with Sir Henry, he uses his 'sister' Beryl to gain his trust and set the trap. Sir Henry was of a different nature to Sir Charles, and Stapleton knew he would not easily scare. Hence he had to be cunning in how he approached him. As Holmes says, ' ... he foresaw that she [Beryl] would be very much more useful to him in the character of a free woman.' (Chapter 12). Post the crime, Holmes says Stapleton carried it out with 'considerable finesse', adding: 'The use of artificial means to make the creature diabolical was a flash of genius upon his part.' When Holmes states: 'A pin, a cork, and a card, and we add him to the Baker Street collection!' (Chapter 13), he actively links himself with Stapleton, 'the naturalist and entomologist who collects rare moths and butterflies' (Frank, 1999). As Frank explains, this is linked to the Darwinian overtones of the novel and the fact the two characters are connected through human nature, with no rational explanation as to why.

An even more intriguing statement from the sleuth is when he announces 'We've laid the family ghost once and for ever.' (Chapter 14). It seems not even he can fail to be drawn into the 'spirit' of the criminal investigation. Furthermore, the logical detective also experiences out-of-body moments in *The Hound of the Baskervilles*, when his 'spirit' hovers over the Ordnance map of Devonshire. This is possibly the first hint of drugs use, emphasised by statements such as 'Sherlock Holmes had, in a very remarkable degree, the power of detaching his mind at will' (Chapter 5). The book does not elaborate, although Conan Doyle's second Holmes novel, *The Sign of the Four*, opens with 'Sherlock Holmes took his bottle from the corner of the mantelpiece and his hypodermic syringe ... he thrust the sharp point home ... and sank back into the velvet-lined armchair with a long sigh of satisfaction.'

Throughout the book it is 'the peasants' who are said to believe in the supernatural hound. Deemed to be closer to nature and less evolved, the implications are that the peasants are unable to utilise science to triumph over the seemingly supernatural elements of nature. It soon transpires, however, that more of the characters believed in the terrible hound than initially thought. Having originally dismissed the legendary Hound of the Baskervilles family legend as of interest 'to a collector of fairy tales', Holmes finds himself 'pale and exultant ... and lips parted in amazement' when faced by the hound. Watson describes the vision: 'A hound it was, an enormous coal-black hound, but not such a hound as mortal eyes have ever seen.' (Chapter 14). Despite one being a doctor and the other an adopter of scientific methods, neither was prepared for the vision that befell them.

As a doctor, Conan Doyle empathised with the pressures that come with such a high profile and key social role. Dr Mortimer in *The Hound of the Baskervilles* explains his reasons for withholding that he'd seen the footprint 'of a gigantic hound' the night of Sir Charles's death': ' ... a man of science shrinks from placing himself in the public position of seeming to endorse a popular superstition.' (Chapter 2). Keenly aware that Holmes is amazed that he, 'a trained man of science, believe[s] it to be supernatural', in his defence, Dr Mortimer states 'that there is some evidence that this may be so'. Proven to be right, this serves to emphasise the complexity of human nature and that science cannot conquer explanations for all happenings.

The characters are complex and, at times, inconsistent in their nature in *The Hound of the Baskervilles*. When you consider the writer, Conan Doyle, there is no wonder at the depths of each creation. So precise and accurate in all he did and thought – much like his most famous creation, Sherlock Holmes – Conan Doyle sought reasons for everything. Having shunned religion early on, Conan Doyle then spent his life feverishly searching for something else and was unwilling to accept that life and death are all there are. He wanted to believe in something beyond this.

With his ever-questioning mind, his conversion to Spiritualism was 'the inescapable outcome of his nature', as one of his earliest biographers Hesketh Pearson wrote in 1930. Conan Doyle was true to himself to the end: Spiritualism was not a whim. Pearson (1930) reports he owned one of the largest libraries of Spiritualist literature in the world and that his conversion to the faith was based on facts alone. It was only after seeing photographs of the Cottingley Fairies that Conan Doyle actually believed in the existence of fairies.

It is fitting that one of the most famous hoaxes that fooled the scientific world, the Piltdown Man of 1912, has a link with Conan Doyle. When scientists discovered fossilised remains in the village of Piltdown near Uckfield in East Sussex, they thought it heralded the link between us and earliest man. It took more than forty years for the scientists to discover the bones were a forgery. Conan Doyle is among the hoaxer suspects and if it was him, he certainly would have demonstrated fallacies in science. Even in 1889, when *The Hound of the Baskervilles* is set, Conan Doyle is beginning to outwardly have doubts in science. In *The Mystery of the Cloomber*, the book ends in Chapter 16 with: 'For what is science? Science is the consensus of opinion of scientific men, and history has shown that it is slow to accept a truth. Science sneered at Newton for twenty years. Science proved mathematically that an iron ship could not swim, and science declared that a steamship could not cross the Atlantic.'

The nature of humans dictates that we follow our beliefs. Conan Doyle believed in evidence first, and commitment to a concept second. He needed evidence for fairies. Likewise, the Piltdown Man scientists needed evidence for the evolution link. It is irrelevant that both sets of evidence proved to be fakes.

Conan Doyle showed throughout his extensive writing career a thorough understanding of science, the supernatural and the flawed nature of man. Much as Holmes sought refuge from his mind through drugs, Conan Doyle found refuge from the torture of science's lack of answers in Spiritualism. This enabled him to rationalise his life, hardships and losses, and die a happy man. Hesketh Pearson (1930) writes that Conan Doyle said on his deathbed: 'I am quite serene and happy. Quite prepared to go or stay, for I know that life and love go on forever.'

Although his conversion to Spiritualism seemed irrational to many of his contemporaries, despite its popularity in the early twentieth century, it was, however, in keeping with his character. All his life he applied logic, summed up neatly by Holmes in *The Hound of the Baskervilles*: 'It is the scientific use of the imagination, but we have always some material basis on which to start our speculations.' Nature and spirit are inseparable; our actions and motives are complex. Influenced by each other, nature and spirit herald an evolutionary history that can only be partially explained by reason. After reading *The Hound of the Baskervilles*, perhaps Conan Doyle and Spiritualism do not seem such an unnatural pairing, after all.

The Sign of the Four

Sherlock Holmes, his method and his mind

Steve Sims

Introduction

While all agree that Sherlock Holmes is the most famous detective in fiction, and arguably the most popular, when we compare his methods with those of the present-day police detective we find that Holmes falls far short of modern standards. Having worked for several years as a frontline CID officer, it is clear to me that by modern standards Sherlock Holmes would fail miserably as a detective. His methodology might match that of the modern crime scene investigator, because in many ways he was ahead of his time in his scientific method of observation and the elimination of suspects in criminal investigation. Where Holmes falls short of modern detective standards is in his ethics and his professional judgment, both of which can be seen as the outcome of a flawed personality.

The Sign of the Four (1890) was the second Sherlock Holmes story written by Arthur Conan Doyle, who became Sir Arthur in 1902 when he was knighted for services to the Boer War. Many regard Sherlock Holmes as one of the greatest literary characters ever portrayed. In Doyle's canon of Sherlock Holmes' works are four novels and 56 stories.

The Sign of the Four involves Sherlock Holmes and his trusted friend Dr John Watson investigating a case of murder, treachery and intrigue surrounding stolen treasure. The story allows Doyle to expand on the detective's character, and introduces the subject of his drug habit. It shows Holmes the man in ways Doyle had not described in the first Sherlock Holmes novel, *A Study in Scarlet*.

The Sign of the Four was first published in the February 1890 *Lippincott's Monthly Magazine*. The story goes that Doyle was commissioned to write the story during a dinner with Oscar Wilde and J. M. Stoddart, an agent for the magazine. Wilde was also commissioned to pen *The Picture of Dorian Gray* at the same dinner, thus making the event notable in literary history. Doyle's novel was published in October 1890 as a book, this time as *The Sign of Four*. No significance is attached to the title change – and since the first edition, the story has been published under both titles.

The Sign of the Four is one of the most popular Sherlock Holmes stories. Translated into many languages, the book is a worldwide best seller and has emerged in many stage, film and TV adaptations over the years – including a Bollywood blockbuster *Neekam* (2005). Novelist Nicholas Meyer also took inspiration from *The Sign of the Four* for his *The Seven-Per-Cent Solution* (1974). The story is a homage to Holmes, in which Sigmund Freud helps Holmes recover from cocaine addiction.

The Sign of the Four is a complex story, and at the very least, a ripping yarn – but looking in to the mind of Sherlock Holmes and his creator, Doyle, throws up a subtext which aficionados of the great detective will continue to debate for years to come.

Investigative style

If Sherlock Holmes was alive today, he would surely be a crime scene investigator – a man of science rather than a brash, fast-punching, shoot-now-ask-questions-later man of action. Holmes says as much himself in the opening pages of *The Sign of the Four*, when he states: 'I examine the data, as an expert, and pronounce a specialist's opinion.' Investigating crime involves methodical work and long hours of painstaking analysis of evidence and the cross-checking of witness statements and alibis. This is work ideally suited to Holmes's character.

Later, Holmes provides one of his most famous quotations. Speaking to Watson, he asks 'How often have I said to you that when you have eliminated the impossible, whatever remains, however improbable, must be the truth?' This truism holds good as well today as when it was written. Many a time a supervising detective has to remind others that their gut feeling, hunch, opinion – or whatever else they might like to call it – does not count. The job of a detective is to follow the evidence, and only the evidence, wherever it may lead.

A detective also requires patience in order to pore over the clues, and a mind that can stand back to observe the larger canvas so as to let a pattern unfold. Holmes certainly has the ability to focus in this way and his attention to detail would make him a good crime scene investigator.

The elimination of one suspect after another, so as to find the real culprit, can take months or years in some cases. The path Holmes was the first to step down as a detective, in striking out the impossible to leave the truth, however improbable, is still one of the principle avenues of detection. Holmes says that whatever is left, however improbable, is the truth, and that is exactly what eliminating suspects down to a single suspect involves. The modern detective cross-references statements from a list of suspects against other witness statements and indisputable known facts, such as forensics, until one remains whose statements do not match those of others.

The police have used a computer system called HOLMES that comprised a database of evidence, such as witness statements, forensics, descriptions of people, and so on, with software that cross-referenced the evidence and produced a list of suspects by pointing out the discrepancies in their answers to questions when compared to those given by other witnesses. It was devised after the 'Yorkshire Ripper' case in response to failures to spot discrepancies in witness statements.

Holmes pronounces himself the last court of appeal in detection. Identifying the villain is one part of a detective's job. The other is gathering and presenting the evidence to gain a conviction in court. I think we can grant our hero a little room for vanity because, as we discover, it is the flaws in Holmes's character that make him the man he is.

Flawed personality

Doyle presents us with Holmes's flawed personality early on in *The Sign of the Four*. From the first line of the first page, we see Holmes as a tormented soul who finds relief from the unbearable pain of being with his seven-per-cent solution of cocaine and immersing himself in detailed studies of the mundane.

Doyle depicts Holmes as a cold, dark and troubled man. In many ways he is an anti-hero and some would find him a dislikeable character if he were real. Psychologists revel in unpicking the strands of the mind that is Sherlock Holmes. Holmes must be one of the few fictional characters who has been the subject of as many, if not more, medical papers as literary criticisms.

Modern psychologists recognise many symptoms of mental disorder submerged in his personality – the diagnoses vary because several conditions have similar symptoms – but some of the conditions for which Holmes shows clear manifestations in his personality include clinical depression, narcissistic personality disorder (NPD) and attention deficit disorder (ADD).

Several clues to Holmes's mental state are laid out in *The Sign of the Four*, and include:

- lack of stimulation by daily routine
- drug abuse
- mood swings
- trouble sustaining friendships or intimate relationships
- a need to seek out high stimulation activities
- taking part in reckless actions without thought of danger to oneself
- having a grandiose sense of self-importance
- having a sense of special entitlement
- lacking empathy
- displaying arrogant attitudes.

Certainly his self-medication with cocaine and morphine is just one among many indicative signs of these disorders.

Conan Doyle, as a medical doctor, may well have kept abreast of developments in medical sciences, including Sigmund Freud's work in the field of psychoanalysis. Freud was becoming well known for his studies at about the time Doyle wrote *The Sign of the Four*, although psychoanalysis was still an infant science. It is surely not unlikely that Conan Doyle knew of Freud's writings and wove that knowledge in to his Sherlock Holmes stories. In order to describe so accurately the signs and symptoms of conditions which were not named until much later in the twentieth century, we can speculate that he may have known someone with these disorders or suffered in some way himself.

Freud did write several papers on the powers of cocaine as an antidepressant, the most well known being *On Coca* (1884), which precedes *The Sign of the Four* by six years. In the 1890s, society had a different view of drugs to the one we hold now. Opiates were freely available from a pharmacy and were not illegal substances, supplied by criminals. To depict Holmes self-medicating in those times would not have had the same resonance as such an act would today for a character of similar status.

Holmes admits that he takes drugs to find refuge from the boredom of day-to-day living, and that he has concocted a protective persona as the world's first and greatest consulting detective to inject some excitement into his bland life. Mood swings are evident in his personality: even Dr Watson, as his friend and confidante, is wary of these moods – only raising his condemnation of Holmes's drug habits when reinforced with Dutch courage from wine with his lunch.

Emotionally, Holmes is cold-hearted – regarding the attractive Miss Morstan impersonally as 'a unit' and not as a woman – and dismisses the idea of sharing his life with a wife because of the distractions marriage might bring to his work as a detective. The work comes first, and he certainly considers himself above the common herd: throughout the story he belittles the talents of Scotland Yard detectives and other contemporary consulting detectives overseas. In a later story, Watson notes, 'sometimes I found myself regarding him as an isolated phenomenon, a brain without a heart, as deficient in human sympathy as he was preeminent in intelligence. His aversion to women and his disinclination to form new friendships were both typical of his unemotional character'.

An assumption of innate superiority is part of the personality of Holmes. Add to that Holmes's clear ability to hyper focus – seen for instance in his monograph *'Upon the Distinction between the Ashes of the Various Tobaccoes'* (sic), an examination of the differences in ash deposits between 140 types of tobacco – and we start to build a picture of a man with a superlative mind but a flawed personality.

Considering another of the signs in our list, the disregard for personal safety, this is exhibited by Holmes throughout the canon and *The Sign of the Four* is no exception.

Fractured story telling

Doyle constructs his story very carefully but has already given the game away to the astute reader in Holmes's first case – *A Study In Scarlet*. 'In solving a problem of this sort, the grand thing is to be able to reason backward. That is a very useful accomplishment, and a very easy one, but people do not practise it much,' Holmes explains to a perplexed Watson.

This paragraph highlights one of the great intellectual accomplishments not only of Sherlock Holmes but also of his creator. Modern readers often overlook the importance of the fact that Doyle uses the device of fractured story telling because this plot device is so common in modern novels, films and TV dramas. Unlike writers such as Dickens, who wrote a straight chronological narrative, Conan Doyle comes in half way through, and reveals the 'back story' in tantalising stages. In this way, Doyle cleverly appears to write his book backwards. He rearranges the chronology of the story to ensure Holmes is set problems he can solve by assessing the already-assembled evidence. In this way, our hero never meets a problem that he cannot resolve. While we are accustomed to writing of this sort, it was very new in its day.

Sometimes, a crack appears in the carefully-wrought plot when Holmes deduces a result that is more a leap in the dark than the result of careful consideration and elimination to leave the only possible answer to his riddle. Let's not forget that although we like to discuss Holmes as though he were a real person, the stories are entertaining fiction, and artistic licence is allowed.

Doyle has another device which he uses to build suspense and maintain the reader's attention: he avoids using the first person. If Holmes had narrated his own stories, we might be privy to his thoughts as the story unfolded and would miss the dramatic surprises in store as we marvel at how he came to his conclusions. With Watson chronicling his investigations, the thought processes of Holmes remain a mystery.

Doyle only reveals to the reader the information needed to move the story on: Watson describes what Holmes is doing and saying but is generally unaware of his companion's reasoning until Holmes chooses to reveal it. Without Watson as narrator, Doyle would have far more trouble in weaving his tales of mystery and maintaining suspense.

So how does fractured story telling work in *The Sign of the Four*? The story starts after Captain Morstan has already gone missing and unravels the events that led up to the point of his disappearance. Then, it is revealed that we are not investigating a disappearance or an abduction, but a continuing intrigue with a past to reveal, a present we are acting out and a future we have yet to see.

Doyle is responsible for some great literary steps forward and this format of fractured story telling is one – where we start in the middle and work backwards as well as forwards to find out the perpetrators of deeds most foul. Another, arguably, is establishing the genre of the reasoning detective. Before Doyle, writers had a story with a beginning, middle and end leading the reader to a conclusion. Now, the reader had to apply some thought as to how the story unfolds and have more involvement in the plot. Doyle is one of the fathers of modern detective mystery thrillers, although some may dispute the honour of being the main progenitor should go to Edgar Allan Poe's C. Auguste Dupin.

Doyle himself modestly defers to Poe when discussing the Dupin stories; he said: 'Each is a root from which a whole literature has developed ... Where was the detective story until Poe breathed the breath of life into it?' Perhaps Doyle is a little coy about his contribution to the genre – Poe did not fully exploit his character in the way that Doyle brought Holmes through his canon of work to his readers.

The gentleman detective ruled supreme until John Buchan raised the stakes with *The Thirty-Nine Steps* (1915) by introducing action man John Hannay – surely the stiff-upper-lipped precursor to James Bond.

Does Holmes have ethics?

Judging by modern standards, it is in the field of ethics that Holmes falls short as a detective. When the newest officer arrives at detective training school, ethics is one of the first subjects for discussion. Everything an officer does has to be framed by professional ethics. One of the main tenets of this code of ethics is that, as a detective, you cannot set yourself up as judge and jury. Your responsibility is to reveal the facts of the matter and then present them before a court.

Whatever the crime, a person's guilt or innocence is a matter for the jury to decide, and Holmes is wrong when he says he is the highest court of appeal in detection, because detection is just one of the many links in the chain of justice. A suspect may have a reason for taking the action that has led them to the steps of the dock, but that does not alter the fact a crime has been committed and that the alleged offender's explanation of his actions is generally viewed as mitigation, not a defence. Holmes is very apt to use his own judgement as to whether to pass on to the police the evidence of crimes which he has detected.

Seen in a modern context, a detective cannot afford to fall short of the highest personal standards when investigating a crime, not least because a failure in ethics presents the defence with a loophole in the case that can lead to a guilty party escaping their rightful punishment. The question is whether Holmes is an impartial defender of justice, or a gentleman detective working for those of his own social class dispensing his own kind of justice.

The Sign of the Four certainly highlights the ethics Holmes displays. The reader has to consider how much reliance to place on judgments and conclusions Holmes makes as a detective with his brain addled by cocaine and morphine.

Holmes goes along with the proposed plan to disburse a treasure obtained by murder – to split the riches, and not to return the gold and gems to their rightful owner in India. An impartial police detective would not take a share of the booty or allow anyone else to do so and would act within the law whatever the social class of those involved in the crime.

Holmes sides with the upper middle class but looks down on the working classes – such as the Baker Street Irregulars; Sherman, the ragged owner of Toby the tracker dog; and steam launch captain Mordechai Smith. Holmes is certainly prepared to benefit from their talents, with no questions asked, and to pay them, but having them in his home is clearly another matter entirely.

Holmes is also walking the line when he tells Thaddeus Sholto that any revelations he cares to make will go no further – without knowing what nefarious deeds the character might admit to. Here we see Holmes taking on the mantle of judge and jury, when he should be open-minded. Sholto mitigates his actions by trying to recompense Miss Morstan against the perceived injustice his brother commits against her, after the death of her father, by stealing her share of the treasure. Holmes works to free Sholto when he is wrongfully arrested for the murder of his brother Bartholomew Sholto, but does nothing about Thaddeus Sholto's involvement in his handling of stolen goods.

Central to the story is the character of Jonathan Small. All the events in *The Sign of the Four* are in some way connected to Small – from the original murder that we eventually discover started the story, to the subsequent murders and loss of the treasure. Doyle has to have Small admit his wrongdoing and to implicate others. If he didn't, no one would know he was an escaped convict, self-confessed murderer, thief and conspirator with other convicts. The repulsive Small seeks revenge against Miss Morstan's father and Major John Sholto, who unjustly stole his treasure while leaving him to rot in a prison overseas. Doyle has not clearly thought through Small's motivation. Greed and honour among thieves are put forward as his driving forces, but Small left his cronies to languish in jail when a chance for them all to escape arose.

Again, Holmes behaves as judge and jury when assuring Small that he can prove he did not kill Bartholomew Sholto. Certainly Holmes seems light on knowledge of the law, even as it existed at the time, but worse, he exhibits the 'god complex' persona of what we would now call narcissistic personality disorder. He puts himself in the role of arbiter of right and wrong and who will and will not receive punishment.

Did the events in *The Sign of the Four* really happen?

The story begins with Holmes injecting cocaine and ends with the suggestion that he is returning to a drug-induced slumber. Is Doyle trying to say that this story is all a product of Holmes's troubled mind, with cocaine surging through his veins to enhance his visions? Holmes has a compromised view of reality as a result of his drug use; to what extent this affects his sense of reality we can only judge from the way Doyle mentions the needle marks on Holmes's arm and Watson's observations that he is more than a casual drug user.

As readers, we must decide whether *The Sign of the Four* is indeed a drug-induced fantasy interweaved with characters, memory fragments and hallucinations. The conclusions we draw do not change the fact that this is an intriguing and absorbing mystery thriller. It hardly matters to the story whether it is a figment of Holmes's imagination or not, but the issue makes us reconsider Doyle's literary style.

All authors of fiction draw on their personal experiences and we know that Doyle, as a physician and as a friend of infamous drug takers like Oscar Wilde, would have a deep knowledge of the effects and dangers of drugs. Nothing in the story is definitive in suggesting this is a fantasy, but one interpretation is that Doyle may have been reaching out to Wilde and others with a warning about abusing drugs.

This interpretation is supported by Doyle's description of the Victorian London of Sherlock Holmes as a city 'besieged by a swirling yellow fog drifting across dun-coloured houses.' Watson reinforces this dream-like vision of London as he rode in a cab from Baker Street to The Lyceum with Holmes and Mrs Morstan: ' ... A dense and drizzly fog lay down low upon the great city. Mud coloured clouds drooped sadly over muddy streets. Down The Strand the lamps were but misty splotches of diffused light, which threw a feeble circular glimmer upon the slimy pavement. The yellow glare from the shop-windows streamed out into the steamy vaporous air, and threw a murky, shifting radiance across the crowded thoroughfare. There was to my mind something eerie and ghost-like in the endless process of faces which flitted across these narrow bars of light – sad faces and glad and haggard and merry. Like all human kind, they flitted from the gloom in to the light, and so back in to the gloom once more.'

Other episodes in *The Sign of the Four* imply a haunted, ethereal cityscape. Let us not forget the curious poison-dart blowing pygmy and the balsamic odour from Sholto's hookah. Both are out of place in Victorian London.

Conclusion

It is a great tribute to Doyle's enduring characterisation of Holmes that critiques of his detection methods and his mental state are possible. It is interesting to compare Holmes with the modern police detective, and fascinating to wonder how much psychiatric medical science was built into the depiction of his character, but only as insights to add enjoyment to the read. Whatever views we take on these matters, we enjoy the story for what it is – a tale of mystery and intrigue.

Conan Doyle in his depiction of Holmes used skills which gave life to a character that has long outlived his creator, and no doubt will long outlive any critics. Doyle quite rightly stands in the front rank of British literature for this achievement.

Principal Characters in
The Hound of the Baskervilles

Sherlock Holmes is the well-known detective of 221b Baker Street and with his trademark pipe and deerstalker he is rigour and analytical mind personified. Disdainful and egotistical, his powers of observation and intuition are famed. He is ably assisted by Dr Watson's meticulous approach to solving crimes. His ego seems to border on arrogance and at times he appears to relish baffling the authorities. Whilst his exterior air is cool and collected this belies a passionate nature beneath. His intellectual approach to solving crimes is by process of deductive reasoning.

Dr John Watson is Sherlock Holmes' loyal sidekick who suffers Holmes' imperious manner with great patience and fortitude. He is Sherlock Holmes' dogsbody in many ways, gathering the minutiae that allows Holmes to come to his brilliant and outstanding conclusions. Dr Watson does not have Holmes' insight and generally acts as a foil to Holmes' startling conclusions. He also doesn't follow the deductive method but rather applies reasoning after the fact. Essentially he provides the main narrative thread but in this investigation Dr Watson is particularly keen to prove himself to his admired friend.

Sir Henry Baskerville is the robust nephew of the late Sir Charles Baskerville. However, by the end of the novel he is as worn out and exhausted by terror of the Baskerville Curse as his uncle before him.

Sir Charles Baskerville is head of the Baskerville estate and a superstitious man terrorised by the curse of the Baskervilles. A well-known philanthropist, Sir Charles had embarked on a number of good works for the area surrounding his estate and needs his nephew Sir Henry to continue this work.

Sir Hugo Baskerville is the villainous ancestor who indulged in debauchery and excess until it eventually killed him. The picture of aristocratic over-indulgence, it is believed that the

Baskerville Curse is revenge for the misdeeds of Sir Hugo. A cruel man with a sadistic streak he kidnapped a young girl he had become infatuated with and imprisoned her. Upon her escape he vowed to give himself to the devil if he could capture her. He rode onto the Moors with his hunting hounds and sometime later was found – the girl having died from fear and exhaustion and a vast ghostly hound hovering over Sir Hugo before killing him.

Dr James Mortimer is the family doctor and executor of the Baskerville Estate. Although untidy and with an unprepossessing air he is a solid and trustworthy man. Fearing for the safety of the Estate's heir Sir Henry, it is Dr Mortimer who appeals to Sherlock Holmes for help. He also reveals that he had found huge footprints near to the body of Sir Charles but did not report them. Dr Mortimer is a phrenologist and hopes one day to study Sherlock Holmes' head.

Mr Jack Stapleton is an entemologist whose intellectual exterior belies a scheming and fearsome interior life. He has an extremely short temper and both Holmes and Watson come to fear him. In many respects he resembles Sir Hugo and is eventually revealed to be related by blood to the Baskerville clan. His scheming plan is to dispose of the living and legitimate Baskervilles so that he can lay claim to the Baskerville fortune.

Miss Stapleton is a great beauty and originally assumed to be Jack Stapleton's sister but is in fact his wife. Fearful of her husband and desperate to prevent another death, she helps both Holmes and Watson with her enigmatic warnings.

Mr John Barrymore is the gaunt domestic factotum of the Baskerville clan. Although in league with a convict brother, he and his wife are harmless.

Mrs Eliza Barrymore is the robust wife of Mr John Barrymore who has looked after generations of the Baskerville family.

Laura Lyons is a beautiful local girl and daughter of Mr Frankland who disowns her when she marries against his will. Abandoned by her husband she turns to Mr Stapleton and Sir Charles for help.

Selden is a murderous criminal whose intent is to escape to South America.

Mr Frankland is Laura's father and a litigator. Demonised by his treatment of Laura he is in all other respects a laughable character within the narrative.

An Arthur Conan Doyle Timeline

1859	1876	1879	1887

Arthur Conan Doyle

Arthur Conan Doyle born

Attends University of Edinburgh Medical School

The Mystery of the Sasanna Valley published

A Study in Scarlet published

UK and Ireland

The Origin of the Species published

First direct telegraph link between Britain and New Zealand

Zulu War begins

Golden Jubilee of Queen Victoria

Europe

Spain declares war on Morocco

Berlin Memorandum proposes armistice in Turkey

A Doll's House by Henrik Ibsen

Triple Alliance of Germany, Austria–Hungary and France ends

Rest of the World

Abolitionist leader John Brown hanged

Alexander Graham Bell patents the telephone

Thomas Edison demonstrates electric light

Japan annexes Iwo Jima

1859	1876	1879	1887

1890 **1891** **1892** **1893**

The Sign of the Four published | Gives up medical practice to write | *The Adventures of Sherlock Holmes* published | *The Adventure of the Final Problem* published

Prince of Wales opens underground station at Stockwell | Britain linked to continent by telephone | Oscar Wilde's *Lady Windermere's Fan* premieres | Beatrix Potter first tells the story of Peter Rabbit

Vincent van Gogh shoots himself | Paul Gauguin departs for Tahiti | Germany, Italy and Austria form Triple Alliance | Russia signs military accord with France

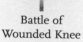

Battle of Wounded Knee | Congress creates US Court of Appeal | General Electrical Company incorporated in New York | Gandhi's first act of civil disobedience

1890 **1891** **1892** **1893**

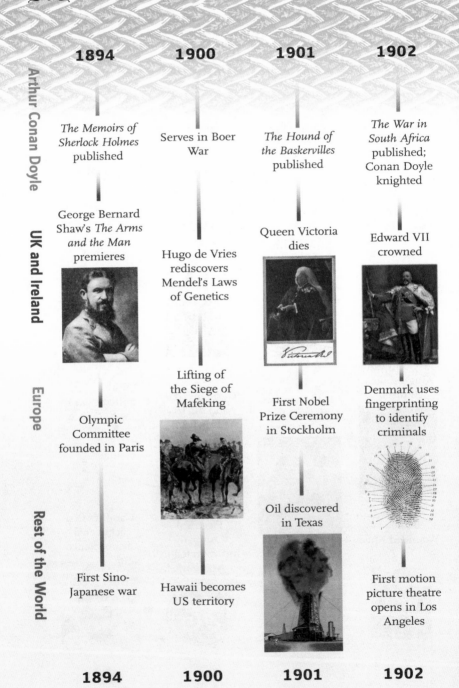

Arthur Conan Doyle

1894

The Memoirs of Sherlock Holmes published

1900

Serves in Boer War

1901

The Hound of the Baskervilles published

1902

The War in South Africa published; Conan Doyle knighted

UK and Ireland

George Bernard Shaw's *The Arms and the Man* premieres

Hugo de Vries rediscovers Mendel's Laws of Genetics

Queen Victoria dies

Edward VII crowned

Europe

Olympic Committee founded in Paris

Lifting of the Siege of Mafeking

First Nobel Prize Ceremony in Stockholm

Denmark uses fingerprinting to identify criminals

Rest of the World

First Sino-Japanese war

Hawaii becomes US territory

Oil discovered in Texas

First motion picture theatre opens in Los Angeles

1894

1900

1901

1902

1904 · 1910 · 1916 · 1930

1904

The Return of Sherlock Holmes published

Peter Pan premieres in London

Anton Chekov's *The Cherry Orchard* opens in Moscow

Wilbur Wright makes first airplane flight

1910

Becomes involved in the Oscar Slater case

Dr Crippen convicted and hanged

British–Russian intervention in Prussia

Tel Aviv founded

1916

Declares belief in spiritualism

Shackleton rescues stranded shipmates

First bombings of Paris by Zeppelin

Allied Forces withdraw from Gallipoli

1930

Dies and is buried in Windlesham

Amy Johnson completes solo flight to Australia

Nazis gain 107 seats in German election

Mickey Mouse comic strip first appears

1904 · 1910 · 1916 · 1930

Dartmoor Prison

Fox Tor Mires ('Grimpen Mire')

Nun's Cross Farm ('Merripit House')

Dartmoor – The Setting of *The Hound of the Baskervilles*

Grimspound
hut circle

Brook Manor

Hayford
Hall

*possible models for
Baskerville Hall*

Fowlescombe

The Hound of the Baskervilles

I

Mr Sherlock Holmes

Mr Sherlock Holmes, who was usually very late in the mornings, save upon those not infrequent occasions when he was up all night, was seated at the breakfast table. I stood upon the hearth-rug and picked up the stick which our visitor had left behind him the night before. It was a fine, thick piece of wood, bulbous-headed, of the sort which is known as a 'Penang lawyer'. Just under the head was a broad silver band nearly an inch across. 'To James Mortimer, MRCS, from his friends of the CCH', was engraved upon it, with the date '1884'. It was just such a stick as the old-fashioned family practitioner used to carry – dignified, solid and reassuring.

'Well, Watson, what do you make of it?'

Holmes was sitting with his back to me, and I had given him no sign of my occupation.

'How did you know what I was doing? I believe you have eyes in the back of your head.'

'I have, at least, a well-polished, silver-plated coffee-pot in front of me,' said he. 'But, tell me, Watson, what do you make of our visitor's stick? Since we have been so unfortunate as to miss him and have no notion of his errand, this accidental souvenir becomes of importance. Let me hear you reconstruct the man by an examination of it.'

'I think,' said I, following as far as I could the methods of my companion, 'that Mr Mortimer is a successful, elderly medical man, well esteemed since those who know him give him this mark of their appreciation.'

'Good!' said Holmes. 'Excellent!'

'I think also that the probability is in favour of his being a country practitioner who does a great deal of his visiting on foot.'

'Why so?'

'Because this stick, though originally a very handsome one has been so knocked about that I can hardly imagine a town practitioner carrying it. The thick iron ferrule is worn down, so it is evident that he has done a great amount of walking with it.'

'Perfectly sound!' said Holmes.

'And then again, there is the "friends of the CCH". I should guess that to be the Something Hunt, the local hunt to whose members he has possibly given some surgical assistance, and which has made him a small presentation in return.'

'Really, Watson, you excel yourself,' said Holmes, pushing back his chair and lighting a cigarette. 'I am bound to say that in all the accounts which you have been so good as to give of my own small achievements you have habitually underrated your own abilities. It may be that you are not yourself luminous, but you are a conductor of light. Some people without possessing genius have a remarkable power of stimulating it. I confess, my dear fellow, that I am very much in your debt.'

He had never said as much before, and I must admit that his words gave me keen pleasure, for I had often been piqued by his indifference to my admiration and to the attempts which I had made to give publicity to his methods. I was proud, too, to think that I had so far mastered his system as to apply it in a way which earned his approval. He now took the stick from my hands and examined it for a few minutes with his naked eyes. Then with an expression of interest he laid down his cigarette, and carrying the cane to the window, he looked over it again with a convex lens.

'Interesting, though elementary,' said he as he returned to his favourite corner of the settee. 'There are certainly one or two indications upon the stick. It gives us the basis for several deductions.'

'Has anything escaped me?' I asked with some self-importance. 'I trust that there is nothing of consequence which I have overlooked?'

'I am afraid, my dear Watson, that most of your conclusions were erroneous. When I said that you stimulated me I meant, to be frank, that in noting your fallacies I was occasionally guided towards the truth. Not that you are entirely wrong in this instance. The man is certainly a country practitioner. And he walks a good deal.'

'Then I was right.'

'To that extent.'

'But that was all.'

'No, no, my dear Watson, not all – by no means all. I would suggest, for example, that a presentation to a doctor is more likely to come from a hospital than from a hunt, and that when the initials CC are placed before that hospital the words Charing Cross very naturally suggest themselves.'

'You may be right.'

'The probability lies in that direction. And if we take this as a working hypothesis we have a fresh basis from which to start our construction of this unknown visitor.'

'Well, then, supposing that CCH does stand for Charing Cross Hospital, what further inferences may we draw?'

'Do none suggest themselves? You know my methods. Apply them!'

'I can only think of the obvious conclusion that the man has practised in town before going to the country.'

'I think that we might venture a little farther than this. Look at it in this light. On what occasion would it be most probable that such a presentation would be made? When would his friends unite to give him a pledge of their goodwill? Obviously at the moment when Dr Mortimer withdrew from the service of the hospital in order to start in practice for himself. We know there has been a presentation. We believe there has been a change from a town hospital to a country practice. Is it, then, stretching our inference too far to say that the presentation was on the occasion of the change?'

'It certainly seems probable.'

'Now, you will observe that he could not have been on the *staff* of the hospital, since only a man well established in a London practice could hold such a position, and such a one would not drift into the country. What was he, then? If he was in the hospital and yet not on the staff he could only have been a house-surgeon or a house-physician – little more than a senior student. And he left five years ago – the date is on the stick. So your grave, middle-aged family practitioner vanishes into thin air, my dear Watson, and there emerges a young fellow under thirty, amiable, unambitious, absent-minded, and the possessor of a favourite dog, which I should describe roughly as being larger than a terrier and smaller than a mastiff.'

I laughed incredulously as Sherlock Holmes leaned back in his settee and blew little wavering rings of smoke up to the ceiling.

'As to the latter part, I have no means of checking you,' said I, 'but at least it is not difficult to find out a few particulars about the man's age and professional career.' From my small medical shelf I took down the *Medical Directory* and turned up the name. There were several Mortimers, but only one who could be our visitor. I read his record aloud.

'Mortimer, James, MRCS, 1882, Grimpen, Dartmoor, Devon. House-surgeon, from 1882 to 1884, at Charing Cross Hospital. Winner of the Jackson Prize for Comparative Pathology, with essay entitled "Is Disease a Reversion?" Corresponding member of the Swedish Patho-

3

logical Society. Author of "Some Freaks of Atavism" (*Lancet*, 1882) and "Do We Progress?" (*Journal of Psychology*, March 1883). Medical officer for the parishes of Grimpen, Thorsley and High Barrow.'

'No mention of that local hunt, Watson,' said Holmes with a mischievous smile, 'but a country doctor, as you very astutely observed. I think that I am fairly justified in my inferences. As to the adjectives, I said, if I remember right, amiable, unambitious and absent-minded. It is my experience that it is only an amiable man in this world who receives testimonials, only an unambitious one who abandons a London career for the country and only an absent-minded one who leaves his stick and not his visiting-card after waiting an hour in your room.'

'And the dog?'

'Has been in the habit of carrying this stick behind his master. Being a heavy stick the dog has held it tightly by the middle, and the marks of his teeth are very plainly visible. The dog's jaw, as shown in the space between these marks, is too broad in my opinion for a terrier and not broad enough for a mastiff. It may have been – yes, by Jove, it is a curly-haired spaniel.'

He had risen and paced the room as he spoke. Now he halted in the recess of the window. There was such a ring of conviction in his voice that I glanced up in surprise.

'My dear fellow, how can you possibly be so sure of that?'

'For the very simple reason that I see the dog himself on our very doorstep, and there is the ring of its owner. Don't move, I beg you, Watson. He is a professional brother of yours, and your presence may be of assistance to me. Now is the dramatic moment of fate, Watson, when you hear a step upon the stair which is walking into your life, and you know not whether for good or ill. What does Dr James Mortimer, the man of science, ask of Sherlock Holmes, the specialist in crime? Come in!'

The appearance of our visitor was a surprise to me, since I had expected a typical country practitioner. He was a very tall, thin man, with a long nose like a beak, which jutted out between two keen, grey eyes, set closely together and sparkling brightly from behind a pair of gold-rimmed glasses. He was clad in a professional but rather slovenly fashion, for his frock-coat was dingy and his trousers frayed. Though young, his long back was already bowed, and he walked with a forward thrust of his head and a general air of peering benevolence. As he entered his eyes fell upon the stick in Holmes's hand, and he ran towards it with an exclamation of joy. 'I am so very glad,' said he. 'I was not sure whether I had left it here or in the Shipping Office. I would not lose that stick for the world.'

'A presentation, I see,' said Holmes.

'Yes, sir.'

'From Charing Cross Hospital?'

'From one or two friends there on the occasion of my marriage.'

'Dear, dear, that's bad!' said Holmes, shaking his head.

Dr Mortimer blinked through his glasses in mild astonishment.

'Why was it bad?'

'Only that you have disarranged our little deductions. Your marriage, you say?'

'Yes, sir. I married, and so left the hospital, and with it all hopes of a consulting practice. It was necessary to make a home of my own.'

'Come, come, we are not so far wrong, after all,' said Holmes. 'And now, Dr James Mortimer – '

'Mr, sir, Mr – a humble mrcs.'

'And a man of precise mind, evidently.'

'A dabbler in science, Mr Holmes, a picker up of shells on the shores of the great unknown ocean. I presume that it is Mr Sherlock Holmes whom I am addressing and not – '

'No, this is my friend Dr Watson.'

'Glad to meet you, sir. I have heard your name mentioned in connection with that of your friend. You interest me very much, Mr Holmes. I had hardly expected so dolichocephalic a skull or such well-marked supra-orbital development. Would you have any objection to my running my finger along your parietal fissure? A cast of your skull, sir, until the original is available, would be an ornament to any anthropological museum. It is not my intention to be fulsome, but I confess that I covet your skull.'

Sherlock Holmes waved our strange visitor into a chair. 'You are an enthusiast in your line of thought, I perceive, sir, as I am in mine,' said he. 'I observe from your forefinger that you make your own cigarettes. Have no hesitation in lighting one.'

The man drew out paper and tobacco and twirled the one up in the other with surprising dexterity. He had long, quivering fingers as agile and restless as the antennae of an insect.

Holmes was silent, but his little darting glances showed me the interest which he took in our curious companion.

'I presume, sir,' said he at last, 'that it was not merely for the purpose of examining my skull that you have done me the honour to call here last night and again today?'

'No, sir, no; though I am happy to have had the opportunity of doing that as well. I came to you, Mr Holmes, because I recognised that I am myself an unpractical man and because I am suddenly confronted with a most serious and extraordinary problem. Recognising, as I do, that you are the second highest expert in Europe – '

'Indeed, sir! May I enquire who has the honour to be the first?' asked Holmes with some asperity.

'To the man of precisely scientific mind the work of Monsieur Bertillon must always appeal strongly.'

'Then had you not better consult him?'

'I said, sir, to the precisely scientific mind. But as a practical man of affairs it is acknowledged that you stand alone. I trust, sir, that I have not inadvertently – '

'Just a little,' said Holmes. 'I think, Dr Mortimer, you would do wisely if without more ado you would kindly tell me plainly what the exact nature of the problem is in which you demand my assistance.'

2

The Curse of the Baskervilles

'I have in my pocket a manuscript,' said Dr James Mortimer.

'I observed it as you entered the room,' said Holmes.

'It is an old manuscript.'

'Early eighteenth century, unless it is a forgery.'

'How can you say that, sir?'

'You have presented an inch or two of it to my examination all the time that you have been talking. It would be a poor expert who could not give the date of a document within a decade or so. You may possibly have read my little monograph upon the subject. I put that at 1730.'

'The exact date is 1742.' Dr Mortimer drew it from his breast-pocket. 'This family paper was committed to my care by Sir Charles Baskerville, whose sudden and tragic death some three months ago created so much excitement in Devonshire. I may say that I was his personal friend as well as his medical attendant. He was a strong-minded man, sir, shrewd, practical, and as unimaginative as I am myself. Yet he took this document very seriously, and his mind was prepared for just such an end as did eventually overtake him.'

Holmes stretched out his hand for the manuscript and flattened it upon his knee.

'You will observe, Watson, the alternative use of the long *s* and the short. It is one of several indications which enabled me to fix the date.'

I looked over his shoulder at the yellow paper and the faded script. At the head was written: 'Baskerville Hall', and below in large, scrawling figures: '1742'.

'It appears to be a statement of some sort.'

'Yes, it is a statement of a certain legend which runs in the Baskerville family.'

'But I understand that it is something more modern and practical upon which you wish to consult me?'

'Most modern. A most practical, pressing matter, which must be decided within twenty-four hours. But the manuscript is short and is intimately connected with the affair. With your permission I will read it to you.'

Holmes leaned back in his chair, placed his fingertips together, and closed his eyes, with an air of resignation. Dr Mortimer turned the manuscript to the light and read in a high, crackling voice the following curious, old-world narrative:

'Of the origin of the Hound of the Baskervilles there have been many statements, yet as I come in a direct line from Hugo Baskerville, and as I had the story from my father, who also had it from his, I have set it down with all belief that it occurred even as is here set forth. And I would have you believe, my sons, that the same Justice which punishes sin may also most graciously forgive it, and that no ban is so heavy but that by prayer and repentance it may be removed. Learn then from this story not to fear the fruits of the past, but rather to be circumspect in the future, that those foul passions whereby our family has suffered so grievously may not again be loosed to our undoing.

Know then that in the time of the Great Rebellion (the history of which by the learned Lord Clarendon I most earnestly commend to your attention) this Manor of Baskerville was held by Hugo of that name, nor can it be gainsaid that he was a most wild, profane, and godless man. This, in truth, his neighbours might have pardoned, seeing that saints have never flourished in those parts, but there was in him a certain wanton and cruel humour which made his name a byword through the West. It chanced that this Hugo came to love (if, indeed, so dark a passion may be known under so bright a name) the daughter of a yeoman who held lands near the Baskerville estate. But the young maiden, being discreet and of good repute, would ever avoid him, for she feared his evil name. So it came to pass that one Michaelmas this Hugo, with five or six of his idle and wicked companions, stole down upon the farm and carried off the maiden, her father and brothers being from home, as he well knew. When they had brought her to the Hall the maiden was placed in an upper chamber, while Hugo and his friends sat down to a long carouse, as was their nightly custom. Now, the poor lass upstairs was like to have her wits turned at the singing and shouting and terrible oaths which came up to her from below, for they say that the words used by Hugo Baskerville, when he was in wine, were such as might blast the man who said them. At last in the stress of her fear she did that which might have daunted the bravest or most active man, for by the aid of the growth of ivy which covered (and still covers) the south wall she came down from under the eaves, and so homeward across the moor, there being three leagues betwixt the Hall and her father's farm.

'It chanced that some little time later Hugo left his guests to carry food and drink – with other worse things, perchance – to his captive, and so found the cage empty and the bird escaped. Then, as it would seem, he became as one that hath a devil, for, rushing down the stairs into the dining-hall, he sprang upon the great table, flagons and trenchers flying before him, and he cried aloud before all the company that he would that very night render his body and soul to the powers of evil if he might but overtake the wench. And while the revellers stood aghast at the fury of the man, one more wicked or, it may be, more drunken than the rest, cried out that they should put the hounds upon her. Whereat Hugo ran from the house, crying to his grooms that they should saddle his mare and unkennel the pack, and giving the hounds a kerchief of the maid's, he swung them to the line, and so off full cry in the moonlight over the moor.

'Now, for some space the revellers stood agape, unable to understand all that had been done in such haste. But anon their bemused wits awoke to the nature of the deed which was like to be done upon the moorlands. Everything was now in an uproar, some calling for their pistols, some for their horses, and some for another flask of wine. But at length some sense came back to their crazed minds, and the whole of them, thirteen in number, took horse and started in pursuit. The moon shone clear above them, and they rode swiftly abreast, taking that course which the maid must needs have taken if she were to reach her own home.

'They had gone a mile or two when they passed one of the night shepherds upon the moorlands, and they cried to him to know if he had seen the hunt. And the man, as the story goes, was so crazed with fear that he could scarce speak, but at last he said that he had indeed seen the unhappy maiden, with the hounds upon her track. "But I have seen more than that," said he, "for Hugo Baskerville passed me upon his black mare, and there ran mute behind him such a hound of hell as God forbid should ever be at my heels."

'So the drunken squires cursed the shepherd and rode onward. But soon their skins turned cold, for there came a sound of galloping across the moor, and the black mare, dabbled with white froth, went past with trailing bridle and empty saddle. Then the revellers rode close together, for a great fear was on them, but they still followed over the moor, though each, had he been alone, would have been right glad to have turned his horse's head. Riding slowly in this fashion, they came at last upon the hounds. These, though known for their valour and their breed, were whimpering in a cluster at the head of a deep dip or goyal, as we call it, upon the moor, some slinking away and some, with starting hackles and staring eyes, gazing down the narrow valley before them.

'The company had come to a halt, more sober men, as you may guess, than when they started. The most of them would by no means advance, but three of them, the boldest, or it may be the most drunken, rode forward down the goyal. Now, it opened into a broad space in which stood two of those great stones, still to be seen there, which were set by certain forgotten peoples in the days of old. The moon was shining bright upon the clearing, and there in the centre lay the unhappy maid where she had fallen, dead of fear and of fatigue. But it was not the sight of her body, nor yet was it that of the body of Hugo Baskerville lying near her, which raised the hair upon the heads of these three daredevil roysterers, but it was that, standing over Hugo, and plucking at his throat, there stood a foul thing, a great, black beast, shaped like a hound, yet larger than any hound that ever mortal eye has rested upon. And even as they looked the thing tore the throat out of Hugo Baskerville, on which, as it turned its blazing eyes and dripping jaws upon them, the three shrieked with fear and rode for dear life, still screaming, across the moor. One, it is said, died that very night of what he had seen, and the other twain were but broken men for the rest of their days.

'Such is the tale, my sons, of the coming of the hound which is said to have plagued the family so sorely ever since. If I have set it down it is because that which is clearly known hath less terror than that which is but hinted at and guessed. Nor can it be denied that many of the family have been unhappy in their deaths, which have been sudden, bloody and mysterious. Yet may we shelter ourselves in the infinite goodness of Providence, which would not forever punish the innocent beyond that third or fourth generation which is threatened in Holy Writ. To that Providence, my sons, I hereby commend you, and I counsel you by way of caution to forbear from crossing the moor in those dark hours when the powers of evil are exalted.

'[This from Hugo Baskerville to his sons Rodger and John, with instructions that they say nothing thereof to their sister Elizabeth.]'

When Dr Mortimer had finished reading this singular narrative he pushed his spectacles up on his forehead and stared across at Mr Sherlock Holmes. The latter yawned and tossed the end of his cigarette into the fire.

'Well?' said he.

'Do you not find it interesting?'

'To a collector of fairy tales.'

Dr Mortimer drew a folded newspaper out of his pocket.

'Now, Mr Holmes, we will give you something a little more recent. This is the *Devon County Chronicle* of May 14th of this year. It is a short account of the facts elicited at the death of Sir Charles Baskerville which occurred a few days before that date.'

My friend leaned a little forward and his expression became intent. Our visitor readjusted his glasses and began:

'The recent sudden death of Sir Charles Baskerville, whose name had been mentioned as the probable Liberal candidate for mid-Devon at the next election, has cast a gloom over the county. Though Sir Charles had resided at Baskerville Hall for a comparatively short period his amiability of character and extreme generosity had won the affection and respect of all who had been brought into contact with him. In these days of *nouveaux riches* it is refreshing to find a case where the scion of an old county family which has fallen upon evil days is able to make his own fortune and to bring it back with him to restore the fallen grandeur of his line. Sir Charles, as is well known, made large sums of money in South African speculation. More wise than those who go on until the wheel turns against them, he realised his gains and returned to England with them. It is only two years since he took up his residence at Baskerville Hall, and it is common talk how large were those schemes of reconstruction and improvement which have been interrupted by his death. Being himself childless, it was his openly expressed desire that the whole countryside should, within his own lifetime, profit by his good fortune, and many will have personal reasons for bewailing his untimely end. His generous donations to local and county charities have been frequently chronicled in these columns.

'The circumstances connected with the death of Sir Charles cannot be said to have been entirely cleared up by the inquest, but at least enough has been done to dispose of those rumours to which local superstition has given rise. There is no reason whatever to suspect foul play, or to imagine that death could be from any but natural causes. Sir Charles was a widower, and a man who may be said to have been in some ways of an eccentric habit of mind. In spite of his considerable wealth he was simple in his personal tastes, and his indoor servants at Baskerville Hall consisted of a married couple named Barrymore, the husband acting as butler and the wife as housekeeper. Their evidence, corroborated by that of several friends, tends to show that Sir Charles's health had for some time been impaired, and points especially to some affection of the heart, manifesting itself in changes of colour, breathlessness and acute attacks of nervous depression. Dr James Mortimer, the friend and medical attendant of the deceased, has given evidence to the same effect.

'The facts of the case are simple. Sir Charles Baskerville was in the habit every night before going to bed of walking down the famous yew alley of Baskerville Hall. The evidence of the Barrymores shows that this had been his custom. On the 4th of May Sir Charles had declared his intention of starting next day for London, and had ordered Barrymore to prepare his luggage. That night he went out as usual for his nocturnal walk, in the course of which he was in the habit of smoking a cigar. He never returned. At twelve o'clock Barrymore, finding the hall door still open, became alarmed and, lighting a lantern, went in search of his master. The day had been wet, and Sir Charles's footmarks were easily traced down the alley. Halfway down this walk there is a gate which leads out on to the moor. There were indications that Sir Charles had stood for some little time here. He then proceeded down the alley, and it was at the far end of it that his body was discovered. One fact which has not been explained is the statement of Barrymore that his master's footprints altered their character from the time that he passed the moor-gate, and that he appeared from thence onward to have been walking upon his toes. One Murphy, a gypsy horse-dealer, was on the moor at no great distance at the time, but he appears by his own confession to have been the worse for drink. He declares that he heard cries but is unable to state from what direction they came. No signs of violence were to be discovered upon Sir Charles's person, and though the doctor's evidence pointed to an almost incredible facial distortion – so great that Dr Mortimer refused at first to believe that it was indeed his friend and patient who lay before him – it was explained that that is a symptom which is not unusual in cases of dyspnoea and death from cardiac exhaustion. This explanation was borne out by the post-mortem examination, which showed long-standing organic disease, and the coroner's jury returned a verdict in accordance with the medical evidence. It is well that this is so, for it is obviously of the utmost importance that Sir Charles's heir should settle at the Hall and continue the good work which has been so sadly interrupted. Had the prosaic finding of the coroner not finally put an end to the romantic stories which have been whispered in connection with the affair, it might have been difficult to find a tenant for Baskerville Hall. It is understood that the next of kin is Mr Henry Baskerville, if he be still alive, the son of Sir Charles Baskerville's younger brother. The young man when last heard of was in America, and enquiries are being instituted with a view to informing him of his good fortune.'

Dr Mortimer refolded his paper and replaced it in his pocket. 'Those are the public facts, Mr Holmes, in connection with the death of Sir Charles Baskerville.'

'I must thank you,' said Sherlock Holmes, 'for calling my attention to a case which certainly presents some features of interest. I had observed some newspaper comment at the time, but I was exceedingly preoccupied by that little affair of the Vatican cameos, and in my anxiety to oblige the Pope I lost touch with several interesting English cases. This article, you say, contains all the public facts?'

'It does.'

'Then let me have the private ones.' He leaned back, put his fingertips together, and assumed his most impassive and judicial expression.

'In doing so,' said Dr Mortimer, who had begun to show signs of some strong emotion, 'I am telling that which I have not confided to anyone. My motive for withholding it from the coroner's enquiry is that a man of science shrinks from placing himself in the public position of seeming to endorse a popular superstition. I had the further motive that Baskerville Hall, as the paper says, would certainly remain untenanted if anything were done to increase its already rather grim reputation. For both these reasons I thought that I was justified in telling rather less than I knew, since no practical good could result from it, but with you there is no reason why I should not be perfectly frank.

'The moor is very sparsely inhabited, and those who live near each other are thrown very much together. For this reason I saw a good deal of Sir Charles Baskerville. With the exception of Mr Frankland, of Lafter Hall, and Mr Stapleton, the naturalist, there are no other men of education within many miles. Sir Charles was a retiring man, but the chance of his illness brought us together, and a community of interests in science kept us so. He had brought back much scientific information from South Africa, and many a charming evening we have spent together discussing the comparative anatomy of the Bushman and the Hottentot.

'Within the last few months it became increasingly plain to me that Sir Charles's nervous system was strained to breaking point. He had taken this legend which I have read you exceedingly to heart – so much so that, although he would walk in his own grounds, nothing would induce him to go out upon the moor at night. Incredible as it may appear to you, Mr Holmes, he was honestly convinced that a dreadful fate overhung his family, and certainly the records which he was able to give of his ancestors were not encouraging. The idea of some ghastly presence constantly haunted him, and on more than one occasion he has asked me whether I had on my medical journeys at night ever seen any strange creature or heard the baying of a hound. The latter question he put to me several times, and always in a voice which vibrated with excitement.

I can well remember driving up to his house in the evening some three weeks before the fatal event. He chanced to be at his hall door. I had descended from my gig and was standing in front of him, when I saw his eyes fix themselves over my shoulder and stare past me with an expression of the most dreadful horror. I whisked round and had just time to catch a glimpse of something which I took to be a large black calf passing at the head of the drive. So excited and alarmed was he that I was compelled to go down to the spot where the animal had been and look around for it. It was gone, however, and the incident appeared to make the worst impression upon his mind. I stayed with him all the evening, and it was on that occasion, to explain the emotion which he had shown, that he confided

13

to my keeping that narrative which I read to you when first I came. I mention this small episode because it assumes some importance in view of the tragedy which followed, but I was convinced at the time that the matter was entirely trivial and that his excitement had no justification.

'It was at my advice that Sir Charles was about to go to London. His heart was, I knew, affected, and the constant anxiety in which he lived, however chimerical the cause of it might be, was evidently having a serious effect upon his health. I thought that a few months among the distractions of town would send him back a new man. Mr Stapleton, a mutual friend who was much concerned at his state of health, was of the same opinion. At the last instant came this terrible catastrophe.

'On the night of Sir Charles's death, Barrymore the butler, who made the discovery, sent Perkins the groom on horseback to me, and as I was sitting up late I was able to reach Baskerville Hall within an hour of the event. I checked and corroborated all the facts which were mentioned at the inquest. I followed the footsteps down the yew alley, I saw the spot at the moor-gate where he seemed to have waited, I remarked the change in the shape of the prints after that point, I noted that there were no other footsteps save those of Barrymore on the soft gravel, and finally I carefully examined the body, which had not been touched until my arrival. Sir Charles lay on his face, his arms out, his fingers dug into the ground, and his features convulsed with some strong emotion to such an extent that I could hardly have sworn to his identity. There was certainly no physical injury of any kind. But one false statement was made by Barrymore at the inquest. He said that there were no traces upon the ground round the body. He did not observe any. But I did – some little distance off, but fresh and clear.'

'Footprints?'

'Footprints.'

'A man's or a woman's?'

Dr Mortimer looked strangely at us for an instant, and his voice sank almost to a whisper as he answered: 'Mr Holmes, they were the footprints of a gigantic hound!'

3

The Problem

I confess at these words a shudder passed through me. There was a thrill in the doctor's voice which showed that he was himself deeply moved by that which he told us. Holmes leaned forward in his excitement and his eyes had the hard, dry glitter which shot from them when he was keenly interested.

'You saw this?'

'As clearly as I see you.'

'And you said nothing?'

'What was the use?'

'How was it that no one else saw it?'

'The marks were some twenty yards from the body and no one gave them a thought. I don't suppose I should have done so had I not known this legend.'

'There are many sheepdogs on the moor?'

'No doubt, but this was no sheepdog.'

'You say it was large?'

'Enormous.'

'But it had not approached the body?'

'No.'

'What sort of night was it?'

'Damp and raw.'

'But not actually raining?'

'No.'

'What is the alley like?'

'There are two lines of old yew hedge, twelve feet high and impenetrable. The walk in the centre is about eight feet across.'

'Is there anything between the hedges and the walk?'

'Yes, there is a strip of grass about six feet broad on either side.'

'I understand that the yew hedge is penetrated at one point by a gate?'

'Yes, the wicket-gate which leads on to the moor.'

'Is there any other opening?'

'None.'

'So that to reach the yew alley one either has to come down it from the house or else to enter it by the moor-gate?'

'There is an exit through a summerhouse at the far end.'

'Had Sir Charles reached this?'

'No; he lay about fifty yards from it.'

'Now, tell me, Dr Mortimer – and this is important – the marks which you saw were on the path and not on the grass?'

'No marks could show on the grass.'

'Were they on the same side of the path as the moor-gate?'

'Yes; they were on the edge of the path on the same side as the moor-gate.'

'You interest me exceedingly. Another point. Was the wicket-gate closed?'

'Closed and padlocked.'

'How high was it?'

'About four feet high.'

'Then anyone could have got over it?'

'Yes.'

'And what marks did you see by the wicket-gate?'

'None in particular.'

'Good heaven! Did no one examine?'

'Yes, I examined, myself.'

'And found nothing?'

'It was all very confused. Sir Charles had evidently stood there for five or ten minutes.'

'How do you know that?'

'Because the ash had twice dropped from his cigar.'

'Excellent! This is a colleague, Watson, after our own heart. But the marks?'

'He had left his own marks all over that small patch of gravel. I could discern no others.'

Sherlock Holmes struck his hand against his knee with an impatient gesture.

'If I had only been there!' he cried. 'It is evidently a case of extraordinary interest, and one which presented immense opportunities to the scientific expert. That gravel path upon which I might have read so much has been long ere this smudged by the rain and defaced by the clogs of curious peasants. Oh, Dr Mortimer, Dr Mortimer, to think that you should not have called me in! You have indeed much to answer for.'

'I could not call you in, Mr Holmes, without disclosing these facts to the world, and I have already given my reasons for not wishing to do so. Besides, besides – '

'Why do you hesitate?'

'There is a realm in which the most acute and most experienced of detectives is helpless.'

'You mean that the thing is supernatural?'

'I did not positively say so.'

'No, but you evidently think it.'

'Since the tragedy, Mr Holmes, there have come to my ears several incidents which are hard to reconcile with the settled order of Nature.'

'For example?'

'I find that before the terrible event occurred several people had seen a creature upon the moor which corresponds with this Baskerville demon, and which could not possibly be any animal known to science. They all agreed that it was a huge creature, luminous, ghastly and spectral. I have cross-examined these men, one of them a hard-headed countryman, one a farrier and one a moorland farmer, who all tell the same story of this dreadful apparition, exactly corresponding to the hell-hound of the legend. I assure you that there is a reign of terror in the district, and that it is a hardy man who will cross the moor at night.'

'And you, a trained man of science, believe it to be supernatural?'

'I do not know what to believe.'

Holmes shrugged his shoulders. 'I have hitherto confined my investigations to this world,' said he. 'In a modest way I have combated evil, but to take on the Father of Evil himself would, perhaps, be too ambitious a task. Yet you must admit that the footmark is material.'

'The original hound was material enough to tug a man's throat out, and yet he was diabolical as well.'

'I see that you have quite gone over to the supernaturalists. But now, Dr Mortimer, tell me this. If you hold these views why have you come to consult me at all? You tell me in the same breath that it is useless to investigate Sir Charles's death and that you desire me to do it.'

'I did not say that I desired you to do it.'

'Then, how can I assist you?'

'By advising me as to what I should do with Sir Henry Baskerville, who arrives at Waterloo Station' – Dr Mortimer looked at his watch – 'in exactly one hour and a quarter.'

'He being the heir?'

'Yes. On the death of Sir Charles we enquired for this young gentleman and found that he had been farming in Canada. From the accounts which have reached us he is an excellent fellow in every way. I speak now not as a medical man but as a trustee and executor of Sir Charles's will.'

'There is no other claimant, I presume?'

'None. The only other kinsman whom we have been able to trace was Rodger Baskerville, the youngest of the three brothers of whom poor Sir Charles was the eldest. The second brother, who died young, is the father of this lad Henry. The third, Rodger, was the black sheep of the family. He came of the old masterful Baskerville strain and was the very image, they tell me, of the family picture of old Hugo. He made England too hot to hold him, fled to Central America, and died there in 1876 of yellow fever. Henry is the last of the Baskervilles. In one hour and five minutes I meet him at Waterloo Station. I have had a wire that he arrived at Southampton this morning. Now, Mr Holmes, what would you advise me to do with him?'

'Why should he not go to the home of his fathers?'

'It seems natural, does it not? And yet, consider that every Baskerville who goes there meets with an evil fate. I feel sure that if Sir Charles could have spoken with me before his death he would have warned me against bringing this, the last of the old race, and the heir to great wealth, to that deadly place. And yet it cannot be denied that the prosperity of the whole poor, bleak countryside depends upon his presence. All the good work which has been done by Sir Charles will crash to the ground if there is no tenant of the Hall. I fear lest I should be swayed too much by my own obvious interest in the matter, and that is why I bring the case before you and ask for your advice.'

Holmes considered for a little time. 'Put into plain words, the matter is this,' said he. 'In your opinion there is a diabolical agency which makes Dartmoor an unsafe abode for a Baskerville – that is your opinion?'

'At least I might go the length of saying that there is some evidence that this may be so.'

'Exactly. But surely, if your supernatural theory be correct, it could work the young man evil in London as easily as in Devonshire. A devil with merely local powers like a parish vestry would be too inconceivable a thing.'

'You put the matter more flippantly, Mr Holmes, than you would probably do if you were brought into personal contact with these things. Your advice, then, as I understand it, is that the young man will be as safe in Devonshire as in London. He comes in fifty minutes. What would you recommend?'

'I recommend, sir, that you take a cab, call off your spaniel who is scratching at my front door, and proceed to Waterloo to meet Sir Henry Baskerville.'

'And then?'

'And then you will say nothing to him at all until I have made up my mind about the matter.'

'How long will it take you to make up your mind?'

'Twenty-four hours. At ten o'clock tomorrow, Dr Mortimer, I will be much obliged to you if you will call upon me here, and it will be of help to me in my plans for the future if you will bring Sir Henry Baskerville with you.'

'I will do so, Mr Holmes.' He scribbled the appointment on his shirt-cuff and hurried off in his strange, peering, absent-minded fashion. Holmes stopped him at the head of the stair.

'Only one more question, Dr Mortimer. You say that before Sir Charles Baskerville's death, several people saw this apparition upon the moor?'

'Three people did.'

'Did any see it after?'

'I have not heard of any.'

'Thank you. Good-morning.'

Holmes returned to his seat with that quiet look of inward satisfaction which meant that he had a congenial task before him.

'Going out, Watson?'

'Unless I can help you.'

'No, my dear fellow, it is at the hour of action that I turn to you for aid. But this is splendid, really unique from some points of view. When you pass Bradley's, would you ask him to send up a pound of the strongest shag tobacco? Thank you. It would be as well if you could make it convenient not to return before evening. Then I should be very glad to compare impressions as to this most interesting problem which has been submitted to us this morning.'

I knew that seclusion and solitude were very necessary for my friend in those hours of intense mental concentration during which he weighed every particle of evidence, constructed alternative theories, balanced one against the other, and made up his mind as to which points were essential and which immaterial. I therefore spent the day at my club and did not return to Baker Street until evening. It was nearly nine o'clock when I found myself in the sitting-room once more.

My first impression as I opened the door was that a fire had broken out, for the room was so filled with smoke that the light of the lamp upon the table was blurred by it. As I entered, however, my fears were set at rest, for it was the acrid fumes of strong coarse tobacco which took me by the throat and set me coughing. Through the haze I had a vague vision of Holmes in his dressing-gown coiled up in an armchair with his black clay pipe between his lips. Several rolls of paper lay around him.

'Caught cold, Watson?' said he.

'No, it's this poisonous atmosphere.'

'I suppose it is pretty thick, now that you mention it.'

'Thick! It is intolerable.'

'Open the window, then! You have been at your club all day, I perceive.'

'My dear Holmes!'

'Am I right?'

'Certainly, but how?'

He laughed at my bewildered expression.

'There is a delightful freshness about you, Watson, which makes it a pleasure to exercise any small powers which I possess at your expense. A gentleman goes forth on a showery and miry day. He returns immaculate in the evening with the gloss still on his hat and his boots. He has been a fixture therefore all day. He is not a man with intimate friends. Where, then, could he have been? Is it not obvious?'

'Well, it is rather obvious.'

'The world is full of obvious things which nobody by any chance ever observes. Where do you think that I have been?'

'A fixture also.'

'On the contrary, I have been to Devonshire.'

'In spirit?'

'Exactly. My body has remained in this armchair and has, I regret to observe, consumed in my absence two large pots of coffee and an incredible amount of tobacco. After you left I sent down to Stanford's for the Ordnance map of this portion of the moor, and my spirit has hovered over it all day. I flatter myself that I could find my way about.'

'A large-scale map, I presume?'

'Very large.' He unrolled one section and held it over his knee. 'Here you have the particular district which concerns us. That is Baskerville Hall in the middle.'

'With a wood round it?'

'Exactly. I fancy the yew alley, though not marked under that name, must stretch along this line, with the moor, as you perceive, upon the right of it. This small clump of buildings here is the hamlet of Grimpen, where our friend Dr Mortimer has his headquarters. Within a radius of five miles there are, as you see, only a very few scattered dwellings. Here is Lafter Hall, which was mentioned in the narrative. There is a house indicated here which may be the residence of the naturalist – Stapleton, if I remember right, was his name. Here are two moorland farmhouses, High Tor and Foulmire. Then fourteen miles away the great convict prison of Princetown. Between and around these scattered points extends the desolate, lifeless moor. This, then, is the stage upon which tragedy has been played, and upon which we may help to play it again.'

'It must be a wild place.'

'Yes, the setting is a worthy one. If the devil did desire to have a hand in the affairs of men – '

'Then you are yourself inclining to the supernatural explanation.'

'The devil's agents may be of flesh and blood, may they not? There are two questions waiting for us at the outset. The one is whether any crime has been committed at all; the second is, what is the crime and how was it committed? Of course, if Dr Mortimer's surmise should be correct, and we are dealing with forces outside the ordinary laws of Nature, there is an end of our investigation. But we are bound to exhaust all other hypotheses before falling back upon this one. I think we'll shut that window again, if you don't mind. It is a singular thing, but I find that a concentrated atmosphere helps a concentration of thought. I have not pushed it to the length of getting into a box to think, but that is the logical outcome of my convictions. Have you turned the case over in your mind?'

'Yes, I have thought a good deal of it in the course of the day.'

'What do you make of it?'

'It is very bewildering.'

'It has certainly a character of its own. There are points of distinction about it. That change in the footprints, for example. What do you make of that?'

'Mortimer said that the man had walked on tiptoe down that portion of the alley.'

'He only repeated what some fool had said at the inquest. Why should a man walk on tiptoe down the alley?'

'What then?'

'He was running, Watson – running desperately, running for his life, running until he burst his heart and fell dead upon his face.'

'Running from what?'

'There lies our problem. There are indications that the man was crazed with fear before ever he began to run.'

'How can you say that?'

'I am presuming that the cause of his fears came to him across the moor. If that were so, and it seems most probable, only a man who had lost his wits would have run from the house instead of towards it. If the gypsy's evidence may be taken as true, he ran with cries for help in the direction where help was least likely to be. Then, again, whom was he waiting for that night, and why was he waiting for him in the yew alley rather than in his own house?'

'You think that he was waiting for someone?'

'The man was elderly and infirm. We can understand his taking an evening stroll, but the ground was damp and the night inclement. Is it natural that he should stand for five or ten minutes, as Dr Mortimer, with more practical sense than I should have given him credit for, deduced from the cigar ash?'

'But he went out every evening.'

'I think it unlikely that he waited at the moor-gate every evening. On the contrary, the evidence is that he avoided the moor. That night he waited there. It was the night before he made his departure for London. The thing takes shape, Watson. It becomes coherent. Might I ask you to hand me my violin, and we will postpone all further thought upon this business until we have had the advantage of meeting Dr Mortimer and Sir Henry Baskerville in the morning.'

4

Sir Henry Baskerville

Our breakfast table was cleared early, and Holmes waited in his dressing-gown for the promised interview. Our clients were punctual to their appointment, for the clock had just struck ten when Dr Mortimer was shown up, followed by the young baronet. The latter was a small, alert, dark-eyed man about thirty years of age, very sturdily built, with thick black eyebrows and a strong, pugnacious face. He wore a ruddy-tinted tweed suit and had the weather-beaten appearance of one who has spent most of his time in the open air, and yet there was something in his steady eye and the quiet assurance of his bearing which indicated the gentleman.

'This is Sir Henry Baskerville,' said Dr Mortimer.

'Why, yes,' said he, 'and the strange thing is, Mr Sherlock Holmes, that if my friend here had not proposed coming round to you this morning I should have come on my own account. I understand that you think out little puzzles, and I've had one this morning which wants more thinking out than I am able to give it.'

'Pray take a seat, Sir Henry. Do I understand you to say that you have yourself had some remarkable experience since you arrived in London?'

'Nothing of much importance, Mr Holmes. Only a joke, as like as not. It was this letter, if you can call it a letter, which reached me this morning.'

He laid an envelope upon the table, and we all bent over it. It was of common quality, greyish in colour. The address, 'Sir Henry Baskerville, Northumberland Hotel', was printed in rough characters; the postmark 'Charing Cross', and the date of posting the preceding evening.

'Who knew that you were going to the Northumberland Hotel?' asked Holmes, glancing keenly across at our visitor.

'No one could have known. We only decided after I met Dr Mortimer.'

'But Dr Mortimer was no doubt already stopping there?'

'No, I had been staying with a friend,' said the doctor. 'There was no possible indication that we intended to go to this hotel.'

'Hum! Someone seems to be very deeply interested in your movements.' Out of the envelope he took a half-sheet of foolscap paper folded into four. This he opened and spread flat upon the table. Across the middle of it a single sentence had been formed by the expedient of pasting printed words upon it. It ran:

As you value your life or your reason keep away from the moor.

The word 'moor' only was printed in ink.

'Now,' said Sir Henry Baskerville, 'perhaps you will tell me, Mr Holmes, what in thunder is the meaning of that, and who it is that takes so much interest in my affairs?'

'What do you make of it, Dr Mortimer? You must allow that there is nothing supernatural about this, at any rate?'

'No, sir, but it might very well come from someone who was convinced that the business is supernatural.'

'What business?' asked Sir Henry sharply. 'It seems to me that all you gentlemen know a great deal more than I do about my own affairs.'

'You shall share our knowledge before you leave this room, Sir Henry. I promise you that,' said Sherlock Holmes. 'We will confine ourselves for the present with your permission to this very interesting document, which must have been put together and posted yesterday evening. Have you yesterday's *Times*, Watson?'

'It is here in the corner.'

'Might I trouble you for it – the inside page, please, with the leading articles?' He glanced swiftly over it, running his eyes up and down the columns. 'Capital article this on free trade. Permit me to give you an extract from it. "You may be cajoled into imagining that your own special trade or your own industry will be encouraged by a protective tariff, but it stands to reason that such legislation must in the long run keep away wealth from the country, diminish the value of our imports, and lower the general conditions of life in this island." What do you think of that, Watson?' cried Holmes in high glee, rubbing his hands together with satisfaction. 'Don't you think that is an admirable sentiment?'

Dr Mortimer looked at Holmes with an air of professional interest, and Sir Henry Baskerville turned a pair of puzzled dark eyes upon me.

'I don't know much about the tariff and things of that kind,' said he, 'but it seems to me we've got a bit off the trail so far as that note is concerned.'

'On the contrary, I think we are particularly hot upon the trail, Sir Henry. Watson here knows more about my methods than you do, but I fear that even he has not quite grasped the significance of this sentence.'

'No, I confess that I see no connection.'

'And yet, my dear Watson, there is so very close a connection that the one is extracted out of the other. "You", "your", "your", "life", "reason", "value", "keep away", "from the". Don't you see now whence these words have been taken?'

'By thunder, you're right! Well, if that isn't smart!' cried Sir Henry.

'If any possible doubt remained it is settled by the fact that "keep away" and "from the" are cut out in one piece.'

'Well, now – so they are!'

'Really, Mr Holmes, this exceeds anything which I could have imagined,' said Dr Mortimer, gazing at my friend in amazement. 'I could understand anyone saying that the words were from a newspaper; but that you should name which, and add that it came from the leading article, is really one of the most remarkable things which I have ever known. How did you do it?'

'I presume, doctor, that you could tell the skull of a Negro from that of an Eskimo?'

'Most certainly.'

'But how?'

'Because that is my special hobby. The differences are obvious. The supra-orbital crest, the facial angle, the maxillary curve, the – '

'But this is my special hobby, and the differences are equally obvious. There is as much difference to my eyes between the leaded bourgeois type of a *Times* article and the slovenly print of an evening halfpenny paper as there could be between your Negro and your Eskimo. The detection of types is one of the most elementary branches of knowledge to the special expert in crime, though I confess that once when I was very young I confused the *Leeds Mercury* with the *Western Morning News*. But a *Times* leader is entirely distinctive, and these words could have been taken from nothing else. As it was done yesterday the strong probability was that we should find the words in yesterday's issue.'

'So far as I can follow you, then, Mr Holmes,' said Sir Henry Baskerville, 'someone cut out this message with a pair of scissors – '

'Nail-scissors,' said Holmes. 'You can see that it was a pair of very short-bladed scissors, since the cutter had to take two snips over "keep away".'

'That is so. Someone, then, cut out the message with a pair of short-bladed scissors, pasted it with paste – '

'Gum,' said Holmes.

'With gum on to the paper. But I want to know why the word "moor" should have been written?'

'Because he could not find it in print. The other words were all simple and might be found in any issue, but "moor" would be less common.'

'Why, of course, that would explain it. Have you read anything else in this message, Mr Holmes?'

'There are one or two indications, and yet the utmost pains have been taken to remove all clues. The address, you observe is printed in rough characters. But *The Times* is a paper which is seldom found in any hands but those of the highly educated. We may take it, therefore, that the letter was composed by an educated man who wished to pose as an uneducated one, and his effort to conceal his own writing suggests that that writing might be known, or come to be known, by you. Again, you will observe that the words are not gummed on in an accurate line, but that some are much higher than others. "Life", for example is quite out of its proper place. That may point to carelessness or it may point to agitation and hurry upon the part of the cutter. On the whole I incline to the latter view, since the matter was evidently important, and it is unlikely that the composer of such a letter would be careless. If he were in a hurry it opens up the interesting question why he should be in a hurry, since any letter posted up to early morning would reach Sir Henry before he would leave his hotel. Did the composer fear an interruption – and from whom?'

'We are coming now rather into the region of guesswork,' said Dr Mortimer.

'Say, rather, into the region where we balance probabilities and choose the most likely. It is the scientific use of the imagination, but we have always some material basis on which to start our speculation. Now, you would call it a guess, no doubt, but I am almost certain that this address has been written in a hotel.'

'How in the world can you say that?'

'If you examine it carefully you will see that both the pen and the ink have given the writer trouble. The pen has spluttered twice in a single word and has run dry three times in a short address, showing that there was very little ink in the bottle. Now, a private pen or ink-bottle is seldom allowed to be in such a state, and the combination of the two must be quite rare. But you know the hotel ink and the hotel pen, where it is rare to get anything else. Yes, I have very little hesitation in saying that could we examine the wastepaper baskets of the hotels around Charing Cross until we found the remains of the mutilated *Times* leader we could lay our hands straight upon the person who sent this singular message. Hallo! Hallo! What's this?'

He was carefully examining the foolscap, upon which the words were pasted, holding it only an inch or two from his eyes.

'Well?'

'Nothing,' said he, throwing it down. 'It is a blank half-sheet of paper, without even a watermark upon it. I think we have drawn as much as we can from this curious letter; and now, Sir Henry, has anything else of interest happened to you since you have been in London?'

'Why, no, Mr Holmes. I think not.'

'You have not observed anyone follow or watch you?'

'I seem to have walked right into the thick of a dime novel,' said our visitor. 'Why in thunder should anyone follow or watch me?'

'We are coming to that. You have nothing else to report to us before we go into this matter?'

'Well, it depends upon what you think worth reporting.'

'I think anything out of the ordinary routine of life well worth reporting.'

Sir Henry smiled.

'I don't know much of British life yet, for I have spent nearly all my time in the States and in Canada. But I hope that to lose one of your boots is not part of the ordinary routine of life over here.'

'You have lost one of your boots?'

'My dear sir,' cried Dr Mortimer, 'it is only mislaid. You will find it when you return to the hotel. What is the use of troubling Mr Holmes with trifles of this kind?'

'Well, he asked me for anything outside the ordinary routine.'

'Exactly,' said Holmes, 'however foolish the incident may seem. You have lost one of your boots, you say?'

'Well, mislaid it, anyhow. I put them both outside my door last night, and there was only one in the morning. I could get no sense out of the chap who cleans them. The worst of it is that I only bought the pair last night in the Strand, and I have never had them on.'

'If you have never worn them, why did you put them out to be cleaned?'

'They were tan boots and had never been varnished. That was why I put them out.'

'Then I understand that on your arrival in London yesterday you went out at once and bought a pair of boots?'

'I did a good deal of shopping. Dr Mortimer here went round with me. You see, if I am to be squire down there I must dress the part, and it may be that I have got a little careless in my ways out West. Among other things I bought these brown boots – gave six dollars for them – and had one stolen before ever I had them on my feet.'

'It seems a singularly useless thing to steal,' said Sherlock Holmes. 'I confess that I share Dr Mortimer's belief that it will not be long before the missing boot is found.'

'And, now, gentlemen,' said the baronet with decision, 'it seems to me that I have spoken quite enough about the little that I know. It is time that you kept your promise and gave me a full account of what we are all driving at.'

'Your request is a very reasonable one,' Holmes answered. 'Dr Mortimer, I think you could not do better than to tell your story as you told it to us.'

Thus encouraged, our scientific friend drew his papers from his pocket and presented the whole case as he had done upon the morning before. Sir Henry Baskerville listened with the deepest attention and with an occasional exclamation of surprise.

'Well, I seem to have come into an inheritance with a vengeance,' said he when the long narrative was finished. 'Of course, I've heard of the hound ever since I was in the nursery. It's the pet story of the family, though I never thought of taking it seriously before. But as to my uncle's death – well, it all seems boiling up in my head, and I can't get it clear yet. You don't seem quite to have made up your mind whether it's a case for a policeman or a clergyman.'

'Precisely.'

'And now there's this affair of the letter to me at the hotel. I suppose that fits into its place.'

'It seems to show that someone knows more than we do about what goes on upon the moor,' said Dr Mortimer.

'And also,' said Holmes, 'that someone is not ill-disposed towards you, since they warn you of danger.'

'Or it may be that they wish, for their own purposes, to scare me away.'

'Well, of course, that is possible also. I am very much indebted to you, Dr Mortimer, for introducing me to a problem which presents several interesting alternatives. But the practical point which we now have to decide, Sir Henry, is whether it is or is not advisable for you to go to Baskerville Hall.'

'Why should I not go?'

'There seems to be danger.'

'Do you mean danger from this family fiend or do you mean danger from human beings?'

'Well, that is what we have to find out.'

'Whichever it is, my answer is fixed. There is no devil in hell, Mr Holmes, and there is no man upon earth who can prevent me from going to the home of my own people, and you may take that to be my final answer.' His dark brows knitted and his face flushed to a dusky red as he spoke. It was evident that the fiery temper of the Baskervilles was not extinct in this their last representative. 'Meanwhile,' said he, 'I have hardly had time to think over all that you have told me. It's a big thing for a man to have to understand and to decide at one sitting. I should like to have a quiet hour by myself to make up my mind. Now, look here, Mr Holmes, it's half-past eleven now and I am going back right away to my hotel. Suppose you and your friend, Dr Watson, come round and lunch with us at two. I'll be able to tell you more clearly then how this thing strikes me.'

'Is that convenient to you, Watson?'

'Perfectly.'

'Then you may expect us. Shall I have a cab called?'

'I'd prefer to walk, for this affair has flurried me rather.'

'I'll join you in a walk, with pleasure,' said his companion.

'Then we meet again at two o'clock. *Au revoir* and good-morning!'

We heard the steps of our visitors descend the stair and the bang of the front door. In an instant Holmes had changed from the languid dreamer to the man of action.

'Your hat and boots, Watson, quick! Not a moment to lose!' He rushed into his room in his dressing-gown and was back again in a few seconds in a frock-coat. We hurried together down the stairs and into the street. Dr Mortimer and Baskerville were still visible about two hundred yards ahead of us in the direction of Oxford Street.

'Shall I run on and stop them?'

'Not for the world, my dear Watson. I am perfectly satisfied with your company if you will tolerate mine. Our friends are wise, for it is certainly a very fine morning for a walk.'

He quickened his pace until we had decreased the distance which divided us by about half. Then, still keeping a hundred yards behind, we followed them into Oxford Street and so down Regent Street. Once our friends stopped and stared into a shop window, upon which Holmes did the same. An instant afterwards he gave a little cry of satisfaction, and, following the direction of his eager eyes, I saw that a hansom cab with a man inside which had halted on the other side of the street was now proceeding slowly onward again.

'There's our man, Watson! Come along! We'll have a good look at him, if we can do no more.'

At that instant I was aware of a bushy black beard and a pair of piercing eyes turned upon us through the side window of the cab. Instantly the trap-door at the top flew up, something was screamed to the driver, and the cab flew madly off down Regent Street. Holmes looked eagerly round for another, but no empty one was in sight. Then he dashed in wild pursuit amid the stream of the traffic, but the start was too great, and already the cab was out of sight.

'There now!' said Holmes bitterly as he emerged panting and white with vexation from the tide of vehicles. 'Was ever such bad luck and such bad management, too? Watson, Watson, if you are an honest man you will record this also and set it against my successes!'

'Who was the man?'

'I have not an idea.'

'A spy?'

'Well, it was evident from what we have heard that Baskerville has been very closely shadowed by someone since he has been in town. How else could it be known so quickly that it was the Northumberland Hotel which he had chosen? If they had followed him the first day I argued that they would follow him also the second. You may have observed that I twice strolled over to the window while Dr Mortimer was reading his legend.'

'Yes, I remember.'

'I was looking out for loiterers in the street, but I saw none. We are dealing with a clever man, Watson. This matter cuts very deep, and though I have not finally made up my mind whether it is a benevolent or a malevolent agency which is in touch with us, I am conscious always of power and design. When our friends left I at once followed them in the hopes of marking down their invisible attendant. So wily was he that he had not trusted himself upon foot, but he had availed himself of a cab so that he could loiter behind or dash past them and so escape their notice. His method had the additional advantage that if they were to take a cab he was all ready to follow them. It has, however, one obvious disadvantage.'

'It puts him in the power of the cabman.'

'Exactly.'

'What a pity we did not get the number!'

'My dear Watson, clumsy as I have been, you surely do not seriously imagine that I neglected to get the number? No. 2704 is our man. But that is no use to us for the moment.'

'I fail to see how you could have done more.'

'On observing the cab I should have instantly turned and walked in the other direction. I should then at my leisure have hired a second cab and followed the first at a respectful distance, or, better still, have driven to the Northumberland Hotel and waited there. When our unknown had followed Baskerville home we should have had the opportunity of playing his own game upon himself and seeing where he made for. As it is, by an indiscreet eagerness, which was taken advantage of with extraordinary quickness and energy by our opponent, we have betrayed ourselves and lost our man.'

We had been sauntering slowly down Regent Street during this conversation, and Dr Mortimer, with his companion, had long vanished in front of us.

'There is no object in our following them,' said Holmes. 'The shadow has departed and will not return. We must see what further cards we have in our hands and play them with decision. Could you swear to that man's face within the cab?'

'I could swear only to the beard.'

'And so could I – from which I gather that in all probability it was a false one. A clever man upon so delicate an errand has no use for a beard save to conceal his features. Come in here, Watson!'

He turned into one of the district messenger offices, where he was warmly greeted by the manager.

'Ah, Wilson, I see you have not forgotten the little case in which I had the good fortune to help you?'

'No, sir, indeed I have not. You saved my good name, and perhaps my life.'

'My dear fellow, you exaggerate. I have some recollection, Wilson, that you had among your boys a lad named Cartwright, who showed some ability during the investigation.'

'Yes, sir, he is still with us.'

'Could you ring him up? – thank you! And I should be glad to have change of this five-pound note.'

A lad of fourteen, with a bright, keen face, had obeyed the summons of the manager. He stood now gazing with great reverence at the famous detective.

'Let me have the *Hotel Directory*,' said Holmes. 'Thank you! Now, Cartwright, there are the names of twenty-three hotels here, all in the immediate neighbourhood of Charing Cross. Do you see?'

'Yes, sir.'

'You will visit each of these in turn.'

'Yes, sir.'

'You will begin in each case by giving the outside porter one shilling. Here are twenty-three shillings.'

'Yes, sir.'

You will tell him that you want to see the wastepaper of yesterday. You will say that an important telegram has miscarried and that you are looking for it. You understand?'

'Yes, sir.'

'But what you are really looking for is the centre page of *The Times* with some holes cut in it with scissors. Here is a copy of *The Times*. It is this page. You could easily recognise it, could you not?'

'Yes, sir.'

'In each case the outside porter will send for the hall porter, to whom also you will give a shilling. Here are twenty-three shillings. You will then learn in possibly twenty cases out of the twenty-three that the waste of the day before has been burned or removed. In the three other cases you will be shown a heap of paper and you will look for this page of *The Times* among it. The odds are enormously against your finding it. There are ten shillings over in case of emergencies. Let me have a report by wire at Baker Street before evening. And now, Watson, it only remains for us to find out by wire the identity of the cabman, No. 2704, and then we will drop into one of the Bond Street picture galleries and fill in the time until we are due at the hotel.'

5

Three Broken Threads

Sherlock Holmes had, in a very remarkable degree, the power of detaching his mind at will. For two hours the strange business in which we had been involved appeared to be forgotten, and he was entirely absorbed in the pictures of the modern Belgian masters. He would talk of nothing but art, of which he had the crudest ideas, from our leaving the gallery until we found ourselves at the Northumberland Hotel.

'Sir Henry Baskerville is upstairs expecting you,' said the clerk. 'He asked me to show you up at once when you came.'

'Have you any objection to my looking at your register?' said Holmes.

'Not in the least.'

The book showed that two names had been added after that of Baskerville. One was Theophilus Johnson and family, of Newcastle; the other Mrs Oldmore and maid, of High Lodge, Alton.

'Surely that must be the same Johnson whom I used to know,' said Holmes to the porter. 'A lawyer, is he not, grey-headed and walks with a limp?'

'No, sir, this is Mr Johnson the coal-owner, a very active gentleman, not older than yourself.'

'Surely you are mistaken about his trade?'

'No, sir; he has used this hotel for many years, and he is very well known to us.'

'Ah, that settles it. Mrs Oldmore, too; I seem to remember the name. Excuse my curiosity, but often in calling upon one friend one finds another.'

'She is an invalid lady, sir. Her husband was once mayor of Gloucester. She always comes to us when she is in town.'

'Thank you; I am afraid I cannot claim her acquaintance. We have established a most important fact by these questions, Watson,' he continued in a low voice as we went upstairs together. 'We know now that the people who are so interested in our friend have not settled down in his own hotel. That means that while they are, as we have seen, very anxious to watch him, they are equally anxious that he should not see them. Now, this is a most suggestive fact.'

'What does it suggest?'

'It suggests – hallo, my dear fellow, what on earth is the matter?'

As we came round the top of the stairs we had run up against Sir Henry Baskerville himself. His face was flushed with anger, and he held an old and dusty boot in one of his hands. So furious was he that he was hardly articulate, and when he did speak it was in a much broader and more Western dialect than any which we had heard from him in the morning.

'Seems to me they are playing me for a sucker in this hotel,' he cried. 'They'll find they've started in to monkey with the wrong man unless they are careful. By thunder, if that chap can't find my missing boot there will be trouble. I can take a joke with the best, Mr Holmes, but they've got a bit over the mark this time.'

'Still looking for your boot?'

'Yes, sir, and mean to find it.'

'But, surely, you said that it was a new brown boot?'

'So it was, sir. And now it's an old black one.'

'What! you don't mean to say – ?'

'That's just what I do mean to say. I only had three pairs in the world – the new brown, the old black and the patent leathers, which I am wearing. Last night they took one of my brown ones, and today they have sneaked one of the black. Well, have you got it? Speak out, man, and don't stand staring!'

An agitated German waiter had appeared upon the scene.

'No, sir; I have made enquiry all over the hotel, but I can hear no word of it.'

'Well, either that boot comes back before sundown or I'll see the manager and tell him that I go right straight out of this hotel.'

'It shall be found, sir – I promise you that if you will have a little patience it will be found.'

'Mind it is, for it's the last thing of mine that I'll lose in this den of thieves. Well, well, Mr Holmes, you'll excuse my troubling you about such a trifle – '

'I think it's well worth troubling about.'

'Why, you look very serious over it.'

'How do you explain it?'

'I just don't attempt to explain it. It seems the very maddest, queerest thing that ever happened to me.'

'The queerest perhaps – ' said Holmes thoughtfully.

'What do you make of it yourself?'

'Well, I don't profess to understand it yet. This case of yours is very complex, Sir Henry. When taken in conjunction with your uncle's death I am not sure that of all the five hundred cases of capital importance which I have handled there is one which cuts so deep. But we hold several threads in our hands, and the odds are that one or other of them guides us to the truth. We may waste time in following the wrong one, but sooner or later we must come upon the right.'

We had a pleasant luncheon in which little was said of the business which had brought us together. It was in the private sitting-room to which we afterwards repaired that Holmes asked Baskerville what were his intentions.

'To go to Baskerville Hall.'

'And when?'

'At the end of the week.'

'On the whole,' said Holmes, 'I think that your decision is a wise one. I have ample evidence that you are being dogged in London, and amid the millions of this great city it is difficult to discover who these people are or what their object can be. If their intentions are evil they might do you a mischief, and we should be powerless to prevent it. You did not know, Dr Mortimer, that you were followed this morning from my house?'

Dr Mortimer started violently.

'Followed! By whom?'

'That, unfortunately, is what I cannot tell you. Have you among your neighbours or acquaintances on Dartmoor any man with a black, full beard?'

'No – or, let me see – why, yes. Barrymore, Sir Charles's butler, is a man with a full, black beard.'

'Ha! Where is Barrymore?'

'He is in charge of the Hall.'

'We had best ascertain if he is really there, or if by any possibility he might be in London.'

'How can you do that?'

'Give me a telegraph form. "Is all ready for Sir Henry?" That will do. Address to Mr Barrymore, Baskerville Hall. What is the nearest telegraph office? Grimpen. Very good, we will send a second wire to the postmaster, Grimpen: "Telegram to Mr Barrymore to be delivered into his own hand. If absent, please return wire to Sir Henry Baskerville, Northumberland Hotel." That should let us know before evening whether Barrymore is at his post in Devonshire or not.'

'That's so,' said Baskerville. 'By the way, Dr Mortimer, who is this Barrymore, anyhow?'

'He is the son of the old caretaker, who is dead. They have looked after the Hall for four generations now. So far as I know, he and his wife are as respectable a couple as any in the county.'

'At the same time,' said Baskerville, 'it's clear enough that so long as there are none of the family at the Hall these people have a mighty fine home and nothing to do.'

'That is true.'

'Did Barrymore profit at all by Sir Charles's will?' asked Holmes.

'He and his wife had five hundred pounds each.'

'Ha! Did they know that they would receive this?'

Yes; Sir Charles was very fond of talking about the provisions of his will.'

'That is very interesting.'

'I hope,' said Dr Mortimer, 'that you do not look with suspicious eyes upon everyone who received a legacy from Sir Charles, for I also had a thousand pounds left to me.'

'Indeed! And anyone else?'

'There were many insignificant sums to individuals, and a large number of public charities. The residue all went to Sir Henry.'

'And how much was the residue?'

'Seven hundred and forty thousand pounds.'

Holmes raised his eyebrows in surprise. 'I had no idea that so gigantic a sum was involved,' said he.

'Sir Charles had the reputation of being rich, but we did not know how very rich he was until we came to examine his securities. The total value of the estate was close on to a million.'

'Dear me! It is a stake for which a man might well play a desperate game. And one more question, Dr Mortimer. Supposing that anything happened to our young friend here – you will forgive the unpleasant hypothesis! – who would inherit the estate?'

'Since Rodger Baskerville, Sir Charles's younger brother, died unmarried, the estate would descend to the Desmonds, who are distant cousins. James Desmond is an elderly clergyman in Westmorland.'

'Thank you. These details are all of great interest. Have you met Mr James Desmond?'

'Yes; he once came down to visit Sir Charles. He is a man of venerable appearance and of saintly life. I remember that he refused to accept any settlement from Sir Charles, though he pressed it upon him.'

'And this man of simple tastes would be the heir to Sir Charles's thousands.'

'He would be the heir to the estate because that is entailed. He would also be the heir to the money unless it were willed otherwise by the present owner, who can, of course, do what he likes with it.'

'And have you made your will, Sir Henry?'

'No, Mr Holmes, I have not. I've had no time, for it was only yesterday that I learned how matters stood. But in any case I feel that the money should go with the title and estate. That was my poor uncle's idea. How is the owner going to restore the glories of the Baskervilles if he has not money enough to keep up the property? House, land and dollars must go together.'

'Quite so. Well, Sir Henry, I am of one mind with you as to the advisability of your going down to Devonshire without delay. There is only one provision which I must make. You certainly must not go alone.'

'Dr Mortimer returns with me.'

'But Dr Mortimer has his practice to attend to, and his house is miles away from yours. With all the goodwill in the world he may be unable to help you. No, Sir Henry, you must take with you someone, a trusty man, who will be always by your side.'

'Is it possible that you could come yourself, Mr Holmes?'

'If matters came to a crisis I should endeavour to be present in person; but you can understand that, with my extensive consulting practice and with the constant appeals which reach me from many quarters, it is impossible for me to be absent from London for an indefinite time. At the present instant one of the most revered names in England is being besmirched by a blackmailer, and only I can stop a disastrous scandal. You will see how impossible it is for me to go to Dartmoor.'

'Whom would you recommend, then?'

Holmes laid his hand upon my arm.

'If my friend would undertake it there is no man who is better worth having at your side when you are in a tight place. No one can say so more confidently than I.'

The proposition took me completely by surprise, but before I had time to answer, Baskerville seized me by the hand and wrung it heartily.

'Well, now, that is real kind of you, Dr Watson,' said he. 'You see how it is with me, and you know just as much about the matter as I do. If you will come down to Baskerville Hall and see me through, I'll never forget it.'

The promise of adventure had always a fascination for me, and I was complimented by the words of Holmes and by the eagerness with which the baronet hailed me as a companion.

'I will come, with pleasure,' said I. 'I do not know how I could employ my time better.'

'And you will report very carefully to me,' said Holmes. 'When a crisis comes, as it will do, I will direct how you shall act. I suppose that by Saturday all might be ready?'

'Would that suit Dr Watson?'

'Perfectly.'

'Then on Saturday, unless you hear to the contrary, we shall meet at the ten-thirty train from Paddington.'

We had risen to depart when Baskerville gave a cry of triumph, and diving into one of the corners of the room he drew a brown boot from under a cabinet.

'My missing boot!' he cried.

'May all our difficulties vanish as easily!' said Sherlock Holmes.

'But it is a very singular thing,' Dr Mortimer remarked. 'I searched this room carefully before lunch.'

'And so did I,' said Baskerville. 'Every inch of it.'

'There was certainly no boot in it then.'

'In that case the waiter must have placed it there while we were lunching.'

The German was sent for but professed to know nothing of the matter, nor could any enquiry clear it up. Another item had been added to that constant and apparently purposeless series of small mysteries which had succeeded each other so rapidly. Setting aside the whole grim story of Sir Charles's death, we had a line of inexplicable incidents all within the limits of two days, which included the receipt of the printed letter, the black-bearded spy in the hansom, the loss of the new brown boot, the loss of the old black boot, and now the return of the new brown boot. Holmes sat in silence in the cab as we drove back to Baker Street, and I knew from his drawn brows and keen face that his mind, like my own, was busy in endeavouring to frame some scheme into which all these strange and apparently disconnected episodes could be fitted. All afternoon and late into the evening he sat lost in tobacco and thought.

Just before dinner two telegrams were handed in. The first ran: 'Have just heard that Barrymore is at the Hall – Baskerville.' The second: 'Visited twenty-three hotels as directed, but sorry to report unable to trace cut sheet of *Times* – Cartwright.'

'There go two of my threads, Watson. There is nothing more stimulating than a case where everything goes against you. We must cast round for another scent.'

'We have still the cabman who drove the spy.'

'Exactly. I have wired to get his name and address from the Official Registry. I should not be surprised if this were an answer to my question.'

The ring at the bell proved to be something even more satisfactory than an answer, however, for the door opened and a rough-looking fellow entered who was evidently the man himself.

'I got a message from the head office that a gent at this address had been inquiring for No. 2704,' said he. 'I've driven my cab this seven years and never a word of complaint. I came here straight from the Yard to ask you to your face what you had against me.'

'I have nothing in the world against you, my good man,' said Holmes. 'On the contrary, I have half a sovereign for you if you will give me a clear answer to my questions.'

'Well, I've had a good day and no mistake,' said the cabman with a grin. 'What was it you wanted to ask, sir?'

'First of all your name and address, in case I want you again.'

'John Clayton, 3 Turpey Street, the Borough. My cab is out of Shipley's Yard, near Waterloo Station.'

Sherlock Holmes made a note of it.

'Now, Clayton, tell me all about the fare who came and watched this house at ten o'clock this morning and afterwards followed the two gentlemen down Regent Street.'

The man looked surprised and a little embarrassed. 'Why there's no good my telling you things, for you seem to know as much as I do already,' said he. 'The truth is that the gentleman told me that he was a detective and that I was to say nothing about him to anyone.'

'My good fellow, this is a very serious business, and you may find yourself in a pretty bad position if you try to hide anything from me. You say that your fare told you that he was a detective?'

'Yes, he did.'

'When did he say this?'

'When he left me.'

'Did he say anything more?'

'He mentioned his name.'

Holmes cast a swift glance of triumph at me. 'Oh, he mentioned his name, did he? That was imprudent. What was the name that he mentioned?'

'His name,' said the cabman, 'was Mr Sherlock Holmes.'

Never have I seen my friend more completely taken aback than by the cabman's reply. For an instant he sat in silent amazement. Then he burst into a hearty laugh.

'A touch, Watson – an undeniable touch!' said he. 'I feel a foil as quick and supple as my own. He got home upon me very prettily that time. So his name was Sherlock Holmes, was it?'

'Yes, sir, that was the gentleman's name.'

'Excellent! Tell me where you picked him up and all that occurred.'

'He hailed me at half-past nine in Trafalgar Square. He said that he was a detective, and he offered me two guineas if I would do exactly what he wanted all day and ask no questions. I was glad enough to agree. First we drove down to the Northland Hotel and waited there until two gentlemen came out and took a cab from the rank. We followed their cab until it pulled up somewhere near here.'

'This very door,' said Holmes.

'Well, I couldn't be sure of that, but I dare say my fare knew all about it. We pulled up halfway down the street and waited an hour and a half. Then the two gentlemen passed us, walking, and we followed down Baker Street and along – '

'I know,' said Holmes.

'Until we got three-quarters down Regent Street. Then my gentleman threw up the trap, and he cried that I should drive right away to Waterloo Station as hard as I could go. I whipped up the mare and we were there under the ten minutes. Then he paid up his two guineas, like a good one, and away he went into the station. Only just as he was leaving he turned round and he said: "It might interest you to know that you have been driving Mr Sherlock Holmes." That's how I come to know the name.'

'I see. And you saw no more of him?'

'Not after he went into the station.'

'And how would you describe Mr Sherlock Holmes?'

The cabman scratched his head. 'Well, he wasn't altogether such an easy gentleman to describe. I'd put him at forty years of age, and he was of a middle height, two or three inches shorter than you, sir. He was dressed like a toff, and he had a black beard, cut square at the end, and a pale face. I don't know as I could say more than that.'

'Colour of his eyes?'

'No, I can't say that.'

'Nothing more that you can remember?'

'No, sir; nothing.'

'Well, then, here is your half-sovereign. There's another one waiting for you if you can bring any more information. Good-night!'

'Good-night, sir, and thank you!'

John Clayton departed chuckling, and Holmes turned to me with a shrug of his shoulders and a rueful smile.

'Snap goes our third thread, and we end where we began,' said he. 'The cunning rascal! He knew our number, knew that Sir Henry Baskerville had consulted me, spotted who I was in Regent Street, conjectured that I had got the number of the cab and would lay my hands on the driver, and so sent back this audacious message. I tell you, Watson, this time we have got a foeman who is worthy of our steel. I've been checkmated in London. I can only wish you better luck in Devonshire. But I'm not easy in my mind about it.'

'About what?'

'About sending you. It's an ugly business, Watson, an ugly dangerous business, and the more I see of it the less I like it. Yes, my dear fellow, you may laugh, but I give you my word that I shall be very glad to have you back safe and sound in Baker Street once more.'

6

Baskerville Hall

Sir Henry Baskerville and Dr Mortimer were ready upon the appointed day, and we started as arranged for Devonshire. Mr Sherlock Holmes drove with me to the station and gave me his last parting injunctions and advice.

'I will not bias your mind by suggesting theories or suspicions, Watson,' said he; 'I wish you simply to report facts in the fullest possible manner to me, and you can leave me to do the theorising.'

'What sort of facts?' I asked.

'Anything which may seem to have a bearing however indirect upon the case, and especially the relations between young Baskerville and his neighbours or any fresh particulars concerning the death of Sir Charles. I have made some enquiries myself in the last few days, but the results have, I fear, been negative. One thing only appears to be certain, and that is that Mr James Desmond, who is the next heir, is an elderly gentleman of a very amiable disposition, so that this persecution does not arise from him. I really think that we may eliminate him entirely from our calculations. There remain the people who will actually surround Sir Henry Baskerville upon the moor.'

'Would it not be well in the first place to get rid of this Barrymore couple?'

'By no means. You could not make a greater mistake. If they are innocent it would be a cruel injustice, and if they are guilty we should be giving up all chance of bringing it home to them. No, no, we will preserve them upon our list of suspects. Then there is a groom at the Hall, if I remember right. There are two moorland farmers. There is our friend Dr Mortimer, whom I believe to be entirely honest, and there is his wife, of whom we know nothing. There is this naturalist, Stapleton, and there is his sister, who is said to be a young lady of attractions. There is Mr Frankland, of Lafter Hall, who is also an unknown factor, and there are one or two other neighbours. These are the folk who must be your very special study.'

'I will do my best.'

'You have arms, I suppose?'

'Yes, I thought it as well to take them.'

'Most certainly. Keep your revolver near you night and day, and never relax your precautions.'

Our friends had already secured a first-class carriage and were waiting for us upon the platform.

'No, we have no news of any kind,' said Dr Mortimer in answer to my friend's questions. 'I can swear to one thing, and that is that we have not been shadowed during the last two days. We have never gone out without keeping a sharp watch, and no one could have escaped our notice.'

'You have always kept together, I presume?'

'Except yesterday afternoon. I usually give up one day to pure amusement when I come to town, so I spent it at the Museum of the College of Surgeons.'

'And I went to look at the folk in the park,' said Baskerville. 'But we had no trouble of any kind.'

'It was imprudent, all the same,' said Holmes, shaking his head and looking very grave. 'I beg, Sir Henry, that you will not go about alone.

Some great misfortune will befall you if you do. Did you get your other boot?'

'No, sir, it is gone forever.'

'Indeed. That is very interesting. Well, goodbye,' he added as the train began to glide down the platform. 'Bear in mind, Sir Henry, one of the phrases in that queer old legend which Dr Mortimer has read to us and avoid the moor in those hours of darkness when the powers of evil are exalted.'

I looked back at the platform when we had left it far behind and saw the tall, austere figure of Holmes standing motionless and gazing after us.

The journey was a swift and pleasant one, and I spent it in making the more intimate acquaintance of my two companions and in playing with Dr Mortimer's spaniel. In a very few hours the brown earth had become ruddy, the brick had changed to granite and red cows grazed in well-hedged fields where the lush grasses and more luxuriant vegetation spoke of a richer, if a damper, climate. Young Baskerville stared eagerly out of the window and cried aloud with delight as he recognised the familiar features of the Devon scenery.

'I've been over a good part of the world since I left it, Dr Watson,' said he; 'but I have never seen a place to compare with it.'

'I never saw a Devonshire man who did not swear by his county,' I remarked.

'It depends upon the breed of men quite as much as on the county,' said Dr Mortimer. 'A glance at our friend here reveals the rounded head of the Celt, which carries inside it the Celtic enthusiasm and power of attachment. Poor Sir Charles's head was of a very rare type, half Gaelic, half Ivernian in its characteristics. But you were very young when you last saw Baskerville Hall, were you not?'

'I was a boy in my teens at the time of my father's death and had never seen the Hall, for he lived in a little cottage on the South Coast. Thence I went straight to a friend in America. I tell you it is all as new to me as it is to Dr Watson, and I'm as keen as possible to see the moor.'

'Are you? Then your wish is easily granted, for there is your first sight of the moor,' said Dr Mortimer, pointing out of the carriage window.

Over the green squares of the fields and the low curve of a wood there rose in the distance a grey, melancholy hill, with a strange jagged summit, dim and vague in the distance, like some fantastic landscape in a dream. Baskerville sat for a long time, his eyes fixed upon it, and I read upon his eager face how much it meant to him, this first sight of that strange spot where the men of his blood had held sway so long and left their mark so deep. There he sat, with his tweed suit and his American accent, in the corner of a prosaic railway-carriage, and yet as I looked at his dark and expressive face I felt more than ever how true a descendant he was of that long line of high-blooded, fiery and masterful men. There were pride, valour and strength in his thick brows, his sensitive nostrils and his large hazel eyes. If on that forbidding moor a difficult and dangerous quest should lie before us, this was at least a comrade for whom one might venture to take a risk with the certainty that he would bravely share it.

The train pulled up at a small wayside station and we all descended. Outside, beyond the low, white fence, a wagonette with a pair of cobs was waiting. Our coming was evidently a great event, for station-master and porters clustered round us to carry out our luggage. It was a sweet, simple country spot, but I was surprised to observe that by the gate there stood two soldierly men in dark uniforms who leaned upon their short rifles and glanced keenly at us as we passed. The coachman, a hard-faced, gnarled little fellow, saluted Sir Henry Baskerville, and in a few minutes we were flying swiftly down the broad, white road. Rolling pasturelands curved upward on either side of us, and old gabled houses peeped out from amid the thick green foliage, but behind the peaceful and sunlit countryside there rose ever, dark against the evening sky, the long, gloomy curve of the moor, broken by the jagged and sinister hills.

The wagonette swung round into a side road, and we curved upward through deep lanes worn by centuries of wheels, high banks on either side, heavy with dripping moss and fleshy hart's-tongue ferns. Bronzing bracken and mottled bramble gleamed in the light of the sinking sun. Still steadily rising, we passed over a narrow granite bridge and skirted a noisy stream which gushed swiftly down, foaming and roaring amid the grey boulders. Both road and stream wound up through a valley dense with scrub oak and fir. At every turn Baskerville gave an exclamation of delight, looking eagerly about him and asking countless questions. To his eyes all seemed beautiful, but to me a tinge of melancholy lay upon the countryside, which bore so clearly the mark of the waning year. Yellow leaves carpeted the lanes and fluttered down upon us as we passed. The rattle of our wheels died away as we drove through drifts of rotting vegetation – sad gifts, as it seemed to me, for Nature to throw before the carriage of the returning heir of the Baskervilles.

'Hallo!' cried Dr Mortimer, 'what is this?'

A steep curve of heath-clad land, an outlying spur of the moor, lay in front of us. On the summit, hard and clear like an equestrian statue upon its pedestal, was a mounted soldier, dark and stern, his rifle poised ready over his forearm. He was watching the road along which we travelled.

'What is this, Perkins?' asked Dr Mortimer.

Our driver half turned in his seat. 'There's a convict escaped from Princetown, sir. He's been out three days now, and the warders watch every road and every station, but they've had no sight of him yet. The farmers about here don't like it, sir, and that's a fact.'

'Well, I understand that they get five pounds if they can give information.'

'Yes, sir, but the chance of five pounds is but a poor thing compared to the chance of having your throat cut. You see, it isn't like any ordinary convict. This is a man that would stick at nothing.'

'Who is he, then?'

'It is Selden, the Notting Hill murderer.'

I remembered the case well, for it was one in which Holmes had taken an interest on account of the peculiar ferocity of the crime and the wanton brutality which had marked all the actions of the assassin. The commutation of his death sentence had been due to some doubts as to his complete sanity, so atrocious was his conduct. Our wagonette had topped a rise and in front of us rose the huge expanse of the moor, mottled with gnarled and craggy cairns and tors. A cold wind swept down from it and set us shivering. Somewhere there, on that desolate plain, was lurking this fiendish man, hiding in a burrow like a wild beast, his heart full of malignancy against the whole race which had cast him out. It needed but this to complete the grim suggestiveness of the barren waste, the chilling wind and the darkling sky. Even Baskerville fell silent and pulled his overcoat more closely around him.

We had left the fertile country behind and beneath us. We looked back on it now, the slanting rays of a low sun turning the streams to threads of gold and glowing on the red earth new turned by the plough and the broad tangle of the woodlands. The road in front of us grew bleaker and wilder over huge russet and olive slopes, sprinkled with giant boulders. Now and then we passed a moorland cottage, walled and roofed with stone, with no creeper to break its harsh outline. Suddenly we looked down into a cuplike depression, patched with stunted oaks and firs which had been twisted and bent by the fury of years of storm. Two high, narrow towers rose over the trees. The driver pointed with his whip.

'Baskerville Hall,' said he.

Its master had risen and was staring with flushed cheeks and shining eyes. A few minutes later we had reached the lodge-gates, a maze of fantastic tracery in wrought iron, with weather-bitten pillars on either side,

blotched with lichens and surmounted by the boars' heads of the Baskervilles. The lodge was a ruin of black granite and bared ribs of rafters,
but facing it was a new building, half constructed, the first fruit of Sir
Charles's South African gold.

Through the gateway we passed into the avenue, where the wheels
were again hushed amid the leaves, and the old trees shot their branches
in a sombre tunnel over our heads. Baskerville shuddered as he looked
up the long, dark drive to where the house glimmered like a ghost at the
farther end.

'Was it here?' he asked in a low voice.

'No, no, the yew alley is on the other side.'

The young heir glanced round with a gloomy face.

'It's no wonder my uncle felt as if trouble were coming on him in
such a place as this,' said he. 'It's enough to scare any man. I'll have a
row of electric lamps up here inside of six months, and you won't know it
again, with a thousand-candlepower Swan and Edison right here in front
of the hall door.'

The avenue opened into a broad expanse of turf, and the house lay
before us. In the fading light I could see that the centre was a heavy block of
building from which a porch projected. The whole front was draped in ivy,
with a patch clipped bare here and there where a window or a coat of arms
broke through the dark veil. From this central block rose the twin towers,
ancient, crenellated and pierced with many loopholes. To right and left of the
turrets were more modern wings of black granite. A dull light shone through
heavy mullioned windows, and from the high chimneys which rose from the
steep, high-angled roof there sprang a single black column of smoke.

'Welcome, Sir Henry! Welcome to Baskerville Hall!'

A tall man had stepped from the shadow of the porch to open the
door of the wagonette. The figure of a woman was silhouetted against the
yellow light of the hall.

She came out and helped the man to hand down our bags.

'You don't mind my driving straight home, Sir Henry?' said Dr
Mortimer. 'My wife is expecting me.'

'Surely you will stay and have some dinner?'

'No, I must go. I shall probably find some work awaiting me. I would
stay to show you over the house, but Barrymore will be a better guide than
I. Goodbye, and never hesitate night or day to send for me if I can be of
service.'

The wheels died away down the drive while Sir Henry and I turned
into the hall, and the door clanged heavily behind us. It was a fine

apartment in which we found ourselves, large, lofty and heavily raftered with huge baulks of age-blackened oak. In the great old-fashioned fireplace behind the high iron dogs a log-fire crackled and snapped. Sir Henry and I held out our hands to it, for we were numb from our long drive. Then we gazed round us at the high, thin window of old stained glass, the oak panelling, the stags' heads, the coats of arms upon the walls, all dim and sombre in the subdued light of the central lamp.

'It's just as I imagined it,' said Sir Henry. 'Is it not the very picture of an old family home? To think that this should be the same hall in which for five hundred years my people have lived. It strikes me solemn to think of it.'

I saw his dark face lit up with a boyish enthusiasm as he gazed about him. The light beat upon him where he stood, but long shadows trailed down the walls and hung like a black canopy above him. Barrymore had returned from taking our luggage to our rooms. He stood in front of us now with the subdued manner of a well-trained servant. He was a remarkable-looking man, tall, handsome, with a square black beard and pale, distinguished features.

'Would you wish dinner to be served at once, sir?'

'Is it ready?'

'In a very few minutes, sir. You will find hot water in your rooms. My wife and I will be happy, Sir Henry, to stay with you until you have made your fresh arrangements, but you will understand that under the new conditions this house will require a considerable staff.'

'What new conditions?'

'I only meant, sir, that Sir Charles led a very retired life, and we were able to look after his wants. You would, naturally, wish to have more company, and so you will need changes in your household.'

'Do you mean that you and your wife wish to leave?'

'Only when it is quite convenient to you, sir.'

'But your family have been with us for several generations, have they not? I should be sorry to begin my life here by breaking an old family connection.'

I seemed to discern some signs of emotion upon the butler's white face.

'I feel that also, sir, and so does my wife. But to tell the truth, sir, we were both very much attached to Sir Charles and his death gave us a shock and made these surroundings very painful to us. I fear that we shall never again be easy in our minds at Baskerville Hall.'

'But what do you intend to do?'

'I have no doubt, sir, that we shall succeed in establishing ourselves in some business. Sir Charles's generosity has given us the means to do so. And now, sir, perhaps I had best show you to your rooms.'

A square balustraded gallery ran round the top of the old hall, approached by a double stair. From this central point two long corridors extended the whole length of the building, from which all the bedrooms opened. My own was in the same wing as Baskerville's and almost next door to it. These rooms appeared to be much more modern than the central part of the house, and the bright paper and numerous candles did something to remove the sombre impression which our arrival had left upon my mind.

But the dining-room which opened out of the hall was a place of shadow and gloom.

It was a long chamber with a step separating the dais where the family sat from the lower portion reserved for their dependants. At one end a minstrels' gallery overlooked it. Black beams shot across above our heads, with smoke-darkened ceiling beyond them. With rows of flaring torches to light it up, and the colour and rude hilarity of an old-time banquet, it might have softened; but now, when two black-clothed gentlemen sat in the little circle of light thrown by a shaded lamp, one's voice became hushed and one's spirit subdued. A dim line of ancestors, in every variety of dress, from the Elizabethan knight to the buck of the Regency, stared down upon us and daunted us by their silent company. We talked little, and I for one was glad when the meal was over and we were able to retire into the modern billiard-room and smoke a cigarette.

'My word, it isn't a very cheerful place,' said Sir Henry. 'I suppose one can tone down to it, but I feel a bit out of the picture at present. I don't wonder that my uncle got a little jumpy if he lived all alone in such a house as this. However, if it suits you, we will retire early tonight, and perhaps things may seem more cheerful in the morning.'

I drew aside my curtains before I went to bed and looked out from my window. It opened upon the grassy space which lay in front of the hall door. Beyond, two copses of trees moaned and swung in a rising wind. A half moon broke through the rifts of racing clouds. In its cold light I saw beyond the trees a broken fringe of rocks, and the long, low curve of the melancholy moor. I closed the curtain, feeling that my last impression was in keeping with the rest.

And yet it was not quite the last. I found myself weary and yet wakeful, tossing restlessly from side to side, seeking for the sleep which would not come. Far away a chiming clock struck out the quarters of the hours, but otherwise a deathly silence lay upon the old house. And then suddenly, in the very dead of the night, there came a sound to my ears, clear, resonant and unmistakable. It was the sob of a woman, the muffled, strangling gasp of one who is torn by an uncontrollable sorrow. I sat up in bed and listened intently. The noise could not have been far away and was certainly in the house. For half an hour I waited with every nerve on the alert, but there came no other sound save the chiming clock and the rustle of the ivy on the wall.

7

The Stapletons of Merripit House

The fresh beauty of the following morning did something to efface from our minds the grim and grey impression which had been left upon both of us by our first experience of Baskerville Hall. As Sir Henry and I sat at breakfast the sunlight flooded in through the high mullioned windows, throwing watery patches of colour from the coats of arms which covered them. The dark panelling glowed like bronze in the golden rays, and it was hard to realise that this was indeed the chamber which had struck such a gloom into our souls upon the evening before.

'I guess it is ourselves and not the house that we have to blame!' said the baronet. 'We were tired with our journey and chilled by our drive, so we took a grey view of the place. Now we are fresh and well, so it is all cheerful once more.'

'And yet it was not entirely a question of imagination,' I answered. 'Did you, for example, happen to hear someone, a woman I think, sobbing in the night?'

'That is curious, for I did when I was half asleep fancy that I heard something of the sort. I waited quite a time, but there was no more of it, so I concluded that it was all a dream.'

'I heard it distinctly, and I am sure that it was really the sob of a woman.'

'We must ask about this right away.' He rang the bell and asked Barrymore whether he could account for our experience. It seemed to me that the pallid features of the butler turned a shade paler still as he listened to his master's question.

'There are only two women in the house, Sir Henry,' he answered. 'One is the scullery-maid, who sleeps in the other wing. The other is my wife, and I can answer for it that the sound could not have come from her.'

And yet he lied as he said it, for it chanced that after breakfast I met Mrs Barrymore in the long corridor with the sun full upon her face. She was a large, impassive, heavy-featured woman with a stern set expression of mouth. But her tell-tale eyes were red and glanced at me from between swollen lids.

It was she, then, who wept in the night, and if she did so her husband must know it. Yet he had taken the obvious risk of discovery in declaring that it was not so. Why had he done this? And why did she weep so bitterly? Already round this pale-faced, handsome, black-bearded man there was gathering an atmosphere of mystery and of gloom. It was he who had been the first to discover the body of Sir Charles, and we had only his word for all the circumstances which led up to the old man's death. Was it possible that it was Barrymore, after all, whom we had seen in the cab in Regent Street? The beard might well have been the same. The cabman had described a somewhat shorter man, but such an impression might easily have been erroneous. How could I settle the point forever? Obviously the first thing to do was to see the Grimpen postmaster and find whether the test telegram had really been placed in Barrymore's own hands. Be the answer what it might, I should at least have something to report to Sherlock Holmes.

Sir Henry had numerous papers to examine after breakfast, so that the time was propitious for my excursion. It was a pleasant walk of four miles along the edge of the moor, leading me at last to a small grey hamlet, in which two larger buildings, which proved to be the inn and the house of Dr Mortimer, stood high above the rest. The postmaster, who was also the village grocer, had a clear recollection of the telegram.

'Certainly, sir,' said he, 'I had the telegram delivered to Mr Barrymore exactly as directed.'

'Who delivered it?'

'My boy here. James, you delivered that telegram to Mr Barrymore at the Hall last week, did you not?'

'Yes, father, I delivered it.'

'Into his own hands?' I asked.

'Well, he was up in the loft at the time, so that I could not put it into his own hands, but I gave it into Mrs Barrymore's hands, and she promised to deliver it at once.'

'Did you see Mr Barrymore?'

'No, sir; I tell you he was in the loft.'

'If you didn't see him, how do you know he was in the loft?'

'Well, surely his own wife ought to know where he is,' said the post-master testily. 'Didn't he get the telegram? If there is any mistake it is for Mr Barrymore himself to complain.'

It seemed hopeless to pursue the enquiry any farther, but it was clear that in spite of Holmes's ruse we had no proof that Barrymore had not been in London all the time. Suppose that it were so – suppose that the same man had been the last who had seen Sir Charles alive, and the first to dog the new heir when he returned to England. What then? Was he the agent of others or had he some sinister design of his own? What interest could he have in persecuting the Baskerville family? I thought of the strange warning clipped out of the leading article of *The Times*. Was that his work or was it possibly the doing of someone who was bent upon counteracting his schemes? The only conceivable motive was that which had been suggested by Sir Henry, that if the family could be scared away a comfortable and permanent home would be secured for the Barrymores. But surely such an explanation as that would be quite inadequate to account for the deep and subtle scheming which seemed to be weaving an invisible net round the young baronet. Holmes himself had said that no more complex case had come to him in all the long series of his sensational investigations. I prayed, as I walked back along the grey, lonely road, that my friend might soon be freed from his preoccupations and able to come down to take this heavy burden of responsibility from my shoulders.

Suddenly my thoughts were interrupted by the sound of running feet behind me and by a voice which called me by name. I turned, expecting to see Dr Mortimer, but to my surprise it was a stranger who was pursuing me.

He was a small, slim, clean-shaven, prim-faced man, flaxen-haired and lean-jawed, between thirty and forty years of age, dressed in a grey suit and wearing a straw hat. A tin box for botanical specimens hung over his shoulder and he carried a green butterfly-net in one of his hands.

'You will, I am sure, excuse my presumption, Dr Watson,' said he as he came panting up to where I stood. 'Here on the moor we are homely folk and do not wait for formal introductions. You may possibly have heard my name from our mutual friend, Mortimer. I am Stapleton, of Merripit House.'

'Your net and box would have told me as much,' said I, 'for I knew that Mr Stapleton was a naturalist. But how did you know me?'

'I have been calling on Mortimer, and he pointed you out to me from the window of his surgery as you passed. As our road lay the same way I thought that I would overtake you and introduce myself. I trust that Sir Henry is none the worse for his journey?'

'He is very well, thank you.'

'We were all rather afraid that after the sad death of Sir Charles the new baronet might refuse to live here. It is asking much of a wealthy man to come down and bury himself in a place of this kind, but I need not tell you that it means a very great deal to the countryside. Sir Henry has, I suppose, no superstitious fears in the matter?'

'I do not think that it is likely.'

'Of course you know the legend of the fiend dog which haunts the family?'

'I have heard it.'

'It is extraordinary how credulous the peasants are about here! Any number of them are ready to swear that they have seen such a creature upon the moor.' He spoke with a smile, but I seemed to read in his eyes that he took the matter more seriously. 'The story took a great hold upon the imagination of Sir Charles, and I have no doubt that it led to his tragic end.'

'But how?'

'His nerves were so worked up that the appearance of any dog might have had a fatal effect upon his diseased heart. I fancy that he really did see something of the kind upon that last night in the yew alley. I feared that some disaster might occur, for I was very fond of the old man, and I knew that his heart was weak.'

'How did you know that?'

'My friend Mortimer told me.'

'You think, then, that some dog pursued Sir Charles, and that he died of fright in consequence?'

'Have you any better explanation?'

'I have not come to any conclusion.'

'Has Mr Sherlock Holmes?'

The words took away my breath for an instant but a glance at the placid face and steadfast eyes of my companion showed that no surprise was intended.

'It is useless for us to pretend that we do not know you, Dr Watson,' said he. 'The records of your detective have reached us here, and you could not celebrate him without being known yourself. When Mortimer told me your name he could not deny your identity. If you are here, then it follows that Mr Sherlock Holmes is interesting himself in the matter, and I am naturally curious to know what view he may take.'

I am afraid that I cannot answer that question.'

'May I ask if he is going to honour us with a visit himself?'

'He cannot leave town at present. He has other cases which engage his attention.'

'What a pity! He might throw some light on that which is so dark to us. But as to your own researches, if there is any possible way in which I can be of service to you I trust that you will command me. If I had any indication of the nature of your suspicions or how you propose to investigate the case, I might perhaps even now give you some aid or advice.'

'I assure you that I am simply here upon a visit to my friend, Sir Henry, and that I need no help of any kind.'

'Excellent!' said Stapleton. 'You are perfectly right to be wary and discreet. I am justly reproved for what I feel was an unjustifiable intrusion, and I promise you that I will not mention the matter again.'

We had come to a point where a narrow grassy path struck off from the road and wound away across the moor. A steep, boulder-sprinkled hill lay upon the right which had in bygone days been cut into a granite quarry. The face which was turned towards us formed a dark cliff, with ferns and brambles growing in its niches. From over a distant rise there floated a grey plume of smoke.

'A moderate walk along this moor-path brings us to Merripit House,' said he. 'Perhaps you will spare an hour that I may have the pleasure of introducing you to my sister.'

My first thought was that I should be by Sir Henry's side. But then I remembered the pile of papers and bills with which his study table was littered. It was certain that I could not help with those. And Holmes had expressly said that I should study the neighbours upon the moor. I accepted Stapleton's invitation, and we turned together down the path.

'It is a wonderful place, the moor,' said he, looking round over the undulating downs, long green rollers, with crests of jagged granite foaming up into fantastic surges. 'You never tire of the moor. You cannot think the wonderful secrets which it contains. It is so vast, and so barren, and so mysterious.'

'You know it well, then?'

'I have only been here two years. The residents would call me a newcomer. We came shortly after Sir Charles settled. But my tastes led me to explore every part of the country round, and I should think that there are few men who know it better than I do.'

'Is it hard to know?'

'Very hard. You see, for example, this great plain to the north here with the queer hills breaking out of it. Do you observe anything remarkable about that?'

'It would be a rare place for a gallop.'

'You would naturally think so and the thought has cost several their lives before now. You notice those bright green spots scattered thickly over it?'

'Yes, they seem more fertile than the rest.'

Stapleton laughed.

'That is the great Grimpen Mire,' said he. 'A false step yonder means death to man or beast. Only yesterday I saw one of the moor ponies wander into it. He never came out. I saw his head for quite a long time craning out of the bog-hole, but it sucked him down at last. Even in dry seasons it is a danger to cross it, but after these autumn rains it is an awful place. And yet I can find my way to the very heart of it and return alive. By George, there is another of those miserable ponies!'

Something brown was rolling and tossing among the green sedges. Then a long, agonised, writhing neck shot upwards and a dreadful cry echoed over the moor. It turned me cold with horror, but my companion's nerves seemed to be stronger than mine.

'It's gone!' said he. 'The mire has him. Two in two days, and many more, perhaps, for they get in the way of going there in the dry weather and never know the difference until the mire has them in its clutches. It's a bad place, the great Grimpen Mire.'

'And you say you can penetrate it?'

'Yes, there are one or two paths which a very active man can take. I have found them out.'

'But why should you wish to go into so horrible a place?'

'Well, you see the hills beyond? They are really islands cut off on all sides by the impassable mire, which has crawled round them in the course of years. That is where the rare plants and the butterflies are, if you have the wit to reach them.'

'I shall try my luck some day.'

He looked at me with a surprised face.

'For God's sake put such an idea out of your mind,' said he. 'Your blood would be upon my head. I assure you that there would not be the least chance of your coming back alive. It is only by remembering certain complex landmarks that I am able to do it.'

'Hallo!' I cried. 'What is that?'

A long, low moan, indescribably sad, swept over the moor. It filled the whole air, and yet it was impossible to say whence it came. From a dull murmur it swelled into a deep roar, and then sank back into a melancholy, throbbing murmur once again. Stapleton looked at me with a curious expression in his face.

'Queer place, the moor!' said he.

'But what is it?'

'The peasants say it is the Hound of the Baskervilles calling for its prey. I've heard it once or twice before, but never quite so loud.'

I looked round, with a chill of fear in my heart, at the huge swelling plain, mottled with the green patches of rushes. Nothing stirred over the vast expanse save a pair of ravens, which croaked loudly from a tor behind us.

'You are an educated man. You don't believe such nonsense as that?' said I. 'What do you think is the cause of so strange a sound?'

'Bogs make queer noises sometimes. It's the mud settling, or the water rising, or something.'

'No, no, that was a living voice.'

'Well, perhaps it was. Did you ever hear a bittern booming?'

'No, I never did.'

'It's a very rare bird – practically extinct – in England now, but all things are possible upon the moor. Yes, I should not be surprised to learn that what we have heard is the cry of the last of the bitterns.'

'It's the weirdest, strangest thing that ever I heard in my life.'

'Yes, it's rather an uncanny place altogether. Look at the hillside yonder. What do you make of those?'

The whole steep slope was covered with grey circular rings of stone, a score of them at least.

'What are they? Sheep-pens?'

'No, they are the homes of our worthy ancestors. Prehistoric man lived thickly on the moor, and as no one in particular has lived there since, we find all his little arrangements exactly as he left them. These are his wigwams with the roofs off. You can even see his hearth and his couch if you have the curiosity to go inside.'

'But it is quite a town. When was it inhabited?'

'Neolithic man – no date.'

'What did he do?'

'He grazed his cattle on these slopes, and he learned to dig for tin when the bronze sword began to supersede the stone axe. Look at the great trench in the opposite hill. That is his mark. Yes, you will find some very singular points about the moor, Dr Watson. Oh, excuse me an instant! It is surely Cyclopides.'

A small fly or moth had fluttered across our path, and in an instant Stapleton was rushing with extraordinary energy and speed in pursuit of it.

To my dismay the creature flew straight for the great mire, and my acquaintance never paused for an instant, bounding from tuft to tuft behind it, his green net waving in the air. His grey clothes and jerky, zigzag, irregular progress made him not unlike some huge moth himself. I was standing watching his pursuit with a mixture of admiration for his extraordinary activity and fear lest he should lose his footing in the treacherous mire when I heard the sound of steps and, turning round, found a woman near me upon the path. She had come from the direction in which the plume of smoke indicated the position of Merripit House, but the dip of the moor had hid her until she was quite close.

I could not doubt that this was the Miss Stapleton of whom I had been told, since ladies of any sort must be few upon the moor, and I remembered that I had heard someone describe her as being a beauty. The woman who approached me was certainly that, and of a most uncommon type. There could not have been a greater contrast between brother and sister, for Stapleton was neutral-tinted, with light hair and grey eyes, while she was darker than any brunette whom I have seen in England – slim, elegant, and tall. She had a proud, finely cut face, so regular that it might have seemed impassive were it not for the sensitive mouth and the beautiful dark, eager eyes. With her perfect figure and elegant dress she was, indeed, a strange apparition upon a lonely moorland path. Her eyes were on her brother as I turned, and then she quickened her pace towards me. I had raised my hat and was about to make some explanatory remark when her own words turned all my thoughts into a new channel.

'Go back!' she said. 'Go straight back to London, instantly.'

I could only stare at her in stupid surprise. Her eyes blazed at me, and she tapped the ground impatiently with her foot.

'Why should I go back?' I asked.

'I cannot explain.' She spoke in a low, eager voice, with a curious lisp in her utterance. 'But for God's sake do what I ask you. Go back and never set foot upon the moor again.'

'But I have only just come.'

'Man, man!' she cried. 'Can you not tell when a warning is for your own good? Go back to London! Start tonight! Get away from this place at all costs! Hush, my brother is coming! Not a word of what I have said. Would you mind getting that orchid for me among the mare's-tails yonder? We are very rich in orchids on the moor, though, of course, you are rather late to see the beauties of the place.'

Stapleton had abandoned the chase and came back to us breathing hard and flushed with his exertions.

'Hallo, Beryl!' said he, and it seemed to me that the tone of his greeting was not altogether a cordial one.

'Well, Jack, you are very hot.'

'Yes, I was chasing a Cyclopides. He is very rare and seldom found in the late autumn. What a pity that I should have missed him!' He spoke unconcernedly, but his small light eyes glanced incessantly from the girl to me.

'You have introduced yourselves, I can see.'

'Yes. I was telling Sir Henry that it was rather late for him to see the true beauties of the moor.'

'Why, who do you think this is?'

'I imagine that it must be Sir Henry Baskerville.'

'No, no,' said I. 'Only a humble commoner, but his friend. My name is Dr Watson.'

A flush of vexation passed over her expressive face. 'We have been talking at cross purposes,' said she.

'Why, you had not very much time for talk,' her brother remarked with the same questioning eyes.

'I talked as if Dr Watson were a resident instead of being merely a visitor,' said she. 'It cannot much matter to him whether it is early or late for the orchids. But you will come on, will you not, and see Merripit House?'

A short walk brought us to it, a bleak moorland house, once the farm of some grazier in the old prosperous days, but now put into repair and turned into a modern dwelling. An orchard surrounded it, but the trees, as is usual upon the moor, were stunted and nipped, and the effect of the whole place was mean and melancholy. We were admitted by a strange, wizened, rusty-coated old manservant, who seemed in keeping with the house. Inside, however, there were large rooms furnished with an elegance in which I seemed to recognise the taste of the lady. As I looked from their windows at the interminable granite-flecked moor rolling unbroken to the farthest horizon I could not but marvel at what could have brought this highly educated man and this beautiful woman to live in such a place.

'Queer spot to choose, is it not?' said he, as if in answer to my thought. 'And yet we manage to make ourselves fairly happy, do we not, Beryl?'

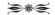

'Quite happy,' said she, but there was no ring of conviction in her words.

'I had a school,' said Stapleton. 'It was in the north country. The work to a man of my temperament was mechanical and uninteresting, but the privilege of living with youth, of helping to mould those young minds and of impressing them with one's own character and ideals was very dear to me. However, the fates were against us. A serious epidemic broke out in the school and three of the boys died. It never recovered from the blow, and much of my capital was irretrievably swallowed up. And yet, if it were not for the loss of the charming companionship of the boys, I could rejoice over my own misfortune, for, with my strong tastes for botany and zoology, I find an unlimited field of work here, and my sister is as devoted to nature as I am. All this, Dr Watson, has been brought upon your head by your expression as you surveyed the moor out of our window.'

'It certainly did cross my mind that it might be a little dull – less for you, perhaps, than for your sister.'

'No, no, I am never dull,' said she quickly.

'We have books, we have our studies, and we have interesting neighbours. Dr Mortimer is a most learned man in his own line. Poor Sir Charles was also an admirable companion. We knew him well and miss him more than I can tell. Do you think that I should intrude if I were to call this afternoon and make the acquaintance of Sir Henry?'

'I am sure that he would be delighted.'

'Then perhaps you would mention that I propose to do so. We may in our humble way do something to make things more easy for him until he becomes accustomed to his new surroundings. Will you come upstairs, Dr Watson, and inspect my collection of Lepidoptera? I think it is the most complete one in the south-west of England. By the time that you have looked through them lunch will be almost ready.'

But I was eager to get back to my charge. The melancholy of the moor, the death of the unfortunate pony, the weird sound which had been associated with the grim legend of the Baskervilles, all these things tinged my thoughts with sadness. Then on the top of these more or less vague impressions there had come the definite and distinct warning of Miss Stapleton, delivered with such intense earnestness that I could not doubt that some grave and deep reason lay behind it. I resisted all pressure to stay for lunch, and I set off at once upon my return journey, taking the grass-grown path by which we had come.

It seems, however, that there must have been some short cut for those who knew it, for before I had reached the road I was astounded to see Miss

Stapleton sitting upon a rock by the side of the track. Her face was beautifully flushed with her exertions and she held her hand to her side.

'I have run all the way in order to cut you off, Dr Watson,' said she. 'I had not even time to put on my hat. I must not stop, or my brother may miss me. I wanted to say to you how sorry I am about the stupid mistake I made in thinking that you were Sir Henry. Please forget the words I said, which have no application whatever to you.'

'But I can't forget them, Miss Stapleton,' said I. 'I am Sir Henry's friend, and his welfare is a very close concern of mine. Tell me why it was that you were so eager that Sir Henry should return to London.'

'A woman's whim, Dr Watson. When you know me better you will understand that I cannot always give reasons for what I say or do.'

'No, no. I remember the thrill in your voice. I remember the look in your eyes. Please, please, be frank with me, Miss Stapleton, for ever since I have been here I have been conscious of shadows all round me. Life has become like that great Grimpen Mire, with little green patches everywhere into which one may sink and with no guide to point the track. Tell me, then, what it was that you meant, and I will promise to convey your warning to Sir Henry.'

An expression of irresolution passed for an instant over her face, but her eyes had hardened again when she answered me.

'You make too much of it, Dr Watson,' said she. 'My brother and I were very much shocked by the death of Sir Charles. We knew him very intimately, for his favourite walk was over the moor to our house. He was deeply impressed with the curse which hung over the family, and when this tragedy came I naturally felt that there must be some grounds for the fears which he had expressed. I was distressed, therefore, when another member of the family came down to live here, and I felt that he should be warned of the danger which he will run. That was all I intended to convey.'

'But what is the danger?'

'You know the story of the hound?'

'I do not believe in such nonsense.'

'But I do. If you have any influence with Sir Henry, take him away from a place which has always been fatal to his family. The world is wide. Why should he wish to live at the place of danger?'

'Because it *is* the place of danger. That is Sir Henry's nature. I fear that unless you can give me some more definite information than this it would be impossible to get him to move.'

'I cannot say anything definite, for I do not know anything definite.'

'I would ask you one more question, Miss Stapleton. If you meant no more than this when you first spoke to me, why should you not wish your brother to overhear what you said? There is nothing to which he, or anyone else, could object.'

'My brother is very anxious to have the Hall inhabited, for he thinks it is for the good of the poor folk upon the moor. He would be very angry if he knew that I have said anything which might induce Sir Henry to go away. But I have done my duty now and I will say no more. I must go back, or he will miss me and suspect that I have seen you. Goodbye!'

She turned and had disappeared in a few minutes among the scattered boulders, while I, with my soul full of vague fears, pursued my way to Baskerville Hall.

8

The First Report of Dr Watson

From this point onward I will follow the course of events by transcribing my own letters to Mr Sherlock Holmes, which lie before me on the table. One page is missing, but otherwise they are exactly as written and show my feelings and suspicions of the moment more accurately than my memory, clear as it is upon these tragic events, can possibly do.

Baskerville Hall, October 13th

MY DEAR HOLMES – My previous letters and telegrams have kept you pretty well up to date as to all that has occurred in this most God-forsaken corner of the world. The longer one stays here the more does the spirit of the moor sink into one's soul, its vastness, and also its grim charm. When you are once out upon its bosom you have left all traces of modern England behind you, but, on the other hand, you are conscious everywhere of the homes and the work of the prehistoric people. On all sides of you as you walk are the houses of these forgotten folk, with their graves and the huge monoliths which are supposed to have marked their temples. As you look at their grey stone huts against the scarred hillsides you leave your own age behind you, and if you were to see a skin-clad, hairy man crawl out from the low door fitting a flint-tipped arrow on to the string of his bow, you would feel that his presence there was more natural than your own. The strange thing is that they should have lived so thickly on what must always have been most unfruitful soil. I am no antiquarian, but I could imagine that they were some unwarlike and harried race who were forced to accept that which none other would occupy.

All this, however, is foreign to the mission on which you sent me and will probably be very uninteresting to your severely practical mind. I can still remember your complete indifference as to whether the sun moved round the earth or the earth round the sun. Let me, therefore, return to the facts concerning Sir Henry Baskerville.

If you have not had any report within the last few days it is because up to today there was nothing of importance to relate. Then a very surprising circumstance occurred, which I shall tell you in due course. But, first of all, I must keep you in touch with some of the other factors in the situation.

One of these, concerning which I have said little, is the escaped convict upon the moor. There is strong reason now to believe that he has got right away, which is a considerable relief to the lonely householders of this district. A fortnight has passed since his flight, during which he has not been seen and nothing has been heard of him. It is surely inconceivable that he could have held out upon the moor during all that time. Of course, so far as his concealment goes there is no difficulty at all. Any one of these stone huts would give him a hiding-place. But there is nothing to eat unless he were to catch and slaughter one of the moor sheep. We think, therefore, that he has gone, and the outlying farmers sleep the better in consequence.

We are four able-bodied men in this household, so that we could take good care of ourselves, but I confess that I have had uneasy moments when I have thought of the Stapletons. They live miles from any help. There is one maid, an old manservant, the sister, and the brother, the latter not a very strong man. They would be helpless in the hands of a desperate fellow like this Notting Hill criminal if he could once effect an entrance. Both Sir Henry and I were concerned at their situation, and it was suggested that Perkins the groom should go over to sleep there, but Stapleton would not hear of it.

The fact is that our friend, the baronet, begins to display a considerable interest in our fair neighbour. It is not to be wondered at, for time hangs heavily in this lonely spot to an active man like him, and she is a very fascinating and beautiful woman. There is something tropical and exotic about her which forms a singular contrast to her cool and unemotional brother. Yet he also gives the idea of hidden fires. He has certainly a very marked influence over her, for I have seen her continually glance at him as she talked as if seeking approbation for what she said. I trust that he is kind to her. There is a dry glitter in his eyes and a firm set of his thin lips, which goes with a positive and possibly a harsh nature. You would find him an interesting study.

He came over to call upon Baskerville on that first day, and the very next morning he took us both to show us the spot where the legend of the wicked Hugo is supposed to have had its origin. It was an excursion of some miles across the moor to a place which is so dismal that it might have suggested the story. We found a short valley between rugged tors which led to an open, grassy space flecked over with the white cotton grass. In the middle of it rose two great stones, worn and sharpened at the upper end until they looked like the huge corroding fangs of some monstrous beast. In every way it corresponded with the scene of the old tragedy. Sir Henry was much interested and asked Stapleton more than once whether he did really believe in the possibility of the interference of the supernatural in the affairs of men. He spoke lightly, but it was evident that he was very much in earnest. Stapleton was guarded in his replies, but it was easy to see that he said less than he might, and that he would not express his whole opinion out of consideration for the feelings of the baronet. He told us of similar cases, where families had suffered from some evil influence, and he left us with the impression that he shared the popular view upon the matter.

On our way back we stayed for lunch at Merripit House, and it was there that Sir Henry made the acquaintance of Miss Stapleton. From the first moment that he saw her he appeared to be strongly attracted by her, and I am much mistaken if the feeling was not mutual. He referred to her again and again on our walk home, and since then hardly a day has passed that we have not seen something of the brother and sister.

They dine here tonight, and there is some talk of our going to them next week. One would imagine that such a match would be very welcome to Stapleton, and yet I have more than once caught a look of the strongest disapprobation in his face when Sir Henry has been paying some attention to his sister. He is much attached to her, no doubt, and would lead a lonely life without her, but it would seem the height of selfishness if he were to stand in the way of her making so brilliant a marriage. Yet I am certain that he does not wish their intimacy to ripen into love, and I have several times observed that he has taken pains to prevent them from being tête-à-tête. By the way, your instructions to me never to allow Sir Henry to go out alone will become very much more onerous if a love affair were to be added to our other difficulties. My popularity would soon suffer if I were to carry out your orders to the letter.

The other day – Thursday, to be more exact – Dr Mortimer lunched with us. He has been excavating a barrow at Long Down and has got a prehistoric skull which fills him with great joy. Never was there such a single-minded enthusiast as he! The Stapletons came in afterwards, and the good doctor took us all to the yew alley at Sir Henry's request to show us exactly how everything occurred upon that fatal night.

It is a long, dismal walk, the yew alley, between two high walls of clipped hedge, with a narrow band of grass upon either side. At the far end is an old tumbledown summerhouse. Halfway down is the moor-gate, where the old gentleman left his cigar-ash. It is a white wooden gate with a latch. Beyond it lies the wide moor. I remembered your theory of the affair and tried to picture all that had occurred. As the old man stood there he saw something coming across the moor, something which terrified him so that he lost his wits and ran and ran until he died of sheer horror and exhaustion. There was the long, gloomy tunnel down which he fled. And from what? A sheepdog of the moor? Or a spectral hound, black, silent and monstrous? Was there a human agency in the matter? Did the pale, watchful Barrymore know more than he cared to say? It was all dim and vague, but always there is the dark shadow of crime behind it.

One other neighbour I have met since I wrote last. This is Mr Frankland, of Lafter Hall, who lives some four miles to the south of us. He is an elderly man, red-faced, white-haired and choleric. His passion is for the British law, and he has spent a large fortune in litigation. He fights for the mere pleasure of fighting and is equally ready to take up either side of a question, so that it is no wonder that he has found it a costly amusement. Sometimes he will shut up a right of way and defy the parish to make him open it. At others he will with his own hands tear down some other man's gate and declare that a path has existed there from time immemorial, defying the owner to prosecute him for trespass. He is learned in old manorial and communal rights, and he applies his knowledge sometimes in favour of the villagers of Fernworthy and sometimes against them, so that he is periodically either carried in triumph down the village street or else burned in effigy, according to his latest exploit. He is said to have about seven lawsuits upon his hands at present, which will probably swallow up the remainder of his fortune and so draw his sting and leave him harmless for the future. Apart from the law he seems a kindly, good-natured person, and I only mention him because you were particular that

I should send some description of the people who surround us. He is curiously employed at present, for, being an amateur astronomer, he has an excellent telescope, with which he lies upon the roof of his own house and sweeps the moor all day in the hope of catching a glimpse of the escaped convict. If he would confine his energies to this all would be well, but there are rumours that he intends to prosecute Dr Mortimer for opening a grave without the consent of the next-of-kin because he dug up the neolithic skull in the barrow on Long Down. He helps to keep our lives from being monotonous and gives a little comic relief where it is badly needed.

And now, having brought you up to date on the escaped convict, the Stapletons, Dr Mortimer and Frankland of Lafter Hall, let me end on that which is most important and tell you more about the Barrymores, and especially about the surprising development of last night.

First of all about the test telegram, which you sent from London in order to make sure that Barrymore was really here. I have already explained that the testimony of the postmaster shows that the test was worthless and that we have no proof one way or the other. I told Sir Henry how the matter stood, and he at once, in his downright fashion, had Barrymore up and asked him whether he had received the telegram himself. Barrymore said that he had.

'Did the boy deliver it into your own hands?' asked Sir Henry.

Barrymore looked surprised, and considered for a little time.

'No,' said he, 'I was in the box-room at the time, and my wife brought it up to me.'

'Did you answer it yourself?'

'No; I told my wife what to answer and she went down to write it.'

In the evening he recurred to the subject of his own accord.

'I could not quite understand the object of your questions this morning, Sir Henry,' said he. 'I trust that they do not mean that I have done anything to forfeit your confidence?'

Sir Henry had to assure him that it was not so and pacify him by giving him a considerable part of his old wardrobe, the London outfit having now all arrived.

Mrs Barrymore is of interest to me. She is a heavy, solid person, very limited, intensely respectable and inclined to be puritanical. You could hardly conceive a less emotional subject. Yet I have told you how, on the first night here, I heard her sobbing bitterly, and since then I have more than once observed traces of tears upon her face. Some deep sorrow gnaws ever at her heart. Sometimes I wonder if she has a guilty memory which haunts her, and sometimes I suspect Barrymore of being a domestic tyrant. I have always felt that there was something singular and question-able in this man's character, but the adventure of last night brings all my suspicions to a head.

And yet it may seem a small matter in itself. You are aware that I am not a very sound sleeper, and since I have been on guard in this house my slumbers have been lighter than ever. Last night, about two in the morning, I was aroused by a stealthy step passing my room. I rose, opened my door and peeped out. A long black shadow was trailing down the corridor. It was thrown by a man who walked softly down the passage with a candle held in his hand. He was in shirt and trousers, with no covering to his feet. I could merely see the outline, but his height told me that it was Barry-more. He walked very slowly and circumspectly, and there was something indescribably guilty and furtive in his whole appearance.

I have told you that the corridor is broken by the balcony which runs round the hall, but that it is resumed upon the farther side. I waited until he had passed out of sight and then I followed him. When I came round the balcony he had reached the end of the farther corridor, and I could see from the glimmer of light through an open door that he had entered one of the rooms. Now, all these rooms are unfurnished and unoccupied so that his expedition became more mysterious than ever. The light shone steadily as if he were standing motionless. I crept down the passage as noiselessly as I could and peeped round the corner of the door.

Barrymore was crouching at the window with the candle held against the glass. His profile was half turned towards me, and his face seemed to be rigid with expectation as he stared out into the blackness of the moor.

For some minutes he stood watching intently. Then he gave a deep groan and with an impatient gesture he put out the light. Instantly I made my way back to my room, and very shortly came the stealthy steps passing once more upon their return journey. Long afterwards when I had fallen into a light sleep I heard a key turn somewhere in a lock, but I could not tell whence the sound came. What it all means I cannot guess, but there is some secret business going on in this house of gloom which sooner or later we shall get to the bottom of. I do not trouble you with my theories, for you asked me to furnish you only with facts. I have had a long talk with Sir Henry this morning, and we have made a plan of campaign founded upon my observations of last night. I will not speak about it just now, but it should make my next report interesting reading.

9

The Light upon the Moor:
The Second Report of Dr Watson

Baskerville Hall, October 15th
MY DEAR HOLMES – If I was compelled to leave you without much news during the early days of my mission you must acknowledge that I am making up for lost time, and that events are now crowding thick and fast upon us. In my last report I ended upon my top note with Barrymore at the window, and now I have quite a budget already which will, unless I am much mistaken, considerably surprise you. Things have taken a turn which I could not have anticipated. In some ways they have within the last forty-eight hours become much clearer and in some ways they have become more complicated. But I will tell you all and you shall judge for yourself.

Before breakfast on the morning following my adventure I went down the corridor and examined the room in which Barrymore had been on the night before. The western window through which he had stared so intently has, I noticed, one peculiarity above all other windows in the house – it commands the nearest outlook on to the moor. There is an opening between two trees which enables one from this point of view to look right down upon it, while from all the other windows it is only a distant glimpse which can be obtained. It follows, therefore, that Barrymore, since only this window would serve the purpose, must have been looking out for something or somebody upon the moor. The night was very dark, so that I can hardly imagine how he could have hoped to see anyone. It had struck me that it was possible that some love intrigue was on foot. That would have accounted for his stealthy movements and also for the uneasiness of his wife. The man is a striking-looking fellow, very well equipped to steal the heart of a country girl, so that this theory seemed to have something to support it. That opening of the door which I had heard after I had returned to my room might mean that he had gone out to keep some clandestine appointment. So I reasoned with myself in the morning, and I tell you the diection of my suspicions, however much the result may have shown that they were unfounded.

But whatever the true explanation of Barrymore's movements might be, I felt that the responsibility of keeping them to myself until I could explain them was more than I could bear. I had an interview with the baronet in his study after breakfast, and I told him all that I had seen. He was less surprised than I had expected.

'I knew that Barrymore walked about nights, and I had a mind to speak to him about it,' said he. 'Two or three times I have heard his steps in the passage, coming and going, just about the hour you name.'

'Perhaps then he pays a visit every night to that particular window,' I suggested.

'Perhaps he does. If so, we should be able to shadow him and see what it is that he is after. I wonder what your friend Holmes would do if he were here.'

'I believe that he would do exactly what you now suggest,' said I. 'He would follow Barrymore and see what he did.'

'Then we shall do it together.'

'But surely he would hear us.'

'The man is rather deaf, and in any case we must take our chance of that. We'll sit up in my room tonight and wait until he passes.' Sir Henry rubbed his hands with pleasure, and it was evident that he hailed the adventure as a relief to his somewhat quiet life upon the moor.

The baronet has been in communication with the architect who prepared the plans for Sir Charles, and with a contractor from London, so that we may expect great changes to begin here soon. There have been decorators and furnishers up from Plymouth, and it is evident that our friend has large ideas and means to spare no pains or expense to restore the grandeur of his family. When the house is renovated and refurnished, all that he will need will be a wife to make it complete. Between ourselves there are pretty clear signs that this will not be wanting if the lady is willing, for I have seldom seen a man more infatuated with a woman than he is with our beautiful neighbour, Miss Stapleton. And yet the course of true love does not run quite as smoothly as one would under the circumstances expect. Today, for example, its surface was broken by a very unexpected ripple, which has caused our friend considerable perplexity and annoyance.

After the conversation which I have quoted about Barrymore, Sir Henry put on his hat and prepared to go out. As a matter of course I did the same.

'What, are *you* coming, Watson?' he asked, looking at me in a curious way.

'That depends on whether you are going on the moor,' said I.

'Yes, I am.'

'Well, you know what my instructions are. I am sorry to intrude, but you heard how earnestly Holmes insisted that I should not leave you, and especially that you should not go alone upon the moor.'

Sir Henry put his hand upon my shoulder, with a pleasant smile.

'My dear fellow,' said he, 'Holmes, with all his wisdom, did not foresee some things which have happened since I have been on the moor. You understand me? I am sure that you are the last man in the world who would wish to be a spoilsport. I must go out alone.'

It put me in a most awkward position. I was at a loss what to say or what to do, and before I had made up my mind he picked up his cane and was gone.

But when I came to think the matter over my conscience reproached me bitterly for having on any pretext allowed him to go out of my sight. I imagined what my feelings would be if I had to return to you and to confess that some misfortune had occurred through my disregard for your instructions. I assure you my cheeks flushed at the very thought. It might not even now be too late to overtake him, so I set off at once in the direction of Merripit House.

I hurried along the road at the top of my speed without seeing anything of Sir Henry, until I came to the point where the moor path branches off. There, fearing that perhaps I had come in the wrong direction after all, I mounted a hill from which I could command a view – the same hill which is cut into the dark quarry. Thence I saw him at once. He was on the moor path about a quarter of a mile off, and a lady was by his side who could only be Miss Stapleton. It was clear that there was already an understanding between them and that they had met by appointment. They were walking slowly along in deep conversation, and I saw her making quick little movements of her hands as if she were very earnest in what she was saying, while he listened intently, and once or twice shook his head in strong dissent. I stood among the rocks watching them, very much puzzled as to what I should do next. To follow them and break into their intimate conversation seemed to be an outrage, and yet my clear duty was never for an instant to let him out of my sight. To act the spy upon a friend was a hateful task. Still, I could see no better course than to observe him from the hill, and to clear my conscience by confessing to him afterwards what I had done. It is true that if any sudden danger had threatened him

I was too far away to be of use, and yet I am sure that you will agree with me that the position was very difficult, and that there was nothing more I could do.

Our friend, Sir Henry, and the lady had halted on the path and were standing deeply absorbed in their conversation, when I was suddenly aware that I was not the only witness of their interview. A wisp of green floating in the air caught my eye, and another glance showed me that it was carried on a stick by a man who was moving among the broken ground. It was Stapleton with his butterfly-net. He was very much closer to the pair than I was, and he appeared to be moving in their direction. At this instant Sir Henry suddenly drew Miss Stapleton to his side. His arm was round her, but it seemed to me that she was straining away from him with her face averted. He stooped his head to hers, and she raised one hand as if in protest. Next moment I saw them spring apart and turn hurriedly round. Stapleton was the cause of the interruption. He was running wildly towards them, his absurd net dangling behind him. He gesticulated and almost danced with excitement in front of the lovers. What the scene meant I could not imagine, but it seemed to me that Stapleton was abusing Sir Henry, who offered explanations, which became more angry as the other refused to accept them. The lady stood by in haughty silence. Finally Stapleton turned upon his heel and beckoned in a peremptory way to his sister, who, after an irresolute glance at Sir Henry, walked off by the side of her brother. The naturalist's angry gestures showed that the lady was included in his displeasure. The baronet stood for a minute looking after them, and then he walked slowly back the way that he had come, his head hanging, the very picture of dejection.

What all this meant I could not imagine, but I was deeply ashamed to have witnessed so intimate a scene without my friend's knowledge. I ran down the hill therefore and met the baronet at the bottom. His face was flushed with anger and his brows were wrinkled, like one who is at his wit's ends what to do.

'Hallo, Watson! Where have you dropped from?' said he. 'You don't mean to say that you came after me in spite of all?'

I explained everything to him: how I had found it impossible to remain behind, how I had followed him, and how I had witnessed all that had occurred. For an instant his eyes blazed at me, but my frankness disarmed his anger, and he broke at last into a rather rueful laugh.

'You would have thought the middle of that prairie a fairly safe place for a man to be private,' said he, 'but, by thunder, the whole countryside seems to have been out to see me do my wooing – and a mighty poor wooing at that! Where had you engaged a seat?'

'I was on that hill.'

'Quite in the back row, eh? But her brother was well up to the front. Did you see him come out on us?'

'Yes, I did.'

'Did he ever strike you as being crazy – this brother of hers?'

'I can't say that he ever did.'

'I dare say not. I always thought him sane enough until today, but you can take it from me that either he or I ought to be in a straitjacket. What's the matter with me, anyhow? You've lived near me for some weeks, Watson. Tell me straight, now! Is there anything that would prevent me from making a good husband to a woman that I loved?'

'I should say not.'

'He can't object to my worldly position, so it must be myself that he has this down on. What has he against me? I never hurt man or woman in my life that I know of. And yet he would not so much as let me touch the tips of her fingers.'

'Did he say so?'

'That, and a deal more. I tell you, Watson, I've only known her these few weeks, but from the first I just felt that she was made for me, and she, too – she was happy when she was with me, and that I'll swear. There's a light in a woman's eyes that speaks louder than words. But he has never let us get together and it was only today for the first time that I saw a chance of having a few words with her alone. She was glad to meet me, but when she did it was not love that she would talk about, and she wouldn't have let me talk about it either if she could have stopped it. She kept coming back to it that this was a place of danger, and that she would never be happy until I had left it. I told her that since I had seen her I was in no hurry to leave it, and that if she really wanted me to go, the only way to work it was for her to arrange to go with me. With that I offered in as many words to marry her, but before she could answer, down came this brother of hers, running at us with a face on him like a madman. He was just white with rage, and those light eyes of his were blazing with fury. What was I doing with the lady? How dared I offer her attentions which were distasteful to her? Did I think that because I was a baronet I could do what I liked? If he had not been her brother I should have known better how to answer him. As it was I told him that my feelings towards his sister were such as I was not ashamed of, and that I hoped that she might honour me by becoming my wife. That seemed to make the matter no better, so then I lost my temper too, and I answered him rather more hotly than I should perhaps, considering that she was standing by. So it ended by his going off with her, as you saw, and here am I as badly puzzled a man as any in this county. Just tell me what it all means, Watson, and I'll owe you more than ever I can hope to pay.'

I tried one or two explanations, but, indeed, I was completely puzzled myself. Our friend's title, his fortune, his age, his character and his appearance are all in his favour, and I know nothing against him unless it be this dark fate which runs in his family. That his advances should be rejected so brusquely without any reference to the lady's own wishes and that the lady should accept the situation without protest is very amazing. However, our conjectures were set at rest by a visit from Stapleton himself that very afternoon. He had come to offer apologies for his rudeness of the morning, and after a long private interview with Sir Henry in his study the upshot of their conversation was that the breach is quite healed, and that we are to dine at Merripit House next Friday as a sign of it.

'I don't say now that he isn't a crazy man,' said Sir Henry; 'I can't forget the look in his eyes when he ran at me this morning, but I must allow that no man could make a more handsome apology than he has done.'

'Did he give any explanation of his conduct?'

'His sister is everything in his life, he says. That is natural enough, and I am glad that he should understand her value. They have always been together, and according to his account he has been a very lonely man with only her as a companion, so that the thought of losing her was really terrible to him. He had not understood, he said, that I was becoming attached to her, but when he saw with his own eyes that it was really so, and that she might be taken away from him, it gave him such a shock that for a time he was not responsible for what he said or did. He was very sorry for all that had passed, and he recognised how foolish and how selfish it was that he should imagine that he could hold a beautiful woman like his sister to himself for her whole life. If she had to leave him he had rather it was to a neighbour like myself than to anyone else. But in any case it was a blow to him and it would take him some time before he could prepare himself to meet it. He would withdraw all opposition upon his part if I would promise for three months to let the matter rest and to be content with cultivating the lady's friendship during that time without claiming her love. This I promised, and so the matter rests.'

So there is one of our small mysteries cleared up. It is something to have touched bottom anywhere in this bog in which we are floundering. We know now why Stapleton looked with disfavour upon his sister's suitor – even when that suitor was so eligible a one as Sir Henry. And now I pass on to another thread which I have extricated out of the tangled skein, the mystery of the sobs in the night, of the tear-stained face of Mrs Barrymore, of the secret journey of the butler to the western lattice window. Congratulate me, my dear Holmes, and tell me that I have not disappointed you as an agent – that you do not regret the confidence which you showed in me when you sent me down. All these things have by one night's work been thoroughly cleared.

I have said 'by one night's work', but, in truth, it was by two nights' work, for on the first we drew entirely blank. I sat up with Sir Henry in his rooms until nearly three o'clock in the morning, but no sound of any sort did we hear except the chiming clock upon the stairs. It was a most melancholy vigil and ended by each of us falling asleep in our chairs. Fortunately we were not discouraged, and we determined to try again. The next night we lowered the lamp and sat smoking cigarettes without making the least sound. It was incredible how slowly the hours crawled by, and yet we were helped through it by the same sort of patient interest which the hunter must feel as he watches the trap into which he hopes the game may wander. One struck, and two, and we had almost for the second time given it up in despair when in an instant we both sat bolt upright in our chairs with all our weary senses keenly on the alert once more. We had heard the creak of a step in the passage.

Very stealthily we heard it pass along until it died away in the distance. Then the baronet gently opened his door and we set out in pursuit. Already our man had gone round the gallery and the corridor was all in darkness. Softly we stole along until we had come into the other wing. We were just in time to catch a glimpse of the tall, black-bearded figure, his shoulders rounded as he tiptoed down the passage. Then he passed through the same door as before, and the light of the candle framed it in the darkness and shot one single yellow beam across the gloom of the corridor. We shuffled cautiously towards it, trying every plank before we dared to put our whole weight upon it. We had taken the precaution of leaving our boots behind us, but, even so, the old boards snapped and creaked beneath our tread. Sometimes it seemed impossible that he should fail to hear our approach. However, the man is fortunately rather deaf, and he was entirely preoccupied in that which he was doing. When at last we reached the door and peeped through we found him crouching at the window, candle in hand, his white, intent face pressed against the pane, exactly as I had seen him two nights before.

We had arranged no plan of campaign, but the baronet is a man to whom the most direct way is always the most natural. He walked into the room, and as he did so Barrymore sprang up from the window with a sharp hiss of his breath and stood, livid and trembling, before us. His dark eyes, glaring out of the white mask of his face, were full of horror and astonishment as he gazed from Sir Henry to me.

'What are you doing here, Barrymore?'

'Nothing, sir.' His agitation was so great that he could hardly speak, and the shadows sprang up and down from the shaking of his candle. 'It was the window, sir. I go round at night to see that they are fastened.'

'On the second floor?'

'Yes, sir, all the windows.'

'Look here, Barrymore,' said Sir Henry sternly, 'we have made up our minds to have the truth out of you, so it will save you trouble to tell it sooner rather than later. Come, now! No lies! What were you doing at that window?'

The fellow looked at us in a helpless way, and he wrung his hands together like one who is in the last extremity of doubt and misery.

'I was doing no harm, sir. I was holding a candle to the window.'

'And why were you holding a candle to the window?'

'Don't ask me, Sir Henry – don't ask me! I give you my word, sir, that it is not my secret, and that I cannot tell it. If it concerned no one but myself I would not try to keep it from you.'

A sudden idea occurred to me, and I took the candle from the trembling hand of the butler.

'He must have been holding it as a signal,' said I. 'Let us see if there is any answer.'

I held it as he had done, and stared out into the darkness of the night. Vaguely I could discern the black bank of the trees and the lighter expanse of the moor, for the moon was behind the clouds. And then I gave a cry of exultation, for a tiny pinpoint of yellow light had suddenly transfixed the dark veil, and glowed steadily in the centre of the black square framed by the window.

'There it is!' I cried.

'No, no, sir, it is nothing – nothing at all!' the butler broke in; 'I assure you, sir – '

'Move your light across the window, Watson!' cried the baronet. 'See, the other moves also! Now, you rascal, do you deny that it is a signal? Come, speak up! Who is your confederate out yonder, and what is this conspiracy that is going on?'

The man's face became openly defiant.

'It is my business, and not yours. I will not tell.'

'Then you leave my employment right away.'

'Very good, sir. If I must I must.'

'And you go in disgrace. By thunder, you may well be ashamed of yourself. Your family has lived with mine for over a hundred years under this roof, and here I find you deep in some dark plot against me.'

'No, no, sir; no, not against you!' It was a woman's voice, and Mrs Barrymore, paler and more horror-struck than her husband, was standing at the door. Her bulky figure in a shawl and skirt might have been comic were it not for the intensity of feeling upon her face.

'We have to go, Eliza. This is the end of it. You can pack our things,' said the butler.

'Oh, John, John, have I brought you to this? It is my doing, Sir Henry – all mine. He has done nothing except for my sake and because I asked him.'

'Speak out, then! What does it mean?'

'My unhappy brother is starving on the moor. We cannot let him perish at our very gates. The light is a signal to him that food is ready for him, and his light out yonder is to show the spot to which to bring it.'

'Then your brother is – '

'The escaped convict, sir – Selden, the criminal.'

'That's the truth, sir,' said Barrymore. 'I said that it was not my secret and that I could not tell it to you. But now you have heard it, and you will see that if there was a plot it was not against you.'

This, then, was the explanation of the stealthy expeditions at night and the light at the window. Sir Henry and I both stared at the woman in amazement. Was it possible that this stolidly respectable person was of the same blood as one of the most notorious criminals in the country?

'Yes, sir, my name was Selden, and he is my younger brother. We humoured him too much when he was a lad and gave him his own way in everything until he came to think that the world was made for his pleasure, and that he could do what he liked in it. Then as he grew older he met wicked companions, and the devil entered into him until he broke my mother's heart and dragged our name in the dirt. From crime to crime he sank lower and lower until it is only the mercy of God which has snatched him from the scaffold; but to me, sir, he was always the little curly-headed boy that I had nursed and played with as an elder sister would. That was why he broke prison, sir. He knew that I was here and that we could not refuse to help him. When he dragged himself here one night, weary and starving, with the warders hard at his heels, what could we do? We took him in and fed him and cared for him. Then you returned, sir, and my brother thought he would be safer on the moor than anywhere else until the hue and cry was over, so he lay in hiding there. But every second night we made sure if he was still there by putting a light in the window, and if there was an answer my husband took out some bread and meat to him. Every day we hoped he would be gone, but as long as he was there we could not desert him. That is the whole truth, as I am an honest Christian woman and you will see that if there is blame in the matter it does not lie with my husband but with me, for whose sake he has done all that he has.'

The woman's words came with an intense earnestness which carried conviction with them.

'Is this true, Barrymore?'

'Yes, Sir Henry. Every word of it.'

'Well, I cannot blame you for standing by your own wife. Forget what I have said. Go to your room, you two, and we shall talk further about this matter in the morning.'

When they were gone we looked out of the window again. Sir Henry had flung it open, and the cold night wind beat in upon our faces. Far away in the black distance there still glowed that one tiny point of yellow light.

'I wonder he dares,' said Sir Henry.

'It may be so placed as to be only visible from here.'

'Very likely. How far do you think it is?'

'Out by the Cleft Tor, I think.'

'Not more than a mile or two off.'

'Hardly that.'

'Well, it cannot be far if Barrymore had to carry out the food to it. And he is waiting, this villain, beside that candle. By thunder, Watson, I am going out to take that man!'

The same thought had crossed my own mind. It was not as if the Barrymores had taken us into their confidence. Their secret had been forced from them. The man was a danger to the community, an unmitigated scoundrel for whom there was neither pity nor excuse. We were only doing our duty in taking this chance of putting him back where he could do no harm. With his brutal and violent nature, others would have to pay the price if we held our hands. Any night, for example, our neighbours the Stapletons might be attacked by him, and it may have been the thought of this which made Sir Henry so keen upon the adventure.

'I will come,' said I.

'Then get your revolver and put on your boots. The sooner we start the better, as the fellow may put out his light and be off.'

In five minutes we were outside the door, starting upon our expedition. We hurried through the dark shrubbery, amid the dull moaning of the autumn wind and the rustle of the falling leaves. The night air was heavy with the smell of damp and decay. Now and again the moon peeped out for an instant, but clouds were driving over the face of the sky, and just as we came out on the moor a thin rain began to fall. The light still burned steadily in front.

'Are you armed?' I asked.

'I have a hunting-crop.'

'We must close in on him rapidly, for he is said to be a desperate fellow. We shall take him by surprise and have him at our mercy before he can resist.'

'I say, Watson,' said the baronet, 'what would Holmes say to this? How about that hour of darkness in which the power of evil is exalted?'

As if in answer to his words there rose suddenly out of the vast gloom of the moor that strange cry which I had already heard upon the borders of the great Grimpen Mire. It came with the wind through the silence of the night, a long, deep mutter then a rising howl, and then the sad moan in which it died away. Again and again it sounded, the whole air throbbing with it, strident, wild and menacing. The baronet caught my sleeve and his face glimmered white through the darkness.

'My God, what's that, Watson?'

'I don't know. It's a sound they have on the moor. I heard it once before.'

It died away, and an absolute silence closed in upon us. We stood straining our ears, but nothing came.

'Watson,' said the baronet, 'it was the cry of a hound.'

My blood ran cold in my veins, for there was a break in his voice which told of the sudden horror which had seized him.

'What do they call this sound?' he asked.

'Who?'

'The folk of the countryside.'

'Oh, they are ignorant people. Why should you mind what they call it?'

'Tell me, Watson. What do they say of it?'

I hesitated but could not escape the question. 'They say it is the cry of the Hound of the Baskervilles.'

He groaned and was silent for a few moments.

'A hound it was,' he said at last, 'but it seemed to come from miles away, over yonder, I think.'

'It was hard to say whence it came.'

'It rose and fell with the wind. Isn't that the direction of the great Grimpen Mire?'

'Yes, it is.'

'Well, it was up there. Come now, Watson, didn't you think yourself that it was the cry of a hound? I am not a child. You need not fear to speak the truth.'

'Stapleton was with me when I heard it last. He said that it might be the calling of a strange bird.'

'No, no, it was a hound. My God, can there be some truth in all these stories? Is it possible that I am really in danger from so dark a cause? You don't believe it, do you, Watson?'

'No, no.'

'And yet it was one thing to laugh about it in London, and it is another to stand out here in the darkness of the moor and to hear such a cry as that. And my uncle! There was the footprint of the hound beside him as he lay. It all fits together. I don't think that I am a coward, Watson, but that sound seemed to freeze my very blood. Feel my hand!'

It was as cold as a block of marble.

'You'll be all right tomorrow.'

'I don't think I'll get that cry out of my head. What do you advise that we do now?'

'Shall we turn back?'

'No, by thunder; we have come out to get our man, and we will do it. We after the convict, and a hell-hound, as likely as not, after us. Come on! We'll see it through if all the fiends of the pit are loose upon the moor.'

We stumbled slowly along in the darkness, with the black loom of the craggy hills around us, and the yellow speck of light burning steadily in front. There is nothing so deceptive as the distance of a light upon a pitch-dark night, and sometimes the glimmer seemed to be far away upon the horizon and sometimes it might have been within a few yards of us. But at last we could see whence it came, and then we knew that we were indeed very close. A guttering candle was stuck in a crevice of the rocks, which flanked it on each side so as to keep the wind from it and also to prevent it from being visible, save in the direction of Baskerville Hall. A boulder of granite concealed our approach, and crouching behind it we gazed over it at the signal light. It was strange to see this single candle burning there in the middle of the moor, with no sign of life near it – just the one straight yellow flame and the gleam of the rock on each side of it.

'What shall we do now?' whispered Sir Henry.

'Wait here. He must be near his light. Let us see if we can get a glimpse of him.'

The words were hardly out of my mouth when we both saw him. Over the rocks, in the crevice of which the candle burned, there was thrust out an evil yellow face, a terrible animal face, all seamed and scored with vile passions. Foul with mire, with a bristling beard and hung with matted hair, it might well have belonged to one of those old savages who dwelt in the burrows on the hillsides. The light beneath him was reflected in his small, cunning eyes, which peered fiercely to right and left through the darkness, like a crafty and savage animal who has heard the steps of the hunters.

Something had evidently aroused his suspicions. It may have been that Barrymore had some private signal which we had neglected to give, or the fellow may have had some other reason for thinking that all was not well, but I could read his fears upon his wicked face. Any instant he might dash out the light and vanish in the darkness. I sprang forward therefore, and Sir Henry did the same. At the same moment the convict screamed out a curse at us and hurled a rock which splintered up against the boulder which had sheltered us. I caught one glimpse of his short, squat, strongly built figure as he sprang to his feet and turned to run. At the same moment by a lucky chance the moon broke through the clouds. We rushed over the brow of the hill, and there was our man running with great speed down the other side, springing over the stones in his way with the activity of a mountain goat. A lucky long shot of my revolver might have crippled him, but I had brought it only to defend myself if attacked and not to shoot an unarmed man who was running away.

We were both fair runners and in good condition, but we soon found that we had no chance of overtaking him. We saw him for a long time in the moonlight, until he was only a small speck moving swiftly among the boulders upon the side of a distant hill. We ran and ran until we were completely blown, but the space between us grew ever wider. Finally we stopped and sat panting on two rocks, while we watched him disappearing in the distance.

And it was at this moment that there occurred a most strange and unexpected thing. We had risen from our rocks and were turning to go home, having abandoned the hopeless chase. The moon was low upon the right, and the jagged pinnacle of a granite tor stood up against the lower curve of its silver disc. There, outlined as black as an ebony statue on that shining background, I saw the figure of a man upon the tor. Do not think that it was a delusion, Holmes. I assure you that I have never in my life seen anything more clearly. As far as I could judge, the figure was that of a tall, thin man. He stood with his legs a little separated, his arms folded, his head bowed, as if he were brooding over that enormous wilderness of peat and granite which lay before him. He might have been the very spirit of that terrible place. It was not the convict. This man was far from the place where the latter had disappeared. Besides, he was a much taller man. With a cry of surprise I pointed him out to the baronet, but in the instant during which I had turned to grasp his arm the man was gone. There was the sharp pinnacle of granite still cutting the lower edge of the moon, but its peak bore no trace of that silent and motionless figure.

I wished to go in that direction and to search the tor, but it was some distance away. The baronet's nerves were still quivering from that cry, which recalled the dark story of his family, and he was not in the mood for fresh adventures. He had not seen this lonely man upon the tor and could not feel the thrill which his strange presence and his commanding attitude had given to me. 'A warder, no doubt,' said he. 'The moor has been thick with them since this fellow escaped.' Well, perhaps his explanation may be the right one, but I should like to have some further proof of it. Today we mean to communicate to the Princetown people where they should look for their missing man, but it is hard lines that we have not actually had the triumph of bringing him back as our own prisoner. Such are the adventures of last night, and you must acknowledge, my dear Holmes, that I have done you very well in the matter of a report. Much of what I tell you is no doubt quite irrelevant, but still I feel that it is best that I should let you have all the facts and leave you to select for yourself those which will be of most service to you in helping you to your conclusions. We are certainly making some progress. So far as the Barrymores go, we have found the motive of their actions, and that has cleared up the situation very much. But the moor with its mysteries and its strange inhabitants remains as inscrutable as ever. Perhaps in my next I may be able to throw some light upon this also. Best of all would it be if you could come down to us.

IO

Extract from the Diary of Dr Watson

So far I have been able to quote from the reports which I have forwarded during these early days to Sherlock Holmes. Now, however, I have arrived at a point in my narrative where I am compelled to abandon this method and to trust once more to my recollections, aided by the diary which I kept at the time. A few extracts from the latter will carry me on to those scenes which are indelibly fixed in every detail upon my memory. I proceed, then, from the morning which followed our abortive chase of the convict and our other strange experiences upon the moor.

October 16th   A dull and foggy day with a drizzle of rain. The house is banked in with rolling clouds, which rise now and then to show the dreary curves of the moor, with thin, silver veins upon the sides of the hills and the distant boulders gleaming where the light strikes upon their wet faces. It is melancholy outside and in. The baronet is in a black reaction after the excitements of the night. I am conscious myself of a weight at my heart and a feeling of impending danger – ever-present danger, which is the more terrible because I am unable to define it.

And have I not cause for such a feeling? Consider the long sequence of incidents which have all pointed to some sinister influence which is at work around us. There is the death of the last occupant of the Hall, fulfilling so exactly the conditions of the family legend, and there are the repeated reports from peasants of the appearance of a strange creature upon the moor. Twice I have with my own ears heard the sound which resembled the distant baying of a hound. It is incredible, impossible, that it should really be outside the ordinary laws of nature. A spectral hound which leaves material footmarks and fills the air with its howling is surely not to be thought of. Stapleton may fall in with such a superstition, and Mortimer also, but if I have one quality upon earth it is common sense, and nothing will persuade me to believe in such a thing. To do so would be to descend to the level of these poor peasants, who are not content with a mere fiend dog but must needs describe him with hell-fire shooting from his mouth and eyes. Holmes would not listen to such fancies, and I am his agent. But facts are facts, and I have twice heard this crying upon the moor. Suppose that there were really some huge hound loose upon it; that would go far to explain everything. But where could such a hound lie concealed, where did it get its food, where did it come from, how was it that no one saw it by day? It must be confessed that the natural explanation offers almost as many difficulties as the other. And always, apart from the hound, there is the fact of the human agency in London, the man in the cab and the letter which warned Sir Henry against the moor. This at least was real, but it might have been the work of a protecting friend as easily as of an enemy. Where is that friend or enemy now? Has he remained in London, or has he followed us down here? Could he – could he be the stranger whom I saw upon the tor?

It is true that I have had only the one glance at him, and yet there are some things to which I am ready to swear. He is no one whom I have seen down here, and I have now met all the neighbours. The figure was far taller than that of Stapleton, far thinner than that of Frankland. Barrymore it might possibly have been, but we had left him behind us, and I am certain that he could not have followed us. A stranger then is still dogging us, just as a stranger dogged us in London. We have never shaken him off. If I could lay my hands upon that man, then at last we might find ourselves at the end of all our difficulties. To this one purpose I must now devote all my energies.

My first impulse was to tell Sir Henry all my plans. My second and wisest one is to play my own game and speak as little as possible to anyone. He is silent and distrait. His nerves have been strangely shaken by that sound upon the moor. I will say nothing to add to his anxieties, but I will take my own steps to attain my own end.

We had a small scene this morning after breakfast. Barrymore asked leave to speak with Sir Henry, and they were closeted in his study some little time. Sitting in the billiard-room, I more than once heard the sound of voices raised, and I had a pretty good idea what the point was which was under discussion. After a time the baronet opened his door and called for me.

'Barrymore considers that he has a grievance,' he said. 'He thinks that it was unfair on our part to hunt his brother-in-law down when he, of his own free will, had told us the secret.'

The butler was standing, very pale but very collected, before us.

'I may have spoken too warmly, sir,' said he, 'and if I have, I am sure that I beg your pardon. At the same time, I was very much surprised when I heard you two gentlemen come back this morning and learned that you had been chasing Selden. The poor fellow has enough to fight against without my putting more upon his track.'

'If you had told us of your own free will it would have been a different thing,' said the baronet, 'you only told us, or rather your wife only told us, when it was forced from you and you could not help yourself.'

'I didn't think you would have taken advantage of it, Sir Henry – indeed I didn't.'

'The man is a public danger. There are lonely houses scattered over the moor, and he is a fellow who would stick at nothing. You only want to get a glimpse of his face to see that. Look at Mr Stapleton's house, for example, with no one but himself to defend it. There's no safety for anyone until he is under lock and key.'

'He'll break into no house, sir. I give you my solemn word upon that. But he will never trouble anyone in this country again. I assure you, Sir Henry, that in a very few days the necessary arrangements will have been made and he will be on his way to South America. For God's sake, sir, I beg of you not to let the police know that he is still on the moor. They have given up the chase there, and he can lie quiet until the ship is ready for him. You can't tell on him without getting my wife and me into trouble. I beg you, sir, to say nothing to the police.'

'What do you say, Watson?'

I shrugged my shoulders. 'If he were safely out of the country it would relieve the taxpayer of a burden.'

'But how about the chance of his holding someone up before he goes?'

'He would not do anything so mad, sir. We have provided him with all that he can want. To commit a crime would be to show where he was hiding.'

'That is true,' said Sir Henry. 'Well, Barrymore – '

'God bless you, sir, and thank you from my heart! It would have killed my poor wife had he been taken again.'

'I guess we are aiding and abetting a felony, Watson? But, after what we have heard I don't feel as if I could give the man up, so there is an end of it. All right, Barrymore, you can go.'

With a few broken words of gratitude the man turned, but he hesitated and then came back.

'You've been so kind to us, sir, that I should like to do the best I can for you in return. I know something, Sir Henry, and perhaps I should have said it before, but it was long after the inquest that I found it out. I've never breathed a word about it yet to mortal man. It's about poor Sir Charles's death.'

The baronet and I were both upon our feet. 'Do you know how he died?'

'No, sir, I don't know that.'

'What then?'

'I know why he was at the gate at that hour. It was to meet a woman.'

'To meet a woman! He?'

'Yes, sir.'

'And the woman's name?'

'I can't give you the name, sir, but I can give you the initials. Her initials were L. L.'

'How do you know this, Barrymore?'

'Well, Sir Henry, your uncle had a letter that morning. He had usually a great many letters, for he was a public man and well known for his kind heart, so that everyone who was in trouble was glad to turn to him. But that morning, as it chanced, there was only this one letter, so I took the more notice of it. It was from Coombe Tracey, and it was addressed in a woman's hand.'

'Well?'

'Well, sir, I thought no more of the matter, and never would have done had it not been for my wife. Only a few weeks ago she was cleaning out Sir Charles's study – it had never been touched since his death – and she found the ashes of a burned letter in the back of the grate. The greater part of it was charred to pieces, but one little slip, the end of a page, hung together, and the writing could still be read, though it was grey on a black ground. It seemed to us to be a postscript at the end of the letter and it said: Please, please, as you are a gentleman, burn this letter, and be at the gate by ten o'clock. Beneath it were signed the initials L. L.'

'Have you got that slip?'

'No, sir, it crumbled all to bits after we moved it.'

'Had Sir Charles received any other letters in the same writing?'

'Well, sir, I took no particular notice of his letters. I should not have noticed this one, only it happened to come alone.'

'And you have no idea who L. L. is?'

'No, sir. No more than you have. But I expect if we could lay our hands upon that lady we should know more about Sir Charles's death.'

'I cannot understand, Barrymore, how you came to conceal this important information.'

'Well, sir, it was immediately after that our own trouble came to us. And then again, sir, we were both of us very fond of Sir Charles, as we well might be considering all that he has done for us. To rake this up couldn't help our poor master, and it's well to go carefully when there's a lady in the case. Even the best of us – '

'You thought it might injure his reputation?'

'Well, sir, I thought no good could come of it. But now you have been kind to us, and I feel as if it would be treating you unfairly not to tell you all that I know about the matter.'

'Very good, Barrymore; you can go.' When the butler had left us Sir Henry turned to me. 'Well, Watson, what do you think of this new light?'

'It seems to leave the darkness rather blacker than before.'

'So I think. But if we can only trace L. L. it should clear up the whole business. We have gained that much. We know that there is someone who has the facts if we can only find her. What do you think we should do?'

'Let Holmes know all about it at once. It will give him the clue for which he has been seeking. I am much mistaken if it does not bring him down.'

I went at once to my room and drew up my report of the morning's conversation for Holmes. It was evident to me that he had been very busy of late, for the notes which I had from Baker Street were few and short, with no comments upon the information which I had supplied and hardly any reference to my mission. No doubt his blackmailing case is absorbing all his faculties. And yet this new factor must surely arrest his attention and renew his interest. I wish that he were here.

October 17th All day today the rain poured down, rustling on the ivy and dripping from the eaves. I thought of the convict out upon the bleak, cold, shelterless moor. Poor devil! Whatever his crimes, he has suffered something to atone for them. And then I thought of that other one – the face in the cab, the figure against the moon. Was he also out in that deluge – the unseen watcher, the man of darkness? In the evening I put on my waterproof and I walked far up on the sodden moor, full of dark imaginings, the rain beating upon my face and the wind whistling about my ears. God help those who wander into the Great Mire now, for even the firm uplands are becoming a morass. I found the black tor upon which I had seen the solitary watcher, and from its craggy summit I looked out myself across the melancholy downs. Rain squalls drifted across their russet face, and the heavy, slate-coloured clouds hung low over the landscape, trailing in grey wreaths down the sides of the fantastic hills. In the distant hollow on the left, half hidden by the mist, the two thin towers of Baskerville Hall rose above the trees. They were the only signs of human life which I could see, save only those prehistoric huts which lay thickly upon the slopes of the hills. Nowhere was there any trace of that lonely man whom I had seen on the same spot two nights before.

As I walked back I was overtaken by Dr Mortimer, driving in his dog-cart over a rough moorland track which led from the outlying farmhouse of Foulmire. He has been very attentive to us, and hardly a day has passed that he has not called at the Hall to see how we were getting on. He insisted upon my climbing into his dog-cart, and he gave me a lift homeward. I found him much troubled over the disappearance of his little spaniel. It had wandered on to the moor and had never come back. I gave him such consolation as I might, but I thought of the pony on the Grimpen Mire, and I do not fancy that he will see his little dog again.

'By the way, Mortimer,' said I as we jolted along the rough road, 'I suppose there are few people living within driving distance of this whom you do not know?'

'Hardly any, I think.'

'Can you, then, tell me the name of any woman whose initials are L. L.?'

He thought for a few minutes.

'No,' said he. 'There are a few gypsies and labouring folk for whom I can't answer, but among the farmers or gentry there is no one whose initials are those. Wait a bit though,' he added after a pause. 'There is Laura Lyons – her initials are L. L. – but she lives in Coombe Tracey.'

'Who is she?' I asked.

'She is Frankland's daughter.'

'What! Old Frankland the crank?'

'Exactly. She married an artist named Lyons, who came sketching on the moor. He proved to be a blackguard and deserted her. The fault from what I hear may not have been entirely on one side. Her father refused to have anything to do with her because she had married without his consent and perhaps for one or two other reasons as well. So, between the old sinner and the young one the girl has had a pretty bad time.'

'How does she live?'

'I fancy old Frankland allows her a pittance, but it cannot be more, for his own affairs are considerably involved. Whatever she may have deserved, one could not allow her to go hopelessly to the bad. Her story got about, and several of the people here did something to enable her to earn an honest living. Stapleton did for one, and Sir Charles for another. I gave a trifle myself. It was to set her up in a typewriting business.'

He wanted to know the object of my enquiries, but I managed to satisfy his curiosity without telling him too much, for there is no reason why we should take anyone into our confidence. Tomorrow morning I shall find my way to Coombe Tracey, and if I can see this Mrs Laura Lyons, of equivocal reputation, a long step will have been made towards clearing one incident in this chain of mysteries. I am certainly developing the wisdom of the serpent, for when Mortimer pressed his questions to an inconvenient extent I asked him casually to what type Frankland's skull belonged, and so heard nothing but craniology for the rest of our drive. I have not lived for years with Sherlock Holmes for nothing.

I have only one other incident to record upon this tempestuous and melancholy day. This was my conversation with Barrymore just now, which gives me one more strong card which I can play in due time.

Mortimer had stayed to dinner, and he and the baronet played écarté afterwards. The butler brought me my coffee into the library, and I took the chance to ask him a few questions.

'Well,' said I, 'has this precious relation of yours departed, or is he still lurking out yonder?'

'I don't know, sir. I hope to heaven that he has gone, for he has brought nothing but trouble here! I've not heard of him since I left out food for him last, and that was three days ago.'

'Did you see him then?'

'No, sir, but the food was gone when next I went that way.'

'Then he was certainly there?'

'So you would think, sir, unless it was the other man who took it.'

I sat with my coffee-cup halfway to my lips and stared at Barrymore.

'You know that there is another man then?'

'Yes, sir; there is another man upon the moor.'

'Have you seen him?'

'No, sir.'

'How do you know of him then?'

'Selden told me of him, sir, a week ago or more. He's in hiding, too, but he's not a convict as far as I can make out. I don't like it, Dr Watson – I tell you straight, sir, that I don't like it.' He spoke with a sudden passion of earnestness.

'Now, listen to me, Barrymore! I have no interest in this matter but that of your master. I have come here with no object except to help him. Tell me, frankly, what it is that you don't like.'

Barrymore hesitated for a moment, as if he regretted his outburst or found it difficult to express his own feelings in words.

'It's all these goings-on, sir,' he cried at last, waving his hand towards the rain-lashed window which faced the moor. 'There's foul play some-where, and there's black villainy brewing, to that I'll swear! Very glad I should be, sir, to see Sir Henry on his way back to London again!'

'But what is it that alarms you?'

'Look at Sir Charles's death! That was bad enough, for all that the coroner said. Look at the noises on the moor at night. There's not a man would cross it after sundown if he was paid for it. Look at this stranger hiding out yonder, and watching and waiting! What's he waiting for? What does it mean? It means no good to anyone of the name of Baskerville, and very glad I shall be to be quit of it all on the day that Sir Henry's new serv-ants are ready to take over the Hall.'

'But about this stranger,' said I. 'Can you tell me anything about him? What did Selden say? Did he find out where he hid, or what he was doing?'

'He saw him once or twice, but he is a deep one and gives nothing away. At first he thought that he was the police, but soon he found that he had some lay of his own. A kind of gentleman he was, as far as he could see, but what he was doing he could not make out.'

'And where did he say that he lived?'

'Among the old houses on the hillside – the stone huts where the old folk used to live.'

'But how about his food?'

'Selden found out that he has got a lad who works for him and brings all he needs. I dare say he goes to Coombe Tracey for what he wants.'

'Very good, Barrymore. We may talk further of this some other time.' When the butler had gone I walked over to the black window, and I looked through a blurred pane at the driving clouds and at the tossing outline of the windswept trees. It is a wild night indoors, and what must it be in a stone hut upon the moor? What passion of hatred can it be which leads a man to lurk in such a place at such a time! And what deep and earnest purpose can he have which calls for such a trial! There, in that hut upon the moor, seems to lie the very centre of that problem which has vexed me so sorely. I swear that another day shall not have passed before I have done all that man can do to reach the heart of the mystery.

II

The Man on the Tor

The extract from my private diary which forms the last chapter has brought my narrative up to the 18th of October, a time when these strange events began to move swiftly towards their terrible conclusion. The incidents of the next few days are indelibly graven upon my recollection, and I can tell them without reference to the notes made at the time. I start them from the day which succeeded that upon which I had established two facts of great importance, the one that Mrs Laura Lyons of Coombe Tracey had written to Sir Charles Baskerville and made an appointment with him at the very place and hour that he met his death, the other that the lurking man upon the moor was to be found among the stone huts upon the hillside. With these two facts in my possession I felt that either my intelligence or my courage must be deficient if I could not throw some further light upon these dark places.

I had no opportunity to tell the baronet what I had learned about Mrs Lyons upon the evening before, for Dr Mortimer remained with him at cards until it was very late. At breakfast, however, I informed him about my discovery and asked him whether he would care to accompany me to Coombe Tracey. At first he was very eager to come, but on second thoughts it seemed to both of us that if I went alone the results might be better. The more formal we made the visit the less information we might obtain. I left Sir Henry behind, therefore, not without some prickings of conscience, and drove off upon my new quest.

When I reached Coombe Tracey I told Perkins to put up the horses, and I made enquiries for the lady whom I had come to interrogate. I had no difficulty in finding her rooms, which were central and well appointed. A maid showed me in without ceremony, and as I entered the sitting-room a lady, who was sitting before a Remington typewriter, sprang up with a pleasant smile of welcome. Her face fell, however, when she saw that I was a stranger, and she sat down again and asked me the object of my visit.

The first impression left by Mrs Lyons was one of extreme beauty. Her eyes and hair were of the same rich hazel colour, and her cheeks, though considerably freckled, were flushed with the exquisite bloom of the brunette, the dainty pink which lurks at the heart of the sulphur rose. Admiration was, I repeat, the first impression. But the second was criticism. There was something subtly wrong with the face, some coarseness of expression, some hardness, perhaps, of eye, some looseness of lip which marred its perfect beauty. But these, of course, are afterthoughts. At the moment I was simply conscious that I was in the presence of a very handsome woman, and that she was asking me the reasons for my visit. I had not quite understood until that instant how delicate my mission was.

'I have the pleasure,' said I, 'of knowing your father.' It was a clumsy introduction, and the lady made me feel it.

'There is nothing in common between my father and me,' she said. 'I owe him nothing, and his friends are not mine. If it were not for the late Sir Charles Baskerville and some other kind hearts I might have starved for all that my father cared.'

'It was about the late Sir Charles Baskerville that I have come here to see you.'

The freckles started out on the lady's face.

'What can I tell you about him?' she asked, and her fingers played nervously over the stops of her typewriter.

'You knew him, did you not?'

'I have already said that I owe a great deal to his kindness. If I am able to support myself it is largely due to the interest which he took in my unhappy situation.'

'Did you correspond with him?'

The lady looked quickly up with an angry gleam in her hazel eyes. 'What is the object of these questions?' she asked sharply.

'The object is to avoid a public scandal. It is better that I should ask them here than that the matter should pass outside our control.'

She was silent and her face was still very pale. At last she looked up with something reckless and defiant in her manner. 'Well, I'll answer,' she said. 'What are your questions?'

'Did you correspond with Sir Charles?'

'I certainly wrote to him once or twice to acknowledge his delicacy and his generosity.'

'Have you the dates of those letters?'

'No.'

'Have you ever met him?'

'Yes, once or twice, when he came into Coombe Tracey. He was a very retiring man, and he preferred to do good by stealth.'

'But if you saw him so seldom and wrote so seldom, how did he know enough about your affairs to be able to help you, as you say that he has done?'

She met my difficulty with the utmost readiness.

'There were several gentlemen who knew my sad history and united to help me. One was Mr Stapleton, a neighbour and intimate friend of Sir Charles's. He was exceedingly kind, and it was through him that Sir Charles learned about my affairs.'

I knew already that Sir Charles Baskerville had made Stapleton his almoner upon several occasions, so the lady's statement bore the impress of truth upon it.

'Did you ever write to Sir Charles asking him to meet you?' I continued.

Mrs Lyons flushed with anger again.

'Really, sir, this is a very extraordinary question.'

'I am sorry, madam, but I must repeat it.'

'Then I answer, certainly not.'

'Not on the very day of Sir Charles's death?'

The flush had faded in an instant, and a deathly face was before me. Her dry lips could not speak the 'No' which I saw rather than heard.

'Surely your memory deceives you,' said I. 'I could even quote a passage of your letter. It ran, "Please, please, as you are a gentleman, burn this letter, and be at the gate by ten o'clock."

I thought that she had fainted, but she recovered herself by a supreme effort.

'Is there no such thing as a gentleman?' she gasped.

'You do Sir Charles an injustice. He *did* burn the letter. But sometimes a letter may be legible even when burned. You acknowledge now that you wrote it?'

'Yes, I did write it,' she cried, pouring out her soul in a torrent of words. 'I did write it. Why should I deny it? I have no reason to be ashamed of it. I wished him to help me. I believed that if I had an interview I could gain his help, so I asked him to meet me.'

'But why at such an hour?'

'Because I had only just learned that he was going to London next day and might be away for months. There were reasons why I could not get there earlier.'

'But why a rendezvous in the garden instead of a visit to the house?'

'Do you think a woman could go alone at that hour to a bachelor's house?'

'Well, what happened when you did get there?'

'I never went.'

'Mrs Lyons!'

'No, I swear it to you on all I hold sacred. I never went. Something intervened to prevent my going.'

'What was that?'

'That is a private matter. I cannot tell it.'

'You acknowledge then that you made an appointment with Sir Charles at the very hour and place at which he met his death, but you deny that you kept the appointment.'

'That is the truth.'

Again and again I cross-questioned her, but I could never get past that point.

'Mrs Lyons,' said I as I rose from this long and inconclusive interview, 'you are taking a very great responsibility and putting yourself in a very false position by not making an absolutely clean breast of all that you know. If I have to call in the aid of the police you will find how seriously you are compromised. If your position is innocent, why did you in the first instance deny having written to Sir Charles upon that date?'

'Because I feared that some false conclusion might be drawn from it and that I might find myself involved in a scandal.'

'And why were you so pressing that Sir Charles should destroy your letter?'

'If you have read the letter you will know.'

'I did not say that I had read all the letter.'

'You quoted some of it.'

'I quoted the postscript. The letter had, as I said, been burned, and it was not all legible. I ask you once again why it was that you were so pressing that Sir Charles should destroy this letter which he received on the day of his death.'

'The matter is a very private one.'

'The more reason why you should avoid a public investigation.'

'I will tell you, then. If you have heard anything of my unhappy history you will know that I made a rash marriage and had reason to regret it.'

'I have heard so much.'

'My life has been one incessant persecution from a husband whom I abhor. The law is upon his side, and every day I am faced by the possibility that he may force me to live with him. At the time that I wrote this letter to Sir Charles I had learned that there was a prospect of my regaining my freedom if certain expenses could be met. It meant everything to me – peace of mind, happiness, self-respect – everything. I knew Sir Charles's generosity, and I thought that if he heard the story from my own lips he would help me.'

'Then how is it that you did not go?'

'Because I received help in the interval from another source.'

'Why, then, did you not write to Sir Charles and explain this?'

'So I should have done had I not seen his death in the paper next morning.'

The woman's story hung coherently together, and all my questions were unable to shake it. I could only check it by finding if she had, indeed, instituted divorce proceedings against her husband at or about the time of the tragedy.

It was unlikely that she would dare to say that she had not been to Baskerville Hall if she really had been, for a trap would be necessary to take her there, and could not have returned to Coombe Tracey until the early hours of the morning. Such an excursion could not be kept secret. The probability was, therefore, that she was telling the truth, or, at least, a part of the truth. I came away baffled and disheartened. Once again I had reached that dead wall which seemed to be built across every path by which I tried to get at the object of my mission. And yet the more I thought of the lady's face and of her manner the more I felt that something was being held back from me.

Why should she turn so pale? Why should she fight against every admission until it was forced from her? Why should she have been so reticent at the time of the tragedy? Surely the explanation of all this could not be as innocent as she would have me believe. For the moment I could proceed no farther in that direction, but must turn back to that other clue which was to be sought for among the stone huts upon the moor.

And that was a most vague direction. I realised it as I drove back and noted how hill after hill showed traces of the ancient people. Barrymore's only indication had been that the stranger lived in one of these abandoned huts, and many hundreds of them are scattered throughout the length and breadth of the moor. But I had my own experience for a guide since it had shown me the man himself standing upon the summit of the black tor. That, then, should be the centre of my search. From there I should explore every hut upon the moor until I lighted upon the right one. If this man were inside it I should find out from his own lips, at the point of my revolver if necessary, who he was and why he had dogged us so long. He might slip away from us in the crowd of Regent Street, but it would puzzle him to do so upon the lonely moor. On the other hand, if I should find the hut and its tenant should not be within it I must remain there, however long the vigil, until he returned. Holmes had missed him in London. It would indeed be a triumph for me if I could run him to earth where my master had failed.

Luck had been against us again and again in this enquiry, but now at last it came to my aid. And the messenger of good fortune was none other than Mr Frankland, who was standing, grey-whiskered and red-faced, outside the gate of his garden, which opened on to the highroad along which I travelled.

'Good-day, Dr Watson,' cried he with unwonted good humour, 'you must really give your horses a rest and come in to have a glass of wine and to congratulate me.'

My feelings towards him were very far from being friendly after what I had heard of his treatment of his daughter, but I was anxious to send Perkins and the wagonette home, and the opportunity was a good one. I alighted and sent a message to Sir Henry that I should walk over in time for dinner. Then I followed Frankland into his dining-room.

'It is a great day for me, sir – one of the red-letter days of my life,' he cried with many chuckles. 'I have brought off a double event. I mean to teach them in these parts that law is law, and that there is a man here who does not fear to invoke it. I have established a right of way through the centre of old Middleton's park, slap across it, sir, within a hundred yards of his own front door. What do you think of that? We'll teach these magnates that they cannot ride roughshod over the rights of the commoners, confound them! And I've closed the wood where the Fernworthy folk used to picnic. These infernal people seem to think that there are no rights of property, and that they can swarm where they like with their papers and their bottles. Both cases decided, Dr Watson, and both in my favour. I haven't had such a day since I had Sir John Morland for trespass because he shot in his own warren.'

'How on earth did you do that?'

'Look it up in the books, sir. It will repay reading – Frankland v. Morland, Court of Queen's Bench. It cost me £200, but I got my verdict.'

'Did it do you any good?'

'None, sir, none. I am proud to say that I had no interest in the matter. I act entirely from a sense of public duty. I have no doubt, for example, that the Fernworthy people will burn me in effigy tonight. I told the police last time they did it that they should stop these disgraceful exhibitions. The County Constabulary is in a scandalous state, sir, and it has not afforded me the protection to which I am entitled. The case of Frankland v. Regina will bring the matter before the attention of the public. I told them that they would have occasion to regret their treatment of me, and already my words have come true.'

'How so?' I asked.

The old man put on a very knowing expression.

'Because I could tell them what they are dying to know; but nothing would induce me to help the rascals in any way.'

I had been casting round for some excuse by which I could get away from his gossip, but now I began to wish to hear more of it. I had seen enough of the contrary nature of the old sinner to understand that any strong sign of interest would be the surest way to stop his confidences.

'Some poaching case, no doubt?' said I with an indifferent manner.

'Ha, ha, my boy, a very much more important matter than that! What about the convict on the moor?'

I stared. 'You don't mean that you know where he is?' said I.

'I may not know exactly where he is, but I am quite sure that I could help the police to lay their hands on him. Has it never struck you that the way to catch that man was to find out where he got his food and so trace it to him?'

He certainly seemed to be getting uncomfortably near the truth. 'No doubt,' said I; 'but how do you know that he is anywhere upon the moor?'

'I know it because I have seen with my own eyes the messenger who takes him his food.'

My heart sank for Barrymore. It was a serious thing to be in the power of this spiteful old busybody. But his next remark took a weight from my mind.

'You'll be surprised to hear that his food is taken to him by a child. I see him every day through my telescope upon the roof. He passes along the same path at the same hour, and to whom should he be going except to the convict?'

Here was luck indeed! And yet I suppressed all appearance of interest. A child! Barrymore had said that our unknown was supplied by a boy. It was on his track, and not upon the convict's, that Frankland had stumbled. If I could get his knowledge it might save me a long and weary hunt. But incredulity and indifference were evidently my strongest cards.

'I should say that it was much more likely that it was the son of one of the moorland shepherds taking out his father's dinner.'

The least appearance of opposition struck fire out of the old autocrat. His eyes looked malignantly at me, and his grey whiskers bristled like those of an angry cat.

'Indeed, sir!' said he, pointing out over the wide-stretching moor. 'Do you see that black tor over yonder? Well, do you see the low hill beyond with the thornbush upon it? It is the stoniest part of the whole moor. Is that a place where a shepherd would be likely to take his station? Your suggestion, sir, is a most absurd one.'

I meekly answered that I had spoken without knowing all the facts. My submission pleased him and led him to further confidences.

'You may be sure, sir, that I have very good grounds before I come to an opinion. I have seen the boy again and again with his bundle. Every day, and sometimes twice a day, I have been able – but wait a moment, Dr Watson. Do my eyes deceive me, or is there at the present moment something moving upon that hillside?'

It was several miles off, but I could distinctly see a small dark dot against the dull green and grey.

'Come, sir, come!' cried Frankland, rushing upstairs. 'You will see with your own eyes and judge for yourself.'

The telescope, a formidable instrument mounted upon a tripod, stood upon the flat leads of the house. Frankland clapped his eye to it and gave a cry of satisfaction.

'Quick, Dr Watson, quick, before he passes over the hill!'

There he was, sure enough, a small urchin with a little bundle upon his shoulder, toiling slowly up the hill. When he reached the crest I saw the ragged uncouth figure outlined for an instant against the cold blue sky. He looked round him with a furtive and stealthy air, as one who dreads pursuit. Then he vanished over the hill.

'Well! Am I right?'

'Certainly, there is a boy who seems to have some secret errand.'

'And what the errand is even a county constable could guess. But not one word shall they have from me, and I bind you to secrecy also, Dr Watson. Not a word! You understand!'

'Just as you wish.'

'They have treated me shamefully – shamefully. When the facts come out in *Frankland* v. *Regina* I venture to think that a thrill of indignation will run through the country. Nothing would induce me to help the police in any way. For all they cared it might have been me, instead of my effigy, which these rascals burned at the stake. Surely you are not going! You will help me to empty the decanter in honour of this great occasion!'

But I resisted all his solicitations and succeeded in dissuading him from his announced intention of walking home with me. I kept the road as long as his eye was on me, and then I struck off across the moor and made for the stony hill over which the boy had disappeared. Everything was working in my favour, and I swore that it should not be through lack of energy or perseverance that I should miss the chance which fortune had thrown in my way.

The sun was already sinking when I reached the summit of the hill, and the long slopes beneath me were all golden-green on one side and grey shadow on the other. A haze lay low upon the farthest skyline, out of which jutted the fantastic shapes of Belliver and Vixen Tor. Over the wide expanse there was no sound and no movement. One great grey bird, a gull or curlew, soared aloft in the blue heaven. He and I seemed to be the only living things between the huge arch of the sky and the desert beneath it. The barren scene, the sense of loneliness, and the mystery and urgency of my task all struck a chill into my heart. The boy was nowhere to be seen. But down beneath me in a cleft of the hills there was a circle of the old stone huts, and in the middle of them there was one which retained sufficient roof to act as a screen against the weather. My heart leaped within me as I saw it. This must be the burrow where the stranger lurked. At last my foot was on the threshold of his hiding-place – his secret was within my grasp.

As I approached the hut, walking as warily as Stapleton would do when with poised net he drew near the settled butterfly, I satisfied myself that the place had indeed been used as a habitation. A vague pathway among the boulders led to the dilapidated opening which served as a door. All was silent within. The unknown might be lurking there, or he might be prowling on the moor. My nerves tingled with the sense of adventure. Throwing aside my cigarette, I closed my hand upon the butt of my revolver and, walking swiftly up to the door, I looked in. The place was empty.

But there were ample signs that I had not come upon a false scent. This was certainly where the man lived. Some blankets rolled in a waterproof lay upon that very stone slab upon which neolithic man had once slumbered. The ashes of a fire were heaped in a rude grate. Beside it lay some cooking utensils and a bucket half-full of water. A litter of empty tins showed that the place had been occupied for some time, and I saw, as my eyes became accustomed to the checkered light, a pannikin and a half-full bottle of spirits standing in the corner. In the middle of the hut a flat stone served the purpose of a table, and upon this stood a small cloth bundle – the same, no doubt, which I had seen through the telescope upon the shoulder of the boy. It contained a loaf of bread, a tinned tongue and two tins of preserved peaches. As I set it down again, after having examined it, my heart leaped to see that beneath it there lay a sheet of paper with writing upon it. I raised it, and this was what I read, roughly scrawled in pencil:

Dr Watson has gone to Coombe Tracey.

For a minute I stood there with the paper in my hands thinking out the meaning of this curt message. It was I, then, and not Sir Henry, who was being dogged by this secret man. He had not followed me himself, but he had set an agent – the boy, perhaps – upon my track, and this was his report. Possibly I had taken no step since I had been upon the moor which had not been observed and reported. Always there was this feeling of an unseen force, a fine net drawn round us with infinite skill and delicacy, holding us so lightly that it was only at some supreme moment that one realised that one was indeed entangled in its meshes.

If there was one report there might be others, so I looked round the hut in search of them. There was no trace, however, of anything of the kind, nor could I discover any sign which might indicate the character or intentions of the man who lived in this singular place, save that he must be of Spartan habits and cared little for the comforts of life. When I thought of the heavy rains and looked at the gaping roof I understood how strong and immutable must be the purpose which had kept him in that inhospitable abode. Was he our malignant enemy, or was he by chance our guardian angel? I swore that I would not leave the hut until I knew.

Outside the sun was sinking low and the west was blazing with scarlet and gold. Its reflection was shot back in ruddy patches by the distant pools which lay amid the great Grimpen Mire. There were the two towers of Baskerville Hall, and there was a distant blur of smoke which marked the village of Grimpen. Between the two, behind the hill, was the house of the Stapletons. All was sweet and mellow and peaceful in the golden evening light, and yet as I looked at them my soul shared none of the peace of nature but quivered at the vagueness and the terror of that interview which every instant was bringing nearer. With tingling nerves, but a fixed purpose, I sat in the dark recess of the hut and waited with sombre patience for the coming of its tenant.

And then at last I heard him. Far away came the sharp clink of a boot striking upon a stone. Then another and yet another, coming nearer and nearer. I shrank back into the darkest corner and cocked the pistol in my pocket, determined not to discover myself until I had an opportunity of seeing something of the stranger. There was a long pause which showed that he had stopped. Then once more the footsteps approached and a shadow fell across the opening of the hut.

'It is a lovely evening, my dear Watson,' said a well-known voice. 'I really think that you will be more comfortable outside than in.'

12

Death on the Moor

For a moment or two I sat breathless, hardly able to believe my ears. Then my senses and my voice came back to me, while a crushing weight of responsibility seemed in an instant to be lifted from my soul. That cold, incisive, ironical voice could belong to but one man in all the world.

'Holmes!' I cried – 'Holmes!'

'Come out,' said he, 'and please be careful with the revolver.'

I stooped under the rude lintel, and there he sat upon a stone outside, his grey eyes dancing with amusement as they fell upon my astonished features. He was thin and worn, but clear and alert, his keen face bronzed by the sun and roughened by the wind. In his tweed suit and cloth cap he looked like any other tourist upon the moor, and he had contrived, with that catlike love of personal cleanliness which was one of his characteristics, that his chin should be as smooth and his linen as perfect as if he were in Baker Street.

'I never was more glad to see anyone in my life,' said I as I wrung him by the hand.

'Or more astonished, eh?'

'Well, I must confess to it.'

'The surprise was not all on one side, I assure you. I had no idea that you had found my occasional retreat, still less that you were inside it, until I was within twenty paces of the door.'

'My footprint, I presume?'

'No, Watson, I fear that I could not undertake to recognise your footprint amid all the footprints of the world. If you seriously desire to deceive me you must change your tobacconist; for when I see the stub of a cigarette marked Bradley, Oxford Street, I know that my friend Watson is in the neighbourhood. You will see it there beside the path. You threw it down, no doubt, at that supreme moment when you charged into the empty hut.'

'Exactly.'

'I thought as much – and knowing your admirable tenacity I was convinced that you were sitting in ambush, a weapon within reach, waiting for the tenant to return. So you actually thought that I was the criminal?'

'I did not know who you were, but I was determined to find out.'

'Excellent, Watson! And how did you localise me? You saw me, perhaps, on the night of the convict hunt, when I was so imprudent as to allow the moon to rise behind me?'

'Yes, I saw you then.'

'And have no doubt searched all the huts until you came to this one?'

'No, your boy had been observed, and that gave me a guide where to look.'

'The old gentleman with the telescope, no doubt. I could not make it out when first I saw the light flashing upon the lens.'

He rose and peeped into the hut. 'Ha, I see that Cartwright has brought up some supplies. What's this paper? So you have been to Coombe Tracey, have you?'

'Yes.'

'To see Mrs Laura Lyons?'

'Exactly.'

'Well done! Our researches have evidently been running on parallel lines, and when we unite our results I expect we shall have a fairly full knowledge of the case.'

'Well, I am glad from my heart that you are here, for indeed the responsibility and the mystery were both becoming too much for my nerves. But how in the name of wonder did you come here, and what have you been doing? I thought that you were in Baker Street working out that case of blackmailing.'

'That was what I wished you to think.'

'Then you use me, and yet do not trust me!' I cried with some bitterness. 'I think that I have deserved better at your hands, Holmes.'

'My dear fellow, you have been invaluable to me in this as in many other cases, and I beg that you will forgive me if I have seemed to play a trick upon you. In truth, it was partly for your own sake that I did it, and it was my appreciation of the danger which you ran which led me to come down and examine the matter for myself. Had I been with Sir Henry and you it is evident that my point of view would have been the same as yours, and my presence would have warned our very formidable opponents to be on their guard. As it is, I have been able to get about as I could not possibly have done had I been living in the Hall, and I remain an unknown factor in the business, ready to throw in all my weight at a critical moment.'

'But why keep me in the dark?'

'For you to know could not have helped us and might possibly have led to my discovery. You would have wished to tell me something, or in your kindness you would have brought me out some comfort or other, and so an unnecessary risk would be run. I brought Cartwright down with me – you remember the little chap at the express office – and he has seen after my simple wants: a loaf of bread and a clean collar. What does man want more? He has given me an extra pair of eyes upon a very active pair of feet, and both have been invaluable.'

'Then my reports have all been wasted!' – My voice trembled as I recalled the pains and the pride with which I had composed them.

Holmes took a bundle of papers from his pocket.

'Here are your reports, my dear fellow, and very well thumbed, I assure you. I made excellent arrangements, and they are only delayed one day upon their way. I must compliment you exceedingly upon the zeal and the intelligence which you have shown over an extraordinarily difficult case.'

I was still rather raw over the deception which had been practised upon me, but the warmth of Holmes's praise drove any anger from my mind. I felt also in my heart that he was right in what he said and that it was really best for our purpose that I should not have known that he was upon the moor.

'That's better,' said he, seeing the shadow rise from my face. 'And now tell me the result of your visit to Mrs Laura Lyons – it was not difficult for me to guess that it was to see her that you had gone, for I am already aware that she is the one person in Coombe Tracey who might be of service to us in the matter. In fact, if you had not gone today it is exceedingly probable that I should have gone tomorrow.'

The sun had set and dusk was settling over the moor. The air had turned chill and we withdrew into the hut for warmth. There sitting together in the twilight, I told Holmes of my conversation with the lady. So interested was he that I had to repeat some of it twice before he was satisfied.

'This is most important,' said he, when I had concluded. 'It fills up a gap which I had been unable to bridge in this most complex affair. You are aware, perhaps, that a close intimacy exists between this lady and the man Stapleton?'

'I did not know of a close intimacy.'

'There can be no doubt about the matter. They meet, they write, there is a complete understanding between them. Now, this puts a very powerful weapon into our hands. If I could only use it to detach his wife –'

'His wife?'

'I am giving you some information now, in return for all that you have given me. The lady who has passed here as Miss Stapleton is in reality his wife.'

'Good heavens, Holmes! Are you sure of what you say? How could he have permitted Sir Henry to fall in love with her?'

'Sir Henry's falling in love could do no harm to anyone except Sir Henry. He took particular care that Sir Henry did not make love to her, as you have yourself observed. I repeat that the lady is his wife and not his sister.'

'But why this elaborate deception?'

'Because he foresaw that she would be very much more useful to him in the character of a free woman.'

All my unspoken instincts, my vague suspicions, suddenly took shape and centred upon the naturalist. In that impassive colourless man, with his straw hat and his butterfly-net, I seemed to see something terrible – a creature of infinite patience and craft, with a smiling face and a murderous heart.

'It is he, then, who is our enemy – it is he who dogged us in London?'

'So I read the riddle.'

'And the warning – it must have come from her!'

'Exactly.'

The shape of some monstrous villainy, half seen, half guessed, loomed through the darkness which had girt me so long.

'But are you sure of this, Holmes? How do you know that the woman is his wife?'

'Because he so far forgot himself as to tell you a true piece of autobiography upon the occasion when he first met you, and I dare say he has many a time regretted it since. He was once a schoolmaster in the north of England. Now, there is no one more easy to trace than a schoolmaster. There are scholastic agencies by which one may identify any man who has been in the profession. A little investigation showed me that a school had come to grief under atrocious circumstances, and that the man who had owned it – the name was different – had disappeared with his wife. The descriptions agreed. When I learned that the missing man was devoted to entomology the identification was complete.'

The darkness was rising, but much was still hidden by the shadows.

'If this woman is in truth his wife, where does Mrs Laura Lyons come in?' I asked.

'That is one of the points upon which your own researches have shed a light. Your interview with the lady has cleared the situation very much. I did not know about a projected divorce between herself and her husband. In that case, regarding Stapleton as an unmarried man, she counted no doubt upon becoming his wife.'

'And when she is undeceived?'

'Why, then we may find the lady of service. It must be our first duty to see her – both of us – tomorrow. Don't you think, Watson, that you are away from your charge rather long? Your place should be at Baskerville Hall.'

The last red streaks had faded away in the west and night had settled upon the moor. A few faint stars were gleaming in a violet sky.

'One last question, Holmes,' I said as I rose. 'Surely there is no need of secrecy between you and me. What is the meaning of it all? What is he after?'

Holmes's voice sank as he answered: 'It is murder, Watson – refined, cold-blooded, deliberate murder. Do not ask me for particulars. My nets are closing upon him, even as his are upon Sir Henry, and with your help he is already almost at my mercy. There is but one danger which can threaten us. It is that he should strike before we are ready to do so. Another day – two at the most – and I have my case complete, but until then guard your charge as closely as ever a fond mother watched her ailing child. Your mission today has justified itself, and yet I could almost wish that you had not left his side. Hark!'

A terrible scream – a prolonged yell of horror and anguish burst out of the silence of the moor. That frightful cry turned the blood to ice in my veins.

'Oh, my God!' I gasped. 'What is it? What does it mean?'

Holmes had sprung to his feet, and I saw his dark, athletic outline at the door of the hut, his shoulders stooping, his head thrust forward, his face peering into the darkness.

'Hush!' he whispered. 'Hush!'

The cry had been loud on account of its vehemence, but it had pealed out from somewhere far off on the shadowy plain. Now it burst upon our ears, nearer, louder, more urgent than before.

'Where is it?' Holmes whispered; and I knew from the thrill of his voice that he, the man of iron, was shaken to the soul. 'Where is it, Watson?'

'There, I think.' I pointed into the darkness.

'No, there!'

Again the agonised cry swept through the silent night, louder and much nearer than ever. And a new sound mingled with it, a deep, muttered rumble, musical and yet menacing, rising and falling like the low, constant murmur of the sea.

'The hound!' cried Holmes. 'Come, Watson, come! Great heavens, if we are too late!'

He had started running swiftly over the moor, and I had followed at his heels. But now from somewhere among the broken ground immediately in front of us there came one last despairing yell, and then a dull, heavy thud. We halted and listened. Not another sound broke the heavy silence of the windless night.

I saw Holmes put his hand to his forehead like a man distracted. He stamped his feet upon the ground.

'He has beaten us, Watson. We are too late.'

'No, no, surely not!'

'Fool that I was to hold my hand. And you, Watson, see what comes of abandoning your charge! But, by Heaven, if the worst has happened we'll avenge him!'

Blindly we ran through the gloom, blundering against boulders, forcing our way through gorse bushes, panting up hills and rushing down slopes, heading always in the direction whence those dreadful sounds had come. At every rise Holmes looked eagerly round him, but the shadows were thick upon the moor, and nothing moved upon its dreary face.

'Can you see anything?'

'Nothing.'

'But, hark, what is that?'

A low moan had fallen upon our ears. There it was again upon our left! On that side a ridge of rocks ended in a sheer cliff which overlooked a stone-strewn slope. On its jagged face was spread-eagled some dark, irregular object. As we ran towards it the vague outline hardened into a definite shape. It was a prostrate man face downward upon the ground, the head doubled under him at a horrible angle, the shoulders rounded and the body hunched together as if in the act of throwing a somersault. So grotesque was the attitude that I could not for the instant realise that that moan had been the passing of his soul. Not a whisper, not a rustle, rose now from the dark figure over which we stooped. Holmes laid his hand upon him and held it up again with an exclamation of horror. The gleam of the match which he struck shone upon his clotted fingers and upon the ghastly pool which widened slowly from the crushed skull of the victim. And it shone upon something else which turned our hearts sick and faint within us – the body of Sir Henry Baskerville!

There was no chance of either of us forgetting that peculiar ruddy tweed suit – the very one which he had worn on the first morning that we had seen him in Baker Street. We caught the one clear glimpse of it, and then the match flickered and went out, even as the hope had gone out of our souls. Holmes groaned, and his face glimmered white through the darkness.

'The brute! the brute!' I cried with clenched hands. 'Oh Holmes, I shall never forgive myself for having left him to his fate.'

'I am more to blame than you, Watson. In order to have my case well rounded and complete, I have thrown away the life of my client. It is the greatest blow which has befallen me in my career. But how *could* I know – how could I know – that he would risk his life alone upon the moor in the face of all my warnings?'

'That we should have heard his screams – my God, those screams! – and yet have been unable to save him! Where is this brute of a hound which drove him to his death? It may be lurking among these rocks at this instant. And Stapleton, where is he? He shall answer for this deed.'

'He shall. I will see to that. Uncle and nephew have been murdered – the one frightened to death by the very sight of a beast which he thought to be supernatural, the other driven to his end in his wild flight to escape from it. But now we have to prove the connection between the man and the beast. Save from what we heard, we cannot even swear to the existence of the latter, since Sir Henry has evidently died from the fall. But, by heavens, cunning as he is, the fellow shall be in my power before another day is past!'

We stood with bitter hearts on either side of the mangled body, overwhelmed by this sudden and irrevocable disaster which had brought all our long and weary labours to so piteous an end. Then as the moon rose we climbed to the top of the rocks over which our poor friend had fallen, and from the summit we gazed out over the shadowy moor, half silver and half gloom. Far away, miles off, in the direction of Grimpen, a single steady yellow light was shining. It could only come from the lonely abode of the Stapletons. With a bitter curse I shook my fist at it as I gazed.

'Why should we not seize him at once?'

'Our case is not complete. The fellow is wary and cunning to the last degree. It is not what we know, but what we can prove. If we make one false move the villain may escape us yet.'

'What can we do?'

'There will be plenty for us to do tomorrow. Tonight we can only perform the last offices to our poor friend.'

Together we made our way down the precipitous slope and approached the body, black and clear against the silvered stones. The agony of those contorted limbs struck me with a spasm of pain and blurred my eyes with tears.

'We must send for help, Holmes! We cannot carry him all the way to the Hall. Good heavens, are you mad?'

He had uttered a cry and bent over the body. Now he was dancing and laughing and wringing my hand. Could this be my stern, self-contained friend? These were hidden fires, indeed!

'A beard! A beard! The man has a beard!'

'A beard?'

'It is not the baronet – it is – why, it is my neighbour, the convict!'

With feverish haste we had turned the body over, and that dripping beard was pointing up to the cold, clear moon. There could be no doubt about the beetling forehead, the sunken animal eyes. It was indeed the same face which had glared upon me in the light of the candle from over the rock – the face of Selden, the criminal.

Then in an instant it was all clear to me. I remembered how the baronet had told me that he had handed his old wardrobe to Barrymore. Barrymore had passed it on in order to help Selden in his escape. Boots, shirt, cap – all were Sir Henry's. The tragedy was still black enough, but this man had at least deserved death by the laws of his country. I told Holmes how the matter stood, my heart bubbling over with thankfulness and joy.

'Then the clothes have been the poor devil's death,' said he. 'It is clear enough that the hound has been laid on from some article of Sir Henry's – the boot which was abstracted in the hotel, in all probability – and so ran this man down. There is one very singular thing, however: How came Selden, in the darkness, to know that the hound was on his trail?'

'He heard him.'

'To hear a hound upon the moor would not work a hard man like this convict into such a paroxysm of terror that he would risk recapture by screaming wildly for help. By his cries he must have run a long way after he knew the animal was on his track. How did he know?'

'A greater mystery to me is why this hound, presuming that all our conjectures are correct – '

'I presume nothing.'

'Well, then, why this hound should be loose tonight. I suppose that it does not always run loose upon the moor. Stapleton would not let it go unless he had reason to think that Sir Henry would be there.'

'My difficulty is the more formidable of the two, for I think that we shall very shortly get an explanation of yours, while mine may remain forever a mystery. The question now is, what shall we do with this poor wretch's body? We cannot leave it here to the foxes and the ravens.'

'I suggest that we put it in one of the huts until we can communicate with the police.'

'Exactly. I have no doubt that you and I could carry it so far. Hallo, Watson, what's this? It's the man himself, by all that's wonderful and audacious! Not a word to show your suspicions – not a word, or my plans crumble to the ground.'

A figure was approaching us over the moor, and I saw the dull red glow of a cigar. The moon shone upon him, and I could distinguish the dapper shape and jaunty walk of the naturalist. He stopped when he saw us, and then came on again.

'Why, Dr Watson, that's not you, is it? You are the last man that I should have expected to see out on the moor at this time of night. But, dear me, what's this? Somebody hurt? Not – don't tell me that it is our friend Sir Henry!'

He hurried past me and stooped over the dead man. I heard a sharp intake of his breath and the cigar fell from his fingers.

'Who – who's this?' he stammered.

'It is Selden, the man who escaped from Princetown.'

Stapleton turned a ghastly face upon us, but by a supreme effort he had overcome his amazement and his disappointment. He looked sharply from Holmes to me. 'Dear me! What a very shocking affair! How did he die?'

'He appears to have broken his neck by falling over these rocks. My friend and I were strolling on the moor when we heard a cry.'

'I heard a cry also. That was what brought me out. I was uneasy about Sir Henry.'

'Why about Sir Henry in particular?' I could not help asking.

'Because I had suggested that he should come over. When he did not come I was surprised, and I naturally became alarmed for his safety when I heard cries upon the moor. By the way' – his eyes darted again from my face to Holmes's – 'did you hear anything else besides a cry?'

'No,' said Holmes; 'did you?'

'No.'

'What do you mean, then?'

'Oh, you know the stories that the peasants tell about a phantom hound, and so on. It is said to be heard at night upon the moor. I was wondering if there were any evidence of such a sound tonight.'

'We heard nothing of the kind,' said I.

'And what is your theory of this poor fellow's death?'

'I have no doubt that anxiety and exposure have driven him off his head. He has rushed about the moor in a crazy state and eventually fallen over here and broken his neck.'

'That seems the most reasonable theory,' said Stapleton, and he gave a sigh which I took to indicate his relief. 'What do you think about it, Mr Sherlock Holmes?'

My friend bowed his compliments. 'You are quick at identification,' said he.

'We have been expecting you in these parts since Dr Watson came down. You are in time to see a tragedy.'

'Yes, indeed. I have no doubt that my friend's explanation will cover the facts. I will take an unpleasant remembrance back to London with me tomorrow.'

'Oh, you return tomorrow?'

'That is my intention.'

'I hope your visit has cast some light upon those occurrences which have puzzled us?'

Holmes shrugged his shoulders.

'One cannot always have the success for which one hopes. An investigator needs facts and not legends or rumours. It has not been a satisfactory case.'

My friend spoke in his frankest and most unconcerned manner. Stapleton still looked hard at him. Then he turned to me.

'I would suggest carrying this poor fellow to my house, but it would give my sister such a fright that I do not feel justified in doing it. I think that if we put something over his face he will be safe until morning.'

And so it was arranged. Resisting Stapleton's offer of hospitality, Holmes and I set off to Baskerville Hall, leaving the naturalist to return alone. Looking back we saw the figure moving slowly away over the broad moor, and behind him that one black smudge on the silvered slope which showed where the man was lying who had come so horribly to his end.

'We're at close grips at last,' said Holmes as we walked together across the moor. 'What a nerve the fellow has! How he pulled himself together in the face of what must have been a paralysing shock when he found that the wrong man had fallen a victim to his plot. I told you in London, Watson, and I tell you now again, that we have never had a foeman more worthy of our steel.'

'I am sorry that he has seen you.'

'And so was I at first. But there was no getting out of it.'

'What effect do you think it will have upon his plans now that he knows you are here?'

'It may cause him to be more cautious, or it may drive him to desperate measures at once. Like most clever criminals, he may be too confident in his own cleverness and imagine that he has completely deceived us.'

'Why should we not arrest him at once?'

'My dear Watson, you were born to be a man of action. Your instinct is always to do something energetic. But supposing, for argument's sake, that we had him arrested tonight, how on earth should we be the better off for that? We could prove nothing against him. There's the devilish cunning of it! If he were acting through a human agent we could get some evidence, but if we were to drag this great dog to the light of day it would not help us in putting a rope round the neck of its master.'

'Surely we have a case.'

'Not a shadow of one – only surmise and conjecture. We should be laughed out of court if we came with such a story and such evidence.'

'There is Sir Charles's death.'

'Found dead without a mark upon him. You and I know that he died of sheer fright, and we know also what frightened him; but how are we to get twelve stolid jurymen to know it? What signs are there of a hound? Where are the marks of its fangs? Of course we know that a hound does not bite a dead body and that Sir Charles was dead before ever the brute overtook him. But we have to *prove* all this, and we are not in a position to do it.'

'Well, then, tonight?'

'We are not much better off tonight. Again, there was no direct connection between the hound and the man's death. We never saw the hound. We heard it, but we could not prove that it was running upon this man's trail. There is a complete absence of motive. No, my dear fellow; we must reconcile ourselves to the fact that we have no case at present, and that it is worth our while to run any risk in order to establish one.'

'And how do you propose to do so?'

'I have great hopes of what Mrs Laura Lyons may do for us when the position of affairs is made clear to her. And I have my own plan as well. Sufficient for tomorrow is the evil thereof; but I hope before the day is past to have the upper hand at last.'

I could draw nothing further from him, and he walked, lost in thought, as far as the Baskerville gates.

'Are you coming up?'

'Yes; I see no reason for further concealment. But one last word, Watson. Say nothing of the hound to Sir Henry. Let him think that Selden's death was as Stapleton would hav us believe. He will have a better nerve for the ordeal which he will have to undergo tomorrow, when he is engaged, if I remember your report aright, to dine with these people.'

'And so am I.'

'Then you must excuse yourself and he must go alone. That will be easily arranged. And now, if we are too late for dinner, I think that we are both ready for our suppers.'

13

Fixing the Nets

Sir Henry was more pleased than surprised to see Sherlock Holmes, for he had for some days been expecting that recent events would bring him down from London. He did raise his eyebrows, however, when he found that my friend had neither any luggage nor any explanations for its absence. Between us we soon supplied his wants, and then over a belated supper we explained to the baronet as much of our experience as it seemed desirable that he should know. But first I had the unpleasant duty of breaking the news to Barrymore and his wife. To him it may have been an unmitigated relief, but she wept bitterly in her apron. To all the world he was the man of violence, half animal and half demon; but to her he always remained the little wilful boy of her own girlhood, the child who had clung to her hand. Evil indeed is the man who has not one woman to mourn him.

'I've been moping in the house all day since Watson went off in the morning,' said the baronet. 'I guess I should have some credit, for I have kept my promise. If I hadn't sworn not to go about alone I might have had a more lively evening, for I had a message from Stapleton asking me over there.'

'I have no doubt that you would have had a more lively evening,' said Holmes drily. 'By the way, I don't suppose you appreciate that we have been mourning over you as having broken your neck?'

Sir Henry opened his eyes. 'How was that?'

'This poor wretch was dressed in your clothes. I fear your servant, who gave them to him, may get into trouble with the police.'

'That is unlikely. There was no mark on any of them, as far as I know.'

'That's lucky for him – in fact, it's lucky for all of you, since you are all on the wrong side of the law in this matter. I am not sure that as a conscientious detective my first duty is not to arrest the whole household. Watson's reports are most incriminating documents.'

'But how about the case?' asked the baronet. 'Have you made anything out of the tangle? I don't know that Watson and I are much the wiser since we came down.'

'I think that I shall be in a position to make the situation rather more clear to you before long. It has been an exceedingly difficult and most complicated business. There are several points upon which we still want light – but it is coming all the same.'

'We've had one experience, as Watson has no doubt told you. We heard the hound on the moor, so I can swear that it is not all empty superstition. I had something to do with dogs when I was out West, and I know one when I hear one. If you can muzzle that one and put him on a chain, I'll be ready to swear you are the greatest detective of all time.'

'I think I will muzzle him and chain him all right if you will give me your help.'

'Whatever you tell me to do, I will do.'

'Very good; and I will ask you also to do it blindly, without always asking the reason.'

'Just as you like.'

'If you will do this I think the chances are that our little problem will soon be solved. I have no doubt – '

He stopped suddenly and stared fixedly up over my head into the air. The lamp beat upon his face, and so intent was it and so still that it might have been that of a clear-cut classical statue, a personification of alertness and expectation.

'What is it?' we both cried.

I could see as he looked down that he was repressing some internal emotion. His features were still composed, but his eyes shone with amused exultation.

'Excuse the admiration of a connoisseur,' said he as he waved his hand towards the line of portraits which covered the opposite wall. 'Watson won't allow that I know anything of art but that is mere jealousy because our views upon the subject differ. Now, these are a really very fine series of portraits.'

'Well, I'm glad to hear you say so,' said Sir Henry, glancing with some surprise at my friend. 'I don't pretend to know much about these things, and I'd be a better judge of a horse or a steer than of a picture. I didn't know that you found time for such things.'

'I know what is good when I see it, and I see it now. That's a Kneller, I'll swear, that lady in the blue silk over yonder, and the stout gentleman with the wig ought to be a Reynolds. They are all family portraits, I presume?'

'Every one.'

'Do you know the names?'

'Barrymore has been coaching me in them, and I think I can say my lessons fairly well.'

'Who is the gentleman with the telescope?'

'That is Rear-Admiral Baskerville, who served under Rodney in the West Indies. The man with the blue coat and the roll of paper is Sir William Baskerville, who was Chairman of Committees of the House of Commons under Pitt.'

'And this Cavalier opposite to me – the one with the black velvet and the lace?'

'Ah, you have a right to know about him. That is the cause of all the mischief, the wicked Hugo, who started the Hound of the Baskervilles. We're not likely to forget him.'

I gazed with interest and some surprise upon the portrait.

'Dear me!' said Holmes, 'he seems a quiet, meek-mannered man enough, but I dare say that there was a lurking devil in his eyes. I had pictured him as a more robust and ruffianly person.'

'There's no doubt about the authenticity, for the name and the date, 1647, are on the back of the canvas.'

Holmes said little more, but the picture of the old roysterer seemed to have a fascination for him, and his eyes were continually fixed upon it during supper. It was not until later, when Sir Henry had gone to his room, that I was able to follow the trend of his thoughts. He led me back into the banqueting-hall, his bedroom candle in his hand, and he held it up against the time-stained portrait on the wall.

'Do you see anything there?'

I looked at the broad plumed hat, the curling love-locks, the white lace collar, and the straight, severe face which was framed between them. It was not a brutal countenance, but it was prim, hard and stern, with a firm-set, thin-lipped mouth and a coldly intolerant eye.

'Is it like anyone you know?'

'There is something of Sir Henry about the jaw.'

'Just a suggestion, perhaps. But wait an instant!' He stood upon a chair, and, holding up the light in his left hand, he curved his right arm over the broad hat and round the long ringlets.

'Good heavens!' I cried in amazement.

The face of Stapleton had sprung out of the canvas.

'Ha, you see it now. My eyes have been trained to examine faces and not their trimmings. It is the first quality of a criminal investigator that he should see through a disguise.'

'But this is marvellous. It might be his portrait.'

'Yes, it is an interesting instance of a throwback, which appears to be both physical and spiritual. A study of family portraits is enough to convert a man to the doctrine of reincarnation. The fellow is a Baskerville – that is evident.'

'With designs upon the succession.'

'Exactly. This chance of the picture has supplied us with one of our most obvious missing links. We have him, Watson, we have him, and I dare swear that before tomorrow night he will be fluttering in our net as helpless as one of his own butterflies. A pin, a cork and a card, and we add him to the Baker Street collection!'

He burst into one of his rare fits of laughter as he turned away from the picture. I have not heard him laugh often, and it has always boded ill to somebody.

I was up betimes in the morning, but Holmes was afoot earlier still, for I saw him, as I dressed, coming up the drive.

'Yes, we should have a full day today,' he remarked, and he rubbed his hands with the joy of action. 'The nets are all in place, and the drag is about to begin. We'll know before the day is out whether we have caught our big, lean-jawed pike, or whether he has got through the meshes.'

'Have you been on the moor already?'

'I have sent a report from Grimpen to Princetown as to the death of Selden. I think I can promise that none of you will be troubled in the matter. And I have also communicated with my faithful Cartwright, who would certainly have pined away at the door of my hut, as a dog does at his master's grave, if I had not set his mind at rest about my safety.'

'What is the next move?'

'To see Sir Henry. Ah, here he is!'

'Good-morning, Holmes,' said the baronet. 'You look like a general who is planning a battle with his chief of staff.'

'That is the exact situation. Watson was asking for orders.'

'And so do I.'

'Very good. You are engaged, as I understand, to dine with our friends the Stapletons tonight.'

'I hope that you will come also. They are very hospitable people, and I am sure that they would be very glad to see you.'

'I fear that Watson and I must go to London.'

'To London?'

'Yes, I think that we should be more useful there at the present juncture.'

The baronet's face perceptibly lengthened. 'I hoped that you were going to see me through this business. The Hall and the moor are not very pleasant places when one is alone.'

'My dear fellow, you must trust me implicitly and do exactly what I tell you. You can tell your friends that we should have been happy to have come with you, but that urgent business required us to be in town. We hope very soon to return to Devonshire. Will you remember to give them that message?'

'If you insist upon it.'

'There is no alternative, I assure you.'

I saw by the baronet's clouded brow that he was deeply hurt by what he regarded as our desertion.

'When do you desire to go?' he asked coldly.

'Immediately after breakfast. We will drive in to Coombe Tracey, but Watson will leave his things as a pledge that he will come back to you. Watson, you will send a note to Stapleton to tell him that you regret that you cannot come.'

'I have a good mind to go to London with you,' said the baronet. 'Why should I stay here alone?'

'Because it is your post of duty. Because you gave me your word that you would do as you were told, and I tell you to stay.'

'All right, then, I'll stay.'

'One more direction! I wish you to drive to Merripit House. Send back your trap, however, and let them know that you intend to walk home.'

'To walk across the moor?'

'Yes.'

'But that is the very thing which you have so often cautioned me not to do.'

'This time you may do it with safety. If I had not every confidence in your nerve and courage I would not suggest it, but it is essential that you should do it.'

'Then I will do it.'

And as you value your life do not go across the moor in any direction save along the straight path which leads from Merripit House to the Grimpen Road, and is your natural way home.'

'I will do just what you say.'

'Very good. I should be glad to get away as soon after breakfast as possible, so as to reach London in the afternoon.'

I was much astounded by this programme, though I remembered that Holmes had said to Stapleton on the night before that his visit would terminate next day. It had not crossed my mind, however, that he would wish me to go with him, nor could I understand how we could both be absent at a moment which he himself declared to be critical. There was nothing for it, however, but implicit obedience; so we bade goodbye to our rueful friend, and a couple of hours afterwards we were at the station of Coombe Tracey and had dispatched the trap upon its return journey. A small boy was waiting upon the platform.

'Any orders, sir?'

'You will take this train to town, Cartwright. The moment you arrive you will send a wire to Sir Henry Baskerville, in my name, to say that if he finds the pocket-book which I have dropped he is to send it by registered post to Baker Street.'

'Yes, sir.'

'And ask at the station office if there is a message for me.'

The boy returned with a telegram, which Holmes handed to me. It ran:

Wire received. Coming down with unsigned warrant. Arrive five-forty
– LESTRADE.

'That is in answer to mine of this morning. He is the best of the professionals, I think, and we may need his assistance. Now, Watson, I think that we cannot employ our time better than by calling upon your acquaintance, Mrs Laura Lyons.'

His plan of campaign was beginning to be evident. He would use the baronet in order to convince the Stapletons that we were really gone, while we should actually return at the instant when we were likely to be needed. That telegram from London, if mentioned by Sir Henry to the Stapletons, must remove the last suspicions from their minds. Already I seemed to see our nets drawing closer around that lean-jawed pike.

Mrs Laura Lyons was in her office, and Sherlock Holmes opened his interview with a frankness and directness which considerably amazed her.

'I am investigating the circumstances which attended the death of the late Sir Charles Baskerville,' said he. 'My friend here, Dr Watson, has informed me of what you have communicated, and also of what you have withheld in connection with that matter.'

'What have I withheld?' she asked defiantly.

'You have confessed that you asked Sir Charles to be at the gate at ten o'clock. We know that that was the place and hour of his death. You have withheld what the connection is between these events.'

'There is no connection.'

'In that case the coincidence must indeed be an extraordinary one. But I think that we shall succeed in establishing a connection, after all. I wish to be perfectly frank with you, Mrs Lyons. We regard this case as one of murder, and the evidence may implicate not only your friend Mr Stapleton but his wife as well.'

The lady sprang from her chair.

'His wife!' she cried.

'The fact is no longer a secret. The person who has passed for his sister is really his wife.'

Mrs Lyons had resumed her seat. Her hands were grasping the arms of her chair, and I saw that the pink nails had turned white with the pressure of her grip.

'His wife!' she said again. 'His wife! He is not a married man.'

Sherlock Holmes shrugged his shoulders.

'Prove it to me! Prove it to me! And if you can do so – !' The fierce flash of her eyes said more than any words.

'I have come prepared to do so,' said Holmes, drawing several papers from his pocket. 'Here is a photograph of the couple taken in York four years ago. It is endorsed "Mr and Mrs Vandeleur", but you will have no difficulty in recognising him, and her also, if you know her by sight. Here are three written descriptions by trustworthy witnesses of Mr and Mrs Vandeleur, who at that time kept St Oliver's private school. Read them and see if you can doubt the identity of these people.'

She glanced at them, and then looked up at us with the set, rigid face of a desperate woman.

'Mr Holmes,' she said, 'this man had offered me marriage on condition that I could get a divorce from my husband. He has lied to me, the villain, in every conceivable way. Not one word of truth has he ever told me. And why – why? I imagined that all was for my own sake. But now I see that I was never anything but a tool in his hands. Why should I preserve faith with him who never kept any with me? Why should I try to shield him from the consequences of his own wicked acts? Ask me what you like, and there is nothing which I shall hold back. One thing I swear to you, and that is that when I wrote the letter I never dreamed of any harm to the old gentleman, who had been my kindest friend.'

'I entirely believe you, madam,' said Sherlock Holmes. 'The recital of these events must be very painful to you, and perhaps it will make it easier if I tell you what occurred, and you can check me if I make any material mistake. The sending of this letter was suggested to you by Stapleton?'

'He dictated it.'

'I presume that the reason he gave was that you would receive help from Sir Charles for the legal expenses connected with your divorce?'

'Exactly.'

'And then after you had sent the letter he dissuaded you from keeping the appointment?'

'He told me that it would hurt his self-respect that any other man should find the money for such an object, and that though he was a poor man himself he would devote his last penny to removing the obstacles which divided us.'

'He appears to be a very consistent character. And then you heard nothing until you read the reports of the death in the paper?'

'No.'

'And he made you swear to say nothing about your appointment with Sir Charles?'

'He did. He said that the death was a very mysterious one, and that I should certainly be suspected if the facts came out. He frightened me into remaining silent.'

'Quite so. But you had your suspicions?'

She hesitated and looked down.

'I knew him,' she said. 'But if he had kept faith with me I should always have done so with him.'

'I think that on the whole you have had a fortunate escape,' said Sherlock Holmes. 'You have had him in your power and he knew it, and yet you are alive. You have been walking for some months very near to the edge of a precipice. We must wish you good-morning now, Mrs Lyons, but it is probable that you will very shortly hear from us again.'

'Our case becomes rounded off, and difficulty after difficulty thins away in front of us,' said Holmes, as later we stood waiting for the arrival of the express from town. 'I shall soon be in the position of being able to put into a single connected narrative one of the most singular and sensational crimes of modern times. Students of criminology will remember the analogous incidents in Grodno, in Little Russia, in the year '66, and of course there are the Anderson murders in North Carolina, but this case possesses some features which are entirely its own. Even now we have no clear case against this very wily man. But I shall be very much surprised if it is not clear enough before we go to bed this night.'

The London express came roaring into the station, and a small, wiry bulldog of a man sprang from a first-class carriage. We all three shook hands, and I saw at once, from the reverential way in which Lestrade gazed at my companion, that he had learned a good deal since the days when they had first worked together. I could well remember the scorn which the theories of the reasoner used then to excite in the practical man.

'Anything good?' he asked.

'The biggest thing for years,' said Holmes. 'We have two hours before we need think of starting. I suggest we might employ it in getting some dinner and then, Lestrade, we will take the London fog out of your throat by giving you a breath of the pure night air of Dartmoor. Never been there? Ah, well, I don't suppose you will forget your first visit.'

14

The Hound of the Baskervilles

One of Sherlock Holmes's defects – if, indeed, one may call it a defect – was that he was exceedingly loath to communicate his full plans to any other person until the instant of their fulfilment. Partly it came no doubt from his own masterful nature, which loved to dominate and surprise those who were around him. Partly also from his professional caution, which urged him never to take any chances. The result, however, was very trying for those who were acting as his agents and assistants. I had often suffered under it, but never more so than during that long drive in the darkness. The great ordeal was in front of us; at last we were about to make our final effort, and yet Holmes had said nothing, and I could only surmise what his course of action would be. My nerves thrilled with anticipation when at last the cold wind upon our faces and the dark, void spaces on either side of the narrow road told me that we were back upon the moor once again. Every stride of the horses and every turn of the wheels was taking us nearer to our supreme adventure.

Our conversation was hampered by the presence of the driver of the hired wagonette, so that we were forced to talk of trivial matters when our nerves were tense with emotion and anticipation. It was a relief to me, after that unnatural restraint, when we at last passed Frankland's house and knew that we were drawing near to the Hall and to the scene of action. We did not drive up to the door but got down near the gate of the avenue.

The wagonette was paid off and ordered to return to Coombe Tracey forthwith, while we started to walk to Merripit House.

'Are you armed, Lestrade?'

The little detective smiled.

'As long as I have my trousers I have a hip-pocket, and as long as I have my hip-pocket I have something in it.'

'Good! My friend and I are also ready for emergencies.'

'You're mighty close about this affair, Mr Holmes. What's the game now?'

'A waiting game.'

'My word, it does not seem a very cheerful place,' said the detective with a shiver, glancing round him at the gloomy slopes of the hill and at the huge lake of fog which lay over the Grimpen Mire. 'I see the lights of a house ahead of us.'

'That is Merripit House and the end of our journey. I must request you to walk on tiptoe and not to talk above a whisper.'

We moved cautiously along the track as if we were bound for the house, but Holmes halted us when we were about two hundred yards from it.

'This will do,' said he. 'These rocks upon the right make an admirable screen.'

'We are to wait here?'

'Yes, we shall make our little ambush here. Get into this hollow, Lestrade. You have been inside the house, have you not, Watson? Can you tell the position of the rooms? What are those latticed windows at this end?'

'I think they are the kitchen windows.'

'And the one beyond, which shines so brightly?'

'That is certainly the dining-room.'

'The blinds are up. You know the lie of the land best. Creep forward quietly and see what they are doing – but for heaven's sake don't let them know that they are watched!'

I tiptoed down the path and stooped behind the low wall which surrounded the stunted orchard. Creeping in its shadow I reached a point whence I could look straight through the uncurtained window.

There were only two men in the room, Sir Henry and Stapleton. They sat with their profiles towards me on either side of the round table. Both of them were smoking cigars, and coffee and wine were in front of them. Stapleton was talking with animation, but the baronet looked pale and distrait. Perhaps the thought of that lonely walk across the ill-omened moor was weighing heavily upon his mind.

As I watched them Stapleton rose and left the room, while Sir Henry filled his glass again and leaned back in his chair, puffing at his cigar. I heard the creak of a door and the crisp sound of boots upon gravel. The steps passed along the path on the other side of the wall under which I crouched. Looking over, I saw the naturalist pause at the door of an outhouse in the corner of the orchard. A key turned in a lock, and as he passed in there was a curious scuffling noise from within. He was only a minute or so inside, and then I heard the key turn once more and he passed me and re-entered the house. I saw him rejoin his guest, and I crept quietly back to where my companions were waiting to tell them what I had seen.

'You say, Watson, that the lady is not there?' Holmes asked when I had finished my report.

'No.'

'Where can she be, then, since there is no light in any other room except the kitchen?'

'I cannot think where she is.'

I have said that over the great Grimpen Mire there hung a dense, white fog. It was drifting slowly in our direction and banked itself up like a wall on that side of us, low but thick and well defined. The moon shone on it, and it looked like a great shimmering ice-field, with the heads of the distant tors as rocks borne upon its surface. Holmes's face was turned towards it, and he muttered impatiently as he watched its sluggish drift.

'It's moving towards us, Watson.'

'Is that serious?'

'Very serious, indeed – the one thing upon earth which could have disarranged my plans. He can't be very long, now. It is already ten o'clock. Our success and even his life may depend upon his coming out before the fog is over the path.'

The night was clear and fine above us. The stars shone cold and bright, while a half-moon bathed the whole scene in a soft, uncertain light. Before us lay the dark bulk of the house, its serrated roof and bristling chimneys hard outlined against the silver-spangled sky. Broad bars of golden light from the lower windows stretched across the orchard and the moor. One of them was suddenly shut off. The servants had left the kitchen. There only remained the lamp in the dining-room where the two men, the murderous host and the unconscious guest, still chatted over their cigars.

Every minute that white woolly plain which covered one-half of the moor was drifting closer and closer to the house. Already the first thin wisps of it were curling across the golden square of the lighted window. The farther wall of the orchard was already invisible, and the trees were standing out of a swirl of white vapour. As we watched it the fog-wreaths came crawling round both corners of the house and rolled slowly into one dense bank on which the upper floor and the roof floated like a strange ship upon a shadowy sea. Holmes struck his hand passionately upon the rock in front of us and stamped his feet in his impatience.

'If he isn't out in a quarter of an hour the path will be covered. In half an hour we won't be able to see our hands in front of us.'

'Shall we move farther back upon higher ground?'

'Yes, I think it would be as well.'

So as the fog-bank flowed onward we fell back before it until we were half a mile from the house, and still that dense white sea, with the moon silvering its upper edge, swept slowly and inexorably on.

'We are going too far,' said Holmes. 'We dare not take the chance of his being overtaken before he can reach us. At all costs we must hold our ground where we are.' He dropped on his knees and clapped his ear to the ground. 'Thank God, I think that I hear him coming.'

A sound of quick steps broke the silence of the moor. Crouching among the stones we stared intently at the silver-tipped bank in front of us. The steps grew louder, and through the fog, as through a curtain, there stepped the man whom we were awaiting. He looked round him in surprise as he emerged into the clear, starlit night. Then he came swiftly along the path, passed close to where we lay, and went on up the long slope behind us. As he walked he glanced continually over either shoulder, like a man who is ill at ease.

'Hist!' cried Holmes, and I heard the sharp click of a cocking pistol. 'Look out! It's coming!'

There was a thin, crisp, continuous patter from somewhere in the heart of that crawling bank. The cloud was within fifty yards of where we lay, and we glared at it, all three, uncertain what horror was about to break from the heart of it. I was at Holmes's elbow, and I glanced for an instant at his face. It was pale and exultant, his eyes shining brightly in the moonlight. But suddenly they started forward in a rigid, fixed stare, and his lips parted in amazement. At the same instant Lestrade gave a yell of terror and threw himself face downward upon the ground. I sprang to my feet, my inert hand grasping my pistol, my mind paralysed by the dreadful shape which had sprung out upon us from the shadows of the fog. A hound it was, an enormous coal-black hound, but not such a hound as mortal eyes have ever seen. Fire burst from its open mouth, its eyes glowed with a smouldering glare, its muzzle and hackles and dewlap were outlined in flickering flame. Never in the delirious dream of a disordered brain could anything more savage, more appalling, more hellish, be conceived than that dark form and savage face which broke upon us out of the wall of fog.

With long bounds the huge black creature was leaping down the track, following hard upon the footsteps of our friend. So paralysed were we by the apparition that we allowed him to pass before we had recovered our nerve. Then Holmes and I both fired together, and the creature gave a hideous howl, which showed that one at least had hit him. He did not pause, however, but bounded onwards. Far away on the path we saw Sir Henry looking back, his face white in the moonlight, his hands raised in horror, glaring helplessly at the frightful thing which was hunting him down.

But that cry of pain from the hound had blown all our fears to the winds. If he was vulnerable he was mortal, and if we could wound him we could kill him. Never have I seen a man run as Holmes ran that night. I am reckoned fleet of foot, but he outpaced me as much as I outpaced the little professional. In front of us as we flew up the track we heard scream after scream from Sir Henry and the deep roar of the hound. I was in time to see the beast spring upon its victim, hurl him to the ground and worry at his throat. But the next instant Holmes had emptied five barrels of his revolver into the creature's flank. With a last howl of agony and a vicious snap in the air, it rolled upon its back, four feet pawing furiously, and then fell limp upon its side. I stooped, panting, and pressed my pistol to the dreadful, shimmering head, but it was useless to press the trigger. The giant hound was dead.

Sir Henry lay insensible where he had fallen. We tore away his collar, and Holmes breathed a prayer of gratitude when we saw that there was no sign of a wound and that the rescue had been in time.

Already our friend's eyelids shivered and he made a feeble effort to move. Lestrade thrust his brandy-flask between the baronet's teeth, and two frightened eyes were looking up at us.

'My God!' he whispered. 'What was it? What, in heaven's name, was it?'

'It's dead, whatever it is,' said Holmes. 'We've laid the family ghost once and forever.'

In mere size and strength it was a terrible creature which was lying stretched before us. It was not a pure bloodhound and it was not a pure mastiff; but it appeared to be a combination of the two – gaunt, savage, and as large as a small lioness. Even now, in the stillness of death, the huge jaws seemed to be dripping with a bluish flame and the small, deep-set, cruel eyes were ringed with fire. I placed my hand upon the glowing muzzle, and as I held them up my own fingers smouldered and gleamed in the darkness.

'Phosphorus,' I said.

'A cunning preparation of it,' said Holmes, sniffing at the dead animal. 'There is no smell which might have interfered with his power of scent. We owe you a deep apology, Sir Henry, for having exposed you to this fright. I was prepared for a hound, but not for such a creature as this. And the fog gave us little time to receive him.'

'You have saved my life.'

'Having first endangered it. Are you strong enough to stand?'

'Give me another mouthful of that brandy and I shall be ready for anything. So! Now, if you will help me up. What do you propose to do?'

'To leave you here. You are not fit for further adventures tonight. If you will wait, one or other of us will go back with you to the Hall.'

He tried to stagger to his feet; but he was still ghastly pale and trembling in every limb. We helped him to a rock, where he sat shivering with his face buried in his hands.

'We must leave you now,' said Holmes. 'The rest of our work must be done, and every moment is of importance. We have our case, and now we only want our man.'

'It's a thousand to one against our finding him at the house,' he continued as we retraced our steps swiftly down the path. 'Those shots must have told him that the game was up.'

'We were some distance off, and this fog may have deadened them.'

'He followed the hound to call him off – of that you may be certain. No, no, he's gone by this time! But we'll search the house and make sure.'

The front door was open, so we rushed in and hurried from room to room, to the amazement of a doddering old manservant, who met us in the passage. There was no light save in the dining-room, but Holmes caught up the lamp and left no corner of the house unexplored. No sign could we see of the man whom we were chasing. On the upper floor, however, one of the bedroom doors was locked.

'There's someone in here,' cried Lestrade. 'I can hear a movement. Open this door!'

A faint moaning and rustling came from within. Holmes struck the door just over the lock with the flat of his foot and it flew open. Pistol in hand, we all three rushed into the room.

But there was no sign within it of that desperate and defiant villain whom we expected to see. Instead we were faced by an object so strange and so unexpected that we stood for a moment staring at it in amazement.

The room had been fashioned into a small museum, and the walls were lined by a number of glass-topped cases full of that collection of butterflies and moths the formation of which had been the relaxation of this complex and dangerous man. In the centre of this room there was an upright beam, which had been placed at some period as a support for the old worm-eaten baulk of timber which spanned the roof. To this post a figure was tied, so swathed and muffled in the sheets which had been used to secure it that one could not for the moment tell whether it was that of a man or a woman. One towel passed round the throat and was secured at the back of the pillar. Another covered the lower part of the face, and over it two dark eyes – eyes full of grief and shame and a dreadful questioning – stared back at us. In a minute we had torn off the gag, unswathed the bonds, and Mrs Stapleton sank upon the floor in front of us. As her beautiful head fell upon her chest I saw the clear red weal of a whiplash across her neck.

'The brute!' cried Holmes. 'Here, Lestrade, your brandy-bottle! Put her in the chair! She has fainted from ill-usage and exhaustion.'

She opened her eyes again.

'Is he safe?' she asked. 'Has he escaped?'

'He cannot escape us, madam.'

'No, no, I did not mean my husband. Sir Henry? Is he safe?'

'Yes.'

'And the hound?'

'It is dead.'

She gave a long sigh of satisfaction.

'Thank God! Thank God! Oh, this villain! See how he has treated me!' She shot her arms out from her sleeves, and we saw with horror that they were all mottled with bruises. 'But this is nothing – nothing! It is my mind and soul that he has tortured and defiled. I could endure it all, ill-usage, solitude, a life of deception, everything, as long as I could still cling to the hope that I had his love, but now I know that in this also I have been his dupe and his tool.' She broke into passionate sobbing as she spoke.

'You bear him no goodwill, madam,' said Holmes. 'Tell us then where we shall find him. If you have ever aided him in evil, help us now and so atone.'

'There is but one place where he can have fled,' she answered. 'There is an old tin mine on an island in the heart of the Mire. It was there that he kept his hound and there also he had made preparations so that he might have a refuge. That is where he would fly.'

The fog-bank lay like white wool against the window. Holmes held the lamp towards it.

'See,' said he. 'No one could find his way into the Grimpen Mire tonight.'

She laughed and clapped her hands. Her eyes and teeth gleamed with fierce merriment.

'He may find his way in, but never out,' she cried. 'How can he see the guiding wands tonight? We planted them together, he and I, to mark the pathway through the Mire. Oh, if I could only have plucked them out today. Then indeed you would have had him at your mercy!'

It was evident to us that all pursuit was in vain until the fog had lifted.

Meanwhile we left Lestrade in possession of the house while Holmes and I went back with the baronet to Baskerville Hall. The story of the Stapletons could no longer be withheld from him, but he took the blow bravely when he learned the truth about the woman whom he had loved. But the shock of the night's adventures had shattered his nerves, and before morning he lay delirious in a high fever under the care of Dr Mortimer. The two of them were destined to travel together round the world before Sir Henry had become once more the hale, hearty man that he had been before he became master of that ill-omened estate.

And now I come rapidly to the conclusion of this singular narrative, in which I have tried to make the reader share those dark fears and vague surmises which clouded our lives so long and ended in so tragic a manner. On the morning after the death of the hound, the fog had lifted and we were guided by Mrs Stapleton to the point where they had found a pathway through the bog. It helped us to realise the horror of this woman's life when we saw the eagerness and joy with which she laid us on her husband's track. We left her standing upon the thin peninsula of firm, peaty soil which tapered out into the widespread bog. From the end of it a small wand planted here and there showed where the path zigzagged from tuft to tuft of rushes among those green-scummed pits and foul quagmires which barred the way to the stranger. Rank reeds and lush, slimy water-plants sent an odour of decay and a heavy miasmatic vapour on to our faces, while a false step plunged us more than once thigh-deep into the dark, quivering mire, which shook for yards in soft undulations around our feet. Its tenacious grip plucked at our heels as we walked, and when we sank into it it was as if some malignant hand was tugging us down into those obscene depths, so grim and purposeful was the clutch in which it held us. Once only we saw a trace that someone had passed that perilous way before us. From amid a tuft of cotton grass which bore it up out of the slime some dark thing was projecting. Holmes sank to his waist as he stepped from the path to seize it, and had we not been there to drag him out he could never have set his foot upon firm land again. He held an old black boot in the air. 'Meyers, Toronto', was printed on the leather inside.

'It is worth a mud bath,' said he. 'It is our friend Sir Henry's missing boot.'

'Thrown there by Stapleton in his flight.'

'Exactly. He retained it in his hand after using it to set the hound upon the track. He fled when he knew the game was up, still clutching it. And he hurled it away at this point of his flight. We know at least that he came so far in safety.'

But more than that we were never destined to know, though there was much which we might surmise. There was no chance of finding footsteps in the mire, for the rising mud oozed swiftly in upon them, but as we at last reached firmer ground beyond the morass we all looked eagerly for them. But no slightest sign of them ever met our eyes. If the earth told a true story, then Stapleton never reached that island of refuge towards which he struggled through the fog upon that last night. Somewhere in the heart of the great Grimpen Mire, down in the foul slime of the huge morass which had sucked him in, this cold and cruel-hearted man is forever buried.

Many traces we found of him in the bog-girt island where he had hid his savage ally. A huge driving-wheel and a shaft half-filled with rubbish showed the position of an abandoned mine. Beside it were the crumbling remains of the cottages of the miners, driven away no doubt by the foul reek of the surrounding swamp. In one of these a staple and chain with a quantity of gnawed bones showed where the animal had been confined.

A skeleton with a tangle of brown hair adhering to it lay among the debris.

'A dog!' said Holmes. 'By Jove, a curly-haired spaniel. Poor Mortimer will never see his pet again. Well, I do not know that this place contains any secret which we have not already fathomed. He could hide his hound, but he could not hush its voice, and hence came those cries which even in daylight were not pleasant to hear. On an emergency he could keep the hound in the out-house at Merripit, but it was always a risk, and it was only on the supreme day, which he regarded as the end of all his efforts, that he dared do it. This paste in the tin is no doubt the luminous mixture with which the creature was daubed. It was suggested, of course, by the story of the family hell-hound, and by the desire to frighten old Sir Charles to death. No wonder the poor devil of a convict ran and screamed, even as our friend did, and as we ourselves might have done, when he saw such a creature bounding through the darkness of the moor upon his track. It was a cunning device, for, apart from the chance of driving your victim to his death, what peasant would venture to enquire too closely into such a creature should he get sight of it, as many have done, upon the moor? I said it in London, Watson, and I say it again now, that never yet have we helped to hunt down a more dangerous man than he who is lying yonder' – he swept his long arm towards the huge mottled expanse of green-splotched bog which stretched away until it merged into the russet slopes of the moor.

15

A Retrospection

It was the end of November, and Holmes and I sat, upon a raw and foggy night, on either side of a blazing fire in our sitting-room in Baker Street. Since the tragic upshot of our visit to Devonshire he had been engaged in two affairs of the utmost importance, in the first of which he had exposed the atrocious conduct of Colonel Upwood in connection with the famous card scandal of the Nonpareil Club, while in the second he had defended the unfortunate Mme Montpensier from the charge of murder which hung over her in connection with the death of her stepdaughter, Mlle Carère, the young lady who, as it will be remembered, was found six months later alive and married in New York. My friend was in excellent spirits over the success which had attended a succession of difficult and important cases, so that I was able to induce him to discuss the details of the Baskerville mystery. I had waited patiently for the opportunity for I was aware that he would never permit cases to overlap, and that his clear and logical mind would not be drawn from its present work to dwell upon memories of the past. Sir Henry and Dr Mortimer were, however, in London, on their way to that long voyage which had been recommended for the restoration of his shattered nerves. They had called upon us that very afternoon, so that it was natural that the subject should come up for discussion.

'The whole course of events,' said Holmes, 'from the point of view of the man who called himself Stapleton was simple and direct, although to us, who had no means in the beginning of knowing the motives of his actions and could only learn part of the facts, it all appeared exceedingly complex. I have had the advantage of two conversations with Mrs Stapleton, and the case has now been so entirely cleared up that I am not aware that there is anything which has remained a secret to us. You will find a few notes upon the matter under the heading B in my indexed list of cases.'

'Perhaps you would kindly give me a sketch of the course of events from memory.'

'Certainly, though I cannot guarantee that I carry all the facts in my mind. Intense mental concentration has a curious way of blotting out what has passed. The barrister who has his case at his fingers' ends and is able to argue with an expert upon his own subject finds that a week or two of the courts will drive it all out of his head once more. So each of my cases displaces the last, and Mlle Carère has blurred my recollection of Baskerville Hall. Tomorrow some other little problem may be submitted to my notice which will in turn dispossess the fair French lady and the infamous Upwood. So far as the case of the hound goes, however, I will give you the course of events as nearly as I can, and you will suggest anything which I may have forgotten.

'My enquiries show beyond all question that the family portrait did not lie, and that this fellow was indeed a Baskerville. He was a son of that Rodger Baskerville, the younger brother of Sir Charles, who fled with a sinister reputation to South America, where he was said to have died unmarried. He did, as a matter of fact, marry, and had one child, this fellow, whose real name is the same as his father's. He married Beryl Garçia, one of the beauties of Costa Rica, and, having purloined a considerable sum of public money, he changed his name to Vandeleur and fled to England, where he established a school in the east of Yorkshire. His reason for attempting this special line of business was that he had struck up an acquaintance with a consumptive tutor upon the voyage home, and that he had used this man's ability to make the undertaking a success. Fraser, the tutor, died, however, and the school which had begun well sank from disrepute into infamy. The Vandeleurs found it convenient to change their name to Stapleton, and he brought the remains of his fortune, his schemes for the future and his taste for entomology to the south of England. I learned at the British Museum that he was a recognised authority upon the subject, and that the name of Vandeleur has been permanently attached to a certain moth which he had, in his Yorkshire days, been the first to describe.

'We now come to that portion of his life which has proved to be of such intense interest to us. The fellow had evidently made enquiry and found that only two lives intervened between him and a valuable estate. When he went to Devonshire his plans were, I believe, exceedingly hazy, but that he meant mischief from the first is evident from the way in which he took his wife with him in the character of his sister. The idea of using her as a decoy was clearly already in his mind, though he may not have been certain how the details of his plot were to be arranged. He meant in the end to have the estate, and he was ready to use any tool or run any risk for that end. His first act was to establish himself as near to his ancestral home as he could, and his second was to cultivate a friendship with Sir Charles Baskerville and with the neighbours.

'The baronet himself told him about the family hound, and so prepared the way for his own death. Stapleton, as I will continue to call him, knew that the old man's heart was weak and that a shock would kill him. So much he had learned from Dr Mortimer. He had heard also that Sir Charles was superstitious and had taken this grim legend very seriously. His ingenious mind instantly suggested a way by which the baronet could be done to death, and yet it would be hardly possible to bring home the guilt to the real murderer.

'Having conceived the idea he proceeded to carry it out with considerable finesse. An ordinary schemer would have been content to work with a savage hound. The use of artificial means to make the creature diabolical was a flash of genius upon his part. The dog he bought in London from Ross and Mangles, the dealers in Fulham Road. It was the strongest and most savage in their possession. He brought it down by the North Devon line and walked a great distance over the moor so as to get it home without exciting any remarks. He had already on his insect hunts learned to penetrate the Grimpen Mire, and so had found a safe hiding-place for the creature. Here he kennelled it and waited his chance.

'But it was some time coming. The old gentleman could not be decoyed outside of his grounds at night. Several times Stapleton lurked about with his hound, but without avail. It was during these fruitless quests that he, or rather his ally, was seen by peasants, and that the legend of the demon dog received a new confirmation. He had hoped that his wife might lure Sir Charles to his ruin, but here she proved unexpectedly independent. She would not endeavour to entangle the old gentleman in a sentimental attachment which might deliver him over to his enemy. Threats and even, I am sorry to say, blows refused to move her. She would have nothing to do with it, and for a time Stapleton was at a deadlock.

'He found a way out of his difficulties through the chance that Sir Charles, who had conceived a friendship for him, made him the minister of his charity in the case of this unfortunate woman, Mrs Laura Lyons. By representing himself as a single man he acquired complete influence over her, and he gave her to understand that in the event of her obtaining a divorce from her husband he would marry her. His plans were suddenly brought to a head by his knowledge that Sir Charles was about to leave the Hall on the advice of Dr Mortimer, with whose opinion he himself pretended to coincide. He must act at once, or his victim might get beyond his power. He therefore put pressure upon Mrs Lyons to write this letter, imploring the old man to give her an interview on the evening before his departure for London. He then, by a specious argument, prevented her from going, and so had the chance for which he had waited.

'Driving back in the evening from Coombe Tracey he was in time to get his hound, to treat it with his infernal paint, and to bring the beast round to the gate at which he had reason to expect that he would find the old gentleman waiting. The dog, incited by its master, sprang over the wicket-gate and pursued the unfortunate baronet, who fled screaming down the yew alley. In that gloomy tunnel it must indeed have been a dreadful sight to see that huge black creature, with its flaming jaws and blazing eyes, bounding after its victim. He fell dead at the end of the alley from heart disease and terror. The hound had kept upon the grassy border while the baronet had run down the path, so that no track but the man's was visible. On seeing him lying still the creature had probably approached to sniff at him, but finding him dead had turned away again. It was then that it left the print which was actually observed by Dr Mortimer. The hound was called off and hurried away to its lair in the Grimpen Mire, and a mystery was left which puzzled the authorities, alarmed the countryside and finally brought the case within the scope of our observation.

'So much for the death of Sir Charles Baskerville. You perceive the devilish cunning of it, for really it would be almost impossible to make a case against the real murderer. His only accomplice was one who could never give him away, and the grotesque, inconceivable nature of the device only served to make it more effective. Both of the women concerned in the case, Mrs Stapleton and Mrs Laura Lyons, were left with a strong suspicion against Stapleton. Mrs Stapleton knew that he had designs upon the old man, and also of the existence of the hound. Mrs Lyons knew neither of these things, but had been impressed by the death occurring at the time of an uncancelled appointment which was only known to him. However, both of them were under his influence, and he had nothing to fear from them. The first half of his task was successfully accomplished but the more difficult still remained.

'It is possible that Stapleton did not know of the existence of an heir in Canada. In any case he would very soon learn it from his friend Dr Mortimer, and he was told by the latter all details about the arrival of Henry Baskerville. Stapleton's first idea was that this young stranger from Canada might possibly be done to death in London without coming down to Devonshire at all. He distrusted his wife ever since she had refused to help him in laying a trap for the old man, and he dared not leave her long out of his sight for fear he should lose his influence over her. It was for this reason that he took her to London with him. They lodged, I find, at the Mexborough Private Hotel, in Craven Street, which was actually one of those called upon by my agent in search of evidence. Here he kept his wife imprisoned in her room while he, disguised in a beard, followed Dr Mortimer to Baker Street and afterwards to the station and to the Northumberland Hotel. His wife had some inkling of his plans; but she had such a fear of her husband – a fear founded upon brutal ill-treatment – that she dare not write to warn the man whom she knew to be in danger. If the letter should fall into Stapleton's hands her own life would not be safe. Eventually, as we know, she adopted the expedient of cutting out the words which would form the message, and addressing the letter in a disguised hand. It reached the baronet, and gave him the first warning of his danger.

'It was very essential for Stapleton to get some article of Sir Henry's attire so that, in case he was driven to use the dog, he might always have the means of setting him upon his track. With characteristic promptness and audacity he set about this at once, and we cannot doubt that the boots or chambermaid of the hotel was well bribed to help him in his design. By chance, however, the first boot which was procured for him was a new one and, therefore, useless for his purpose. He then had it returned and obtained another – a most instructive incident, since it proved conclusively to my mind that we were dealing with a real hound, as no other supposition could explain this anxiety to obtain an old boot and this indifference to a new one. The more *outré* and grotesque an incident is the more carefully it deserves to be examined, and the very point which appears to complicate a case is, when duly considered and scientifically handled, the one which is most likely to elucidate it.

'Then we had the visit from our friends next morning, shadowed always by Stapleton in the cab. From his knowledge of our rooms and of my appearance, as well as from his general conduct, I am inclined to think that Stapleton's career of crime has been by no means limited to this single Baskerville affair. It is suggestive that during the last three years there have been four considerable burglaries in the West Country, for none of which was any criminal ever arrested. The last of these, at Folkestone Court, in May, was remarkable for the cold-blooded pistolling of the page, who surprised the masked and solitary burglar. I cannot doubt that Stapleton recruited his waning resources in this fashion, and that for years he has been a desperate and dangerous man.

'We had an example of his readiness of resource that morning when he got away from us so successfully, and also of his audacity in sending back my own name to me through the cabman. From that moment he understood that I had taken over the case in London, and that therefore there was no chance for him there. He returned to Dartmoor and awaited the arrival of the baronet.'

'One moment!' said I. 'You have, no doubt, described the sequence of events correctly, but there is one point which you have left unexplained. What became of the hound when its master was in London?'

'I have given some attention to this matter and it is undoubtedly of importance. There can be no question that Stapleton had a confidant, though it is unlikely that he ever placed himself in his power by sharing all his plans with him. There was an old manservant at Merripit House, whose name was Anthony. His connection with the Stapletons can be traced for several years, as far back as the schoolmastering days, so that he must have been aware that his master and mistress were really husband and wife. This man has disappeared and has escaped from the country. It is suggestive that Anthony is not a common name in England, while Antonio is so in all Spanish or Spanish-American countries. The man, like Mrs Stapleton herself, spoke good English, but with a curious lisping accent. I have myself seen this old man cross the Grimpen Mire by the path which Stapleton had marked out. It is very probable, therefore, that in the absence of his master it was he who cared for the hound, though he may never have known the purpose for which the beast was used.

'The Stapletons then went down to Devonshire, whither they were soon followed by Sir Henry and you. One word now as to how I stood myself at that time. It may possibly recur to your memory that when I examined the paper upon which the printed words were fastened I made a close inspection for the watermark. In doing so I held it within a few inches of my eyes, and was conscious of a faint smell of the scent known as white jessamine. There are seventy-five perfumes which it is very necessary that a criminal expert should be able to distinguish from each other, and cases have more than once within my own experience depended upon their prompt recognition. The scent suggested the presence of a lady, and already my thoughts began to turn towards the Stapletons. Thus I had made certain of the hound, and had guessed at the criminal before ever we went to the West Country.

'It was my game to watch Stapleton. It was evident, however, that I could not do this if I were with you, since he would be keenly on his guard. I deceived everybody, therefore, yourself included, and I came down secretly when I was supposed to be in London. My hardships were not so great as you imagined, though such trifling details must never interfere with the investigation of a case. I stayed for the most part at Coombe Tracey, and only used the hut upon the moor when it was necessary to be near the scene of action. Cartwright had come down with me, and in his disguise as a country boy he was of great assistance to me. I was dependent upon him for food and clean linen. When I was watching Stapleton, Cartwright was frequently watching you, so that I was able to keep my hand upon all the strings.

'I have already told you that your reports reached me rapidly, being forwarded instantly from Baker Street to Coombe Tracey. They were of great service to me, and especially that one incidentally truthful piece of biography of Stapleton's. I was able to establish the identity of the man and the woman and knew at last exactly how I stood. The case had been considerably complicated through the incident of the escaped convict and the relations between him and the Barrymores. This also you cleared up in a very effective way, though I had already come to the same conclusions from my own observations.

'By the time that you discovered me upon the moor I had a complete knowledge of the whole business, but I had not a case which could go to a jury. Even Stapleton's attempt upon Sir Henry that night which ended in the death of the unfortunate convict did not help us much in proving murder against our man. There seemed to be no alternative but to catch him red-handed, and to do so we had to use Sir Henry, alone and apparently unprotected, as a bait. We did so, and at the cost of a severe shock to our client we succeeded in completing our case and driving Stapleton to his destruction. That Sir Henry should have been exposed to this is, I must confess, a reproach to my management of the case, but we had no means of foreseeing the terrible and paralysing spectacle which the beast presented, nor could we predict the fog which enabled him to burst upon us at such short notice. We succeeded in our object at a cost which both the specialist and Dr Mortimer assure me will be a temporary one. A long journey may enable our friend to recover not only from his shattered nerves but also from his wounded feelings. His love for the lady was deep and sincere, and to him the saddest part of all this black business was that he should have been deceived by her.

'It only remains to indicate the part which she had played throughout. There can be no doubt that Stapleton exercised an influence over her which may have been love or may have been fear, or very possibly both, since they are by no means incompatible emotions. It was, at least, absolutely effective. At his command she consented to pass as his sister, though he found the limits of his power over her when he endeavoured to make her the direct accessory to murder. She was ready to warn Sir Henry so far as she could without implicating her husband, and again and again she tried to do so. Stapleton himself seems to have been capable of jealousy, and when he saw the baronet paying court to the lady, even though it was part of his own plan, still he could not help interrupting with a passionate outburst which revealed the fiery soul which his self-contained manner so cleverly concealed. By encouaging the intimacy he made it certain that Sir Henry would frequently come to Merripit House and that he would sooner or later get the opportunity which he desired. On the day of the crisis, however, his wife turned suddenly against him. She had learned something of the death of the convict, and she knew that the hound was being kept in the out-house on the evening that Sir Henry was coming to dinner. She taxed her husband with his intended crime, and a furious scene followed in which he showed her for the first time that she had a rival in his love. Her fidelity turned in an instant to bitter hatred, and he saw that she would betray him. He tied her up, therefore, that she might have no chance of warning Sir Henry, and he hoped, no doubt, that when the whole countryside put down the baronet's death to the curse of his family, as they certainly would do, he could win his wife back to accept an accomplished fact and to keep silent upon what she knew. In this I fancy that in any case he made a miscalculation, and that, if we had not been there, his doom would none the less have been sealed. A woman of Spanish blood does not condone such an injury so lightly. And now, my dear Watson, without referring to my notes, I cannot give you a more detailed account of this curious case. I do not know that anything essential has been left unexplained.'

'He could not hope to frighten Sir Henry to death as he had done the old uncle with his bogey hound.'

'The beast was savage and half-starved. If its appearance did not frighten its victim to death, at least it would paralyse the resistance which might be offered.'

'No doubt. There only remains one difficulty. If Stapleton came into the succession, how could he explain the fact that he, the heir, had been living unannounced under another name so close to the property? How could he claim it without causing suspicion and enquiry?'

'It is a formidable difficulty, and I fear that you ask too much when you expect me to solve it. The past and the present are within the field of my enquiry, but what a man may do in the future is a hard question to answer. Mrs Stapleton had heard her husband discuss the problem on several occasions. There were three possible courses. He might claim the property from South America, establish his identity before the British authorities there and so obtain the fortune without ever coming to England at all; or he might adopt an elaborate disguise during the short time that he need be in London; or, again, he might furnish an accomplice with the proofs and papers, putting him in as heir, and retaining a claim upon some proportion of his income. We cannot doubt from what we know of him that he would have found some way out of the difficulty. And now, my dear Watson, we have had some weeks of severe work, and for one evening, I think, we may turn our thoughts into more pleasant channels. I have a box for *Les Huguenots*. Have you heard the De Reszkes? Might I trouble you then to be ready in half an hour, and we can stop at Marcini's for a little dinner on the way?'

The Sign of the Four

I

The Science of Deduction

Sherlock Holmes took his bottle from the corner of the mantelpiece and his hypodermic syringe from its neat morocco case. With his long, white, nervous fingers he adjusted the delicate needle and rolled back his left shirt-cuff. For some little time his eyes rested thoughtfully upon the sinewy forearm and wrist, all dotted and scarred with innumerable puncture-marks. Finally, he thrust the sharp point home, pressed down the tiny piston, and sank back into the velvet-lined armchair with a long sigh of satisfaction.

Three times a day for many months I had witnessed this performance, but custom had not reconciled my mind to it. On the contrary, from day to day I had become more irritable at the sight, and my conscience swelled nightly within me at the thought that I had lacked the courage to protest. Again and again I had registered a vow that I should deliver my soul upon the subject; but there was that in the cool, nonchalant air of my companion which made him the last man with whom one would care to take anything approaching to a liberty. His great powers, his masterly manner, and the experience which I had had of his many extraordinary qualities, all made me diffident and backward in crossing him.

Yet upon that afternoon, whether it was the Beaune which I had taken with my lunch, or the additional exasperation produced by the extreme deliberation of his manner, I suddenly felt that I could hold out no longer.

'Which is it today,' I asked, 'morphine or cocaine?'

He raised his eyes languidly from the old black-leather volume which he had opened.

'It is cocaine,' he said, 'a seven-per-cent solution. Would you care to try it?'

'No, indeed,' I answered, brusquely. 'My constitution has not got over the Afghan campaign yet. I cannot afford to throw any extra strain upon it.'

He smiled at my vehemence. 'Perhaps you are right, Watson,' he said. 'I suppose that its influence is physically a bad one. I find it, however, so transcendently stimulating and clarifying to the mind that its secondary action is a matter of small moment.'

'But consider!' I said, earnestly. 'Count the cost! Your brain may, as you say, be roused and excited, but it is a pathological and morbid process, which involves increased tissue-change, and may at last leave a permanent weakness. You know, too, what a black reaction comes upon you. Surely the game is hardly worth the candle. Why should you, for a mere passing pleasure, risk the loss of those great powers with which you have been endowed? Remember that I speak not only as one comrade to another, but as a medical man to one for whose constitution he is to some extent answerable.'

He did not seem offended. On the contrary, he put his fingertips together, and leaned his elbows on the arms of his chair, like one who has a relish for conversation.

'My mind,' he said, 'rebels at stagnation. Give me problems, give me work, give me the most abstruse cryptogram, or the most intricate analysis, and I am in my own proper atmosphere. I can dispense then with artificial stimulants. But I abhor the dull routine of existence. I crave for mental exaltation. That is why I have chosen my own particular profession, or rather created it, for I am the only one in the world.'

'The only unofficial detective?' I said, raising my eyebrows.

'The only unofficial consulting detective,' he answered. 'I am the last and highest court of appeal in detection. When Gregson or Lestrade or Athelney Jones are out of their depths which, by the way, is their normal state – the matter is laid before me. I examine the data, as an expert, and pronounce a specialist's opinion. I claim no credit in such cases. My name figures in no newspaper. The work itself, the pleasure of finding a field for my peculiar powers, is my highest reward. But you have yourself had some experience of my methods of work in the Jefferson Hope case.'

'Yes, indeed,' said I, cordially. 'I was never so struck by anything in my life. I even embodied it in a small brochure, with the somewhat fantastic title of "A Study in Scarlet".'

He shook his head sadly.

'I glanced over it,' said he. 'Honestly, I cannot congratulate you upon it. Detection is, or ought to be, an exact science and should be treated in the same cold and unemotional manner. You have attempted to tinge it with romanticism, which produces much the same effect as if you worked a love story or an elopement into the fifth proposition of Euclid.'

'But the romance was there,' I remonstrated. 'I could not tamper with the facts.'

'Some facts should be suppressed, or, at least, a just sense of proportion should be observed in treating them. The only point in the case which deserved mention was the curious analytical reasoning from effects to causes by which I succeeded in unravelling it.'

I was annoyed at this criticism of a work which had been specially designed to please him. I confess, too, that I was irritated by the egotism which seemed to demand that every line of my pamphlet should be devoted to his own special doings. More than once during the years that I had lived with him in Baker Street I had observed that a small vanity underlay my companion's quiet and didactic manner. I made no remark, however, but sat nursing my wounded leg. I had had a Jezail bullet through it some time before, and, though it did not prevent me from walking, it ached wearily at every change of the weather.

'My practice has extended recently to the Continent,' said Holmes, after a while, filling up his old brier-root pipe. 'I was consulted last week by François le Villard, who, as you probably know, has come rather to the front lately in the French detective service. He has all the Celtic power of quick intuition, but he is deficient in the wide range of exact knowledge which is essential to the higher developments of his art. The case was concerned with a will, and possessed some features of interest. I was able to refer him to two parallel cases, the one at Riga in 1857 and the other at St Louis in 1871, which have suggested to him the true solution. Here is the letter which I had this morning acknowledging my assistance.'

He tossed over, as he spoke, a crumpled sheet of foreign notepaper. I glanced my eyes down it, catching a profusion of notes of admiration, with stray 'magnifiques', 'coup-de-maîtres' and 'tours-de-force', all testifying to the ardent admiration of the Frenchman.

'He speaks as a pupil to his master,' said I.

'Oh, he rates my assistance too highly,' said Sherlock Holmes, lightly. 'He has considerable gifts himself. He possesses two out of the three qualities necessary for the ideal detective. He has the power of observation and that of deduction. He is only wanting in knowledge, and that may come in time. He is now translating my small works into French.'

'Your works?'

'Oh, didn't you know?' he cried, laughing. 'Yes, I have been guilty of several monographs. They are all upon technical subjects. Here, for example, is one "Upon the Distinction Between the Ashes of the Various Tobaccos". In it I enumerate a hundred and forty forms of cigar, cigarette and pipe tobacco, with coloured plates illustrating the difference in the ash. It is a point which is continually turning up in criminal trials and which is sometimes of supreme importance as a clue. If you can say definitely, for example, that some murder had been done by a man who was smoking an Indian lunkah, it obviously narrows your field of search. To the trained eye there is as much difference between the black ash of a Trichinopoly and the white fluff of bird's-eye as there is between a cabbage and a potato.'

'You have an extraordinary genius for minutiae,' I remarked.

'I appreciate their importance. Here is my monograph upon the tracing of footsteps, with some remarks upon the uses of plaster of Paris as a preserver of impresses. Here, too, is a curious little work upon the influence of a trade upon the form of the hand, with lithotypes of the hands of slaters, sailors, cork-cutters, compositors, weavers and diamond-polishers. That is a matter of great practical interest to the scientific detective – especially in cases of unclaimed bodies, or in discovering the antecedents of criminals. But I weary you with my hobby.'

'Not at all,' I answered, earnestly. 'It is of the greatest interest to me, especially since I have had the opportunity of observing your practical application of it. But you spoke just now of observation and deduction. Surely the one to some extent implies the other.'

'Why, hardly,' he answered, leaning back luxuriously in his armchair and sending up thick blue wreaths from his pipe. 'For example, observation shows me that you have been to the Wigmore Street Post Office this morning, but deduction lets me know that when there you dispatched a telegram.'

'Right!' said I. 'Right on both points! But I confess that I don't see how you arrived at it. It was a sudden impulse upon my part, and I have mentioned it to no one.'

'It is simplicity itself,' he remarked, chuckling at my surprise – 'so absurdly simple that an explanation is superfluous; and yet it may serve to define the limits of observation and of deduction. Observation tells me that you have a little reddish mould adhering to your instep. Just opposite the Wigmore Street office they have taken up the pavement and thrown up some earth, which lies in such a way that it is difficult to avoid treading in it in entering. The earth is of this peculiar reddish tint which is found as far as I know nowhere else in the neighbourhood. So much is observation. The rest is deduction.'

'How, then, did you deduce the telegram?'

'Why, of course I knew that you had not written a letter, since I sat opposite to you all morning. I see also in your open desk there that you have a sheet of stamps and a thick bundle of postcards. What could you go into the post-office for, then, but to send a wire? Eliminate all other factors, and the one which remains must be the truth.'

'In this case it certainly is so,' I replied, after a little thought. 'The thing, however, is, as you say, of the simplest. Would you think me impertinent if I were to put your theories to a more severe test?'

'On the contrary,' he answered; 'it would prevent me from taking a second dose of cocaine. I should be delighted to look into any problem which you might submit to me.'

'I have heard you say that it is difficult for a man to have any object in daily use without leaving the impress of his individuality upon it in such a way that a trained observer might read it. Now, I have here a watch which has recently come into my possession. Would you have the kindness to let me have an opinion upon the character or habits of the late owner?'

I handed him over the watch with some slight feeling of amusement in my heart, for the test was, as I thought, an impossible one, and I intended it as a lesson against the somewhat dogmatic tone which he occasionally assumed. He balanced the watch in his hand, gazed hard at the dial, opened the back, and examined the works, first with his naked eyes and then with a powerful convex lens. I could hardly keep from smiling at his crestfallen face when he finally snapped the case to and handed it back.

'There are hardly any data,' he remarked. 'The watch has been recently cleaned, which robs me of my most suggestive facts.'

'You are right,' I answered. 'It was cleaned before being sent to me.'

In my heart I accused my companion of putting forward a most lame and impotent excuse to cover his failure. What data could he expect from an uncleaned watch?

'Though unsatisfactory, my research has not been entirely barren,' he observed, staring up at the ceiling with dreamy, lack-lustre eyes. 'Subject to your correction, I should judge that the watch belonged to your elder brother, who inherited it from your father.'

'That you gather, no doubt, from the H.W. upon the back?'

'Quite so. The W. suggests your own name. The date of the watch is nearly fifty years back and the initials are as old as the watch; so it was made for the last generation. Jewellery usually descends to the eldest son, and he is most likely to have the same name as the father. Your father has, if I remember right, been dead many years. It has, therefore, been in the hands of your eldest brother.'

'Right, so far,' said I. 'Anything else?'

'He was a man of untidy habits – very untidy and careless. He was left with good prospects, but he threw away his chances, lived for some time in poverty with occasional short intervals of prosperity, and, finally, taking to drink, he died. That is all I can gather.'

I sprang from my chair and limped impatiently about the room with considerable bitterness in my heart.

'This is unworthy of you, Holmes,' I said. 'I could not have believed that you would have descended to this. You have made enquiries into the history of my unhappy brother, and you now pretend to deduce this knowledge in some fanciful way. You cannot expect me to believe that you have read all this from his old watch! It is unkind, and, to speak plainly, has a touch of charlatanism in it.'

'My dear doctor,' said he, kindly, 'pray accept my apologies. Viewing the matter as an abstract problem, I had forgotten how personal and painful a thing it might be to you. I assure you, however, that I never even knew that you had a brother until you handed me the watch.'

'Then how in the name of all that is wonderful did you get these facts? They are absolutely correct in every particular.'

'Ah, that is good luck. I could only say what was the balance of probability. I did not at all expect to be accurate.'

'But it was not mere guesswork?'

'No, no: I never guess. It is a shocking habit – destructive to the logical faculty. What seems strange to you is only so because you do not follow my train of thought or observe the small facts upon which large inferences may depend. For example, I began by stating that your brother was careless. When you observe the lower part of that watch-case you notice that it is not only dinted in two places, but it is cut and marked all over from the habit of keeping other hard objects, such as coins or keys, in the same pocket. Surely it is no great feat to assume that a man who treats a fifty-guinea watch so cavalierly must be a careless man. Neither is it a very far-fetched inference that a man who inherits one article of such value is pretty well provided for in other respects.'

I nodded, to show that I followed his reasoning.

'It is very customary for pawnbrokers in England, when they take a watch, to scratch the number of the ticket with a pinpoint upon the inside of the case. It is more handy than a label, as there is no risk of the number being lost or transposed. There are no fewer than four such numbers visible to my lens on the inside of this case. Inference – that your brother was often at low water. Secondary inference – that he had occasional bursts of prosperity, or he could not have redeemed the pledge. Finally, I ask you to look at the inner plate, which contains the keyhole. Look at the thousands of scratches all round the hole – marks where the key has slipped. What sober man's key could have scored those grooves? But you will never see a drunkard's watch without them.

He winds it at night, and he leaves these traces of his unsteady hand. Where is the mystery in all this?'

'It is as clear as daylight,' I answered. 'I regret the injustice which I did you. I should have had more faith in your marvellous faculty. May I ask whether you have any professional enquiry on foot at present?'

'None. Hence the cocaine. I cannot live without brainwork. What else is there to live for? Stand at the window here. Was ever such a dreary, dismal, unprofitable world? See how the yellow fog swirls down the street and drifts across the dun-coloured houses. What could be more hopelessly prosaic and material? What is the use of having powers, doctor, when one has no field upon which to exert them? Crime is commonplace, existence is commonplace, and no qualities save those which are commonplace have any function upon earth.'

I had opened my mouth to reply to this tirade, when, with a crisp knock, our landlady entered, bearing a card upon the brass salver.

'A young lady for you, sir,' she said, addressing my companion.

'Miss Mary Morstan,' he read. 'Hum! I have no recollection of the name. Ask the young lady to step up, Mrs Hudson. Don't go, doctor. I should prefer that you remain.'

2

The Statement of the Case

Miss Morstan entered the room with a firm step and an outward composure of manner. She was a blonde young lady, small, dainty, well gloved, and dressed in the most perfect taste. There was, however, a plainness and simplicity about her costume which bore with it a suggestion of limited means. The dress was a sombre greyish beige, untrimmed and unbraided, and she wore a small turban of the same dull hue, relieved only by a suspicion of white feather in the side. Her face had neither regularity of feature nor beauty of complexion, but her expression was sweet and amiable and her large blue eyes were singularly spiritual and sympathetic. In an experience of women which extends over many nations and three separate continents, I have never looked upon a face which gave a clearer promise of a refined and sensitive nature. I could not but observe that, as she took the seat which Sherlock Holmes placed for her, her lip trembled, her hand quivered and she showed every sign of intense inward agitation.

'I have come to you, Mr Holmes,' she said, 'because you once enabled my employer, Mrs Cecil Forrester, to unravel a little domestic complication. She was much impressed by your kindness and skill.'

'Mrs Cecil Forrester,' he repeated, thoughtfully. 'I believe that I was of some slight service to her. The case, however, as I remember it, was a very simple one.'

'She did not think so. But at least you cannot say the same of mine. I can hardly imagine anything more strange, more utterly inexplicable, than the situation in which I find myself.'

Holmes rubbed his hands and his eyes glistened. He leaned forward in his chair with an expression of extraordinary concentration upon his clear-cut, hawklike features.

'State your case,' said he, in brisk, business tones.

I felt that my position was an embarrassing one.

'You will, I am sure, excuse me,' I said, rising from my chair.

To my surprise, the young lady held up her gloved hand to detain me.

'If your friend,' she said, 'would be good enough to stop, he might be of inestimable service to me.'

I relapsed into my chair.

'Briefly,' she continued, 'the facts are these. My father was an officer in an Indian regiment, who sent me home when I was quite a child. My mother was dead, and I had no relative in England. I was placed, however, in a comfortable boarding establishment at Edinburgh, and there I remained until I was seventeen years of age. In the year 1878 my father, who was senior captain of his regiment, obtained twelve months' leave and came home. He telegraphed to me from London that he had arrived all safe, and directed me to come down at once, giving the Langham Hotel as his address. His message, as I remember, was full of kindness and love. On reaching London I drove to the Langham, and was informed that Captain Morstan was staying there, but that he had gone out the night before and had not returned. I waited all day without news of him. That night, on the advice of the manager of the hotel, I communicated with the police, and next morning we advertised in all the papers. Our enquiries led to no result; and from that day to this no word has ever been heard of my unfortunate father. He came home with his heart full of hope, to find some peace, some comfort, and instead – ' She put her hand to her throat, and a choking sob cut short the sentence.

'The date?' asked Holmes, opening his notebook.

'He disappeared upon the 3rd of December 1878 – nearly ten years ago.'

'His luggage?'

'Remained at the hotel. There was nothing in it to suggest a clue – some clothes, some books and a considerable number of curiosities from the Andaman Islands. He had been one of the officers in charge of the convict guard there.'

'Had he any friends in town?'

'Only one that we know of – Major Sholto, of his own regiment, the 34th Bombay Infantry. The major had retired some little time before, and lived at Upper Norwood. We communicated with him, of course, but he did not even know that his brother officer was in England.'

'A singular case,' remarked Holmes.

'I have not yet described to you the most singular part. About six years ago – to be exact, upon the 4th of May 1882 – an advertisement appeared in *The Times* asking for the address of Miss Mary Morstan, and stating that it would be to her advantage to come forward. There was no name or address appended. I had at that time just entered the family of Mrs Cecil Forrester in the capacity of governess. By her advice I published my address in the advertisement column. The same day there arrived through the post a small cardboard box addressed to me, which I found to contain a very large and lustrous pearl. No word of writing was enclosed. Since then every year upon the same date there has always appeared a similar box, containing a similar pearl, without any clue as to the sender. They have been pronounced by an expert to be of a rare variety and of consider-able value. You can see for yourselves that they are very handsome.'

She opened a flat box as she spoke, and showed me six of the finest pearls that I had ever seen.

'Your statement is most interesting,' said Sherlock Holmes. 'Has anything else occurred to you?'

'Yes, and no later than today. That is why I have come to you. This morning I received this letter, which you will perhaps read for yourself.'

'Thank you,' said Holmes. 'The envelope, too, please. Postmark, London, S.W. Date, July 7. Hum! Man's thumbmark on corner – probably postman. Best quality paper. Envelopes at sixpence a packet. Particular man in his stationery. No address. "Be at the third pillar from the left outside the Lyceum Theatre tonight at seven o'clock. If you are distrustful bring two friends. You are a wronged woman, and shall have justice. Do not bring police. If you do, all will be in vain. Your unknown friend." Well, really, this is a very pretty little mystery! What do you intend to do, Miss Morstan?'

'That is exactly what I want to ask you.'

'Then we shall most certainly go – you and I and – yes, why, Dr Watson is the very man. Your correspondent says two friends. He and I have worked together before.'

'But would he come?' she asked, with something appealing in her voice and expression.

'I shall be proud and happy,' said I, fervently, 'if I can be of any service.'

'You are both very kind,' she answered. 'I have led a retired life, and have no friends whom I could appeal to. If I am here at six it will do, I suppose?'

'You must not be later,' said Holmes. 'There is one other point, however. Is this handwriting the same as that upon the pearl-box addresses?'

'I have them here,' she answered, producing half a dozen pieces of paper.

'You are certainly a model client. You have the correct intuition. Let us see, now.' He spread out the papers upon the table, and gave little, darting glances from one to the other. 'They are disguised hands, except the letter,' he said, presently; 'but there can be no question as to the authorship. See how the irrepressible Greek *e* will break out, and see the twirl of the final *s*. They are undoubtedly by the same person. I should not like to suggest false hopes, Miss Morstan, but is there any resemblance between this hand and that of your father?'

'Nothing could be more unlike.'

'I expected to hear you say so. We shall look out for you, then, at six. Pray allow me to keep the papers. I may look into the matter before then. It is only half-past three. *Au revoir*, then.'

'*Au revoir*,' said our visitor; and with a bright, kindly glance from one to the other of us, she replaced her pearl-box in her bosom and hurried away.

Standing at the window, I watched her walking briskly down the street, until the grey turban and white feather were but a speck in the sombre crowd.

'What a very attractive woman!' I exclaimed, turning to my companion.

He had lit his pipe again, and was leaning back with drooping eyelids. 'Is she?' he said, languidly; 'I did not observe.'

'You really are an automaton – a calculating machine,' I cried. 'There is something positively inhuman in you at times.'

144

He smiled gently.

'It is of the first importance,' he said, 'not to allow your judgement to be biased by personal qualities. A client is to me a mere unit, a factor in a problem. The emotional qualities are antagonistic to clear reasoning. I assure you that the most winning woman I ever knew was hanged for poisoning three little children for their insurance money, and the most repellent man of my acquaintance is a philanthropist who has spent nearly a quarter of a million upon the London poor.'

'In this case, however – '

'I never make exceptions. An exception disproves the rule. Have you ever had occasion to study character in handwriting? What do you make of this fellow's scribble?'

'It is legible and regular,' I answered. 'A man of business habits and some force of character.'

Holmes shook his head.

'Look at his long letters,' he said. 'They hardly rise above the common herd. That *d* might be an *a*, and that *l* an *e*. Men of character always differentiate their long letters, however illegibly they may write. There is vacillation in his *k*s and self-esteem in his capitals. I am going out now. I have some few references to make. Let me recommend this book – one of the most remarkable ever penned. It is Winwood Reade's *Martydom of Man*. I shall be back in an hour.'

I sat in the window with the volume in my hand, but my thoughts were far from the daring speculations of the writer. My mind ran upon our late visitor – her smiles, the deep, rich tones of her voice, the strange mystery which overhung her life. If she were seventeen at the time of her father's disappearance she must be seven-and-twenty now – a sweet age, when youth has lost its self-consciousness and become a little sobered by experience. So I sat and mused, until such dangerous thoughts came into my head that I hurried away to my desk and plunged furiously into the latest treatise upon pathology. What was I, an army surgeon with a weak leg and a weaker banking account, that I should dare to think of such things? She was a unit, a factor – nothing more. If my future were black, it was better surely to face it like a man than to attempt to brighten it by mere will-o'-the-wisps of the imagination.

3

In Quest of a Solution

It was half-past five before Holmes returned. He was bright, eager, and in excellent spirits, a mood which in his case alternated with fits of the blackest depression.

'There is no great mystery in this matter,' he said, taking the cup of tea which I had poured out for him; 'the facts appear to admit of only one explanation.'

'What! you have solved it already?'

'Well, that would be too much to say. I have discovered a suggestive fact, that is all. It is, however, very suggestive. The details are still to be added. I have just found, on consulting the back files of *The Times*, that Major Sholto, of Upper Norwood, late of the 34th Bombay Infantry, died upon the 28th of April 1882.'

'I may be very obtuse, Holmes, but I fail to see what this suggests.'

'No? You surprise me. Look at it in this way, then. Captain Morstan disappears. The only person in London whom he could have visited is Major Sholto. Major Sholto denies having heard that he was in London. Four years later Sholto dies. *Within a week of his death* Captain Morstan's daughter receives a valuable present, which is repeated from year to year, and now culminates in a letter which describes her as a wronged woman. What wrong can it refer to except this deprivation of her father? And why should the presents begin immediately after Sholto's death, unless it is that Sholto's heir knows something of the mystery and desires to make compensation? Have you any alternative theory which will meet the facts?'

'But what a strange compensation! And how strangely made! Why, too, should he write a letter now, rather than six years ago? Again, the letter speaks of giving her justice. What justice can she have? It is too much to suppose that her father is still alive. There is no other injustice in her case that you know of.'

'There are difficulties; there are certainly difficulties,' said Sherlock Holmes, pensively; 'but our expedition of tonight will solve them all. Ah, here is a four-wheeler, and Miss Morstan inside. Are you all ready? Then we had better go down, for it is a little past the hour.'

I picked up my hat and my heaviest stick, but I observed that Holmes took his revolver from his drawer and slipped it into his pocket. It was clear that he thought that our night's work might be a serious one.

Miss Morstan was muffled in a dark cloak, and her sensitive face was composed, but pale. She must have been more than woman if she did not feel some uneasiness at the strange enterprise upon which we were embarking, yet her self-control was perfect, and she readily answered the few additional questions which Sherlock Holmes put to her.

'Major Sholto was a very particular friend of papa's,' she said. 'His letters were full of allusions to the major. He and papa were in command of the troops at the Andaman Islands, so they were thrown a great deal together. By the way, a curious paper was found in papa's desk which no one could understand. I don't suppose that it is of the slightest importance, but I thought you might care to see it, so I brought it with me. It is here.'

Holmes unfolded the paper carefully and smoothed it out upon his knee. He then very methodically examined it all over with his double lens.

'It is paper of native Indian manufacture,' he remarked. 'It has at some time been pinned to a board. The diagram upon it appears to be a plan of part of a large building with numerous halls, corridors and passages. At one point is a small cross done in red ink, and above it is "3.37 from left" in faded pencil-writing. In the left-hand corner is a curious hieroglyphic like four crosses in a line with their arms touching. Beside it is written, in very rough and coarse characters, "The sign of the four – Jonathan Small, Mahomet Singh, Abdullah Khan, Dost Akbar". No, I confess that I do not see how this bears upon the matter. Yet it is evidently a document of importance. It has been kept carefully in a pocket-book, for the one side is as clean as the other.'

'It was in his pocket-book that we found it.'

'Preserve it carefully, then, Miss Morstan, for it may prove to be of use to us. I begin to suspect that this matter may turn out to be much deeper and more subtle than I at first supposed. I must reconsider my ideas.'

He leaned back in the cab, and I could see by his drawn brow and his vacant eye that he was thinking intently. Miss Morstan and I chatted in an undertone about our present expedition and its possible outcome, but our companion maintained his impenetrable reserve until the end of our journey.

It was a September evening, and not yet seven o'clock, but the day had been a dreary one, and a dense drizzly fog lay low upon the great city. Mud-coloured clouds drooped sadly over the muddy streets. Down the Strand the lamps were but misty splotches of diffused light, which threw a feeble circular glimmer upon the slimy pavement. The yellow glare from the shop-windows streamed out into the steamy, vaporous air and threw a murky, shifting radiance across the crowded thoroughfare. There was, to my mind, something eerie and ghostlike in the endless procession of faces which flitted across these narrow bars of light – sad faces and glad, haggard and merry. Like all human kind, they flitted from the gloom into the light, and so back into the gloom once more. I am not subject to impressions, but the dull, heavy evening, with the strange business upon which we were engaged, combined to make me nervous and depressed. I could see from Miss Morstan's manner that she was suffering from the same feeling. Holmes alone could rise superior to petty influences. He held his open notebook upon his knee, and from time to time he jotted down figures and memoranda in the light of his pocket-lantern.

At the Lyceum Theatre the crowds were already thick at the side-entrances. In front a continuous stream of hansoms and four-wheelers were rattling up, discharging their cargoes of shirt-fronted men and beshawled, bediamonded women. We had hardly reached the third pillar, which was our rendezvous, before a small, dark, brisk man in the dress of a coachman accosted us.

'Are you the parties who come with Miss Morstan?' he asked.

'I am Miss Morstan, and these two gentlemen are my friends,' said she.

He bent a pair of wonderfully penetrating and questioning eyes upon us.

'You will excuse me, miss,' he said, with a certain dogged manner, 'but I was to ask you to give me your word that neither of your companions is a police officer.'

'I give you my word on that,' she answered.

He gave a shrill whistle, on which a street arab led across a four-wheeler and opened the door. The man who had addressed us mounted to the box, while we took our places inside. We had hardly done so before the driver whipped up his horse, and we plunged away at a furious pace through the foggy streets.

The situation was a curious one. We were driving to an unknown place, on an unknown errand. Yet our invitation was either a complete hoax – which was an inconceivable hypothesis or else we had good reason to think that important issues might hang upon our journey. Miss Morstan's demeanour was as resolute and collected as ever. I endeavoured to cheer and amuse her by reminiscences of my adventures in Afghanistan; but, to tell the truth, I was myself so excited at our situation, and so curious as to our destination, that my stories were slightly involved. To this day she declares that I told her one moving anecdote as to how a musket looked into my tent at the dead of night, and how I fired a double-barrelled tiger cub at it. At first I had some idea as to the direction in which we were driving; but soon, what with our pace, the fog, and my own limited knowledge of London, I lost my bearings, and knew nothing, save that we seemed to be going a very long way. Sherlock Holmes was never at fault, however, and he muttered the names as the cab rattled through squares and in and out by tortuous by-streets.

'Rochester Row,' said he. 'Now Vincent Square. Now we come out on the Vauxhall Bridge Road. We are making for the Surrey side, apparently. Yes. I thought so. Now we are on the bridge. You can catch glimpses of the river.'

We did indeed get a fleeting view of a stretch of the Thames, with the lamps shining upon the broad, silent water; but our cab dashed on, and was soon involved in a labyrinth of streets upon the other side.

'Wandsworth Road,' said my companion. 'Priory Road. Larkhall Lane. Stockwell Place. Robert Street. Coldharbour Lane. Our quest does not appear to take us to very fashionable regions.

We had indeed reached a questionable and forbidding neighbourhood. Long lines of dull brick houses were only relieved by the coarse glare and tawdry brilliancy of public-houses at the corners. Then came rows of two-storeyed villas, each with a fronting of miniature garden, and then again interminable lines of new, staring brick buildings – the monster tentacles which the giant city was throwing out into the country. At last the cab drew up at the third house in a new terrace. None of the other houses were inhabited, and that at which we stopped was as dark as its neighbours, save for a single glimmer in the kitchen-window. On our knocking, however, the door was instantly thrown open by a Hindu servant, clad in a yellow turban, white, loose-fitting clothes, and a yellow sash. There was something strangely incongruous in this Oriental figure framed in the commonplace doorway of a third-rate suburban dwelling-house.

'The sahib awaits you,' said he, and even as he spoke there came a high, piping voice from some inner room.

'Show them in to me, khitmutgar,' it cried. 'Show them straight in to me.'

4

The Story of the Bald-Headed Man

We followed the Indian down a sordid and common passage, ill-lit and worse furnished, until he came to a door upon the right, which he threw open. A blaze of yellow light streamed out upon us, and in the centre of the glare there stood a small man with a very high head, a bristle of red hair all round the fringe of it, and a bald, shining scalp which shot out from among it like a mountain-peak from fir trees. He writhed his hands together as he stood, and his features were in a perpetual jerk – now smiling, now scowling, but never for an instant in repose. Nature had given him a pendulous lip, and a too visible line of yellow and irregular teeth, which he strove feebly to conceal by constantly passing his hand over the lower part of his face. In spite of his obtrusive baldness, he gave the impression of youth. In point of fact, he had just turned his thirtieth year.

'Your servant, Miss Morstan,' he kept repeating, in a thin, high voice. 'Your servant, gentlemen. Pray step into my little sanctum. A small place, miss, but furnished to my own liking. An oasis of art in the howling desert of South London.'

We were all astonished by the appearance of the apartment into which he invited us. In that sorry house it looked as out-of-place as a diamond of the first water in a setting of brass. The richest and glossiest of curtains and tapestries draped the walls, looped back here and there to expose some richly mounted painting or Oriental vase. The carpet was of amber and black, so soft and so thick that the foot sank pleasantly into it, as into a bed of moss. Two great tiger-skins thrown athwart it increased the suggestion of Eastern luxury, as did a huge hookah which stood upon a mat in the corner. A lamp in the fashion of a silver dove was hung from an almost invisible golden wire in the centre of the room. As it burned it filled the air with a subtle and aromatic odour.

'Mr Thaddeus Sholto,' said the little man, still jerking and smiling. 'That is my name. You are Miss Morstan, of course. And these gentlemen – '

'This is Mr Sherlock Holmes, and this Dr Watson.'

'A doctor, eh?' cried he, much excited. 'Have you your stethoscope? Might I ask you – would you have the kindness? I have grave doubts as to my mitral valve, if you would be so very good. The aortic I may rely upon, but I should value your opinion upon the mitral.'

I listened to his heart, as requested, but was unable to find anything amiss, save, indeed, that he was in an ecstasy of fear, for he shivered from head to foot.

'It appears to be normal,' I said. 'You have no cause for uneasiness.'

'You will excuse my anxiety, Miss Morstan,' he remarked, airily. 'I am a great sufferer, and I have long had suspicions as to that valve. I am delighted to hear that they are unwarranted. Had your father, Miss Morstan, refrained from throwing a strain upon his heart, he might have been alive now.'

I could have struck the man across the face, so hot was I at this callous and offhand reference to so delicate a matter. Miss Morstan sat down, and her face grew white to the lips.

'I knew in my heart that he was dead,' said she.

'I can give you every information,' said he; 'and what is more, I can do you justice; and I will, too, whatever Brother Bartholomew may say. I am so glad to have your friends here, not only as an escort to you, but also as witnesses to what I am about to do and say. The three of us can show a bold front to Brother Bartholomew. But let us have no outsiders – no police or officials. We can settle everything satisfactorily among ourselves, without any interference. Nothing would annoy Brother Bartholomew more than any publicity.'

He sat down upon a low settee, and blinked at us enquiringly with his weak, watery blue eyes.

'For my part,' said Holmes, 'whatever you may choose to say will go no farther.'

I nodded to show my agreement.

'That is well! That is well!' said he. 'May I offer you a glass of Chianti, Miss Morstan? Or of Tokay? I keep no other wines. Shall I open a flask? No? Well, then, I trust that you have no objection to tobacco smoke, to the balsamic odour of the Eastern tobacco. I am a little nervous, and I find my hookah an invaluable sedative.'

He applied a taper to the great bowl, and the smoke bubbled merrily through the rosewater. We sat all three in a semi-circle, with our heads advanced and our chins upon our hands, while the strange, jerky little fellow, with his high, shining head, puffed uneasily in the centre.

'When I first determined to make this communication to you,' said he, 'I might have given you my address; but I feared that you might disregard my request and bring unpleasant people with you. I took the liberty, therefore, of making an appointment in such a way that my man Williams might be able to see you first. I have complete confidence in his discretion, and he had orders, if he were dissatisfied, to proceed no further in the matter. You will excuse these precautions, but I am a man of somewhat retiring, and I might even say refined, tastes, and there is nothing more unaesthetic than a policeman. I have a natural shrinking from all forms of rough materialism. I seldom come in contact with the rough crowd. I live, as you see, with some little atmosphere of elegance around me. I may call myself a patron of the arts. It is my weakness. The landscape is a genuine Corot, and, though a connoisseur might perhaps throw a doubt upon that Salvator Rosa, there cannot be the least question about the Bouguereau. I am partial to the modern French school.'

'You will excuse me, Mr Sholto,' said Miss Morstan, 'but I am here at your request to learn something which you desire to tell me. It is very late, and I should desire the interview to be as short as possible.'

'At the best, it must take some time,' he answered; 'for we shall certainly have to go to Norwood and see Brother Bartholomew. We shall all go and try if we can get the better of Brother Bartholomew. He is very angry with me for taking the course which has seemed right to me. I had quite high words with him last night. You cannot imagine what a terrible fellow he is when he is angry.'

'If we are to go to Norwood, it would perhaps be as well to start at once,' I ventured to remark.

He laughed until his ears were quite red.

'That would hardly do,' he cried. 'I don't know what he would say if I brought you in that sudden way. No, I must prepare you by showing you how we all stand to each other. In the first place, I must tell you that there are several points in the story of which I am myself ignorant. I can only lay the facts before you as far as I know them myself.

'My father was, as you may have guessed, Major John Sholto, once of the Indian Army. He retired some eleven years ago, and came to live at Pondicherry Lodge, in Upper Norwood. He had prospered in India, and brought back with him a considerable sum of money, a large collection of valuable curiosities and a staff of native servants. With these advantages he bought himself a house and lived in great luxury. My twin brother Bartholomew and I were the only children.

'I very well remember the sensation which was caused by the disappearance of Captain Morstan. We read the details in the papers, and knowing that he had been a friend of our father's, we discussed the case freely in his presence. He used to join in our speculations as to what could have happened. Never for an instant did we suspect that he had the whole secret hidden in his own breast, that of all men he alone knew the fate of Arthur Morstan.

'We did know, however, that some mystery, some positive danger, overhung our father. He was very fearful of going out alone, and he always employed two prizefighters to act as porters at Pondicherry Lodge. Williams, who drove you tonight, was one of them. He was once light-weight champion of England. Our father would never tell us what it was he feared, but he had a most marked aversion to men with wooden legs. On one occasion he actually fired his revolver at a wooden-legged man, who proved to be a harmless tradesman canvassing for orders. We had to pay a large sum to hush the matter up. My brother and I used to think this a mere whim of my father's; but events have since led us to change our opinion.

'Early in 1882 my father received a letter from India which was a great shock to him. He nearly fainted at the breakfast-table when he opened it, and from that day he sickened to his death. What was in the letter we could never discover, but I could see as he held it that it was short and written in a scrawling hand. He had suffered for years from an enlarged spleen, but he now became rapidly worse, and towards the end of April we were informed that he was beyond all hope, and that he wished to make a last communication to us.

'When we entered his room he was propped up with pillows and breathing heavily. He besought us to lock the door and to come upon either side of the bed. Then, grasping our hands, he made a remarkable statement to us, in a voice which was broken as much by emotion as by pain. I shall try and give it to you in his own very words.

' "I have only one thing," he said, "which weighs upon my mind at this supreme moment. It is my treatment of poor Morstan's orphan. The cursed greed which has been my besetting sin through life has withheld from her the treasure, half at least of which should have been hers. And yet I have made no use of it myself, so blind and foolish a thing is avarice. The mere feeling of possession has been so dear to me that I could not bear to share it with another. See that chaplet tipped with pearls beside the quinine-bottle? Even that I could not bear to part with, although I had got it out with the design of sending it to her. You, my sons, will give her a fair share of the Agra treasure. But send her nothing – not even the chaplet – until I am gone. After all, men have been as bad as this and have recovered.

' "I will tell you how Morstan died," he continued. "He had suffered for years from a weak heart, but he concealed it from everyone. I alone knew it. When in India, he and I, through a remarkable chain of circumstances, came into possession of a considerable treasure. I brought it over to England, and on the night of Morstan's arrival he came straight over here to claim his share. He walked over from the station, and was admitted by my faithful old Lal Chowdar, who is now dead. Morstan and I had a difference of opinion as to the division of the treasure, and we came to heated words. Morstan had sprung out of his chair in a paroxysm of anger, when he suddenly pressed his hand to his side, his face turned a dusky hue and he fell backwards, cutting his head against the corner of the treasure-chest. When I stooped over him I found, to my horror, that he was dead.

' "For a long time I sat half distracted, wondering what I should do. My first impulse was, of course, to call for assistance; but I could not but recognise that there was every chance that I would be accused of his murder. His death at the moment of a quarrel, and the gash in his head, would be black against me. Again, an official enquiry could not be made without bringing out some facts about the treasure, which I was particularly anxious to keep secret. He had told me that no soul upon earth knew where he had gone. There seemed to be no necessity why any soul ever should know.

' "I was still pondering over the matter, when, looking up, I saw my servant, Lal Chowdar, in the doorway. He stole in and bolted the door behind him. 'Do not fear, sahib,' he said; 'no one need know that you have killed him. Let us hide him away, and who is the wiser?' 'I did not kill him,' said I. Lal Chowdar shook his head and smiled. 'I heard it all, sahib,' said he; 'I heard you quarrel, and I heard the blow. But my lips are sealed. All are asleep in the house. Let us put him away together.' That was enough to decide me. If my own servant could not believe my innocence, how could I hope to make it good before twelve foolish tradesmen in a jury-box? Lal Chowdar and I disposed of the body that night and within a few days the London papers were full of the mysterious disappearance of Captain Morstan. You will see from what I say that I can hardly be blamed in the matter. My fault lies in the fact that we concealed not only the body but also the treasure, and that I have clung to Morstan's share as well as to my own. I wish you, therefore, to make restitution. Put your ears down to my mouth. The treasure is hidden in— "

'At this instant a horrible change came over his expression; his eyes stared wildly, his jaw dropped, and he yelled, in a voice which I can never forget, "Keep him out! For Christ's sake, keep him out!" We both stared round at the window behind us upon which his gaze was fixed. A face was looking in at us out of the darkness. We could see the whitening of the nose where it was pressed against the glass. It was a bearded, hairy face, with wild, cruel eyes and an expression of concentrated malevolence. My brother and I rushed towards the window, but the man was gone. When we returned to my father, his head had dropped and his pulse had ceased to beat.

'We searched the garden that night, but found no sign of the intruder, save that just under the window a single footmark was visible in the flower-bed. But for that one trace, we might have thought that our imaginations had conjured up that wild, fierce face. We soon, however, had another and a more striking proof that there were secret agencies at work all round us. The window of my father's room was found open in the morning, his cupboards and boxes had been rifled, and upon his chest was fixed a torn piece of paper, with the words "The sign of the four" scrawled across it. What the phrase meant, or who our secret visitor may have been, we never knew. As far as we can judge, none of my father's property had been actually stolen, though everything had been turned out. My brother and I naturally associated this peculiar incident with the fear which haunted my father during his life; but it is still a complete mystery to us.'

The little man stopped to relight his hookah, and puffed thoughtfully for a few moments. We had all sat absorbed, listening to his extraordinary narrative. At the short account of her father's death Miss Morstan had turned deadly white, and for a moment I feared that she was about to faint. She rallied, however, on drinking a glass of water which I quietly poured out for her from a Venetian carafe upon the side-table. Sherlock Holmes leaned back in his chair with an abstracted expression and the lids drawn low over his glittering eyes. As I glanced at him I could not but think how, on that very day, he had complained bitterly of the commonplaceness of life. Here at least was a problem which would tax his sagacity to the utmost. Mr Thaddeus Sholto looked from one to the other of us with an obvious pride at the effect which his story had produced, and then continued, between the puffs of his overgrown pipe.

'My brother and I,' said he, 'were, as you may imagine, much excited as to the treasure which my father had spoken of. For weeks and for months we dug and delved in every part of the garden without discovering its whereabouts. It was maddening to think that the hiding-place was on his very lips at the moment that he died. We could judge the splendour of the missing riches by the chaplet which he had taken out. Over this chaplet Brother Bartholomew and I had some little discussion. The pearls were evidently of great value, and he was averse to parting with them, for, between friends, my brother was himself a little inclined to my father's fault. He thought, too, that if we parted with the chaplet it might give rise to gossip, and finally bring us into trouble. It was all that I could do to persuade him to let me find out Miss Morstan's address and send her a detached pearl at fixed intervals, so that at least she might never feel destitute.'

'It was a kindly thought,' said our companion, earnestly; 'it was extremely good of you.'

The little man waved his hand deprecatingly.

'We were your trustees,' he said; 'that was the view which I took of it, though Brother Bartholomew could not altogether see it in that light. We had plenty of money ourselves. I desired no more. Besides, it would have been such bad taste to have treated a young lady in so scurvy a fashion. *Le mauvais goût mène au crime.* The French have a very neat way of putting these things. Our difference of opinion on this subject went so far that I thought it best to set up rooms for myself; so I left Pondicherry Lodge, taking the old khitmutgar and Williams with me. Yesterday, however, I learned that an event of extreme importance has occurred. The treasure has been discovered. I instantly communicated with Miss Morstan, and it only remains for us to drive out to Norwood and demand our share. I explained my views last night to Brother Bartholomew, so we shall be expected, if not welcome, vistors.'

Mr Thaddeus Sholto ceased, and sat twitching on his luxurious settee. We all remained silent, with our thoughts upon the new development which the mysterious business had taken. Holmes was the first to spring to his feet.

'You have done well, sir, from first to last,' said he. 'It is possible that we may be able to make you some small return by throwing some light upon that which is still dark to you. But, as Miss Morstan remarked just now, it is late, and we had best put the matter through without delay.'

Our new acquaintance very deliberately coiled up the tube of his hookah and produced from behind a curtain a very long, befrogged top-coat with astrakhan collar and cuffs. This he buttoned tightly up, in spite of the extreme closeness of the night, and finished his attire by putting on a rabbit-skin cap with hanging lappets which covered the ears, so that no part of him was visible save his mobile and peaky face.

'My health is somewhat fragile,' he remarked, as he led the way down the passage. 'I am compelled to be a valetudinarian.'

Our cab was awaiting us outside, and our programme was evidently prearranged, for the driver started off at once at a rapid pace. Thaddeus Sholto talked incessantly, in a voice which rose high above the rattle of the wheels.

'Bartholomew is a clever fellow,' said he. 'How do you think he found out where the treasure was? He had come to the conclusion that it was somewhere indoors: so he worked out all the cubic space of the house, and made measurements everywhere, so that not one inch should be unaccounted for. Among other things, he found that the height of the building was seventy-four feet, but on adding together the heights of all the separate rooms, and making every allowance for the space between, which he ascertained by borings, he could not bring the total to more than seventy feet. There were four feet unaccounted for. These could only be at the top of the building. He knocked a hole, therefore, in the lath and plaster ceiling of the highest room, and there, sure enough, he came upon another little garret above it, which had been sealed up and was known to no one. In the centre stood the treasure-chest, resting upon two rafters. He lowered it through the hole, and there it lies. He computes the value of the jewels at not less than half a million sterling.'

At the mention of this gigantic sum we all stared at one another open-eyed. Miss Morstan, could we secure her rights, would change from a needy governess to the richest heiress in England. Surely it was the place of a loyal friend to rejoice at such news; yet I am ashamed to say that selfishness took me by the soul, and that my heart turned as heavy as lead within me. I stammered out some few halting words of congratulation, and then sat downcast, with my head drooped, deaf to the babble of our new acquaintance. He was clearly a confirmed hypochondriac, and I was dreamily conscious that he was pouring forth interminable trains of symptoms, and imploring information as to the composition and action of innumerable quack nostrums, some of which he bore about in a leather case in his pocket. I trust that he may not remember any of the answers which I gave him that night. Holmes declares that he overheard me caution him against the great danger of taking more than two drops of castor-oil, while I recommended strychnine in large doses as a sedative. However that may be, I was certainly relieved when our cab pulled up with a jerk and the coachman sprang down to open the door.

'This, Miss Morstan, is Pondicherry Lodge,' said Mr Thaddeus Sholto, as he handed her out.

5

The Tragedy of Pondicherry Lodge

It was nearly eleven o'clock when we reached this final stage of our night's adventures. We had left the damp fog of the great city behind us, and the night was fairly fine. A warm wind blew from the westward, and heavy clouds moved slowly across the sky, with half a moon peeping occasionally through the rifts. It was clear enough to see for some distance, but Thaddeus Sholto took down one of the side-lamps from the carriage to give us a better light upon our way.

Pondicherry Lodge stood in its own grounds, and was girt round with a very high stone wall topped with broken glass. A single narrow iron-clamped door formed the only means of entrance. On this our guide knocked with a peculiar postman-like rat-tat.

'Who is there?' cried a gruff voice from within.

'It is I, McMurdo. You surely know my knock by this time.'

There was a grumbling sound and a clanking and jarring of keys. The door swung heavily back, and a short, deep-chested man stood in the opening, with the yellow light of the lantern shining upon his protruded face and twinkling, distrustful eyes.

'That you, Mr Thaddeus? But who are the others? I had no orders about them from the master.'

'No, McMurdo? You surprise me! I told my brother last night that I should bring some friends.'

'He hain't been out o' his room today, Mr Thaddeus, and I have no orders. You know very well that I must stick to regulations. I can let you in, but your friends they must just stop where they are.'

This was an unexpected obstacle. Thaddeus Sholto looked about him in a perplexed and helpless manner.

'This is too bad of you, McMurdo!' he said. 'If I guarantee them, that is enough for you. There is the young lady, too. She cannot wait on the public road at this hour.'

'Very sorry, Mr Thaddeus,' said the porter, inexorably. 'Folk may be friends o' yours, and yet no friends o' the master's. He pays me well to do my duty, and my duty I'll do. I don't know none o' your friends.'

'Oh, yes, you do, McMurdo,' cried Sherlock Holmes, genially. 'I don't think you can have forgotten me. Don't you remember the amateur who fought three rounds with you at Alison's rooms on the night of your benefit four years back?'

'Not Mr Sherlock Holmes!' roared the prizefighter. 'God's truth! how could I have mistook you? If instead o' standin' there so quiet you had just stepped up and given me that cross-hit of yours under the jaw, I'd ha' known you without a question. Ah, you're one that has wasted your gifts, you have! You might have aimed high, if you had joined the fancy.'

'You see, Watson, if all else fails me, I have still one of the scientific professions open to me,' said Holmes, laughing. 'Our friend won't keep us out in the cold now, I am sure.'

'In you come, sir, in you come – you and your friends,' he answered. 'Very sorry, Mr Thaddeus, but orders are very strict. Had to be certain of your friends before I let them in.'

Inside, a gravel path wound through desolate grounds to a huge clump of a house, square and prosaic, all plunged in shadow save where a moonbeam struck one corner and glimmered in a garret window. The vast size of the building, with its gloom and its deathly silence, struck a chill to the heart. Even Thaddeus Sholto seemed ill at ease, and the lantern quivered and rattled in his hand.

'I cannot understand it,' he said. 'There must be some mistake. I distinctly told Bartholomew that we should be here, and yet there is no light in his window. I do not know what to make of it.'

'Does he always guard the premises in this way?' asked Holmes.

'Yes, he has followed my father's custom. He was the favourite son, you know, and I sometimes think that my father may have told him more than he ever told me. That is Bartholomew's window up there where the moonshine strikes. It is quite bright, but there is no light from within, I think.'

'None,' said Holmes. 'But I see the glint of a light in that little window beside the door.'

'Ah, that is the housekeeper's room. That is where old Mrs Bernstone sits. She can tell us all about it. But perhaps you would not mind waiting here for a minute or two, for if we all go in together, and she has had no word of our coming, she may be alarmed. But, hush! what is that?'

He held up the lantern, and his hand shook until the circles of light flickered and wavered all round us. Miss Morstan seized my wrist, and we all stood, with thumping hearts, straining our ears. From the great black house there sounded through the silent night the saddest and most pitiful of sounds the shrill, broken whimpering of a frightened woman.

'It is Mrs Bernstone,' said Sholto. 'She is the only woman in the house. Wait here. I shall be back in a moment.'

He hurried for the door, and knocked in his peculiar way. We could see a tall old woman admit him, and sway with pleasure at the very sight of him.

'Oh, Mr Thaddeus, sir, I am so glad you have come! I am so glad you have come, Mr Thaddeus, sir!'

We heard her reiterated rejoicings until the door was closed and her voice died away into a muffled monotone.

Our guide had left us the lantern. Holmes swung it slowly round, and peered keenly at the house, and at the great rubbish-heaps which cumbered the grounds. Miss Morstan and I stood together, and her hand was in mine. A wondrous subtle thing is love, for here were we two, who had never seen each other before that day, between whom no word or even look of affection had ever passed, and yet now in an hour of trouble our hands instinctively sought for each other. I have marvelled at it since, but at the time it seemed the most natural thing that I should go out to her so, and, as she has often told me, there was in her also the instinct to turn to me for comfort and protection. So we stood hand in hand, like two children, and there was peace in our hearts for all the dark things that surrounded us.

'What a strange place!' she said, looking round.

'It looks as though all the moles in England had been let loose in it. I have seen something of the sort on the side of a hill near Ballarat, where the prospectors had been at work.'

'And from the same cause,' said Holmes. 'These are the traces of the treasure-seekers. You must remember that they were six years looking for it. No wonder that the grounds look like a gravel-pit.'

At that moment the door of the house burst open, and Thaddeus Sholto came running out, with his hands thrown forward and terror in his eyes.

'There is something amiss with Bartholomew!' he cried. 'I am frightened! My nerves cannot stand it.'

He was, indeed, half blubbering with fear, and his twitching, feeble face peeping out from the great astrakhan collar had the helpless, appealing expression of a terrified child.

'Come into the house,' said Holmes, in his crisp, firm way.

'Yes, do!' pleaded Thaddeus Sholto. 'I really do not feel equal to giving directions.'

We all followed him into the housekeeper's room, which stood upon the left-hand side of the passage. The old woman was pacing up and down with a scared look and restless, picking fingers, but the sight of Miss Morstan appeared to have a soothing effect upon her.

'God bless your sweet, calm face!' she cried, with a hysterical sob. 'It does me good to see you. Oh, but I have been sorely tried this day!'

Our companion patted her thin, work-worn hand, and murmured some few words of kindly, womanly comfort, which brought the colour back into the other's bloodless cheeks.

'Master has locked himself in, and will not answer me,' she explained. 'All day I have waited to hear from him, for he often likes to be alone; but an hour ago I feared that something was amiss, so I went up and peeped through the keyhole. You must go up, Mr Thaddeus – you must go up and look for yourself. I have seen Mr Bartholomew Sholto in joy and in sorrow for ten long years, but I never saw him with such a face on him as that.'

Sherlock Holmes took the lamp and led the way, for Thaddeus Sholto's teeth were chattering in his head. So shaken was he that I had to pass my hand under his arm as we went up the stairs, for his knees were trembling under him. Twice as we ascended Holmes whipped his lens out of his pocket and carefully examined marks which appeared to me to be mere shapeless smudges of dust upon the coconut-matting which served as a stair-carpet. He walked slowly from step to step, holding the lamp low, and shooting keen glances to right and left. Miss Morstan had remained behind with the frightened housekeeper.

The third flight of stairs ended in a straight passage of some length, with a great picture in Indian tapestry upon the right of it and three doors upon the left. Holmes advanced along it in the same slow and methodical way, while we kept close at his heels, with our long, black shadows streaming backwards down the corridor. The third door was that which we were seeking. Holmes knocked without receiving any answer, and then tried to turn the handle and force it open. It was locked on the inside, however, and by a broad and powerful bolt, as we could see when we set our lamp up against it. The key being turned, however, the hole was not entirely closed. Sherlock Holmes bent down to it, and instantly rose again with a sharp intaking of the breath.

'There is something devilish in this, Watson,' said he, more moved than I had ever before seen him. 'What do you make of it?'

I stooped to the hole, and recoiled in horror. Moonlight was streaming into the room, and it was bright with a vague and shifty radiance. Looking straight at me, and suspended, as it were, in the air, for all beneath was in shadow, there hung a face – the very face of our companion Thaddeus.

There was the same high, shining head, the same circular bristle of red hair, the same bloodless countenance. The features were set, however, in a horrible smile, a fixed and unnatural grin, which in that still and moonlit room was more jarring to the nerves than any scowl or contortion. So like was the face to that of our little friend that I looked round at him to make sure that he was indeed with us. Then I recalled to mind that he had mentioned to us that his brother and he were twins.

'This is terrible!' I said to Holmes. 'What is to be done?'

'The door must come down,' he answered, and, springing against it, he put all his weight upon the lock.

It creaked and groaned, but did not yield. Together we flung ourselves upon it once more, and this time it gave way with a sudden snap, and we found ourselves within Bartholomew Sholto's chamber.

It appeared to have been fitted up as a chemical laboratory. A double line of glass-stoppered bottles was drawn up upon the wall opposite the door, and the table was littered over with Bunsen burners, test-tubes and retorts. In the corners stood carboys of acid in wicker baskets. One of these appeared to leak or to have been broken, for a stream of dark-coloured liquid had trickled out from it, and the air was heavy with a peculiarly pungent, tar-like odour. A set of steps stood at one side of the room, in the midst of a litter of lath and plaster, and above them there was an opening in the ceiling large enough for a man to pass through. At the foot of the steps a long coil of rope was thrown carelessly together.

By the table, in a wooden armchair, the master of the house was seated all in a heap, with his head sunk upon his left shoulder, and that ghastly, inscrutable smile upon his face. He was stiff and cold and had clearly been dead many hours. It seemed to me that not only his features, but all his limbs, were twisted and turned in the most fantastic fashion. By his hand upon the table there lay a peculiar instrument – a brown, close-grained stick, with a stone head like a hammer, rudely lashed on with coarse twine. Beside it was a torn sheet of notepaper with some words scrawled upon it. Holmes glanced at it, and then handed it to me.

'You see,' he said, with a significant raising of the eyebrows.

In the light of the lantern I read, with a thrill of horror, 'The sign of the four.'

'In God's name, what does it all mean?' I asked.

'It means murder,' said he, stooping over the dead man. 'Ah! I expected it. Look here!'

He pointed to what looked like a long, dark thorn stuck in the skin just above the ear.

'It looks like a thorn,' said I.

'It is a thorn. You may pick it out. But be careful, for it is poisoned.'

I took it up between my finger and thumb. It came away from the skin so readily that hardly any mark was left behind. One tiny speck of blood showed where the puncture had been.

'This is all an insoluble mystery to me,' said I. 'It grows darker instead of clearer.'

'On the contrary,' he answered, 'it clears every instant. I only require a few missing links to have an entirely connected case.'

We had almost forgotten our companion's presence since we entered the chamber. He was still standing in the doorway, the very picture of terror, wringing his hands and moaning to himself. Suddenly, however, he broke out into a sharp, querulous cry.

'The treasure is gone!' he said. 'They have robbed him of the treasure! There is the hole through which we lowered it. I helped him to do it! I was the last person who saw him! I left him here last night, and I heard him lock the door as I came downstairs.'

'What time was that?'

'It was ten o'clock. And now he is dead, and the police will be called in, and I shall be suspected of having had a hand in it. Oh, yes, I am sure I shall. But you don't think so, gentlemen? Surely, you don't think that it was I? Is it likely that I would have brought you here if it were I? Oh, dear! oh, dear! I know that I shall go mad!'

He jerked his arms and stamped his feet in a kind of convulsive frenzy.

'You have no reason for fear, Mr Sholto,' said Holmes kindly, putting his hand upon his shoulder; 'take my advice and drive down to the station to report the matter to the police. Offer to assist them in every way. We shall wait here until your return.'

The little man obeyed in a half-stupefied fashion, and we heard him stumbling down the stairs in the dark.

6
Sherlock Holmes Gives a Demonstration

'Now, Watson,' said Holmes, rubbing his hands, 'we have half an hour to ourselves. Let us make good use of it. My case is, as I have told you, almost complete; but we must not err on the side of over-confidence. Simple as the case seems now, there may be something deeper underlying it.'

'Simple!' I ejaculated.

'Surely,' said he, with something of the air of a clinical professor expounding to his class. 'Just sit in the corner there, that your footprints may not complicate matters. Now to work! In the first place, how did these folk come, and how did they go? The door has not been opened since last night. What of the window?' He carried the lamp across to it, muttering his objections aloud the while, but addressing them to himself rather than to me. 'Window is snibbed on the inner side. Framework is solid. No hinges at the side. Let us open it. No water-pipe near. Roof quite out of reach. Yet a man has mounted by the window. It rained a little last night. Here is the print of a foot in mould upon the sill. And here is a circular muddy mark, and here again upon the floor, and here again by the table. See here, Watson! This is really a very pretty demonstration.'

I looked at the round, well-defined muddy discs.

'That is not a footmark,' said I.

'It is something much more valuable to us. It is the impression of a wooden stump. You see here on the sill is the boot-mark, a heavy boot with a broad metal heel, and beside it is the mark of the timber toe.'

'It is the wooden-legged man.'

'Quite so. But there has been someone else – a very able and efficient ally. Could you scale that wall, doctor?'

I looked out of the open window. The moon still shone brightly on that angle of the house. We were a good sixty feet from the ground, and, look where I would, I could see no foothold, nor as much as a crevice in the brickwork.

'It is absolutely impossible,' I answered.

'Without aid it is so. But suppose you had a friend up here who lowered you this good stout rope which I see in the corner, securing one end of it to this great hook in the wall. Then, I think, if you were an active man, you might swarm up, wooden leg and all. You would depart, of course, in the same fashion, and your ally would draw up the rope, untie it from the hook, shut the window, snib it on the inside, and get away in the way that he originally came. As a minor point, it may be noted,' he continued, fingering the rope, 'that our wooden-legged friend, though a fair climber, was not a professional sailor. His hands were far from horny. My lens discloses more than one blood-mark, especially towards the end of the rope, from which I gather that he slipped down with such velocity that he took the skin off his hand.'

'This is all very well,' said I; 'but the thing becomes more unintelligible than ever. How about this mysterious ally? How came he into the room?'

'Yes, the ally!' repeated Holmes, pensively. 'There are features of interest about this ally. He lifts the case from the regions of the commonplace. I fancy that this ally breaks fresh ground in the annals of crime in this country – though parallel cases suggest themselves from India, and, if my memory serves me, from Senegambia.'

'How came he, then?' I reiterated. 'The door is locked; the window is inaccessible. Was it through the chimney?'

'The grate is much too small,' he answered. 'I had already considered that possibility.'

'How, then?' I persisted.

'You will not apply my precept,' he said, shaking his head. 'How often have I said to you that when you have eliminated the impossible, whatever remains, *however improbable*, must be the truth? We know that he did not come through the door, the window, or the chimney. We also know that he could not have been concealed in the room, as there is no concealment possible. Whence, then, did he come?'

'He came through the hole in the roof!' I cried.

'Of course he did. He must have done so. If you will have the kindness to hold the lamp for me, we shall now extend our researches to the room above – the secret room in which the treasure was found.'

He mounted the steps, and, seizing a rafter with either hand, he swung himself up into the garret. Then, lying on his face, he reached down for the lamp, and held it while I followed him.

The chamber in which we found ourselves was about ten feet one way and six the other. The floor was formed by the rafters, with thin lath and plaster between, so that in walking one had to step from beam to beam. The roof ran up to an apex, and was evidently the inner shell of the true roof to the house. There was no furniture of any sort, and the accumulated dust of years lay thick upon the floor.

165

'Here you are, you see,' said Sherlock Holmes, putting his hand against the sloping wall. 'This is a trap-door which leads out on to the roof. I can press it back, and here is the roof itself, sloping at a gentle angle. This, then, is the way by which Number One entered. Let us see if we can find some other traces of his individuality.'

He held down the lamp to the floor, and as he did so I saw for the second time that night a startled, surprised look come over his face. For myself, as I followed his gaze, my skin was cold under my clothes. The floor was covered thickly with the prints of a naked foot – clear, well defined, perfectly formed, but scarce half the size of those of an ordinary man.

'Holmes,' I said, in a whisper, 'a child has done this horrid thing.'

He had recovered his self-possession in an instant.

'I was staggered for the moment,' he said, 'but the thing is quite natural. My memory failed me, or I should have been able to foretell it. There is nothing more to be learned here. Let us go down.'

'What is your theory, then, as to those footmarks?' I asked, eagerly, when we had regained the lower room once more.

'My dear Watson, try a little analysis yourself,' said he, with a touch of impatience. 'You know my methods. Apply them, and it will be instructive to compare results.'

'I cannot conceive anything which will cover the facts,' I answered.

'It will be clear enough to you soon,' he said, in an offhand way. 'I think that there is nothing else of importance here, but I will look.'

He whipped out his lens and a tape measure, and hurried about the room on his knees, measuring, comparing, examining, with his long, thin nose only a few inches from the planks, and his beady eyes gleaming and deep-set like those of a bird. So swift, silent and furtive were his movements, like those of a trained bloodhound picking out a scent, that I could not but think what a terrible criminal he would have made had he turned his energy and sagacity against the law instead of exerting them in its defence. As he hunted about he kept muttering to himself, and finally he broke out into a loud crow of delight.

'We are certainly in luck,' said he. 'We ought to have very little trouble now. Number One has had the misfortune to tread in the creosote. You can see the outline of the edge of his small foot here at the side of this evil-smelling mess. The carboy has been cracked, you see, and the stuff has leaked out.'

'What then?' I asked.

'Why, we have got him, that's all,' said he. 'I know a dog that would follow that scent to the world's end. If a pack can track a trailed herring across a shire, how far can a specially trained hound follow so pungent a smell as this? It sounds like a sum in the rule of three. The answer should give us the – But, halloa! here are the accredited representatives of the law.'

Heavy steps and the clamour of loud voices were audible from below, and the hall door shut with a loud crash.

'Before they come,' said Holmes, 'just put your hand here on this poor fellow's arm, and here on his leg. What do you feel?'

'The muscles are as hard as a board,' I answered.

'Quite so. They are in a state of extreme contraction, far exceeding the usual rigor mortis. Coupled with this distortion of the face, this Hippocratic smile, or *risus sardonicus*, as the old writers called it, what conclusion would it suggest to your mind?'

'Death from some powerful vegetable alkaloid,' I answered; 'some strychnine-like substance which would produce tetanus.'

'That was the idea which occurred to me the instant I saw the drawn muscles of the face. On getting into the room I at once looked for the means by which the poison had entered the system. As you saw, I discovered a thorn which had been driven or shot with no great force into the scalp. You observe that the part struck was that which would be turned towards the hole in the ceiling if the man were erect in his chair. Now examine this thorn.'

I took it up gingerly and held it in the light of the lantern. It was long, sharp and black, with a glazed look near the point as though some gummy substance had dried upon it. The blunt end had been trimmed and rounded off with a knife.

'Is that an English thorn?' he asked.

'No, it certainly is not.'

'With all these data you should be able to draw some just inference. But here are the regulars; so the auxiliary forces may beat a retreat.'

As he spoke, the steps which had been coming nearer sounded loudly in the passage, and a very stout, portly man in a grey suit strode heavily into the room. He was red-faced, burly and plethoric, with a pair of very small, twinkling eyes, which looked keenly out from between swollen and puffy pouches. He was closely followed by an inspector in uniform, and by the still palpitating Thaddeus Sholto.

'Here's a business!' he cried, in a muffled, husky voice. 'Here's a pretty business! But who are all these? Why, the house seems to be as full as a rabbit-warren!'

'I think you must recollect me, Mr Athelney Jones,' said Holmes, quietly.

'Why, of course I do!' he wheezed. 'It's Mr Sherlock Holmes, the theorist. Remember you! I'll never forget how you lectured us all on causes and inferences and effects in the Bishopgate jewel case. It's true you set us on the right track; but you'll own now that it was more by good luck than good guidance.'

'It was a piece of very simple reasoning.'

'Oh, come, now, come! Never be ashamed to own up. But what is all this? Bad business! Bad business! Stern facts here – no room for theories. How lucky that I happened to be out at Norwood over another case! I was at the station when the message arrived. What d'you think the man died of?'

'Oh, this is hardly a case for me to theorise over,' said Holmes, drily.

'No, no. Still, we can't deny that you hit the nail on the head sometimes. Dear me! Door locked, I understand. Jewels worth half a million missing. How was the window?'

'Fastened; but there are steps on the sill.'

'Well, well, if it was fastened the steps could have nothing to do with the matter. That's common sense. Man might have died in a fit; but then the jewels are missing. Ha! I have a theory. These flashes come upon me at times. Just step outside, sergeant, and you, Mr Sholto. Your friend can remain. What do you think of this, Holmes? Sholto was, on his own confession, with his brother last night. The brother died in a fit, on which Sholto walked off with the treasure! How's that?'

'On which the dead man very considerately got up and locked the door on the inside.'

'Hum! There's a flaw there. Let us apply common sense to the matter. This Thaddeus Sholto was with his brother; there *was* a quarrel: so much we know. The brother is dead and the jewels are gone. So much also we know. No one saw the brother from the time Thaddeus left him. His bed had not been slept in. Thaddeus is evidently in a most disturbed state of mind. His appearance is – well, not attractive. You see that I am weaving my web round Thaddeus. The net begins to close upon him.'

'You are not quite in possession of the facts yet,' said Holmes. 'This splinter of wood, which I have every reason to believe to be poisoned, was in the man's scalp where you still see the mark; this card, inscribed as you see it, was on the table, and beside it lay this rather curious stone-headed instrument. How does all that fit into your theory?'

'Confirms it in every respect,' said the fat detective, pompously. 'House is full of Indian curiosities. Thaddeus brought this up, and if this splinter be poisonous, Thaddeus may as well have made murderous use of it as any other man. The card is some hocus-pocus – a blind, as like as not. The only question is, how did he depart. Ah, of course, here is a hole in the roof.'

With great activity, considering his bulk, he sprang up the steps and squeezed through into the garret, and immediately afterwards we heard his exulting voice proclaiming that he had found the trap-door.

'He can find something,' remarked Holmes, shrugging his shoulders; 'he has occasional glimmerings of reason. *Il n'y a pas des sots si incommodes que ceux qui ont de l'esprit!*'

'You see!' said Athelney Jones, reappearing down the steps again; 'facts are better than theories, after all. My view of the case is confirmed. There is a trap-door communicating with the roof, and it is partly open.'

'It was I who opened it.'

'Oh, indeed! You did notice it, then?' He seemed a little crestfallen at the discovery. 'Well, whoever noticed it, it shows how our gentleman got away. Inspector!'

'Yes, sir,' from the passage.

'Ask Mr Sholto to step this way – Mr Sholto, it is my duty to inform you that anything which you may say will be used against you. I arrest you in the Queen's name as being concerned in the death of your brother.'

'There, now! Didn't I tell you?' cried the poor little man, throwing out his hands, and looking from one to the other of us.

'Don't trouble yourself about it, Mr Sholto,' said Holmes; 'I think that I can engage to clear you of the charge.'

'Don't promise too much, Mr Theorist, don't promise too much!' snapped the detective. 'You may find it a harder matter than you think.'

'Not only will I clear him, Mr Jones, but I will make you a free present of the name and description of one of the two people who were in this room last night. His name, I have every reason to believe, is Jonathan Small. He is a poorly educated man, small, active, with his right leg off, and wearing a wooden stump which is worn away upon the inner side. His left boot has a coarse, square-toed sole, with an iron band round the heel. He is a middle-aged man, much sunburned, and has been a convict. These few indications may be of some assistance to you, coupled with the fact that there is a good deal of skin missing from the palm of his hand. The other man – '

'Ah! the other man?' asked Athelney Jones, in a sneering voice, but impressed none the less, as I could easily see, by the precision of the other's manner.

'Is a rather curious person,' said Sherlock Holmes, turning upon his heel. 'I hope before very long to be able to introduce you to the pair of them. A word with you, Watson.'

He led me out to the head of the stair.

'This unexpected occurrence,' he said, 'has caused us rather to lose sight of the original purpose of our journey.'

'I have just been thinking so,' I answered; 'it is not right that Miss Morstan should remain in this stricken house.'

'No. You must escort her home. She lives with Mrs Cecil Forrester, in Lower Camberwell, so it is not very far. I will wait for you here if you will drive out again. Or perhaps you are too tired?'

'By no means. I don't think I could rest until I know more of this fantastic business. I have seen something of the rough side of life, but I give you my word that this quick succession of strange surprises tonight has shaken my nerve completely. I should like, however, to see the matter through with you, now that I have got so far.'

'Your presence will be of great service to me,' he answered. 'We shall work the case out independently, and leave this fellow Jones to exult over any mare's-nest which he may choose to construct. When you have dropped Miss Morstan, I wish you to go to No. 3, Pinchin Lane, down near the water's edge at Lambeth. The third house on the right-hand side is a bird-stuffer's; Sherman is the name. You will see a weasel holding a young rabbit in the window. Knock old Sherman up, and tell him, with my compliments, that I want Toby at once. You will bring Toby back in the cab with you.'

'A dog, I suppose?'

'Yes, a queer mongrel, with a most amazing power of scent. I would rather have Toby's help than that of the whole detective force of London.'

'I shall bring him then,' said I. 'It is one now. I ought to be back before three, if I can get a fresh horse.'

'And I,' said Holmes, 'shall see what I can learn from Mrs Bernstone, and from the Indian servant, who, Mr Thaddeus tells me, sleeps in the next garret. Then I shall study the great Jones's methods and listen to his not-too-delicate sarcasms. "*Wir sind gewohnt dass die Menschen verhöhnen was sie nicht verstehen.*" Goethe is always pithy.'

7

The Episode of the Barrel

The police had brought a cab with them, and in this I escorted Miss Morstan back to her home. After the angelic fashion of women, she had borne trouble with a calm face as long as there was someone weaker than herself to support, and I had found her bright and placid by the side of the frightened housekeeper. In the cab, however, she first turned faint, and then burst into a passion of weeping – so sorely had she been tried by the adventures of the night. She has told me since that she thought me cold and distant upon that journey. She little guessed the struggle within my breast, or the effort of self-restraint which held me back. My sympathies and my love went out to her, even as my hand had in the garden. I felt that years of the conventionalities of life could not teach me to know her sweet, brave nature as had this one day of strange experiences. Yet there were two thoughts which sealed the words of affection upon my lips. She was weak and helpless, shaken in mind and nerve. It was to take her at a disadvantage to obtrude love upon her at such a time. Worse still, she was rich. If Holmes's researches were successful, she would be an heiress. Was it fair, was it honourable, that a half-pay surgeon should take such advantage of an intimacy which chance had brought about? Might she not look upon me as a mere vulgar fortune-seeker? I could not bear to risk that such a thought should cross her mind. This Agra treasure intervened like an impassable barrier between us.

It was nearly two o'clock when we reached Mrs Cecil Forrester's. The servants had retired hours ago, but Mrs Forrester had been so interested by the strange message which Miss Morstan had received that she had sat up in the hope of her return. She opened the door herself, a middle-aged, graceful woman, and it gave me joy to see how tenderly her arm stole round the other's waist, and how motherly was the voice in which she greeted her. She was clearly no mere paid dependant but an honoured friend. I was introduced, and Mrs Forrester earnestly begged me to step in and to tell her our adventures. I explained, however, the importance of my errand, and pro7ised faithfully to call and report any progress which we might make with the case. As we drove away I stole a glance back, and I still seem to see that little group on the step – the two graceful, clinging figures, the half-opened door, the hall light shining through stained glass, the barometer and the bright stair-rods. It was soothing to catch even that passing glimpse of a tranquil English home in the midst of the wild, dark business which had absorbed us.

And the more I thought of what had happened, the wilder and darker it grew. I reviewed the whole extraordinary sequence of events as I rattled on through the silent, gas-lit streets. There was the original problem: that, at least, was pretty clear now. The death of Captain Morstan, the sending of the pearls, the advertisement, the letter – we had had light upon all those events. They had only led us, however, to a deeper and far more tragic mystery. The Indian treasure, the curious plan found among Morstan's baggage, the strange scene at Major Sholto's death, the rediscovery of the treasure immediately followed by the murder of the discoverer, the very singular accompaniments to the crime, the footsteps, the remarkable weapons, the words upon the card, corresponding with those upon Captain Morstan's chart – here was, indeed, a labyrinth in which a man less singularly endowed than my fellow-lodger might well despair of ever finding the clue.

Pinchin Lane was a row of shabby, two-storeyed brick houses in the lower quarter of Lambeth. I had to knock for some time at No. 3 before I could make any impression. At last, however, there was the glint of a candle behind the blind, and a face looked out at the upper window.

'Go on, you drunken vagabond,' said the face. 'If you kick up any more row, I'll open the kennels and let out forty-three dogs upon you.'

'If you'll let one out, it's just what I have come for,' said I.

'Go on!' yelled the voice. 'So help me gracious, I have a wiper in this bag, an' I'll drop it on your 'ead if you don't hook it!'

'But I want a dog,' I cried.

'I won't be argued with!' shouted Mr Sherman. 'Now, stand clear; for when I say "Three", down goes the wiper.'

'Mr Sherlock Holmes – ' I began; but the words had a most magical effect, for the window instantly slammed down, and within a minute the door was unbarred and open. Mr Sherman was a lanky, lean old man, with stooping shoulders, a stringy neck and blue-tinted glasses.

'A friend of Mr Sherlock is always welcome,' said he. 'Step in, sir. Keep clear of the badger, for he bites. Ah, naughty, naughty! would you take a nip at the gentleman?' This to a stoat, which thrust its wicked head and red eyes between the bars of its cage. 'Don't mind that, sir; it's only a slow-worm. It hain't got no fangs, so I gives it the run o' the room, for it keeps the beetles down. You must not mind my bein' just a little short wi' you at first, for I'm guyed at by the children, and there's many a one just comes down this lane to knock me up. What was it that Mr Sherlock Holmes wanted, sir?'

'He wanted a dog of yours.'

'Ah! that would be Toby.'

'Yes, "Toby" was the name.'

'Toby lives at No. 7 on the left here.'

He moved slowly forward with his candle among the queer animal family which he had gathered round him. In the uncertain, shadowy light I could see dimly that there were glancing, glimmering eyes peeping down at us from every cranny and corner. Even the rafters above our heads were lined by solemn fowls, who lazily shifted their weight from one leg to the other as our voices disturbed their slumbers.

Toby proved to be an ugly, long-haired, lop-eared creature, half spaniel and half lurcher, brown and white in colour, with a very clumsy, waddling gait. It accepted, after some hesitation, a lump of sugar which the old naturalist handed to me, and, having thus sealed an alliance, it followed me to the cab, and made no difficulties about accompanying me. It had just struck three on the Palace clock when I found myself back once more at Pondicherry Lodge. The ex-prizefighter McMurdo had, I found, been arrested as an accessory, and both he and Mr Sholto had been marched off to the station. Two constables guarded the narrow gate, but they allowed me to pass with the dog on my mentioning the detective's name.

Holmes was standing on the doorstep, with his hands in his pockets, smoking his pipe.

'Ah, you have him there!' said he. 'Good dog, then! Athelney Jones has gone. We have had an immense display of energy since you left. He has arrested not only friend Thaddeus, but the gatekeeper, the housekeeper and the Indian servant. We have the place to ourselves, but for a sergeant upstairs. Leave the dog here and come up.'

We tied Toby to the hall table, and re-ascended the stairs. The room was as we had left it, save that a sheet had been draped over the central figure. A weary-looking police sergeant reclined in the corner.

'Lend me your bull's-eye, sergeant,' said my companion. 'Now tie this bit of cord round my neck, so as to hang it in front of me. Thank you. Now I must kick off my boots and stockings. Just you carry them down with you, Watson. I am going to do a little climbing. And dip my handkerchief into the creosote. That will do. Now come up into the garret with me for a moment.'

We clambered up through the hole. Holmes turned his light once more upon the footsteps in the dust.

'I wish you particularly to notice these footmarks,' he said. 'Do you observe anything noteworthy about them?'

'They belong,' I said, 'to a child or a small woman.'

'Apart from their size, though. Is there nothing else?'

'They appear to be much as other footmarks.'

'Not at all. Look here! This is the print of a right foot in the dust. Now I make one with my naked foot beside it. What is the chief difference?'

'Your toes are all cramped together. The other print has each toe distinctly divided.'

'Quite so. That is the point. Bear that in mind. Now, would you kindly step over to that flap-window and smell the edge of the woodwork? I shall stay over here, as I have this handkerchief in my hand.'

I did as he directed, and was instantly conscious of a strong tarry smell.

'That is where he put his foot in getting out. If you can trace him, I should think that Toby will have no difficulty. Now run downstairs, loose the dog, and look out for Blondin.'

By the time that I got out into the grounds Sherlock Holmes was on the roof, and I could see him like an enormous glow-worm crawling very slowly along the ridge. I lost sight of him behind a stack of chimneys, but he presently reappeared, and then vanished once more upon the opposite side. When I made my way round there I found him seated at one of the corner eaves.

'That you, Watson?' he cried.

'Yes.'

'This is the place. What is that black thing down there?'

'A water-barrel.'

'Top on it?'

'Yes.'

'No sign of a ladder?'

'No.'

'Confound the fellow! It's a most breakneck place. I ought to be able to come down where he could climb up. The water-pipe feels pretty firm. Here goes, anyhow.'

There was a scuffling of feet, and the lantern began to come steadily down the side of the wall. Then with a light spring he came on to the barrel, and from there to the earth.

'It was easy to follow him,' he said, drawing on his stockings and boots. 'Tiles were loosened the whole way along, and in his hurry he had dropped this. It confirms my diagnosis, as you doctors express it.'

The object which he held up to me was a small pocket or pouch woven out of coloured grasses, and with a few tawdry beads strung round it. In shape and size it was not unlike a cigarette-case. Inside were half a dozen spines of dark wood, sharp at one end and rounded at the other, like that which had struck Bartholomew Sholto.

'They are hellish things,' said he. 'Look out that you don't prick yourself. I'm delighted to have them, for the chances are that they are all he has. There is the less fear of you or me finding one in our skin before long. I would sooner face a Martini bullet myself. Are you game for a six-mile trudge, Watson?'

'Certainly,' I answered.

'Your leg will stand it?'

'Oh, yes.'

'Here you are, doggy! Good old Toby! Smell it, Toby, smell it!' He pushed the creosote handkerchief under the dog's nose, while the creature stood with its fluffy legs separated, and with a most comical cock to its head, like a connoisseur sniffing the *bouquet* of a famous vintage. Holmes then threw the handkerchief to a distance, fastened a stout cord to the mongrel's collar, and led him to the foot of the water-barrel. The creature instantly broke into a succession of high, tremulous yelps, and, with his nose on the ground and his tail in the air, pattered off upon the trail at a pace which strained his leash and kept us at the top of our speed.

The east had been gradually whitening, and we could now see some distance in the cold, grey light. The square, massive house, with its black, empty windows and high, bare walls, towered up, sad and forlorn, behind us. Our course led right across the grounds, in and out among the trenches and pits with which they were scarred and intersected. The whole place, with its scattered dirt-heaps and ill-grown shrubs, had a blighted, ill-omened look which harmonised with the black tragedy which hung over it.

On reaching the boundary wall Toby ran along, whining eagerly, underneath its shadow, and stopped finally in a corner screened by a young beech. Where the two walls joined, several bricks had been loosened, and the crevices left were worn down and rounded upon the lower side, as though they had frequently been used as a ladder. Holmes clambered up, and, taking the dog from me, he dropped it over upon the other side.

'There's the print of wooden-leg's hand,' he remarked, as I mounted up beside him. 'You see the slight smudge of blood upon the white plaster. What a lucky thing it is that we have had no very heavy rain since yesterday! The scent will lie upon the road in spite of their eight-and-twenty hours' start.'

I confess that I had my doubts myself when I reflected upon the great traffic which had passed along the London road in the interval. My fears were soon appeased, however. Toby never hesitated or swerved, but waddled on in his peculiar rolling fashion. Clearly, the pungent smell of the creosote rose high above all other contending scents.

'Do not imagine,' said Holmes, 'that I depend for my success in this case upon the mere chance of one of these fellows having put his foot in the chemical. I have knowledge now which would enable me to trace them in many different ways. This, however, is the readiest, and, since fortune has put it into our hands, I should be culpable if I neglected it. It has, however, prevented the case from becoming the pretty little intellectual problem which it at one time promised to be. There might have been some credit to be gained out of it, but for this too palpable clue.'

'There is credit, and to spare,' said I. 'I assure you, Holmes, that I marvel at the means by which you obtain your results in this case, even more than I did in the Jefferson Hope murder. The thing seems to me to be deeper and more inexplicable. How, for example, could you describe with such confidence the wooden-legged man?'

'Pshaw, my dear boy! it was simplicity itself. I don't wish to be theatrical. It is all patent and above-board. Two officers who are in command of a convict guard learn an important secret as to buried treasure. A map is drawn for them by an Englishman named Jonathan Small. You remember that we saw the name upon the chart in Captain Morstan's possession. He had signed it on behalf of himself and his associates – the sign of the four, as he somewhat dramatically called it. Aided by this chart, the officers – or one of them – gets the treasure and brings it to England, leaving, we will suppose, some condition under which he received it unfulfilled. Now, then, why did not Jonathan Small get the treasure himself? The answer is obvious. The chart is dated at a time when Morstan was brought into close association with convicts. Jonathan Small did not get the treasure because he and his associates were themselves convicts and could not get away.'

'But this is mere speculation,' said I.

'It is more than that. It is the only hypothesis which covers the facts. Let us see how it fits in with the sequel. Major Sholto remains at peace for some years, happy in the possession of his treasure. Then he receives a letter from India which gives him a great fright. What was that?'

'A letter to say that the men whom he had wronged had been set free.'

'Or had escaped. That is much more likely, for he would have known what their term of imprisonment was. It would not have been a surprise to him. What does he do then? He guards himself against a wooden-legged man – a white man, mark you, for he mistakes a white tradesman for him, and actually fires a pistol at him. Now, only one white man's name is on the chart. The others are Hindus or Mohammedans. There is no other white man. Therefore, we may say with confidence that the wooden-legged man is identical with Jonathan Small. Does the reasoning strike you as being faulty?'

'No: it is clear and concise.'

'Well, now, let us put ourselves in the place of Jonathan Small. Let us look at it from his point of view. He comes to England with the double idea of regaining what he would consider to be his rights, and of having his revenge upon the man who had wronged him. He found out where Sholto lived, and very possibly he established communications with someone inside the house. There is this butler, Lal Rao, whom we have not seen. Mrs Bernstone gives him a far from good character. Small could not find out, however, where the treasure was hid, for no one ever knew, save the major and one faithful servant who had died. Suddenly, Small learns that the major is on his deathbed. In a frenzy lest the secret of the treasure die with him, he runs the gauntlet of the guards, makes his way to the dying man's window, and is only deterred from entering by the presence of his two sons. Mad with hate, however, against the dead man, he enters the room that night, searches his private papers in the hope of discovering some memorandum relating to the treasure, and finally leaves a memento of his visit in the short inscription upon the card. He had doubtless planned beforehand that, should he slay the major, he would leave some such record upon the body as a sign that it was not a common murder, but, from the point of view of the four associates, something in the nature of an act of justice. Whimsical and bizarre conceits of this kind are common enough in the annals of crime, and usually afford valuable indications as to the criminal. Do you follow all this?'

'Very clearly.'

'Now, what could Jonathan Small do? He could only continue to keep a secret watch upon the efforts made to find the treasure. Possibly he leaves England and only comes back at intervals. Then comes the discovery of the garret, and he is instantly informed of it. We again trace the presence of some confederate in the household. Jonathan, with his wooden leg, is utterly unable to reach the lofty room of Bartholomew Sholto. He takes

177

with him, however, a rather curious associate, who gets over this difficulty, but dips his naked foot into creosote, whence come Toby, and a six-mile limp for a half-pay officer with a damaged *tendo Achillis*.'

'But it was the associate, and not Jonathan, who committed the crime.'

'Quite so. And rather to Jonathan's disgust, to judge by the way he stamped about when he got into the room. He bore no grudge against Bartholomew Sholto, and would have preferred if he could have been simply bound and gagged. He did not wish to put his head in a halter. There was no help for it, however: the savage instincts of his companion had broken out, and the poison had done its work: so Jonathan Small left his record, lowered the treasure-box to the ground, and followed it himself. That was the train of events as far as I can decipher them. Of course, as to his personal appearance he must be middle-aged, and must be sunburned after serving his time in such an oven as the Andamans. His height is readily calculated from the length of his stride, and we know that he was bearded. His hairiness was the one point which impressed itself upon Thaddeus Sholto when he saw him at the window. I don't know that there is anything else.'

'The associate?'

'Ah, well, there is no great mystery in that. But you will know all about it soon enough. How sweet the morning air is! See how that one little cloud floats like a pink feather from some gigantic flamingo. Now the red rim of the sun pushes itself over the London cloud-bank. It shines on a good many folk, but on none, I dare bet, who are on a stranger errand than you and I. How small we feel, with our petty ambitions and strivings, in the presence of the great elemental forces of nature! Are you well up in your Jean Paul?'

'Fairly so. I worked back to him through Carlyle.'

'That was like following the brook to the parent lake. He makes one curious but profound remark. It is that the chief proof of man's real greatness lies in his perception of his own smallness. It argues, you see, a power of comparison and of appreciation which is in itself a proof of nobility. There is much food for thought in Richter. You have not a pistol, have you?'

'I have my stick.'

'It is just possible that we may need something of the sort if we get to their lair. Jonathan I shall leave to you, but if the other turns nasty I shall shoot him dead.'

He took out his revolver as he spoke, and having loaded two of the chambers, he put it back into the right-hand pocket of his jacket.

We had during this time been following the guidance of Toby down the half-rural villa-lined roads which lead to the metropolis. Now, however, we were beginning to come among continuous streets, where labourers and dockmen were already astir, and slatternly women were taking down shutters and brushing doorsteps. At the square-topped corner public-houses business was just beginning, and rough-looking men were emerging, rubbing their sleeves across their beards after their morning wet. Strange dogs sauntered up and stared wonderingly at us as we passed, but our inimitable Toby looked neither to the right nor to the left, but trotted onwards with his nose to the ground and an occasional eager whine which spoke of a hot scent.

We had traversed Streatham, Brixton, Camberwell, and now found ourselves in Kennington Lane, having borne away through the side-streets to the east of the Oval. The men whom we pursued seemed to have taken a curiously zig-zag road, with the idea probably of escaping observation. They had never kept to the main road if a parallel side-street would serve their turn. At the foot of Kennington Lane they had edged away to the left through Bond Street and Miles Street. Where the latter street turns into Knight's Place, Toby ceased to advance, but began to run backwards and forwards with one ear cocked and the other drooping, the very picture of canine indecision. Then he waddled round in circles, looking up to us from time to time, as if to ask for sympathy in his embarrassment.

'What the deuce is the matter with the dog?' growled Holmes. 'They surely would not take a cab, or go off in a balloon.'

'Perhaps they stood here for some time,' I suggested.

'Ah! it's all right. He's off again,' said my companion, in a tone of relief.

He was indeed off, for after sniffing round again he suddenly made up his mind, and darted away with an energy and determination such as he had not yet shown. The scent appeared to be much hotter than before, for he had not even to put his nose on the ground, but tugged at his leash and tried to break into a run. I could see by the gleam in Holmes's eyes that he thought we were nearing the end of our journey.

Our course now ran down Nine Elms until we came to Broderick and Nelson's large timber-yard, just past the White Eagle tavern. Here the dog, frantic with excitement, turned down through the side gate into the enclosure, where the sawyers were already at work. On the dog raced through sawdust and shavings, down an alley, round a passage, between two wood-piles, and finally, with a triumphant yelp, sprang upon a large barrel which still stood upon the hand-trolley on which it had been brought.

With lolling tongue and blinking eyes, Toby stood upon the cask, looking from one to the other of us for some sign of appreciation. The staves of the barrel and the wheels of the trolley were smeared with a dark liquid, and the whole air was heavy with the smell of creosote.

Sherlock Holmes and I looked blankly at each other, and then burst simultaneously into an uncontrollable fit of laughter.

8

The Baker Street Irregulars

'What now?' I asked. 'Toby has lost his character for infallibility.'

'He acted according to his lights,' said Holmes, lifting him down from the barrel and walking him out of the timber-yard. 'If you consider how much creosote is carted about London in one day, it is no great wonder that our trail should have been crossed. It is much used now, especially for the seasoning of wood. Poor Toby is not to blame.'

'We must get on the main scent again, I suppose.'

'Yes. And, fortunately, we have no distance to go. Evidently what puzzled the dog at the corner of Knight's Place was that there were two different trails running in opposite directions. We took the wrong one. It only remains to follow the other.'

There was no difficulty about this. On being led to the place where he had committed his fault, Toby cast about in a wide circle and finally dashed off in a fresh direction.

'We must take care that he does not now bring us to the place where the creosote-barrel came from,' I observed.

'I had thought of that. But you notice that he keeps on the pavement, whereas the barrel passed down the roadway. No, we are on the true scent now.'

It tended down towards the riverside, running through Belmont Place and Prince's Street. At the end of Broad Street it ran right down to the water's edge, where there was a small wooden wharf. Toby led us to the very edge of this, and there stood whining, looking out on the dark current beyond.

'We are out of luck,' said Holmes. 'They have taken to a boat here.'

Several small punts and skiffs were lying about in the water and on the edge of the wharf. We took Toby round to each in turn, but though he sniffed earnestly, he made no sign.

Close to the rude landing-stage was a small brick house, with a wooden placard slung out through the second window. Mordecai Smith was printed across it in large letters, and unneath, *Boats to hire by the hour or day.* A second inscription above the door informed us that a steam launch was kept – a statement which was confirmed by a great pile of coke upon the jetty. Sherlock Holmes looked slowly round, and his face assumed an ominous expression.

'This looks bad,' said he. 'These fellows are sharper than I expected. They seem to have covered their tracks. There has, I fear, been preconcerted management here.'

He was approaching the door of the house, when it opened, and a little curly-headed lad of six came running out, followed by a stoutish, red-faced woman with a large sponge in her hand.

'You come back and be washed, Jack,' she shouted. 'Come back, you young imp; for if your father comes home and finds you like that, he'll let us hear of it.'

'Dear little chap!' cried Holmes, strategically. 'What a rosy-cheeked young rascal! Now, Jack, is there anything you would like?'

The youth pondered for a moment.

'I'd like a shillin',' said he.

'Nothing you would like better?'

'I'd like two shillin' better,' the prodigy answered, after some thought.

'Here you are, then! Catch! – A fine child, Mrs Smith!'

'Lor' bless you, sir, he is that, and forward. He gets almost too much for me to manage, 'specially when my man is away days at a time.'

'Away, is he?' said Holmes, in a disappointed voice. 'I am sorry for that, for I wanted to speak to Mr Smith.'

'He's been away since yesterday mornin', sir, and, truth to tell, I am beginning to feel frightened about him. But if it was about a boat, sir, maybe I could serve as well.'

'I wanted to hire his steam launch.'

'Why, bless you, sir, it is in the steam launch that he has gone. That's what puzzles me; for I know there ain't more coals in her than would take her to about Woolwich and back. If he'd been away in the barge I'd ha' thought nothin'; for many a time a job has taken him as far as Gravesend, and then if there was much doin' there he might ha' stayed over. But what good is a steam launch without coals?'

'He might have bought some at a wharf down the river.'

'He might, sir, but it weren't his way. Many a time I've heard him call out at the prices they charge for a few odd bags. Besides, I don't like that wooden-legged man, wi' his ugly face and outlandish talk. What did he want always knockin' about here for?'

'A wooden-legged man?' said Holmes, with bland surprise.

'Yes, sir, a brown, monkey-faced chap that's called more'n once for my old man. It was him that roused him up yesternight, and, what's more, my man knew he was comin', for he had steam up in the launch. I tell you straight, sir, I don't feel easy in my mind about it.'

'But, my dear Mrs Smith,' said Holmes, shrugging his shoulders, you are frightening yourself about nothing. How could you possibly tell that it was the wooden-legged man who came in the night? I don't quite understand how you can be so sure.'

'His voice, sir. I knew his voice, which is kind o' thick and foggy. He tapped at the winder – about three it would be. "Show a leg, matey," says he: "time to turn out guard." My old man woke up Jim – that's my eldest – and away they went, without so much as a word to me. I could hear the wooden leg clackin' on the stones.'

'And was this wooden-legged man alone?'

'Couldn't say, I am sure, sir. I didn't hear no one else.'

'I am sorry, Mrs Smith, for I wanted a steam launch, and I have heard good reports of the – Let me see, what is her name?'

'The *Aurora*, sir.'

'Ah! She's not that old green launch with a yellow line, very broad in the beam?'

'No, indeed. She's as trim a little thing as any on the river. She's been fresh painted, black with two red streaks.'

'Thanks. I hope that you will hear soon from Mr Smith. I am going down the river, and if I should see anything of the *Aurora* I shall let him know that you are uneasy. A black funnel, you say?'

'No, sir. Black with a white band.'

'Ah, of course. It was the sides which were black. Good-morning, Mrs Smith. There is a boatman here with a wherry, Watson. We shall take it and cross the river.'

'The main thing with people of that sort,' said Holmes, as we sat in the sheets of the wherry, 'is never to let them think that their information can be of the slightest importance to you. If you do, they will instantly shut up like an oyster. If you listen to them under protest, as it were, you are very likely to get what you want.'

'Our course now seems pretty clear,' said I.

'What would you do, then?'

'I would engage a launch and go down the river on the track of the *Aurora*.'

'My dear fellow, it would be a colossal task. She may have touched at any wharf on either side of the stream between here and Greenwich. Below the bridge there is a perfect labyrinth of landing-places for miles. It would take you days and days to exhaust them, if you set about it alone.'

'Employ the police, then.'

'No. I shall probably call Athelney Jones in at the last moment. He is not a bad fellow, and I should not like to do anything which would injure him professionally. But I have a fancy for working it out myself, now that we have gone so far.'

'Could we advertise, then, asking for information from wharfingers?'

'Worse and worse! Our men would know that the chase was hot at their heels, and they would be off out of the country. As it is, they are likely enough to leave, but as long as they think they are perfectly safe they will be in no hurry. Jones's energy will be of use to us there, for his view of the case is sure to push itself into the daily press, and the runaways will think that everyone is off on the wrong scent.'

'What are we to do, then?' I asked, as we landed near Millbank Penitentiary.

'Take this hansom, drive home, have some breakfast, and get an hour's sleep. It is quite on the cards that we may be afoot tonight again. Stop at a telegraph-office, cabby! We will keep Toby, for he may be of use to us yet.'

We pulled up at the Great Peter Street post-office, and Holmes dispatched his wire.

'Whom do you think that is to?' he asked, as we resumed our journey.

'I am sure I don't know.'

'You remember the Baker Street division of the detective police force whom I employed in the Jefferson Hope case?'

'Well?' said I, laughing.

'This is just the case where they might be invaluable. If they fail, I have other resources; but I shall try them first. That wire was to my dirty little lieutenant, Wiggins, and I expect that he and his gang will be with us before we have finished our breakfast.'

It was between eight and nine o'clock now, and I was conscious of a strong reaction after the successive excitements of the night. I was limp and weary, befogged in mind and fatigued in body. I had not the professional enthusiasm which carried my companion on, nor could I look at the matter as a mere abstract intellectual problem. As far as the death of Bartholomew Sholto went, I had heard little good of him, and could feel no intense antipathy to his murderers. The treasure, however, was a different matter. That, or part of it, belonged rightfully to Miss Morstan. While there was a chance of recovering it I was ready to devote my life to the one object. True, if I found it, it would probably put her for ever beyond my reach. Yet it would be a petty and selfish love which would be influenced by such a thought as that. If Holmes could work to find the criminals, I had a tenfold stronger reason to urge me on to find the treasure.

A bath at Baker Street and a complete change freshened me up wonderfully. When I came down to our room I found the breakfast laid and Holmes pouring out the coffee.

'Here it is,' said he, laughing and pointing to an open newspaper. 'The energetic Jones and the ubiquitous reporter have fixed it up between them. But you have had enough of the case. Better have your ham and eggs first.'

I took the paper from him and read the short notice, which was headed: Mysterious Business at Upper Norwood.

About twelve o'clock last night [said the *Standard*], Mr Bartholomew Sholto, of Pondicherry Lodge, Upper Norwood, was found dead in his room under circumstances which point to foul play. As far as we can learn, no actual traces of violence were found upon Mr Sholto's person, but a valuable collection of Indian gems which the deceased gentleman had inherited from his father has been carried off. The discovery was first made by Mr Sherlock Holmes and Dr Watson, who had called at the house with Mr Thaddeus Sholto, brother of the deceased. By a singular piece of good fortune, Mr Athelney Jones, the well-known member of the detective police force, happened to be at the Norwood Police Station, and was on the ground within half an hour of the first alarm. His trained and experienced faculties were at once directed towards the detection of the criminals, with the gratifying result that the brother, Thaddeus Sholto, has already been arrested, together with the housekeeper, Mrs Bernstone, an Indian butler named Lal Rao, and a porter, or gatekeeper, named McMurdo. It is quite certain that the thief or thieves were well acquainted with the house, for Mr Jones's well-known technical knowledge and his powers of minute observation have enabled him to prove conclusively that the miscreants could not have entered by the door or by the window, but must have made their way across the roof of the building, and so through a trap-door into a room which communicated with that in which the body was found. This fact, which has been very clearly made out, proves conclusively that it was no mere haphazard burglary. The prompt and energetic action of the officers of the law shows the great advantage of the presence on such occasions of a single vigorous and masterful mind. We cannot but think that it supplies an argument to those who would wish to see our detectives more decentralised and so brought into closer and more effective touch with the cases which it is their duty to investigate.

'Isn't it gorgeous?' said Holmes, grinning over his coffee cup. 'What do you think of it?'

'I think that we have had a close shave ourselves of being arrested for the crime.'

'So do I. I wouldn't answer for our safety now, if he should happen to have another of his attacks of energy.'

At this moment there was a loud ring at the bell, and I could hear Mrs Hudson, our landlady, raising her voice in a wail of expostulation and dismay.

'By heavens, Holmes,' said I, half rising, 'I believe that they are really after us.'

'No, it's not quite so bad as that. It is the unofficial force – the Baker Street irregulars.'

As he spoke, there came a swift pattering of naked feet upon the stairs, a clatter of high voices, and in rushed a dozen dirty and ragged little street arabs. There was some show of discipline among them, despite their tumultuous entry, for they instantly drew up in line and stood facing us with expectant faces. One of their number, taller and older than the others, stood forward with an air of lounging superiority which was very funny in such a disreputable little scarecrow.

'Got your message, sir,' said he, 'and brought 'em on sharp. Three bob and a tanner for tickets.'

'Here you are,' said Holmes, producing some silver. 'In future they can report to you, Wiggins, and you to me. I cannot have the house invaded in this way. However, it is just as well that you should all hear the instructions. I want to find the whereabouts of a steam launch called the *Aurora*, owner Mordecai Smith, black with two red streaks, funnel black with a white band. She is down the river somewhere. I want one boy to be at Mordecai Smith's landing-stage opposite Millbank to say if the boat comes back. You must divide it out among yourselves, and do both banks thoroughly. Let me know the moment you have news. Is that all clear?'

'Yes, guv'nor,' said Wiggins.

'The old scale of pay, and a guinea to the boy who finds the boat. Here's a day in advance. Now, off you go!'

He handed them a shilling each, and away they buzzed down the stairs, and I saw them a moment later streaming down the street.

'If the launch is above water they will find her,' said Holmes, as he rose from the table and lit his pipe. 'They can go everywhere, see everything, overhear everyone. I expect to hear before evening that they have spotted her. In the meanwhile, we can do nothing but await results. We cannot pick up the broken trail until we find either the *Aurora* or Mr Mordecai Smith.'

'Toby could eat these scraps, I dare say. Are you going to bed, Holmes?'

'No; I am not tired. I have a curious constitution. I never remember feeling tired by work, though idleness exhausts me completely. I am going to smoke and to think over this queer business to which my fair client has introduced us. If ever man had an easy task, this of ours ought to be. Wooden-legged men are not so common, but the other man must, I should think, be absolutely unique.'

'That other man again!'

'I have no wish to make a mystery of him to you, anyway. But you must have formed your own opinion. Now, do consider the data. Diminutive footmarks, toes never fettered by boots, naked feet, stone-headed wooden mace, great agility, small poisoned darts. What do you make of all this?'

'A savage!' I exclaimed. 'Perhaps one of those Indians who were the associates of Jonathan Small.'

'Hardly that,' said he. 'When first I saw signs of strange weapons, I was inclined to think so; but the remarkable character of the footmarks caused me to reconsider my views. Some of the inhabitants of the Indian Peninsula are small men, but none could have left such marks as that. The Hindu proper has long and thin feet. The sandal-wearing Mohammedan has the great toe well separated from the others, because the thong is commonly passed between. These little darts, too, could only be shot in one way. They are from a blow-pipe. Now, then, where are we to find our savage?'

'South America,' I hazarded.

He stretched his hand up, and took down a bulky volume from the shelf.

'This is the first volume of a gazetteer which is now being published. It may be looked upon as the very latest authority. What have we here? "Andaman Islands, situated 340 miles to the north of Sumatra, in the Bay of Bengal." Hum! hum! What's all this? Moist climate, coral reefs, sharks, Port Blair, convict barracks, Rutland Island, cottonwoods – Ah, here we are! "The aborigines of the Andaman Islands may perhaps claim the distinction of being the smallest race upon this earth, though some anthropologists prefer the Bushmen of Africa, the Digger Indians of America, and the Tierra del Fuegians. The average height is rather below four feet, although many full-grown adults may be found who are very much smaller than this. They are a fierce, morose and intractable people, though capable of forming most devoted friendships when their confidence has once been gained." Mark that, Watson. Now, then, listen to this. "They are naturally hideous, having large, misshapen heads, small, fierce eyes and distorted features. Their feet and hands, however, are remarkably small. So intractable and fierce are they, that all the efforts of the British officials have failed to win them over in any degree. They have always been a terror to shipwrecked crews, braining the survivors with their stone-headed clubs or shooting them with their poisoned arrows. These massacres are invariably concluded by a cannibal feast." Nice, amiable people, Watson! If this fellow had been left to his own unaided devices, this affair might have taken an even more ghastly turn. I fancy that, even as it is, Jonathan Small would give a good deal not to have employed him.'

'But how came he to have so singular a companion?'

'Ah, that is more than I can tell. Since, however, we had already determined that Small had come from the Andamans, it is not so very wonderful that this islander should be with him. No doubt we shall know all about it in time. Look here, Watson; you look regularly done. Lie down there on the sofa, and see if I can put you to sleep.'

He took up his violin from the corner, and as I stretched myself out he began to play some low, dreamy, melodious air – his own, no doubt, for he had a remarkable gift for improvisation. I have a vague remembrance of his gaunt limbs, his earnest face, and the rise and fall of his bow. Then I seemed to be floated peacefully away upon a soft sea of sound, until I found myself in dreamland, with the sweet face of Mary Morstan looking down upon me.

9

A Break in the Chain

It was late in the afternoon before I woke, strengthened and refreshed. Sherlock Holmes still sat exactly as I had left him, save that he had laid aside his violin and was deep in a book. He looked across at me as I stirred, and I noticed that his face was dark and troubled.

'You have slept soundly,' he said. 'I feared that our talk would wake you.'

'I heard nothing,' I answered. 'Have you had fresh news, then?'

'Unfortunately, no. I confess that I am surprised and disappointed. I expected something definite by this time. Wiggins has just been up to report. He says that no trace can be found of the launch. It is a provoking check, for every hour is of importance.'

'Can I do anything? I am perfectly fresh now, and quite ready for another night's outing.'

'No; we can do nothing. We can only wait. If we go ourselves, the message might come in our absence, and delay be caused. You can do what you will, but I must remain on guard.'

'Then I shall run over to Camberwell and call upon Mrs Cecil Forrester. She asked me to yesterday.'

'On Mrs Cecil Forrester?' asked Holmes with the twinkle of a smile in his eyes.

'Well, of course, on Miss Morstan too. They were to hear what happened.'

'I would not tell them too much,' said Holmes. 'Women are never to be entirely trusted – not the best of them.'

I did not pause to argue over this atrocious sentiment.

'I shall be back in an hour or two,' I remarked.

'All right! Good luck! But, I say, if you are crossing the water you may as well return Toby, for I don't think it is at all likely that we shall have any use for him now.'

I took our mongrel accordingly, and left him, together with a half-sovereign, at the old naturalist's in Pinchin Lane. At Camberwell I found

Miss Morstan a little weary after her night's adventures, but very eager to hear the news. Mrs Forrester, too, was full of curiosity. I told them all that we had done, suppressing, however, the more dreadful parts of the tragedy. Thus, although I spoke of Mr Sholto's death, I said nothing of the exact manner and method of it. With all my omissions, however, there was enough to startle and amaze them.

'It is a romance!' cried Mrs Forrester. 'An injured lady, half a million in treasure, a black cannibal and a wooden-legged ruffian. They take the place of the conventional dragon or wicked earl.'

'And two knight-errants to the rescue,' added Miss Morstan, with a bright glance at me.

'Why, Mary, your fortune depends upon the issue of this search. I don't think that you are nearly excited enough. Just imagine what it must be to be so rich, and to have the world at your feet!'

It sent a little thrill of joy to my heart to notice that she showed no sign of elation at the prospect. On the contrary, she gave a toss of her proud head, as though the matter were one in which she took small interest.

'It is for Mr Thaddeus Sholto that I am anxious,' she said. 'Nothing else is of any consequence; but I think that he has behaved most kindly and honourably throughout. It is our duty to clear him of this dreadful and unfounded charge.'

It was evening before I left Camberwell, and quite dark by the time I reached home. My companion's book and pipe lay by his chair, but he had disappeared. I looked about in the hope of seeing a note, but there was none.

'I suppose that Mr Sherlock Holmes has gone out?' I said to Mrs Hudson as she came up to lower the blinds.

'No, sir. He has gone to his room, sir. Do you know, sir,' sinking her voice into an impressive whisper, 'I am afraid for his health.'

'Why so, Mrs Hudson?'

'Well, he's that strange, sir. After you was gone he walked and he walked, up and down and up and down, until I was weary of the sound of his footstep. Then I heard him talking to himself and muttering, and every time the bell rang out he came on the stairhead with, "What is that, Mrs Hudson?" And now he has slammed off to his room, but I can hear him walking away the same as ever. I hope he's not going to be ill, sir. I ventured to say something to him about cooling medicine, but he turned on me, sir, with such a look that I don't know however I got out of the room.'

'I don't think that you have any cause to be uneasy, Mrs Hudson,' I answered. 'I have seen him like this before. He has some small matter upon his mind which makes him restless.'

I tried to speak lightly to our worthy landlady, but I was myself somewhat uneasy when through the long night I still from time to time heard the dull sound of his tread, and knew how his keen spirit was chafing against this involuntary inaction.

At breakfast-time he looked worn and haggard, with a little fleck of feverish colour upon either cheek.

'You are knocking yourself up, old man,' I remarked. 'I heard you marching about in the night.'

'No, I could not sleep,' he answered. 'This infernal problem is consuming me. It is too much to be baulked by so petty an obstacle, when all else had been overcome. I know the men, the launch, everything; and yet I can get no news. I have set other agencies at work, and used every means at my disposal. The whole river has been searched on either side, but there is no news, nor has Mrs Smith heard of her husband. I shall come to the conclusion soon that they have scuttled the craft. But there are objections to that.'

'Or that Mrs Smith has put us on a wrong scent.'

'No, I think that may be dismissed. I had enquiries made and there is a launch of that description.'

'Could it have gone up the river?'

'I have considered that possibility too, and there is a search-party who will work up as far as Richmond. If no news comes today, I shall start off myself tomorrow, and go for the men rather than the boat. But surely, surely, we shall hear something.'

We did not, however. Not a word came to us either from Wiggins or from the other agencies. There were articles in most of the papers upon the Norwood tragedy. They all appeared to be rather hostile to the unfortunate Thaddeus Sholto. No fresh details were to be found, however, in any of them, save that an inquest was to be held upon the following day. I walked over to Camberwell in the evening to report our ill-success to the ladies, and on my return I found Holmes dejected and somewhat morose. He would hardly reply to my questions, and busied himself all the evening in an abstruse chemical analysis which involved much heating of retorts and distilling of vapours, ending at last in a smell which fairly drove me out of the apartment. Up to the small hours of the morning I could hear the clinking of his test-tubes, which told me that he was still engaged in his malodorous experiment.

In the early dawn I woke with a start, and was surprised to find him standing by my bedside, clad in a rude sailor dress with a pea-jacket and a coarse red scarf round his neck.

'I am off down the river, Watson,' said he. 'I have been turning it over in my mind, and I can see only one way out of it. It is worth trying, at all events.'

'Surely I can come with you, then?' said I.

'No; you can be much more useful if you will remain here as my representative. I am loath to go, for it is quite on the cards that some message may come during the day, though Wiggins was despondent about it last night. I want you to open all notes and telegrams, and to act on your own judgement if any news should come. Can I rely upon you?'

'Most certainly.'

'I am afraid that you will not be able to wire to me, for I can hardly tell yet where I may find myself. If I am in luck, however, I may not be gone so very long. I shall have news of some sort or other before I get back.'

I had heard nothing of him by breakfast-time. On opening the *Standard*, however, I found that there was a fresh allusion to the business.

With reference to the Upper Norwood tragedy [it remarked], we have reason to believe that the matter promises to be even more complex and mysterious than was originally supposed. Fresh evidence has shown that it is quite impossible that Mr Thaddeus Sholto could have been in any way concerned in the matter. He and the housekeeper, Mrs Bernstone, were both released yesterday evening. It is believed, however, that the police have a clue as to the real culprits, and that it is being prosecuted by Mr Athelney Jones, of Scotland Yard, with all his well-known energy and sagacity. Further arrests may be expected at any moment.

'That is satisfactory so far as it goes,' thought I. 'Friend Sholto is safe, at any rate. I wonder what the fresh clue may be, though it seems to be a stereotyped form whenever the police have made a blunder.'

I tossed the paper down upon the table, but at that moment my eye caught an advertisement in the agony column. It ran in this way:

LOST – Whereas Mordecai Smith, boatman, and his son Jim, left Smith's Wharf at or about three o'clock last Tuesday morning in the steam launch *Aurora*, black with two red stripes, funnel black with a white band, the sum of five pounds will be paid to anyone who can give information to Mrs Smith, at Smith's Wharf or at 221b Baker Street, as to the whereabouts of the said Mordecai Smith and the launch *Aurora*.

This was clearly Holmes's doing. The Baker Street address was enough to prove that. It struck me as rather ingenious, because it might be read by the fugitives without their seeing in it more than the natural anxiety of a wife for her missing husband.

It was a long day. Every time that a knock came to the door or a sharp step passed in the street, I imagined that it was either Holmes returning or an answer to his advertisement. I tried to read, but my thoughts would wander oft to our strange quest and to the ill-assorted and villainous pair whom we were pursuing. Could there be, I wondered, some radical flaw in my companion's reasoning? Might he not be suffering from some huge self-deception? Was it not possible that his nimble and speculative mind had built up this wild theory upon faulty premises? I had never known him to be wrong, and yet the keenest reasoner may occasionally be deceived. He was likely, I thought, to fall into error through the over-refinement of his logic – his preference for a subtle and bizarre explanation when a plainer and more commonplace one lay ready to his hand. Yet, on the other hand, I had myself seen the evidence, and I had heard the reasons for his deductions. When I looked back on the long chain of curious circumstances, many of them trivial in themselves, but all tending in the same direction, I could not disguise from myself that even if Holmes's explanation were incorrect the true theory must be equally *outré* and startling.

At three o'clock in the afternoon there was a loud peal at the bell, an authoritative voice in the hall, and, to my surprise, no less a person than Mr Athelney Jones was shown up to me. Very different was he, however, from the brusque and masterful professor of common sense who had taken over the case so confidently at Upper Norwood. His expression was downcast, and his bearing meek and even apologetic.

'Good-day, sir; good-day,' said he. 'Mr Sherlock Holmes is out, I understand?'

'Yes, and I cannot be sure when he will be back. But perhaps you would care to wait. Take that chair and try one of these cigars.'

'Thank you; I don't mind if I do,' said he, mopping his face with a red bandanna handkerchief.

'And a whisky and soda?'

'Well, half a glass. It is very hot for the time of year; and I have had a good deal to worry and try me. You know my theory about this Norwood case?'

'I remember that you expressed one.'

'Well, I have been obliged to reconsider it. I had my net drawn tightly round Mr Sholto, sir, when pop he went through a hole in the middle of it. He was able to prove an alibi which could not be shaken. From the time that he left his brother's room he was never out of sight of someone or other. So it could not be he who climbed over roofs and through trap-doors. It's a very dark case, and my professional credit is at stake. I should be very glad of a little assistance.'

'We all need help sometimes,' said I.

'Your friend Mr Sherlock Holmes is a wonderful man, sir,' said he, in a husky and confidential voice. 'He's a man who is not to be beat. I have known that young man go into a good many cases, but I never saw the case yet that he could not throw a light upon. He is irregular in his methods, and a little quick perhaps in jumping at theories; but, on the whole, I think he would have made a most promising officer and I don't care who knows it. I have had a wire from him this morning, by which I understand that he has got some clue to this Sholto business. Here is his message.'

He took the telegram out of his pocket, and handed it to me. It was dated from Poplar at twelve o'clock. 'Go to Baker Street at once,' it said. 'If I have not returned, wait for me. I am close on the track of the Sholto gang. You can come with us tonight if you want to be in at the finish.'

'This sounds well. He has evidently picked up the scent again,' said I.

'Ah, then he has been at fault too,' exclaimed Jones, with evident satisfaction. 'Even the best of us are thrown off sometimes. Of course this may prove to be a false alarm; but it is my duty as an officer of the law to allow no chance to slip. But there is someone at the door. Perhaps this is he.'

A heavy step was heard ascending the stair, with a great wheezing and rattling as from a man who was sorely put to it for breath. Once or twice he stopped, as though the climb were too much for him, but at last he made his way to our door and entered. His appearance corresponded to the sounds which we had heard. He was an aged man, clad in seafaring garb, with an old pea-jacket buttoned up to his throat. His back was bowed, his knees were shaky, and his breathing was painfully asthetic. As he leaned upon a thick oaken cudgel, his shoulders heaved in the effort to draw the air into his lungs. He had a coloured scarf round his chin, and I could see little of his face save a pair of keen dark eyes overhung by bushy white brows, and long grey side-whiskers. Altogether he gave me the impression of a respectable master mariner who had fallen into years and poverty.

'What is it, my man?' I asked.

He looked about him in the slow methodical fashion of old age.

'Is Mr Sherlock Holmes here?' said he.

193

'No; but I am acting for him. You can tell me any message you have for him.'

'It was to him himself I was to tell it,' said he.

'But I tell you I am acting for him. Was it about Mordecai Smith's boat?'

'Yes. I knows well where it is. An' I knows where the men he is after are. An' I knows where the treasure is. I knows all about it.'

'Then tell me, and I shall let him know.'

'It was to him I was to tell it,' he repeated, with the petulant obstinacy of a very old man.

'Well, you must wait for him.'

'No, no; I ain't goin' to lose a whole day to please no one. If Mr Holmes ain't here, then Mr Holmes must find it all out for himself. I don't care about the look of either of you, and I won't tell a word.'

He shuffled towards the door, but Athelney Jones got in front of him.

'Wait a bit, my friend,' said he. 'You have important information, and you must not walk off. We shall keep you, whether you like it or not, until our friend returns.'

The old man made a little run towards the door, but as Athelney Jones put his broad back up against it he recognised the uselessness of resistance.

'Pretty sort o' treatment this!' he cried, stamping his stick. 'I come here to see a gentleman, and you two, who I never saw in my life, seize me and treat me in this fashion!'

'You will be none the worse,' I said. 'We shall recompense you for the loss of your time. Sit over here on the sofa, and you will not have long to wait.'

He came across sullenly enough, and seated himself with his face resting on his hands. Jones and I resumed our cigars and our talk. Suddenly, however, Holmes's voice broke in upon us.

'I think that you might offer me a cigar too,' he said.

We both started in our chairs. There was Holmes sitting close to us with an air of quiet amusement.

'Holmes!' I exclaimed. 'You here! But where is the old man?'

'Here is the old man,' said he, holding out a heap of white hair. 'Here he is – wig, whiskers, eyebrows and all. I thought my disguise was pretty good, but I hardly expected that it would stand that test.'

'Ah, you rogue!' cried Jones, highly delighted. 'You would have made an actor, and a rare one. You had the proper workhouse cough, and those weak legs of yours are worth ten pounds a week. I thought I knew the glint of your eye, though. You didn't get away from us so easily, you see.'

'I have been working in that get-up all day,' said he, lighting his cigar. 'You see, a good many of the criminal classes begin to know me – especially since our friend here took to publishing some of my cases: so I can only go on the war-path under some simple disguise like this. You got my wire?'

'Yes; that was what brought me here.'

'How has your case prospered?'

'It has all come to nothing. I have had to release two of my prisoners, and there is no evidence against the other two.'

'Never mind. We shall give you two others in the place of them. But you must put yourself under my orders. You are welcome to all the official credit, but you must act on the lines that I point out. Is that agreed?'

'Entirely, if you will help me to the men.'

'Well, then, in the first place I shall want a fast police boat – a steam launch – to be at the Westminster Stairs at seven o'clock.'

'That is easily managed. There is always one about there; but I can step across the road and telephone to make sure.'

'Then I shall want two staunch men, in case of resistance.'

'There will be two or three in the boat. What else?'

'When we secure the men we shall get the treasure. I think that it would be a pleasure to my friend here to take the box round to the young lady to whom half of it rightfully belongs. Let her be the first to open it. Eh, Watson?'

'It would be a great pleasure to me.'

'Rather an irregular proceeding,' said Jones, shaking his head. 'However, the whole thing is irregular, and I suppose we must wink at it. The treasure must afterwards be handed over to the authorities until after the official investigation.'

'Certainly. That is easily managed. One other point. I should much like to have a few details about this matter from the lips of Jonathan Small himself. You know I like to work the details of my cases out. There is no objection to my having an unofficial interview with him, either here in my rooms or elsewhere, as long as he is efficiently guarded?'

'Well, you are master of the situation. I have had no proof yet of the existence of this Jonathan Small. However, if you can catch him, I don't see how I can refuse you an interview with him.'

'That is understood, then?'

'Perfectly. Is there anything else?'

'Only that I insist upon your dining with us. It will be ready in half an hour. I have oysters and a brace of grouse, with something a little choice in white wines. Watson, you have never yet recognised my merits as a housekeeper.'

IO

The End of the Islander

Our meal was a merry one. Holmes could talk exceedingly well when he chose, and that night he did choose. He appeared to be in a state of nervous exaltation. I have never known him so brilliant. He spoke on a quick succession of subjects – on miracle plays, on medieval pottery, on Stradivarius violins, on the Buddhism of Ceylon, and on the warships of the future – handling each as though he had made a special study of it. His bright humour marked the reaction from his black depression of the preceding days. Athelney Jones proved to be a sociable soul in his hours of relaxation, and faced his dinner with the air of a *bon vivant*. For myself, I felt elated at the thought that we were nearing the end of our task, and I caught something of Holmes's gaiety. None of us alluded during dinner to the cause which had brought us together.

When the cloth was cleared, Holmes glanced at his watch, and filled up three glasses with port.

'One bumper,' said he, 'to the success of our little expedition. And now it is high time we were off. Have you a pistol, Watson?'

'I have my old service-revolver in my desk.'

'You had best take it, then. It is well to be prepared. I see that the cab is at the door. I ordered it for half-past six.'

It was a little past seven before we reached the Westminster Wharf, and found our launch awaiting us. Holmes eyed it critically.

'Is there anything to mark it as a police-boat?'

'Yes; that green lamp at the side.'

'Then take it off.'

The small change was made, we stepped on board, and the ropes were cast off. Jones, Holmes and I sat in the stern. There was one man at the rudder, one to tend the engines, and two burly police inspectors forward.

'Where to?' asked Jones.

'To the Tower. Tell them to stop opposite to Jacobson's Yard.'

Our craft was evidently a very fast one. We shot past the long lines of loaded barges as though they were stationary. Holmes smiled with satisfaction as we overhauled a river steamer and left her behind us.

'We ought to be able to catch anything on the river,' he said.

'Well, hardly that. But there are not many launches to beat us.'

'We shall have to catch the *Aurora*, and she has a name for being a clipper. I will tell you how the land lies, Watson. You recollect how annoyed I was at being baulked by so small a thing?'

'Yes.'

'Well, I gave my mind a thorough rest by plunging into a chemical analysis. One of our greatest statesmen has said that a change of work is the best rest. So it is. When I had succeeded in dissolving the hydro-carbon which I was at work at, I came back to the problem of the Sholtos, and thought the whole matter out again. My boys had been up the river and down the river without result. The launch was not at any landing-stage or wharf, nor had it returned. Yet it could hardly have been scuttled to hide their traces, though that always remained as a possible hypoth-esis if all else failed. I knew that this man Small had a certain degree of low cunning, but I did not think him capable of anything in the nature of delicate finesse. That is usually a product of higher education. I then reflected that since he had certainly been in London some time as we had evidence that he maintained a continual watch over Pondicherry Lodge – he could hardly leave at a moment's notice, but would need some little time, if it were only a day, to arrange his affairs. That was the balance of probability, at any rate.'

'It seems to me to be a little weak,' said I: 'it is more probable that he had arranged his affairs before ever he set out upon his expedition.'

'No, I hardly think so. This lair of his would be too valuable a retreat in case of need for him to give it up until he was sure that he could do without it. But a second consideration struck me. Jonathan Small must have felt that the peculiar appearance of his companion, however much he may have top-coated him, would give rise to gossip, and possibly be associated with this Norwood tragedy. He was quite sharp enough to see that. They had started from their headquarters under cover of darkness, and he would wish to get back before it was broad light. Now, it was past three o'clock, according to Mrs Smith, when they got the boat. It would be quite bright, and people would be about in an hour or so. Therefore, I argued, they did not go very far. They paid Smith well to hold his tongue, reserved his launch for the final escape and hurried to their lodgings with the treasure-box. In a couple of nights, when they had time to see what view the papers took, and whether there was any suspicion, they would make their way under cover of darkness to some ship at Gravesend or in the Downs, where no doubt they had already arranged for passages to America or the Colonies.'

'But the launch? They could not have taken that to their lodgings.'

'Quite so. I argued that the launch must be no great way off, in spite of its invisibility. I then put myself in the place of Small, and looked at it as a man of his capacity would. He would probably consider that to send back the launch or to keep it at a wharf would make pursuit easy if the police did happen to get on his track. How, then, could he conceal the launch and yet have her at hand when wanted? I wondered what I should do myself if I were in his shoes. I could only think of one way of doing it. I might hand the launch over to some boat-builder or repairer, with directions to make a trifling change in her. She would then be removed to his shed or yard, and so be effectually concealed, while at the same time I could have her at a few hours' notice.'

'That seems simple enough.'

'It is just these very simple things which are extremely liable to be over-looked. However, I determined to act on the idea. I started at once, in this harmless seaman's rig, and enquired at all the yards down the river. I drew blank at fifteen but at the sixteenth – Jacobson's – I learned that the *Aurora* had been handed over to them two days ago by a wooden-legged man, with some trivial directions as to her rudder. "There ain't naught amiss with her rudder," said the foreman. "There she lies, with the red streaks." At that moment who should come down but Mordecai Smith, the missing owner! He was rather the worse for liquor. I should not, of course, have known him, but he bellowed out his name and the name of his launch. "I want her tonight at eight o'clock," said he – "eight o'clock sharp, mind, for I have two gentlemen who won't be kept waiting." They had evidently paid him well, for he was very flush of money, chucking shillings about to the men. I followed him some distance, but he subsided into an alehouse; so I went back to the yard, and happening to pick up one of my boys on the way, I stationed him as a sentry over the launch. He is to stand at the water's edge and wave his handkerchief to us when they start. We shall be lying off in the stream, and it will be a strange thing if we do not take men, treasure and all.'

'You have planned it all very neatly, whether they are the right men or not,' said Jones; 'but if the affair were in my hands I should have had a body of police in Jacobson's Yard, and arrested them when they came down.'

'Which would have been never. This man Small is a pretty shrewd fellow. He would send a scout on ahead, and if anything made him suspicious he would lie snug for another week.'

'But you might have stuck to Mordecai Smith, and so been led to their hiding-place,' said I.

'In that case I should have wasted my day. I think that it is a hundred to one against Smith knowing where they live. As long as he has liquor and good pay, why should he ask questions? They send him messages what to do. No, I thought over every possible course, and this is the best.'

While this conversation had been proceeding, we had been shooting the long series of bridges which span the Thames. As we passed the City the last rays of the sun were gilding the cross upon the summit of St Paul's. It was twilight before we reached the Tower.

'That is Jacobson's Yard,' said Holmes, pointing to a bristle of masts and rigging on the Surrey side. 'Cruise gently up and down here under cover of this string of lighters.' He took a pair of night-glasses from his pocket and gazed some time at the shore. 'I see my sentry at his post,' he remarked, 'but no sign of a handkerchief.'

'Suppose we go downstream a short way and lie in wait for them,' said Jones, eagerly.

We were all eager by this time, even the policemen and stokers, who had a very vague idea of what was going forward.

'We have no right to take anything for granted,' Holmes answered. 'It is certainly ten to one that they go downstream, but we cannot be certain. From this point we can see the entrance of the yard, and they can hardly see us. It will be a clear night with plenty of light. We must stay where we are. See how the folk swarm over yonder in the gas-light.'

'They are coming from work in the yard.'

'Dirty-looking rascals, but I suppose everyone has some little immortal spark concealed about him. You would not think it, to look at them. There is no *a priori* probability about it. A strange enigma is man!'

'Someone calls him a soul concealed in an animal,' I suggested.

'Winwood Reade is good upon the subject,' said Holmes. 'He remarks that, while the individual man is an insoluble puzzle, in the aggregate he becomes a mathematical certainty. You can, for example, never foretell what any one man will do, but you can say with precision what an average number will be up to. Individuals vary, but percentages remain constant. So says the statistician. But do I see a handkerchief? Surely there is a white flutter over yonder.'

'Yes, it is your boy,' I cried. 'I can see him plainly.'

'And there is the *Aurora*,' exclaimed Holmes, 'and going like the devil! Full speed ahead, engineer. Make after that launch with the yellow light. By heaven, I shall never forgive myself if she proves to have the heels of us!'

She had slipped unseen through the yard-entrance and passed behind two or three small craft, so that she had fairly got her speed up before we saw her. Now she was flying down the stream, near in to the shore, going at a tremendous rate. Jones looked gravely at her and shook his head.

'She is very fast,' he said. 'I doubt if we shall catch her.'

'We *must* catch her!' cried Holmes, between his teeth. 'Heap it on, stokers! Make her do all she can! If we burn the boat, we must have them!'

We were fairly after her now. The furnaces roared, and the powerful engines whizzed and clanked, like a great metallic heart. Her sharp, steep prow cut through the still river-water and sent two rolling waves to right and to left of us. With every throb of the engines we sprang and quivered like a living thing. One great yellow lantern in our bows threw a long, flickering funnel of light in front of us. Right ahead a dark blur upon the water showed where the *Aurora* lay, and the swirl of white foam behind her spoke of the pace at which she was going. We flashed past barges, steamers, merchant vessels, in and out, behind this one and round the other. Voices hailed us out of the darkness, but still the *Aurora* thundered on, and still we followed close upon her track.

'Pile it on, men, pile it on!' cried Holmes, looking down into the engine-room, while the fierce glow from below beat upon his eager, aquiline face. 'Get every pound of steam you can.'

'I think we gain a little,' said Jones, with his eyes on the *Aurora*.

'I am sure of it,' said I. 'We shall be up with her in a very few minutes.'

At that moment, however, as our evil fate would have it, a tug with three barges in tow blundered in between us. It was only by putting our helm hard down that we avoided a collision and before we could round them and recover our way the *Aurora* had gained a good two hundred yards. She was still, however, well in view, and the murky, uncertain twilight was settling into a clear starlit night. Our boilers were strained to their utmost, and the frail shell vibrated and creaked with the fierce energy which was driving us along. We had shot through the Pool, past the West India Docks, down the long Deptford Reach, and up again after rounding the Isle of Dogs. The dull blur in front of us resolved itself now clearly enough into the dainty *Aurora*. Jones turned our searchlight upon her, so that we could plainly see the figures upon her deck. One man sat by the stern, with something black between his knees, over which he stooped. Beside him lay a dark mass, which looked like a Newfoundland dog. The boy held the tiller, while against the red glare of the furnace I could see old Smith, stripped to the waist and shovelling coals for dear life. They may have had some doubt at first as to whether we were really pursuing them, but now as we followed every winding and turning which they took there could no longer be any question about it. At Greenwich we were about three hundred paces behind them. At Blackwall we could not have been more than two hundred and fifty. I have coursed many creatures in many countries during my chequered career, but never did sport give me such a wild thrill as this mad, flying manhunt down the Thames. Steadily we drew in upon them, yard by yard. In the silence of the night we could hear the panting and clanking of their machinery. The man in the stern still crouched upon the deck, and his arms were moving as though he were busy, while every now and then he would look up and measure with a glance the distance which still separated us. Nearer we came and nearer. Jones yelled to them to stop. We were not more than four boat's-lengths behind them, both boats flying at a tremendous pace. It was a clear reach of the river, with Barking Level upon one side and the melancholy Plumstead Marshes upon the other. At our hail the man in the stern sprang up from the deck and shook his two clenched fists at us, cursing the while in a high, cracked voice. He was a good-sized, powerful man, and as he stood poising himself with legs astride, I could see that, from the thigh downwards, there was but a wooden stump upon the right side. At the sound of his strident, angry cries, there was a movement in the huddled bundle upon the deck. It straightened itself into a little black man – the smallest I have ever seen – with a great, misshapen head and a shock of tangled dishevelled hair. Holmes had already drawn his revolver, and I whipped out mine at the sight of this savage, distorted creature. He was wrapped in some sort of a dark ulster or blanket, which left only his face exposed; but that face was enough to give a man a sleepless night. Never have I seen features so deeply marked with all bestiality and cruelty. His small eyes glowed and burned with a sombre light, and his thick lips were writhed back from his teeth, which grinned and chattered at us with half-animal fury.

'Fire if he raises his hand,' said Holmes quietly.

We were within a boat's-length by this time, and almost within touch of our quarry. I can see the two of them now as they stood: the white man with his legs far apart, shrieking out curses, and the unhallowed dwarf with his hideous face, and his strong, yellow teeth gnashing at us in the light of our lantern.

It was well that we had so clear a view of him. Even as we looked he plucked out from under his covering a short, round piece of wood, like a school ruler, and clapped it to his lips. Our pistols rang out together. He whirled round, threw up his arms and, with a kind of choking cough, fell sideways into the stream. I caught one glimpse of his venomous, menacing eyes amid the white swirl of the waters. At the same moment the wooden-legged man threw himself upon the rudder and put it hard down, so that his boat made straight in for the southern bank, while we shot past her stern, only clearing her by a few feet. We were round after her in an instant, but she was already nearly at the bank. It was a wild and desolate place, where the moon glimmered upon a wide expanse of marshland, with pools of stagnant water and beds of decaying vegetation. The launch, with a dull thud, ran up upon the mud-bank, with her bow in the air and her stern flush with the water. The fugitive sprang out, but his stump instantly sank its whole length into the sodden soil. In vain he struggled and writhed. Not one step could he possibly take either forwards or backwards. He yelled in impotent rage, and kicked frantically into the mud with his other foot; but his struggles only bored his wooden pin the deeper into the sticky bank. When we brought our launch alongside he was so firmly anchored that it was only by throwing the end of a rope over his shoulder that we were able to haul him out and to drag him like some evil fish over our side. The two Smiths, father and son, sat sullenly in their launch, but came aboard meekly enough when commanded. The *Aurora* herself we hauled off and made fast to our stern. A solid iron chest of Indian workmanship stood upon the deck. This, there could be no question, was the same that had contained the ill-omened treasure of the Sholtos. There was no key, but it was of considerable weight, so we transferred it carefully to our own little cabin. As we steamed slowly upstream again we flashed our searchlight in every direction, but there was no sign of the Islander. Somewhere in the dark ooze at the bottom of the Thames lie the bones of that strange visitor to our shores.

'See here,' said Holmes, pointing to the wooden hatchway. 'We were hardly quick enough with our pistols.' There, sure enough, just behind where we had been standing, stuck one of those murderous darts which we knew so well. It must have whizzed between us at the instant we fired. Holmes smiled at it and shrugged his shoulders in his easy fashion, but I confess that it turned me sick to think of the horrible death which had passed so close to us that night.

II

The Great Agra Treasure

Our captive sat in the cabin opposite to the iron box which he had done so much and waited so long to gain. He was a sunburned reckless-eyed fellow, with a network of lines and wrinkles all over his mahogany features which told of a hard, open-air life. There was a singular prominence about his bearded chin which marked a man who was not to be easily turned from his purpose. His age may have been fifty or thereabouts, for his black, curly hair was thickly shot with grey. His face in repose was not an unpleasing one, though his heavy brows and aggressive chin gave him, as I had lately seen, a terrible expression when moved to anger. He sat now with his handcuffed hands upon his lap, and his head sunk upon his breast, while he looked with his keen, twinkling eyes at the box which had been the cause of his ill-doings. It seemed to me that there was more sorrow than anger in his rigid and contained countenance. Once he looked up at me with a gleam of something like humour in his eyes.

'Well, Jonathan Small,' said Holmes, lighting a cigar, 'I am sorry that it has come to this.'

'And so am I, sir,' he answered, frankly. 'I don't believe that I can swing over the job. I give you my word on the Book that I never raised hand against Mr Sholto. It was that little hellhound Tonga who shot one of his cursed darts into him. I had no part in it, sir. I was as grieved as if it had been my blood-relation. I welted the little devil with the slack end of the rope for it, but it was done and I could not undo it again.'

'Have a cigar,' said Holmes; 'and you had best take a pull out of my flask, for you are very wet. How could you expect so small and weak a man as this black fellow to overpower Mr Sholto and hold him while you were climbing the rope?'

'You seem to know as much about it as if you were there, sir. The truth is that I hoped to find the room clear. I knew the habits of the house pretty well, and it was the time when Mr Sholto usually went down to his supper. I shall make no secret of the business. The best defence that I can make is just the simple truth. Now, if it had been the old major I would have swung for him with a light heart. I would have thought no more of knifing him than of smoking this cigar. But it's cursed hard that I should be lagged over this young Sholto with whom I had no quarrel whatever.'

'You are under the charge of Mr Athelney Jones, of Scotland Yard. He is going to bring you up to my rooms, and I shall ask you for a true account of the matter. You must make a clean breast of it, for if you do I hope that I may be of use to you. I think I can prove that the poison acts so quickly that the man was dead before ever you reached the room.'

'That he was, sir. I never got such a turn in my life as when I saw him grinning at me with his head on his shoulder as I climbed through the window. It fairly shook me, sir. I'd have half killed Tonga for it if he had not scrambled off. That was how he came to leave his club, and some of his darts, too, as he tells me, which I dare say helped to put you on our track; though how you kept on it is more than I can tell. I don't feel no malice against you for it. But it does seem a queer thing,' he added, with a bitter smile, 'that I, who have a fair claim to half a million of money, should spend the first half of my life building a breakwater in the Andamans, and am like to spend the other half digging drains at Dartmoor. It was an evil day for me when first I clapped eyes upon the merchant Achmet and had to do with the Agra treasure, which never brought anything but a curse yet upon the man who owned it. To him it brought murder, to Major Sholto it brought fear and guilt, to me it has meant slavery for life.'

At this moment Athelney Jones thrust his face and shoulders into the tiny cabin.

'Quite a family party,' he remarked. 'I think I shall have a pull at that flask, Holmes. Well, I think we may all congratulate each other. Pity we didn't take the other alive: but there was no choice. I say, Holmes, you must confess that you cut it rather fine. It was all we could do to overhaul her.'

'All is well that ends well,' said Holmes. 'But I certainly did not know that the *Aurora* was such a clipper.'

'Smith says she is one of the fastest launches on the river, and that if he had had another man to help him with the engines we should never have caught her. He swears he knew nothing of this Norwood business.'

'Neither he did,' cried our prisoner – 'not a word. I chose his launch because I heard that she was a flier. We told him nothing; but we paid him well, and he was to get something handsome if we reached our vessel, the *Esmeralda*, at Gravesend, outward bound for the Brazils.'

'Well, if he has done no wrong we shall see that no wrong comes to him. If we are pretty quick in catching our men, we are not so quick in condemning them.' It was amusing to notice how the consequential Jones was already beginning to give himself airs on the strength of the capture. From the slight smile which played over Sherlock Holmes's face, I could see that the speech had not been lost upon him.

'We will be at Vauxhall Bridge presently,' said Jones, 'and shall land you, Dr Watson, with the treasure-box. I need hardly tell you that I am taking a very grave responsibility upon myself in doing this. It is most irregular; but of course an agreement is an agreement. I must, however, as a matter of duty, send an inspector with you, since you have so valuable a charge. You will drive, no doubt?'

'Yes, I shall drive.'

'It is a pity there is no key, that we may make an inventory first. You will have to break it open. Where is the key, my man?'

'At the bottom of the river,' said Small shortly.

'Hum! There was no use your giving this unnecessary trouble. We have had work enough already through you. However, doctor, I need not warn you to be careful. Bring the box back with you to the Baker Street rooms. You will find us there, on our way to the station.'

They landed me at Vauxhall, with my heavy iron box, and with a bluff, genial inspector as my companion. A quarter of an hour's drive brought us to Mrs Cecil Forrester's. The servant seemed surprised at so late a visitor. Mrs Cecil Forrester was out for the evening, she explained, and likely to be very late. Miss Morstan, however, was in the drawing-room; so to the drawing-room I went, box in hand, leaving the obliging inspector in the cab.

She was seated by the open window, dressed in some sort of white diaphanous material, with a little touch of scarlet at the neck and waist. The soft light of a shaded lamp fell upon her as she leaned back in the basket chair, playing over her sweet, grave face, and tinting with a dull, metallic sparkle the rich coils of her luxuriant hair. One white arm and hand drooped over the side of the chair, and her whole pose and figure spoke of an absorbing melancholy. At the sound of my footfall she sprang to her feet, however, and a bright flush of surprise and of pleasure coloured her pale cheeks.

'I heard a cab drive up,' she said. 'I thought that Mrs Forrester had come back very early, but I never dreamed that it might be you. What news have you brought me?'

'I have brought something better than news,' said I, putting down the box upon the table and speaking jovially and boisterously, though my heart was heavy within me. 'I have brought you something which is worth all the news in the world. I have brought you a fortune.'

She glanced at the iron box.

'Is that the treasure, then?' she asked, coolly enough.

'Yes, this is the great Agra treasure. Half of it is yours and half is Thaddeus Sholto's. You will have a couple of hundred thousand each. Think of that! an annuity of ten thousand pounds. There will be few richer young ladies in England. Is it not glorious?'

I think that I must have been rather overacting my delight, and that she detected a hollow ring in my congratulations, for I saw her eyebrows rise a little, and she glanced at me curiously.

'If I have it,' said she, 'I owe it to you.'

'No, no,' I answered, 'not to me but to my friend Sherlock Holmes. With all the will in the world, I could never have followed up a clue which has taxed even his analytical genius. As it was, we very nearly lost it at the last moment.'

'Pray sit down and tell me all about it, Dr Watson,' said she.

I narrated briefly what had occurred since I had seen her last. Holmes's new method of search, the discovery of the *Aurora*, the appearance of Athelney Jones, our expedition in the evening and the wild chase down the Thames. She listened with parted lips and shining eyes to my recital of our adventures. When I spoke of the dart which had so narrowly missed us, she turned so white that I feared that she was about to faint.

'It is nothing,' she said, as I hastened to pour her out some water. 'I am all right again. It was a shock to me to hear that I had placed my friends in such horrible peril.'

'That is all over,' I answered. 'It was nothing. I will tell you no more gloomy details. Let us turn to something brighter. There is the treasure. What could be brighter than that? I got leave to bring it with me, thinking that it would interest you to be the first to see it.'

'It would be of the greatest interest to me,' she said. There was no eagerness in her voice, however. It had struck her, doubtless, that it might seem ungracious upon her part to be indifferent to a prize which had cost so much to win. 'What a pretty box!' she said, stooping over it. 'This is Indian work, I suppose?'

'Yes; it is Benares metalwork.'

'And so heavy!' she exclaimed, trying to raise it. 'The box alone must be of some value. Where is the key?'

'Small threw it into the Thames,' I answered. 'I must borrow Mrs Forrester's poker.'

There was in the front a thick and broad hasp, wrought in the image of a sitting Buddha. Under this I thrust the end of the poker and twisted it outward as a lever. The hasp sprang open with a loud snap. With trembling fingers I flung back the lid. We both stood gazing in astonishment. The box was empty!

No wonder that it was heavy. The ironwork was two-thirds of an inch thick all round. It was massive, well made and solid, like a chest constructed to carry things of great price, but not one shred or crumb of metal or jewellery lay within it. It was absolutely and completely empty.

'The treasure is lost,' said Miss Morstan, calmly.

As I listened to the words and realised what they meant, a great shadow seemed to pass from my soul. I did not know how this Agra treasure had weighed me down, until now that it was finally removed. It was selfish, no doubt, disloyal, wrong, but I could realise nothing save that the golden barrier was gone from between us.

'Thank God!' I ejaculated from my very heart.

She looked at me with a quick, questioning smile.

'Why do you say that?' she asked.

'Because you are within my reach again,' I said, taking her hand. She did not withdraw it. 'Because I love you, Mary, as truly as ever a man loved a woman. Because this treasure, these riches, sealed my lips. Now that they are gone I can tell you how I love you. That is why I said, "Thank God."'

'Then I say "Thank God," too,' she whispered, as I drew her to my side.

Whoever had lost a treasure, I knew that night that I had gained one.

12
The Strange Story of Jonathan Small

A very patient man was that inspector in the cab, for it was a weary time before I rejoined him. His face clouded over when I showed him the empty box.

'There goes the reward!' said he, gloomily. 'Where there is no money there is no pay. This night's work would have been worth a tenner each to Sam Brown and me if the treasure had been there.'

'Mr Thaddeus Sholto is a rich man,' I said; 'he will see that you are rewarded, treasure or no.'

The inspector shook his head despondently, however. 'It's a bad job,' he repeated; 'and so Mr Athelney Jones will think.'

His forecast proved to be correct, for the detective looked blank enough when I got to Baker Street and showed him the empty box. They had only just arrived, Holmes, the prisoner, and he, for they had changed their plans so far as to report themselves at a station upon the way. My companion lounged in his armchair with his usual listless expression, while Small sat stolidly opposite to him with his wooden leg cocked over his sound one. As I exhibited the empty box he leaned back in his chair and laughed aloud.

'This is your doing, Small,' said Athelney Jones, angrily.

'Yes, I have put it away where you shall never lay hand on it,' he cried, exultantly. 'It is my treasure, and if I can't have the loot I'll take darned good care that no one else does. I tell you that no living man has any right to it, unless it is three men who are in the Andaman convict-barracks and myself. I know now that I cannot have the use of it, and I know that they cannot. I have acted all through for them as much as for myself. It's been the sign of the four with us always. Well, I know that they would have had me do just what I have done, and throw the treasure into the Thames rather than let it go to kith or kin of Sholto or Morstan. It was not to make them rich that we did for Achmet. You'll find the treasure where the key is, and where little Tonga is. When I saw that your launch must catch us, I put the loot away in a safe place. There are no rupees for you this journey.'

'You are deceiving us, Small,' said Athelney Jones, sternly. 'If you had wished to throw the treasure into the Thames, it would have been easier for you to have thrown box and all.'

'Easier for me to throw, and easier for you to recover,' he answered, with a shrewd, sidelong look. 'The man that was clever enough to hunt me down is clever enough to pick an iron box from the bottom of a river. Now that they are scattered over five miles or so, it may be a harder job. It went to my heart to do it, though. I was half mad when you came up with us. However, there's no good grieving over it. I've had ups in my life, and I've had downs, but I've learned not to cry over spilled milk.'

'This is a very serious matter, Small,' said the detective. 'If you had helped justice, instead of thwarting it in this way, you would have had a better chance at your trial.'

'Justice!' snarled the ex-convict. 'A pretty justice! Whose loot is this, if it is not ours? Where is the justice that I should give it up to those who have never earned it? Look how I have earned it! Twenty long years in that fever-ridden swamp, all day at work under the mangrove tree, all night chained up in the filthy convict-huts, bitten by mosquitoes, racked with ague, bullied by every cursed black-faced policeman who loved to take it out of a white man. That was how I earned the Agra treasure, and you talk to me of justice because I cannot bear to feel that I have paid this price only that another may enjoy it! I would rather swing a score of times, or have one of Tonga's darts in my hide, than live in a convict's cell and feel that another man is at his ease in a palace with the money that should be mine.'

Small had dropped his mask of stoicism, and all this came out in a wild whirl of words, while his eyes blazed and the handcuffs clanked together with the impassioned movement of his hands. I could understand, as I saw the fury and the passion of the man, that it was no groundless or unnatural terror which had possessed Major Sholto when he first learned that the injured convict was upon his track.

'You forget that we know nothing of all this,' said Holmes, quietly. 'We have not heard your story, and we cannot tell how far justice may originally have been on your side.'

'Well, sir, you have been very fair-spoken to me, though I can see that I have you to thank that I have these bracelets upon my wrists. Still, I bear no grudge for that. It is all fair and above-board. If you want to hear my story, I have no wish to hold it back. What I say to you is God's truth, every word of it. Thank you, you can put the glass beside me here, and I'll put my lips to it if I am dry.

'I am a Worcestershire man myself, born near Pershore. I dare say you would find a heap of Smalls living there now if you were to look. I have often thought of taking a look round there, but the truth is that I was never much of a credit to the family, and I doubt if they would be so very glad to see me. They were all steady, chapel-going folk, small farmers, well known and respected over the countryside, while I was always a bit of a rover. At last, however, when I was about eighteen, I gave them no more trouble, for I got into a mess over a girl, and could only get out of it again by taking the Queen's shilling and joining the 3rd Buffs, which was just starting for India.

'I wasn't destined to do much soldiering, however. I had just got past the goose-step, and learned to handle my musket, when I was fool enough to go swimming in the Ganges. Luckily for me, my company sergeant, John Holder, was in the water at the same time, and he was one of the finest swimmers in the service. A crocodile took me, just as I was halfway across, and nipped off my right leg as clean as a surgeon could have done it, just above the knee. What with the shock and the loss of blood, I fainted, and should have been drowned if Holder had not caught hold of me and paddled for the bank. I was five months in hospital over it, and when at last I was able to limp out of it with this timber toe strapped to my stump I found myself invalided out of the army and unfitted for any active occupation.

'I was, as you can imagine, pretty down on my luck at this time, for I was a useless cripple, though not yet in my twentieth year. However, my misfortune soon proved to be a blessing in disguise. A man named Abel White, who had come out there as an indigo-planter, wanted an overseer to look after his coolies and keep them up to their work. He happened to be a friend of our colonel's who had taken an interest in me since the accident. To make a long story short, the colonel recommended me strongly for the post, and, as the work was mostly to be done on horseback, my leg was no great obstacle, for I had enough knee left to keep a good grip on the saddle. What I had to do was to ride over the plantation, to keep an eye on the men as they worked and to report the idlers. The pay was fair, I had comfortable quarters and altogether I was content to spend the remainder of my life in indigo-planting. Mr Abel White was a kind man, and he would often drop into my little shanty and smoke a pipe with me, for white folk out there feel their hearts warm to each other as they never do here at home.

'Well, I was never in luck's way long. Suddenly, without a note of warning, the great mutiny broke upon us. One month India lay as still and peaceful, to all appearance, as Surrey or Kent; the next there were two hundred thousand black devils let loose, and the country was a perfect hell. Of course you know all about it, gentlemen – a deal more than I do, very like, since reading is not in my line. I only know what I saw with my own eyes. Our plantation was at a place called Muttra, near the border of the North West Provinces. Night after night the whole sky was alight with the burning bungalows, and day after day we had small companies of Europeans passing through our estate with their wives and children, on their way to Agra, where were the nearest troops. Mr Abel White was an obstinate man. He had it in his head that the affair had been exaggerated, and that it would blow over as suddenly as it had sprung up. There he sat on his verandah, drinking whisky-pegs and smoking cheroots, while the country was in a blaze about him. Of course, we stuck by him, I and Dawson, who, with his wife, used to do the bookwork and the managing.

Well, one fine day the crash came. I had been away on a distant plantation and was riding slowly home in the evening when my eye fell upon something all huddled together at the bottom of a steep nullah. I rode down to see what it was, and the cold struck through my heart when I found it was Dawson's wife, all cut into ribbons and half-eaten by jackals and native dogs. A little farther up the road Dawson himself was lying on his face, quite dead, with an empty revolver in his hand, and four sepoys lying across each other in front of him. I reined up my horse, wondering which way I should turn; but at that moment I saw thick smoke curling up from Abel White's bungalow, and the flames beginning to burst through the roof. I knew then that I could do my employer no good, but would only throw my own life away if I meddled in the matter. From where I stood I could see hundreds of the black fiends, with their red coats still on their backs, dancing and howling round the burning house. Some of them pointed at me, and a couple of bullets sang past my head: so I broke away across the paddy-fields, and found myself late at night safe within the walls at Agra.

'As it proved, however, there was no great safety here either. The whole country was up like a swarm of bees. Wherever the English could collect in little bands, they held just the ground that their guns commanded. Everywhere else they were helpless fugitives. It was a fight of the millions against the hundreds; and the cruellest part of it was that these men that we fought against, foot, horse and gunners, were our own picked troops, whom we had taught and trained, handling our own weapons and blowing our own bugle-calls. At Agra there were the 3rd Bengal Fusiliers, some Sikhs, two troops of horse and a battery of artillery. A volunteer corps of clerks and merchants had been formed, and this I joined, wooden leg and all. We went out to meet the rebels at Shahgunge early in July, and we beat them back for a time, but our powder gave out and we had to fall back upon the city.

'Nothing but the worst news came to us from every side – which is not to be wondered at, for if you look at the map you will see that we were right in the heart of it. Lucknow is rather better than a hundred miles to the east, and Cawnpore about as far to the south. From every point on the compass there was nothing but torture and murder and outrage.

'The city of Agra is a great place, swarming with fanatics and fierce devil-worshippers of all sorts. Our handful of men were lost among the narrow, winding streets. Our leader moved across the river, therefore, and took up his position in the old fort of Agra. I don't know if any of you gentlemen have ever read or heard anything of that old fort. It is a very queer place – the queerest that ever I was in, and I have been in some rum corners, too. First of all, it is enormous in size. I should think that the enclosure must be acres and acres. There is a modern part, which took all our garrison, women, children, stores and everything else, with plenty of room over. But the modern part is nothing like the size of the old quarter, where nobody goes, and which is given over to the scorpions and the centipedes. It is all full of great, deserted halls, and winding passages, and long corridors twisting in and out, so that it is easy enough for folk to get lost in it. For this reason it was seldom that anyone went into it, though now and again a party with torches might go exploring.

'The river washes along the front of the old fort, and so protects it, but on the sides and behind there are many doors, and these had to be guarded, of course, in the old quarter as well as in that which was actually held by our troops. We were short-handed, with hardly men enough to man the angles of the building and to serve the guns. It was impossible for us, therefore, to station a strong guard at every one of the innumerable gates. What we did was to organise a central guardhouse in the middle of the fort, and to leave each gate under the charge of one white man and two or three natives. I was selected to take charge during certain hours of the night of a small isolated door upon the south-west side of the building. Two Sikh troopers were placed under my command, and I was instructed if anything went wrong to fire my musket, when I might rely upon help coming at once from the central guard. As the guard was a good two hundred paces away, however, and as the space between was cut up into a labyrinth of passages and corridors, I had great doubts as to whether they could arrive in time to be of any use in case of an actual attack.

'Well, I was pretty proud at having this small command given me, since I was a raw recruit and a game-legged one at that. For two nights I kept the watch with my Punjabis. They were tall, fierce-looking chaps, Mahomet Singh and Abdullah Khan by name, both old fighting-men who had borne arms against us at Chilian Wallah. They could talk English pretty well, but I could get little out of them. They preferred to stand together and jabber all night in their queer Sikh lingo. For myself, I used to stand outside the gateway looking down on the broad, winding river and on the twinkling lights of the great city. The beating of drums, the rattle of tom-toms and the yells and howls of the rebels, drunk with opium and with bhang, were enough to remind us all night of our dangerous neighbours across the stream. Every two hours the officer of the night used to come round to all the posts, to make sure that all was well.

'The third night of my watch was dark and dirty, with a small, driving rain. It was dreary work standing in the gateway hour after hour in such weather. I tried again and again to make my Sikhs talk, but without much success. At two in the morning the rounds passed, and broke for a moment the weariness of the night. Finding that my companions would not be led into conversation, I took out my pipe and laid down my musket to strike a match. In an instant the two Sikhs were upon me. One of them snatched my firelock up and levelled it at my head, while the other held a great knife to my throat and swore between his teeth that he would plunge it into me if I moved a step.

'My first thought was that these fellows were in league with the rebels, and that this was the beginning of an assault. If our door were in the hands of the sepoys the place must fall, and the women and children be treated as they were in Cawnpore. Maybe you gentlemen think that I am just making out a case for myself, but I give you my word that when I thought of that, though I felt the point of the knife at my throat, I opened my mouth with the intention of giving a scream, if it was my last one, which might alarm the main guard. The man who held me seemed to know my thoughts for, even as I braced myself to it, he whispered: "Don't make a noise. The fort is safe enough. There are no rebel dogs on this side of the river." There was the ring of truth in what he said, and I knew that if I raised my voice I was a dead man. I could read it in the fellow's brown eyes. I waited, therefore, in silence, to see what it was that they wanted from me.

'"Listen to me, sahib," said the taller and fiercer of the pair, the one whom they called Abdullah Khan. "You must either be with us now, or you must be silenced for ever. The thing is too great a one for us to hesitate. Either you are heart and soul with us on your oath on the cross of the Christians, or your body this night shall be thrown into the ditch, and we shall pass over to our brothers in the rebel army. There is no middle way. Which is it to be – death or life? We can only give you three minutes to decide, for the time is passing, and all must be done before the rounds come again."

'"How can I decide?" said I. "You have not told me what you want of me. But I tell you now that if it is anything against the safety of the fort I will have no truck with it, so you can drive home your knife, and welcome."

'"It is nothing against the fort," said he. "We only ask you to do that which your countrymen come to this land for. We ask you to be rich. If you will be one of us this night, we will swear to you upon the naked knife, and by the threefold oath which no Sikh was ever known to break, that you shall have your fair share of the loot. A quarter of the treasure shall be yours. We can say no fairer."

' "But what is the treasure, then?" I asked. "I am as ready to be rich as you can be, if you will but show me how it can be done."

' "You will swear, then," said he, "by the bones of your father, by the honour of your mother, by the cross of your faith, to raise no hand and speak no word against us, either now or afterwards?"

' "I will swear it," I answered, "provided that the fort is not endangered."

' "Then, my comrade and I will swear that you shall have a quarter of the treasure, which shall be equally divided among the four of us."

' "There are but three," said I.

' "No; Dost Akbar must have his share. We can tell the tale to you while we await them. Do you stand at the gate, Mahomet Singh, and give notice of their coming. The thing stands thus, sahib, and I tell it to you because I know that an oath is binding upon a Feringhee, and that we may trust you. Had you been a lying Hindu, though you had sworn by all the gods in their false temples, your blood would have been upon the knife and your body in the water. But the Sikh knows the Englishman, and the Englishman knows the Sikh. Hearken, then, to what I have to say.

' "There is a rajah in the northern provinces who has much wealth, though his lands are small. Much has come to him from his father, and more still he has set by himself, for he is of a low nature, and hoards his gold rather than spend it. When the troubles broke out he would be friends both with the lion and the tiger – with the sepoy and with the Company's Raj. Soon, however, it seemed to him that the white men's day was come, for through all the land he could hear of nothing but of their death and their overthrow. Yet, being a careful man, he made such plans that, come what might, half at least of his treasure should be left to him. That which was in gold and silver he kept by him in the vaults of his palace; but the most precious stones and the choicest pearls that he had he put in an iron box and sent it by a trusty servant, who, under the guise of a merchant, should take it to the fort at Agra, there to lie until the land is at peace. Thus, if the rebels won he would have his money; but if the Company conquered, his jewels would be saved to him. Having thus divided his hoard, he threw himself into the cause of the sepoys, since they were strong upon his borders. By his doing this, mark you, sahib, his property becomes the due of those who have been true to their salt.

' "This pretended merchant, who travels under the name of Achmet, is now in the city of Agra, and desires to gain his way into the fort. He has with him as travelling-companion my foster-brother, Dost Akbar, who knows his secret. Dost Akbar has promised this night to lead him to a side-postern of the fort, and has chosen this one for his purpose. Here he will come presently and here he will find Mahomet Singh and myself awaiting him. The place is lonely, and none shall know of his coming. The world shall know of the merchant, Achmet, no more, but the great treasure of the rajah shall be divided among us. What say you to it, sahib?"

'In Worcestershire the life of a man seems a great and sacred thing; but it is very different when there is fire and blood all round you, and you have been used to meeting death at every turn. Whether Achmet the merchant lived or died was a thing as light as air to me, but at the talk about the treasure my heart turned to it, and I thought of what I might do in the old country with it, and how my folk would stare when they saw their ne'er-do-well coming back with his pockets full of gold moidores. I had, therefore, already made up my mind. Abdullah Khan, however, thinking that I hesitated, pressed the matter more closely.

' "Consider, sahib," said he, "that if this man is taken by the commandant he will be hung or shot, and his jewels taken by the government, so that no man will be a rupee the better for them. Now, since we do the taking of him, why should we not do the rest as well? The jewels will be as well with us as in the Company's coffers. There will be enough to make every one of us rich men and great chiefs. No one can know about the matter, for here we are cut off from all men. What could be better for the purpose? Say again, then, sahib, whether you are with us, or if we must look upon you as an enemy."

' "I am with you heart and soul," said I.

' "It is well," he answered, handing me back my firelock. "You see that we trust you, for your word, like ours, is not to be broken. We have now only to wait for my brother and the merchant."

' "Does your brother know, then, of what you will do?" I asked.

' "The plan is his. He has devised it. We will go to the gate and share the watch with Mahomet Singh."

'The rain was still falling steadily, for it was just the beginning of the wet season. Brown, heavy clouds were drifting across the sky, and it was hard to see more than a stone-cast. A deep moat lay in front of our door, but the water was in places nearly dried up, and it could easily be crossed. It was strange to me to be standing there with those two wild Punjabis waiting for the man who was coming to his death.

'Suddenly my eye caught the glint of a shaded lantern at the other side of the moat. It vanished among the mound-heaps, and then appeared again coming slowly in our direction.

' "Here they are!" I exclaimed.

' "You will challenge him, sahib, as usual," whispered Abdullah. "Give him no cause for fear. Send us in with him, and we shall do the rest while you stay here on guard. Have the lantern ready to uncover, that we may be sure that it is indeed the man."

'The light had flickered onwards, now stopping and now advancing, until I could see two dark figures upon the other side of the moat. I let them scramble down the sloping bank, splash through the mire, and climb halfway up to the gate, before I challenged them.

' "Who goes there?" said I, in a subdued voice.

' "Friends," came the answer. I uncovered my lantern and threw a flood of light upon them. The first was an enormous Sikh, with a black beard which swept nearly down to his cummerbund. Outside of a show I have never seen so tall a man. The other was a little, fat, round fellow, with a great yellow turban, and a bundle in his hand, done up in a shawl. He seemed to be all in a quiver with fear, for his hands twitched as if he had the ague, and his head kept turning to left and right with two bright little twinkling eyes, like a mouse when he ventures out from his hole. It gave me the chills to think of killing him, but I thought of the treasure, and my heart set as hard as a flint within me. When he saw my white face he gave a little chirrup of joy, and came running up towards me.

' "Your protection, sahib," he panted; "your protection for the unhappy merchant Achmet. I have travelled across Rajputana that I might seek the shelter of the fort at Agra. I have been robbed and beaten and abused because I have been the friend of the Company. It is a blessed night this when I am once more in safety – I and my poor possessions."

' "What have you in the bundle?" I asked.

' "An iron box," he answered, "which contains one or two little family matters which are of no value to others, but which I should be sorry to lose. Yet I am not a beggar; and I shall reward you, young sahib, and your governor also, if he will give me the shelter I ask."

'I could not trust myself to speak longer with the man. The more I looked at his fat, frightened face, the harder did it seem that we should slay him in cold blood. It was best to get it over.

' "Take him to the main guard," said I. The two Sikhs closed in upon him on each side, and the giant walked behind while they marched in through the dark gateway. Never was a man so compassed round with death. I remained at the gateway with the lantern.

'I could hear the measured tramp of their footsteps sounding through the lonely corridors. Suddenly it ceased, and I heard voices and a scuffle, with the sound of blows. A moment later there came, to my horror, a rush of footsteps coming in my direction, with the loud breathing of a running man. I turned my lantern down the long, straight passage, and there was the fat man, running like the wind, with a smear of blood across his face, and close at his heels, bounding like a tiger, the great, black-bearded Sikh, with a knife flashing in his hand. I have never seen a man run so fast as that little merchant. He was gaining on the Sikh, and I could see that if he once passed me and got to the open air he would save himself yet. My heart softened to him, but again the thought of his treasure turned me hard and bitter. I cast my firelock between his legs as he raced past, and he rolled twice over like a shot rabbit. Ere he could stagger to his feet the Sikh was upon him, and buried his knife twice in his side. The man never uttered moan nor moved muscle, but lay where he had fallen. I think myself that he may have broken his neck with the fall. You see, gentlemen, that I am keeping my promise. I am telling you every word of the business just exactly as it happened, whether it is in my favour or not.'

He stopped, and held out his manacled hands for the whisky and water which Holmes had brewed for him. For myself I confess that I had now conceived the utmost horror of the man, not only for this cold-blooded business in which he had been concerned but even more for the somewhat flippant and careless way in which he narrated it. Whatever punishment was in store for him, I felt that he might expect no sympathy from me. Sherlock Holmes and Jones sat with their hands upon their knees, deeply interested in the story, but with the same disgust written upon their faces. He may have observed it, for there was a touch of defiance in his voice and manner as he proceeded.

'It was all very bad, no doubt,' said he. 'I should like to know how many fellows in my shoes would have refused a share of this loot when they knew that they would have their throats cut for their pains. Besides, it was my life or his when once he was in the fort. If he had got out, the whole business would come to light, and I should have been court-martialled and shot as likely as not; for people were not very lenient at a time like that.'

'Go on with your story,' said Holmes, shortly.

'Well, we carried him in, Abdullah, Akbar and I. A fine weight he was, too, for all that he was so short. Mahomet Singh was left to guard the door. We took him to a place which the Sikhs had already prepared. It was some distance off, where a winding passage leads to a great empty hall, the brick walls of which were all crumbling to pieces. The earth floor had sunk in at one place, making a natural grave, so we left Achmet the merchant there, having first covered him over with loose bricks. This done, we all went back to the treasure.

'It lay where he had dropped it when he was first attacked. The box was the same which now lies open upon your table. A key was hung by a silken cord to that carved handle upon the top. We opened it, and the light of the lantern gleamed upon a collection of gems such as I read of and thought about when I was a little lad at Pershore. It was blinding to look upon them. When we had feasted our eyes we took them all out and made a list of them. There were one hundred and forty-three diamonds of the first water, including one which has been called, I believe, "the Great Mogul", and is said to be the second largest stone in existence. Then there were ninety-seven very fine emeralds, and one hundred and seventy rubies, some of which, however, were small. There were forty carbuncles, two hundred and ten sapphires, sixty-one agates and a great quantity of beryls, onyxes, cat's-eyes, turquoises and other stones, the very names of which I did not know at the time though I have become more familiar with them since. Besides this, there were nearly three hundred very fine pearls, twelve of which were set in a gold coronet. By the way, these last had been taken out of the chest, and were not there when I recovered it.

'After we had counted our treasures we put them back into the chest and carried them to the gateway to show them to Mahomet Singh. Then we solemnly renewed our oath to stand by each other and be true to our secret. We agreed to conceal our loot in a safe place until the country should be at peace again, and then to divide it equally among ourselves. There was no use dividing it at present, for if gems of such value were found upon us it would cause suspicion, and there was no privacy in the fort nor any place where we could keep them. We carried the box, therefore, into the same hall where we had buried the body, and there, under certain bricks in the best-preserved wall, we made a hollow and put our treasure. We made careful note of the place, and next day I drew four plans, one for each of us, and put the sign of the four of us at the bottom, for we had sworn that we should each always act for all, so that none might take advantage. That is an oath that I can put my hand to my heart and swear that I have never broken.

'Well, there's no use my telling you gentlemen what came of the Indian Mutiny. After Wilson took Delhi and Sir Colin relieved Lucknow the back of the business was broken. Fresh troops came pouring in, and Nana Sahib made himself scarce over the frontier. A flying column under Colonel Greathed came round to Agra and cleared the Pandies away from it. Peace seemed to be settling upon the country, and we four were beginning to hope that the time was at hand when we might safely go off with our share of the plunder. In a moment, however, our hopes were shattered by our being arrested as the murderers of Achmet.

'It came about in this way. When the rajah put his jewels into the hands of Achmet, he did it because he knew that he was a trusty man. They are suspicious folk in the East, however; so what does this rajah do but take a second even more trusty servant and set him to play the spy upon the first? The second man was ordered never to let Achmet out of his sight, and he followed him like his shadow. He went after him that night and saw him pass through the doorway. Of course, he thought he had taken refuge in the fort, and applied for admission there himself next day, but could find no trace of Achmet. This seemed to him so strange that he spoke about it to a sergeant of guides, who brought it to the ears of the commandant. A thorough search was quickly made and the body was discovered. Thus at the very moment that we thought that all was safe we were all four seized and brought to trial on a charge of murder – three of us because we had held the gate that night, and the fourth because he was known to have been in the company of the murdered man. Not a word about the jewels came out at the trial, for the rajah had been deposed and driven out of India; so no one had any particular interest in them. The murder, however, was clearly made out, and it was certain that we must all have been concerned in it. The three Sikhs got penal servitude for life, and I was condemned to death, though my sentence was afterwards commuted into the same as the others.

'It was rather a queer position that we found ourselves in then. There we were all four tied by the leg and with precious little chance of ever getting out again, while we each held a secret which might have put each of us in a palace if we could only have made use of it. It was enough to make a man eat his heart out to have to stand the kick and the cuff of every petty jack-in-office, to have rice to eat and water to drink, when that gorgeous fortune was ready for him outside, just waiting to be picked up. It might have driven me mad; but I was always a pretty stubborn one, so I just held on and bided my time.

'At last it seemed to me to have come. I was changed from Agra to Madras, and from there to Blair Island in the Andamans. There are very few white convicts at this settlement and, as I had behaved well from the first, I soon found myself a sort of privileged person. I was given a hut in Hope Town, which is a small place on the slopes of Mount Harriet, and I was left pretty much to myself. It is a dreary, fever-stricken place, and all beyond our little clearings was infested with wild cannibal natives, who were ready enough to blow a poisoned dart at us if they saw a chance.

There was digging and ditching and yam-planting, and a dozen other things to be done, so we were busy enough all day; though in the evening we had a little time to ourselves. Among other things I learned to dispense drugs for the surgeon, and picked up a smattering of his knowledge. All the time I was on the lookout for a chance of escape; but it is hundreds of miles from any other land, and there is little or no wind in those seas: so it was a terribly difficult job to get away.

'The surgeon, Dr Somerton, was a fast, sporting young chap, and the other young officers would meet in his rooms of an evening and play cards. The surgery, where I used to make up my drugs, was next to his sitting-room, with a small window between us. Often, if I felt lonesome, I used to turn out the lamp in the surgery, and then, standing there, I could hear their talk and watch their play. I am fond of a hand at cards myself, and it was almost as good as having one to watch the others. There was Major Sholto, Captain Morstan and Lieutenant Bromley Brown, who were in command of the native troops, and there was the surgeon himself, and two or three prison-officials, crafty old hands who played a nice, sly, safe game. A very snug little party they used to make.

'Well, there was one thing which very soon struck me, and that was that the soldiers used always to lose and the civilians to win. Mind, I don't say there was anything unfair, but so it was. These prison-chaps had done little else than play cards ever since they had been at the Andamans, and they knew each other's game to a point, while the others just played to pass the time and threw their cards down anyhow. Night after night the soldiers got up poorer men, and the poorer they got the more keen they were to play. Major Sholto was the hardest hit. He used to pay in notes and gold at first, but soon it came to notes of hand and for big sums. He sometimes would win for a few deals, just to give him heart, and then the luck would set in against him worse than ever. All day he would wander about as black as thunder, and he took to drinking a deal more than was good for him.

'One night he lost even more heavily than usual. I was sitting in my hut when he and Captain Morstan came stumbling along on the way to their quarters. They were bosom friends, those two, and never far apart. The major was raving about his losses.

' "It's all up, Morstan," he was saying, as they passed my hut. "I shall have to send in my papers. I am a ruined man."

' "Nonsense, old chap!" said the other, slapping him upon the shoulder. "I've had a nasty facer myself, but – " That was all I could hear, but it was enough to set me thinking.

'A couple of days later Major Sholto was strolling on the beach: so I took the chance of speaking to him.

'"I wish to have your advice, major," said I.

'"Well, Small, what is it?" he asked, taking his cheroot from his lips.

'"I wanted to ask you, sir," said I, "who is the proper person to whom hidden treasure should be handed over. I know where half a million's worth lies, and, as I cannot use it myself, I thought perhaps the best thing that I could do would be to hand it over to the proper authorities, and then perhaps they would get my sentence shortened for me."

'"Half a million, Small?" he gasped, looking hard at me to see if I was in earnest.

'"Quite that, sir – in jewels and pearls. It lies there ready for anyone. And the queer thing about it is that the real owner is outlawed and cannot hold property, so that it belongs to the first comer."

'"To government, Small," he stammered, "to government." But he said it in a halting fashion, and I knew in my heart that I had got him.

'"You think, then, sir, that I should give the information to the governor-general?" said I, quietly.

'"Well, well, you must not do anything rash, or that you might repent. Let me hear all about it, Small. Give me the facts."

'I told him the whole story, with small changes, so that he could not identify the places. When I had finished he stood stock-still and full of thought. I could see by the twitch of his lip that there was a struggle going on within him.

'"This is a very important matter, Small," he said at last. "You must not say a word to anyone about it, and I shall see you again soon."

'Two nights later he and his friend, Captain Morstan, came to my hut in the dead of the night with a lantern.

'"I want you just to let Captain Morstan hear that story from your own lips, Small," said he.

'I repeated it as I had told it before.

'"It rings true, eh?" said he. "It's good enough to act upon?"

'Captain Morstan nodded.

'"Look here, Small," said the major. "We have been talking it over, my friend here and I, and we have come to the conclusion that this secret of yours is hardly a government matter, after all, but is a private concern of your own, which, of course, you have the power of disposing of as you think best. Now the question is: What price would you ask for it? We might be inclined to take it up, and at least look into it, if we could agree as to terms." He tried to speak in a cool, careless way, but his eyes were shining with excitement and greed.

' "Why, as to that, gentlemen," I answered, trying also to be cool, but feeling as excited as he did, "there is only one bargain which a man in my position can make. I shall want you to help me to my freedom, and to help my three companions to theirs. We shall then take you into partnership, and give you a fifth share to divide between you."

' "Hum!" said he. "A fifth share! That is not very tempting."

' "It would come to fifty thousand apiece," said I.

' "But how can we gain your freedom? You know very well that you ask an impossibility."

' "Nothing of the sort," I answered. "I have thought it all out to the last detail. The only bar to our escape is that we can get no boat fit for the voyage, and no provisions to last us for so long a time. There are plenty of little yachts and yawls at Calcutta or Madras which would serve our turn well. Do you bring one over. We shall engage to get aboard her by night, and if you will drop us on any part of the Indian coast you will have done your part of the bargain."

' "If there were only one," he said.

' "None or all," I answered. "We have sworn it. The four of us must always act together."

' "You see, Morstan," said he, "Small is a man of his word. He does not flinch from his friends. I think we may very well trust him."

' "It's a dirty business," the other answered. "Yet, as you say, the money will save our commissions handsomely."

' "Well, Small," said the major, "we must, I suppose, try and meet you. We must first, of course, test the truth of your story. Tell me where the box is hid, and I shall get leave of absence and go back to India in the monthly relief-boat to enquire into the affair."

' "Not so fast," said I, growing colder as he got hot. "I must have the consent of my three comrades. I tell you that it is four or none with us."

' "Nonsense!" he broke in. "What have three black fellows to do with our agreement?"

' "Black or blue," said I, "they are in with me, and we all go together."

'Well, the matter ended by a second meeting, at which Mahomet Singh, Abdullah Khan and Dost Akbar were all present. We talked the matter over again, and at last we came to an arrangement. We were to provide both the officers with charts of the part of the Agra fort, and mark the place in the wall where the treasure was hid. Major Sholto was to go to India to test our story. If he found the box he was to leave it there, to send out a small yacht provisioned for a voyage, which was to lie off Rutland

Island and to which we were to make our way, and finally to return to his duties. Captain Morstan was then to apply for leave of absence, to meet us at Agra, and there we were to have a final division of the treasure, he taking the major's share as well as his own. All this we sealed by the most solemn oaths that the mind could think or the lips utter. I sat up all night with paper and ink, and by the morning I had the two charts all ready, signed with the sign of the four – that is, of Abdullah, Akbar, Mahomet and myself.

'Well, gentlemen, I weary you with my long story, and I know that my friend Mr Jones is impatient to get me safely stowed in chokey. I'll make it as short as I can. The villain Sholto went off to India, but he never came back again. Captain Morstan showed me his name among a list of passengers in one of the mail-boats very shortly afterwards. His uncle had died, leaving him a fortune, and he had left the army; yet he could stoop to treat five men as he had treated us. Morstan went over to Agra shortly afterwards, and found, as we expected, that the treasure was indeed gone. The scoundrel had stolen it all, without carrying out one of the conditions on which we had sold him the secret. From that day I lived only for vengeance. I thought of it by day and I nursed it by night. It became an overpowering, absorbing passion with me. I cared nothing for the law – nothing for the gallows. To escape, to track down Sholto, to have my hand upon his throat – that was my one thought. Even the Agra treasure had come to be a smaller thing in my mind than the slaying of Sholto.

'Well, I have set my mind on many things in this life, and never one which I did not carry out. But it was weary years before my time came. I have told you that I had picked up something of medicine. One day when Dr Somerton was down with a fever a little Andaman Islander was picked up by a convict-gang in the woods. He was sick to death, and had gone to a lonely place to die. I took him in hand, though he was as venomous as a young snake, and after a couple of months I got him all right and able to walk. He took a kind of fancy to me then, and would hardly go back to his woods but was always hanging about my hut. I learned a little of his lingo from him, and this made him all the fonder of me.

'Tonga – for that was his name – was a fine boatman, and owned a big, roomy canoe of his own. When I found that he was devoted to me and would do anything to serve me, I saw my chance of escape. I talked it over with him. He was to bring his boat round on a certain night to an old wharf which was never guarded, and there he was to pick me up. I gave him directions to have several gourds of water and a lot of yams, coconuts and sweet potatoes.

223

'He was staunch and true, was little Tonga. No man ever had a more faithful mate. On the night named he had his boat at the wharf. As it chanced, however, there was one of the convict-guard down there – a vile Pathan who had never missed a chance of insulting and injuring me. I had always vowed vengeance, and now I had my chance. It was as if fate had placed him in my way that I might pay my debt before I left the island. He stood on the bank with his back to me and his carbine on his shoulder. I looked about for a stone to beat out his brains with, but none could I see.

'Then a queer thought came into my head, and showed me where I could lay my hand on a weapon. I sat down in the darkness and unstrapped my wooden leg. With three long hops I was on him. He put his carbine to his shoulder, but I struck him full, and knocked the whole front of his skull in. You can see the split in the wood now where I hit him. We both went down together, for I could not keep my balance; but when I got up I found him lying quiet enough. I made for the boat, and in an hour we were well out at sea. Tonga had brought all his earthly possessions with him, his arms and his gods. Among other things, he had a long bamboo spear and some Andaman coconut-matting, with which I made a sort of a sail. For ten days we were beating about, trusting to luck, and on the eleventh we were picked up by a trader which was going from Singapore to Jeddah with a cargo of Malay pilgrims. They were a rum crowd, and Tonga and I soon managed to settle down among them. They had one very good quality: they let you alone and asked no questions.

'Well, if I were to tell you all the adventures that my little chum and I went through, you would not thank me, for I would have you here until the sun was shining. Here and there we drifted about the world, something always turning up to keep us from London. All the time, however, I never lost sight of my purpose. I would dream of Sholto at night. A hundred times I have killed him in my sleep. At last, however, some three or four years ago, we found ourselves in England. I had no great difficulty in finding where Sholto lived, and I set to work to discover whether he had realised the treasure, or if he still had it. I made friends with someone who could help me – I name no names, for I don't want to get anyone else in a hole – and I soon found that he still had the jewels. Then I tried to get at him in many ways; but he was pretty sly, and had always two prizefighters, besides his sons and his khitmutgar, on guard over him.

'One day, however, I got word that he was dying. I hurried at once to the garden, mad that he should slip out of my clutches like that, and, looking through the window, I saw him lying in his bed, with his sons on each side of him. I'd have come through and taken my chance with the three of them, only even as I looked at him his jaw dropped and I knew that he was gone. I got into his room the same night, though, and I searched his papers to see if there was any record of where he had hidden our jewels. There was not a line, however, so I came away, bitter and savage as a man could be. Before I left I bethought me that if I ever met my Sikh friends again it would be a satisfaction to know that I had left some mark of our hatred; so I scrawled down the sign of the four of us, as it had been on the chart, and I pinned it on his bosom. It was too much that he should be taken to the grave without some token from the men whom he had robbed and befooled.

'We earned a living at this time by my exhibiting poor Tonga at fairs and other such places as the black cannibal. He would eat raw meat and dance his war-dance, so we always had a hatful of pennies after a day's work. I still heard all the news from Pondicherry Lodge, and for some years there was no news to hear, except that they were hunting for the treasure. At last, however, came what we had waited for so long. The treasure had been found. It was up at the top of the house, in Mr Bartholomew Sholto's chemical laboratory. I came at once and had a look at the place, but I could not see how, with my wooden leg, I was to make my way up to it. I learned, however, about a trap-door in the roof, and also about Mr Sholto's supper-hour. It seemed to me that I could manage the thing easily through Tonga. I brought him out with me with a long rope wound round his waist. He could climb like a cat, and he soon made his way through the roof, but, as ill-luck would have it, Bartholomew Sholto was still in the room, to his cost. Tonga thought he had done something very clever in killing him, for when I came up by the rope I found him strutting about as proud as a peacock. Very much surprised was he when I made at him with the rope's end and cursed him for a little bloodthirsty imp. I took the treasure box and let it down, and then slid down myself, having first left the sign of the four upon the table, to show that the jewels had come back at last to those who had most right to them. Tonga then pulled up the rope, closed the window and made off the way that he had come.

'I don't know that I have anything else to tell you. I had heard a waterman speak of the speed of Smith's launch, the *Aurora*, so I thought she would be a handy craft for our escape. I engaged with old Smith, and was to give him a big sum if he got us safe to our ship. He knew, no doubt, that there was some screw loose, but he was not in our secrets. All this is the truth, and if I tell it to you gentlemen, it is not to amuse you – for you have not done me a very good turn – but it is because I believe the best defence I can make is just to hold back nothing, but let all the world know how badly I have myself been served by Major Sholto, and how innocent I am of the death of his son.'

'A very remarkable account,' said Sherlock Holmes. 'A fitting wind-up to an extremely interesting case. There is nothing at all new to me in the latter part of your narrative except that you brought your own rope. That I did not know. By the way, I had hoped that Tonga had lost all his darts; yet he managed to shoot one at us in the boat.'

'He had lost them all, sir, except the one which was in his blow-pipe at the time.'

'Ah, of course,' said Holmes. 'I had not thought of that.'

'Is there any other point which you would like to ask about?' asked the convict, affably.

'I think not, thank you,' my companion answered.

'Well, Holmes,' said Athelney Jones, 'you are a man to be humoured, and we all know that you are a connoisseur of crime; but duty is duty, and I have gone rather far in doing what you and your friend asked me. I shall feel more at ease when we have our storyteller here safe under lock and key. The cab still waits, and there are two inspectors downstairs. I am much obliged to you both for your assistance. Of course, you will be wanted at the trial. Good-night to you.'

'Good-night, gentlemen both,' said Jonathan Small.

'You first, Small,' remarked the wary Jones as they left the room. 'I'll take particular care that you don't club me with your wooden leg, whatever you may have done to the gentleman at the Andaman Isles.'

'Well, and there is the end of our little drama,' I remarked, after we had sat some time smoking in silence. 'I fear that it may be the last investigation in which I shall have the chance of studying your methods. Miss Morstan has done me the honour to accept me as a husband in prospective.'

Holmes gave a most dismal groan. 'I feared as much,' said he. 'I really cannot congratulate you.'

I was a little hurt. 'Have you any reason to be dissatisfied with my choice?' I asked.

'Not at all. I think she is one of the most charming young ladies I ever met, and might have been most useful in such work as we have been doing. She had a decided genius that way; witness the way in which she preserved that Agra plan from all the other papers of her father. But love is an emotional thing, and whatever is emotional is opposed to that true, cold reason which I place above all things. I should never marry myself, lest I bias my judgement.'

'I trust,' said I, laughing, 'that my judgement may survive the ordeal. But you look weary.'

'Yes, the reaction is already upon me. I shall be as limp as a rag for a week.'

'Strange,' said I, 'how terms of what in another man I should call laziness alternate with your fits of splendid energy and vigour.'

'Yes,' he answered, 'there are in me the makings of a very fine loafer, and also of a pretty spry sort of a fellow. I often think of those lines of old Goethe:

Schade dass die Natur nur einen Mensch aus dir schuf, Denn zum würdigen Mann war und zum Schelmen der Stoff.

'By the way, apropos of this Norwood business, you see that they had, as I surmised, a confederate in the house, who could be none other than Lal Rao, the butler: so Jones actually has the undivided honour of having caught one fish in his great haul.'

'The division seems rather unfair,' I remarked. 'You have done all the work in this business. I get a wife out of it, Jones gets the credit; pray what remains for you?'

'For me,' said Sherlock Holmes, 'there still remains the cocaine bottle.' And he stretched his long, white hand up for it.

A Scandal in Bohemia

I

To Sherlock Holmes she is always *the* woman. I have seldom heard him mention her under any other name. In his eyes she eclipses and predominates the whole of her sex. It was not that he felt any emotion akin to love for Irene Adler. All emotions, and that one particularly, were abhorrent to his cold, precise but admirably balanced mind. He was, I take it, the most perfect reasoning and observing machine that the world has seen, but as a lover he would have placed himself in a false position. He never spoke of the softer passions, save with a gibe and a sneer. They were admirable things for the observer – excellent for drawing the veil from men's motives and actions. But for the trained reasoner to admit such intrusions into his own delicate and finely adjusted temperament was to introduce a distracting factor which might throw a doubt upon all his mental results. Grit in a sensitive instrument, or a crack in one of his own high-power lenses, would not be more disturbing than a strong emotion in a nature such as his. And yet there was but one woman to him, and that woman was the late Irene Adler, of dubious and questionable memory.

I had seen little of Holmes lately. My marriage had drifted us away from each other. My own complete happiness, and the home-centred interests which rise up around the man who first finds himself master of his own establishment, were sufficient to absorb all my attention, while Holmes, who loathed every form of society with his whole Bohemian soul, remained in our lodgings in Baker Street, buried among his old books, and alternating from week to week between cocaine and ambition, the drowsiness of the drug and the fierce energy of his own keen nature. He was still, as ever, deeply attracted by the study of crime, and occupied his immense faculties and extraordinary powers of observation in following out those clues and clearing up those mysteries which had been abandoned as hopeless by the official police. From time to time I heard some vague account of his doings: of his summons to Odessa in the case of the Trepoff murder, of his clearing up of the singular tragedy of the Atkinson brothers at Trincomalee and, finally, of the mission which he had accomplished so delicately and successfully for the reigning family of Holland.

Beyond these signs of his activity, however, which I merely shared with all the readers of the daily press, I knew little of my former friend and companion.

One night – it was on the twentieth of March 1888 – I was returning from a journey to a patient (for I had now returned to civil practice), when my way led me through Baker Street. As I passed the well-remembered door, which must always be associated in my mind with my wooing, and with the dark incidents of the Study in Scarlet, I was seized with a keen desire to see Holmes again, and to know how he was employing his extraordinary powers. His rooms were brilliantly lit and, even as I looked up, I saw his tall, spare figure pass twice in dark silhouette against the blind. He was pacing the room swiftly, eagerly, with his head sunk upon his chest and his hands clasped behind him. To me, who knew his every mood and habit, his attitude and manner told their own story. He was at work again. He had risen out of his drug-created dreams and was hot upon the scent of some new problem. I rang the bell and was shown up to the chamber which had formerly been in part my own.

His manner was not effusive. It seldom was; but he was glad, I think, to see me. With hardly a word spoken, but with a kindly eye, he waved me to an armchair, threw across his case of cigars, and indicated a spirit case and a gasogene in the corner. Then he stood before the fire and looked me over in his singular introspective fashion.

'Wedlock suits you,' he remarked. 'I think, Watson, that you have put on seven and a half pounds since I saw you.'

'Seven!' I answered.

'Indeed, I should have thought a little more. Just a trifle more, I fancy, Watson. And in practice again, I observe. You did not tell me that you intended to go into harness.'

'Then, how do you know?'

'I see it, I deduce it. How do I know that you have been getting yourself very wet lately, and that you have a most clumsy and careless servant girl?'

'My dear Holmes,' said I, 'this is too much. You would certainly have been burned had you lived a few centuries ago. It is true that I had a country walk on Thursday and came home in a dreadful mess, but as I have changed my clothes I can't imagine how you deduce it. As to Mary Jane, she is incorrigible, and my wife has given her notice, but there, again, I fail to see how you work it out.'

He chuckled to himself and rubbed his long, nervous hands together.

'It is simplicity itself,' said he; 'my eyes tell me that on the inside of your left shoe, just where the firelight strikes it, the leather is scored by six almost parallel cuts. Obviously they have been caused by someone who has very carelessly scraped round the edges of the sole in order to remove crusted mud from it. Hence, you see, my double deduction that you had been out in vile weather and that you had a particularly malignant boot-slitting specimen of the London slavey. As to your practice, if a gentleman walks into my rooms smelling of iodoform, with a black mark of nitrate of silver upon his right forefinger and a bulge on the right side of his top-hat to show where he has secreted his stethoscope, I must be dull, indeed, if I do not pronounce him to be an active member of the medical profession.'

I could not help laughing at the ease with which he explained his process of deduction. 'When I hear you give your reasons,' I remarked, 'the thing always appears to me to be so ridiculously simple that I could easily do it myself, though at each successive instance of your reasoning I am baffled until you explain your process. And yet I believe that my eyes are as good as yours.'

'Quite so,' he answered, lighting a cigarette, and throwing himself down into an armchair. 'You see, but you do not observe. The distinction is clear. For example, you have frequently seen the steps which lead up from the hall to this room.'

'Frequently.'

'How often?'

'Well, some hundreds of times.'

'Then how many are there?'

'How many? I don't know.'

'Quite so! You have not observed. And yet you have seen. That is just my point. Now, I know that there are seventeen steps, because I have both seen and observed. By the way, since you are interested in these little problems, and since you are good enough to chronicle one or two of my trifling experiences, you may be interested in this.' He threw over a sheet of thick, pink-tinted notepaper which had been lying open upon the table. 'It came by the last post,' said he. 'Read it aloud.'

The note was undated, and without either signature or address.

'There will call upon you tonight, at a quarter to eight o'clock [it said], a gentleman who desires to consult you upon a matter of the very deepest moment. Your recent services to one of the royal houses of Europe have shown that you are one who may safely be trusted with matters which are of an importance which can hardly be exaggerated. This account of you we have from all quarters received. Be in your chamber then at that hour, and do not take it amiss if your visitor wear a mask.'

'This is indeed a mystery,' I remarked. 'What do you imagine it means?'

'I have no data yet. It is a capital mistake to theorise before one has data. Insensibly one begins to twist facts to suit theories, instead of theories to suit facts. But the note itself. What do you deduce from it?'

I carefully examined the writing, and the paper upon which it was written.

'The man who wrote it was presumably well to do,' I remarked, endeavouring to imitate my companion's processes. 'Such paper could not be bought under half a crown a packet. It is peculiarly strong and stiff.'

'Peculiar – that is the very word,' said Holmes. 'It is not an English paper at all. Hold it up to the light.'

I did so, and saw a large E with a small g, a P and a large G with a small t woven into the texture of the paper.

'What do you make of that?' asked Holmes.

'The name of the maker, no doubt; or his monogram, rather.'

'Not at all. The G with the small t stands for *Gesellschaft*, which is the German for Company. It is a customary contraction like our Co. P, of course, stands for *Papier*. Now for the Eg. Let us glance at our *Continental Gazetteer*.' He took down a heavy brown volume from his shelves. 'Eglow, Eglonitz – here we are, Egria. It is in a German-speaking country – in Bohemia, not far from Carlsbad. "Remarkable as being the scene of the death of Wallenstein, and for its numerous glass-factories and paper-mills." Ha, ha, my boy, what do you make of that?' His eyes sparkled, and he sent up a great blue triumphant cloud from his cigarette.

'The paper was made in Bohemia,' I said.

'Precisely. And the man who wrote the note is a German. Do you note the peculiar construction of the sentence – "This account of you we have from all quarters received." A Frenchman or Russian could not have written that. It is the German who is so uncourteous to his verbs. It only remains, therefore, to discover what is wanted by this German who writes upon Bohemian paper and prefers wearing a mask to showing his face. And here he comes, if I am not mistaken, to resolve all our doubts.'

As he spoke there was the sharp sound of horses' hoofs and grating wheels against the curb, followed by a sharp pull at the bell. Holmes whistled.

'A pair, by the sound,' said he. 'Yes,' he continued, glancing out of the window. 'A nice little brougham and a pair of beauties. A hundred

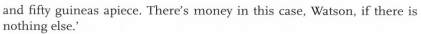

and fifty guineas apiece. There's money in this case, Watson, if there is nothing else.'

'I think that I had better go, Holmes.'

'Not a bit, doctor. Stay where you are. I am lost without my Boswell. And this promises to be interesting. It would be a pity to miss it.'

'But your client — '

'Never mind him. I may want your help, and so may he. Here he comes. Sit down in that armchair, doctor, and give us your best attention.'

A slow and heavy step, which had been heard upon the stairs and in the passage, paused immediately outside the door. Then there was a loud and authoritative tap.

'Come in!' said Holmes.

A man entered who could hardly have been less than six feet six inches in height, with the chest and limbs of a Hercules. His dress was rich with a richness which would, in England, be looked upon as akin to bad taste. Heavy bands of astrakhan were slashed across the sleeves and fronts of his double-breasted coat, while the deep blue cloak which was thrown over his shoulders was lined with flame-coloured silk and secured at the neck with a brooch which consisted of a single flaming beryl. Boots which extended halfway up his calves, and which were trimmed at the tops with rich brown fur, completed the impression of barbaric opulence which was suggested by his whole appearance. He carried a broad-brimmed hat in his hand, while he wore across the upper part of his face, extending down past the cheekbones, a black vizard mask, which he had apparently adjusted that very moment, for his hand was still raised to it as he entered. From the lower part of the face he appeared to be a man of strong character, with a thick, hanging lip, and a long, straight chin suggestive of resolution pushed to the length of obstinacy.

'You had my note?' he asked with a deep harsh voice and a strongly marked German accent. 'I told you that I would call.' He looked from one to the other of us, as if uncertain which to address.

'Pray take a seat,' said Holmes. 'This is my friend and colleague, Dr Watson, who is occasionally good enough to help me in my cases. Whom have I the honour to address?'

'You may address me as the Count von Kramm, a Bohemian nobleman. I understand that this gentleman, your friend, is a man of honour and discretion, whom I may trust with a matter of the most extreme importance.? If not, I should much prefer to communicate with you alone.'

I rose to go, but Holmes caught me by the wrist and pushed me back into my chair. 'It is both, or none,' said he. 'You may say before this gentleman anything which you may say to me.'

The count shrugged his broad shoulders. 'Then I must begin,' said he, 'by binding you both to absolute secrecy for two years; at the end of that time the matter will be of no importance. At present it is not too much to say that it is of such weight it may have an influence upon European history.'

'I promise,' said Holmes.

'And I.'

'You will excuse this mask,' continued our strange visitor. 'The august person who employs me wishes his agent to be unknown to you, and I may confess at once that the title by which I have just called myself is not exactly my own.'

'I was aware of it,' said Holmes dryly.

'The circumstances are of great delicacy, and every precaution has to be taken to quench what might grow to be an immense scandal and seriously compromise one of the reigning families of Europe. To speak plainly, the matter implicates the great House of Ormstein, hereditary kings of Bohemia.'

'I was also aware of that,' murmured Holmes, settling himself down in his armchair and closing his eyes.

Our visitor glanced with some apparent surprise at the languid, lounging figure of the man who had been no doubt depicted to him as the most incisive reasoner and most energetic agent in Europe.

Holmes slowly reopened his eyes and looked impatiently at his gigantic client. 'If your majesty would condescend to state your case,' he remarked, 'I should be better able to advise you.'

The man sprang from his chair and paced up and down the room in uncontrollable agitation. Then, with a gesture of desperation, he tore the mask from his face and hurled it upon the ground. 'You are right,' he cried; 'I am the king. Why should I attempt to conceal it?'

'Why, indeed?' murmured Holmes. 'Your majesty had not spoken before I was aware that I was addressing Wilhelm Gottsreich Sigismond von Ormstein, Grand Duke of Cassel-Felstein, and hereditary King of Bohemia.'

'But you can understand,' said our strange visitor, sitting down once more and passing his hand over his high white forehead, 'you can understand that I am not accustomed to doing such business in my own person. Yet the matter was so delicate that I could not confide it to an agent without putting myself in his power. I have come *incognito* from Prague for the purpose of consulting you.'

'Then, pray consult,' said Holmes, shutting his eyes once more.

'The facts are briefly these: Some five years ago, during a lengthy visit to Warsaw, I made the acquaintance of the well-known adventuress, Irene Adler. The name is no doubt familiar to you.'

'Kindly look her up in my index, doctor,' murmured Holmes without opening his eyes. For many years he had adopted a system of docketing all paragraphs concerning men and things, so that it was difficult to name a subject or a person on which he could not at once furnish information. In this case I found her biography sandwiched in between that of a Hebrew rabbi and that of a staff-commander who had written a monograph upon deep-sea fishes.

'Let me see,' said Holmes. 'Hum! Born in New Jersey in the year 1858. Contralto – hum! La Scala, hum! Prima donna Imperial Opera of Warsaw – yes! Retired from operatic stage – ha! Living in London – quite so! Your majesty, as I understand, became entangled with this young person, wrote her some compromising letters, and is now desirous of getting those letters back.'

'Precisely so. But how — '

'Was there a secret marriage?'

'None.'

'No legal papers or certificates?'

'None.'

'Then I fail to follow your majesty. If this young person should produce her letters for blackmailing or other purposes, how is she to prove their authenticity?'

'There is the writing.'

'Pooh, pooh! Forgery.'

'My private notepaper.'

'Stolen.'

'My own seal.'

'Imitated.'

'My photograph.'

'Bought.'

'We were both in the photograph.'

'Oh, dear! That is very bad! Your majesty has indeed committed an indiscretion.'

'I was mad – insane.'

'You have compromised yourself seriously.'

'I was only crown prince then. I was young. I am but thirty now.'

'It must be recovered.'

'We have tried and failed.'

'Your majesty must pay. It must be bought.'

'She will not sell.'

'Stolen, then.'

'Five attempts have been made. Twice burglars in my pay ransacked her house. Once we diverted her luggage when she travelled. Twice she has been waylaid. There has been no result.'

'No sign of it?'

'Absolutely none.'

Holmes laughed. 'It is quite a pretty little problem,' said he.

'But a very serious one to me,' returned the king reproachfully.

'Very, indeed. And what does she propose to do with the photograph?'

'To ruin me.'

'But how?'

'I am about to be married.'

'So I have heard.'

'To Clotilde Lothman von Saxe-Meningen, second daughter of the King of Scandinavia. You may know the strict principles of her family. She is herself the very soul of delicacy. A shadow of a doubt as to my conduct would bring the matter to an end.'

'And Irene Adler?'

'Threatens to send them the photograph. And she will do it. I know that she will do it. You do not know her, but she has a soul of steel. She has the face of the most beautiful of women, and the mind of the most resolute of men. Rather than I should marry another woman, there are no lengths to which she would not go – none.'

'You are sure that she has not sent it yet?'

'I am sure.'

'And why?'

'Because she has said that she would send it on the day when the betrothal was publicly proclaimed. That will be next Monday.'

'Oh, then we have three days yet,' said Holmes with a yawn. 'That is very fortunate, as I have one or two matters of importance to look into just at present. Your majesty will, of course, stay in London for the present?'

'Certainly. You will find me at the Langham, under the name of the Count von Kramm.'

'Then I shall drop you a line to let you know how we progress.'

'Pray do so. I shall be all anxiety.'

'Then, as to money?'

'You have *carte blanche*.'

'Absolutely?'

'I tell you that I would give one of the provinces of my kingdom to have that photograph.'

'And for present expenses?'

The king took a heavy chamois-leather bag from under his cloak and laid it on the table. 'There are three hundred pounds in gold and seven hundred in notes,' he said.

Holmes scribbled a receipt upon a sheet of his notebook and handed it to him. 'And mademoiselle's address?' he asked.

'Is Briony Lodge, Serpentine Avenue, St John's Wood.'

Holmes took a note of it. 'One other question,' said he. 'Was the photograph a cabinet?'

'It was.'

'Then, good-night, your majesty, and I trust that we shall soon have some good news for you. And good-night, Watson,' he added, as the wheels of the royal brougham rolled down the street. 'If you will be good enough to call tomorrow afternoon at three o'clock I should like to chat this little matter over with you.'

2

At three o'clock precisely I was at Baker Street, but Holmes had not yet returned. The landlady informed me that he had left the house shortly after eight o'clock in the morning. I sat down beside the fire, however, with the intention of awaiting him, however long he might be. I was already deeply interested in his inquiry, for, though it was surrounded by none of the grim and strange features which were associated with the two crimes which I had elsewhere recorded, still, the nature of the case and the exalted station of his client gave it a character of its own. Indeed, apart from the nature of the investigation which my friend had on hand, there was something in his masterly grasp of a situation, and his keen, incisive reasoning, which made it a pleasure to me to study his system of work, and to follow the quick, subtle methods by which he disentangled the most inextricable mysteries. So accustomed was I to his invariable success that the very possibility of his failing had ceased to enter into my head.

It was close upon four before the door opened, and a drunken-looking groom, ill-kempt and side-whiskered, with an inflamed face and disreputable clothes, walked into the room. Accustomed as I was to my friend's amazing powers in the use of disguises, I had to look three times before I was certain that it was indeed he. With a nod he vanished into the

bedroom, whence he emerged in five minutes tweed-suited and respectable, as of old. Putting his hands into his pockets, he stretched out his legs
in front of the fire and laughed heartily for some minutes.

'Well, really!' he cried, and then he choked and laughed again until he
was obliged to lie back, limp and helpless, in the chair.

'What is it?'

'It's quite too funny. I am sure you could never guess how I employed
my morning, or what I ended by doing.'

'I can't imagine. I suppose that you have been watching the habits,
and perhaps the house, of Miss Irene Adler.'

'Quite so; but the sequel was rather unusual. I will tell you, however.
I left the house a little after eight o'clock this morning in the character of
a groom out of work. There is a wonderful sympathy and freemasonry
among horsey men. Be one of them, and you will know all that there is
to know. I soon found Briony Lodge. It is a *bijou* villa, with a garden at
the back, but built out in front right up to the road, two storeys. Chubb
lock to the door. Large sitting-room on the right side, well furnished, with
long windows almost to the floor, and those preposterous English window
fasteners which a child could open. Behind there was nothing remarkable, save that the passage window could be reached from the top of the
coach-house. I walked round it and examined it closely from every point
of view, but without noting anything else of interest.

'I then lounged down the street and found, as I expected, that there
was a mews in a lane which runs down by one wall of the garden. I lent
the ostlers a hand in rubbing down their horses, and received in exchange
twopence, a glass of half-and-half, two fills of shag tobacco, and as much
information as I could desire about Miss Adler, to say nothing of half a
dozen other people in the neighbourhood in whom I was not in the least
interested, but whose biographies I was compelled to listen to.'

'And what of Irene Adler?' I asked.

'Oh, she has turned all the men's heads down in that part. She is
the daintiest thing under a bonnet on this planet. So says the Serpentine Mews, to a man. She lives quietly, sings at concerts, drives out at five
every day, and returns at seven sharp for dinner. Seldom goes out at other
times, except when she sings. Has only one male visitor, but a good deal
of him. He is dark, handsome and dashing, never calls less than once a
day, and often twice. He is a Mr Godfrey Norton, of the Inner Temple. See
the advantages of a cabman as a confidant. They had driven him home a
dozen times from Serpentine Mews, and knew all about him. When I had
listened to all they had to tell, I began to walk up and down near Briony

Lodge once more, and to think over my plan of campaign.

'This Godfrey Norton was evidently an important factor in the matter. He was a lawyer. That sounded ominous. What was the relation between them, and what the object of his repeated visits? Was she his client, his friend or his mistress? If the former, she had probably transferred the photograph to his keeping. If the latter, it was less likely. On the issue of this question depended whether I should continue my work at Briony Lodge or turn my attention to the gentleman's chambers in the Temple. It was a delicate point, and it widened the field of my inquiry. I fear that I bore you with these details, but I have to let you see my little difficulties if you are to understand the situation.'

'I am following you closely,' I answered.

'I was still balancing the matter in my mind when a hansom cab drove up to Briony Lodge, and a gentleman sprang out. He was a remark-ably handsome man, dark, aquiline and moustached – evidently the man of whom I had heard. He appeared to be in a great hurry, shouted to the cabman to wait, and brushed past the maid who opened the door with the air of a man who was thoroughly at home.

'He was in the house about half an hour, and I could catch glimpses of him in the windows of the sitting-room, pacing up and down, talking excitedly and waving his arms. Of her I could see nothing. Presently he emerged, looking even more flurried than before. As he stepped up to the cab, he pulled a gold watch from his pocket and looked at it earnestly. "Drive like the devil," he shouted, "first to Gross & Hankey's in Regent Street, and then to the Church of St Monica in the Edgeware Road. Half a guinea if you do it in twenty minutes!"

'Away they went, and I was just wondering whether I should not do well to follow them when up the lane came a neat little landau, the coachman with his coat only half-buttoned, and his tie under his ear, while all the tags of his harness were sticking out of the buckles. It hadn't pulled up before she shot out of the hall door and into it. I only caught a glimpse of her at the moment, but she was a lovely woman, with a face that a man might die for.

' "The Church of St Monica, John," she cried, "and half a sovereign if you reach it in twenty minutes."

'This was quite too good to lose, Watson. I was just balancing whether I should run for it, or whether I should perch behind her landau when a cab came through the street. The driver looked twice at such a shabby fare, but I jumped in before he could object. "The Church of St Monica," said I, "and half a sovereign if you reach it in twenty minutes."

It was twenty-five minutes to twelve, and of course it was clear enough what was in the wind.

'My cabby drove fast. I don't think I ever drove faster, but the others were there before us. The cab and the landau with their steaming horses were in front of the door when I arrived. I paid the man and hurried into the church. There was not a soul there save the two whom I had followed and a surpliced clergyman, who seemed to be expostulating with them. They were all three standing in a knot in front of the altar. I lounged up the side aisle like any other idler who has dropped into a church. Suddenly, to my surprise, the three at the altar faced round to me, and Godfrey Norton came running as hard as he could towards me.

' "Thank God," he cried. "You'll do. Come! Come!"

' "What then?" I asked.

' "Come, man, come, only three minutes, or it won't be legal."

'I was half-dragged up to the altar, and before I knew where I was I found myself mumbling responses which were whispered in my ear, and vouching for things of which I knew nothing, and generally assisting in the secure tying up of Irene Adler, spinster, to Godfrey Norton, bachelor. It was all done in an instant, and there was the gentleman thanking me on the one side and the lady on the other, while the clergyman beamed on me in front. It was the most preposterous position in which I ever found myself in my life, and it was the thought of it that started me laughing just now. It seems that there had been some informality about their licence, that the clergyman absolutely refused to marry them without a witness of some sort, and that my lucky appearance saved the bridegroom from having to sally out into the streets in search of a best man. The bride gave me a sovereign, and I mean to wear it on my watch-chain in memory of the occasion.'

'This is a very unexpected turn of affairs,' said I; 'and what then?'

'Well, I found my plans very seriously menaced. It looked as if the pair might take an immediate departure, and so necessitate very prompt and energetic measures on my part. At the church door, however, they separated, he driving back to the Temple, and she to her own house. "I shall drive out in the park at five as usual," she said as she left him. I heard no more. They drove away in different directions, and I went off to make my own arrangements.'

'Which are?'

'Some cold beef and a glass of beer,' he answered, ringing the bell. 'I have been too busy to think of food, and I am likely to be busier still this evening. By the way, doctor, I shall want your co-operation.'

'I shall be delighted.'

'You don't mind breaking the law?'

'Not in the least.'

'Nor running a chance of arrest?'

'Not in a good cause.'

'Oh, the cause is excellent!'

'Then I am your man.'

'I was sure that I might rely on you.'

'But what is it you wish?'

'When Mrs Turner has brought in the tray I will make it clear to you ... Now,' he said as he turned hungrily on the simple fare that our landlady had provided, 'I must discuss it while I eat, for I have not much time. It is nearly five now. In two hours we must be on the scene of action. Miss Irene, or Madame, rather, returns from her drive at seven. We must be at Briony Lodge to meet her.'

'And what then?'

'You must leave that to me. I have already arranged what is to occur. There is only one point on which I must insist. You must not interfere, come what may. You understand?'

'I am to be neutral?'

'To do nothing whatever. There will probably be some small unpleasantness. Do not join in it. It will end in my being conveyed into the house. Four or five minutes afterwards the sitting-room window will open. You are to station yourself close to that open window.'

'Yes.'

'You are to watch me, for I will be visible to you.'

'Yes.'

'And when I raise my hand – so – you will throw into the room what I give you to throw, and will, at the same time, raise the cry of fire. You quite follow me?'

'Entirely.'

'It is nothing very formidable,' he said, taking a long cigar-shaped roll from his pocket. 'It is an ordinary plumber's smoke-rocket, fitted with a cap at either end to make it self-lighting. Your task is confined to that. When you raise your cry of fire, it will be taken up by quite a number of people. You may then walk to the end of the street, and I will rejoin you in ten minutes. I hope that I have made myself clear?'

'I am to remain neutral, to get near the window, to watch you, and at the signal to throw in this object, then to raise the cry of fire, and to await you at the corner of the street.'

'Precisely.'

'Then you may entirely rely on me.'

'That is excellent. I think, perhaps, it is almost time that I prepare for the new role I have to play.'

He disappeared into his bedroom and returned in a few minutes in the character of an amiable and simple-minded nonconformist clergyman. His broad black hat, his baggy trousers, his white tie, his sympathetic smile and general look of peering and benevolent curiosity were such as Mr John Hare alone could have equalled. It was not merely that Holmes changed his costume. His expression, his manner, his very soul seemed to vary with every fresh part that he assumed. The stage lost a fine actor, even as science lost an acute reasoner, when he became a specialist in crime.

It was a quarter past six when we left Baker Street, and it still wanted ten minutes to the hour when we found ourselves in Serpentine Avenue. It was already dusk, and the lamps were just being lit as we paced up and down in front of Briony Lodge, waiting for the coming of its occupant. The house was just such as I had pictured it from Sherlock Holmes' succinct description, but the locality appeared to be less private than I expected. On the contrary, for a small street in a quiet neighbourhood, it was remark-ably animated. There was a group of shabbily dressed men smoking and laughing in a corner, a scissors-grinder with his wheel, two guardsmen who were flirting with a nurse-girl, and several well-dressed young men who were lounging up and down with cigars in their mouths.

'You see,' remarked Holmes, as we paced to and fro in front of the house, 'this marriage rather simplifies matters. The photograph becomes a double-edged weapon now. The chances are that she would be as averse to its being seen by Mr Godfrey Norton, as our client is to its coming to the eyes of his princess. Now the question is, Where are we to find the photograph?'

'Where, indeed?'

'It is most unlikely that she carries it about with her. It is cabinet size. Too large for easy concealment about a woman's dress. She knows that the king is capable of having her waylaid and searched. Two attempts of the sort have already been made. We may take it, then, that she does not carry it about with her.'

'Where, then?'

'Her banker or her lawyer. There is that double possibility. But I am inclined to think neither. Women are naturally secretive, and they like to do their own secreting. Why should she hand it over to anyone else? She could trust her own guardianship, but she could not tell what indirect or political influence might be brought to bear upon a businessman. Besides, remember that she had resolved to use it within a few days. It must be where she can lay her hands upon it. It must be in her own house.'

'But it has twice been burgled.'

'Pshaw! They did not know how to look.'

'But how will you look?'

'I will not look.'

'What then?'

'I will get her to show me.'

'But she will refuse.'

'She will not be able to. But I hear the rumble of wheels. It is her carriage. Now carry out my orders to the letter.'

As he spoke the gleam of the sidelights of a carriage came round the curve of the avenue. It was a smart little landau which rattled up to the door of Briony Lodge. As it pulled up, one of the loafing men at the corner dashed forward to open the door in the hope of earning a copper, but was elbowed away by another loafer, who had rushed up with the same intention. A fierce quarrel broke out, which was increased by the two guardsmen, who took sides with one of the loungers, and by the scissors-grinder, who was equally hot upon the other side. A blow was struck, and in an instant the lady, who had stepped from her carriage, was the centre of a little knot of flushed and struggling men, who struck savagely at each other with their fists and sticks. Holmes dashed into the crowd to protect the lady; but, just as he reached her, he gave a cry and dropped to the ground, with the blood running freely down his face. At his fall the guardsmen took to their heels in one direction and the loungers in the other, while a number of better dressed people, who had watched the scuffle without taking part in it, crowded in to help the lady and to attend to the injured man. Irene Adler, as I will still call her, had hurried up the steps; but she stood at the top with her superb figure outlined against the lights of the hall, looking back into the street.

'Is the poor gentleman much hurt?' she asked.

'He is dead,' cried several voices.

'No, no, there's life in him!' shouted another. 'But he'll be gone before you can get him to hospital.'

'He's a brave fellow,' said a woman. 'They would have had the lady's purse and watch if it hadn't been for him. They were a gang, and a rough one, too. Ah, he's breathing now.'

'He can't lie in the street. May we bring him in, ma'am?'

'Surely. Bring him into the sitting-room. There is a comfortable sofa.

This way, please!'

Slowly and solemnly he was borne into Briony Lodge and laid out in the principal room, while I still observed the proceedings from my post by the window. The lamps had been lit, but the blinds had not been drawn, so that I could see Holmes as he lay upon the couch. I do not know whether he was seized with compunction at that moment for the part he was playing, but I know that I never felt more heartily ashamed of myself in my life than when I saw the beautiful creature against whom I was conspiring and observed the grace and kindliness with which she waited upon the injured man. And yet it would be the blackest treachery to Holmes to draw back now from the part which he had entrusted to me. I hardened my heart, and took the smoke-rocket from under my ulster. After all, I thought, we are not injuring her. We are but preventing her from injuring another.

Holmes had sat up upon the couch, and I saw him motion like a man who is in need of air. A maid rushed across and threw open the window. At the same instant I saw him raise his hand and at the signal I tossed my rocket into the room with a cry of 'Fire!' The word was no sooner out of my mouth than the whole crowd of spectators, well dressed and ill – gentlemen, ostlers and servant maids – joined in a general shriek of 'Fire!' Thick clouds of smoke curled through the room and out at the open window. I caught a glimpse of rushing figures, and a moment later the voice of Holmes from within assuring them that it was a false alarm. Slipping through the shouting crowd I made my way to the corner of the street, and in ten minutes was rejoiced to find my friend's arm in mine and relieved to get away from the scene of uproar. He walked swiftly and in silence for some few minutes until we had turned down one of the quiet streets which lead towards the Edgeware Road.

'You did it very nicely, doctor,' he remarked. 'Nothing could have been better. It is all right.'

'You have the photograph?'

'I know where it is.'

'And how did you find out?'

'She showed me, as I told you she would.'

'I am still in the dark.'

'I do not wish to make a mystery,' said he, laughing. 'The matter was perfectly simple. You, of course, saw that everyone in the street was an accomplice. They were all engaged for the evening.'

'I guessed as much.'

'Then, when the row broke out, I had a little moist red paint in the palm of my hand. I rushed forward, fell down, clapped my hand to my face, and became a piteous spectacle. It is an old trick.'

'That also I could fathom.'

'Then they carried me in. She was bound to have me in. What else could she do? And into her sitting-room, which was the very room which I suspected. It lay between that and her bedroom, and I was determined to see which. They laid me on a couch, I motioned for air, they were compelled to open the window, and you had your chance.'

'How did that help you?'

'It was all-important. When a woman thinks that her house is on fire, her instinct is at once to rush to the thing which she values most. It is a perfectly overpowering impulse, and I have more than once taken advantage of it. In the case of the Darlington Substitution Scandal it was of use to me, and also in the Arnsworth Castle business. A married woman grabs at her baby; an unmarried one reaches for her jewel-box. Now it was clear to me that our lady of today had nothing in the house more precious to her than what we are in quest of. She would rush to secure it. The alarm of fire was admirably done. The smoke and shouting were enough to shake nerves of steel. She responded beautifully. The photograph is in a recess behind a sliding panel just above the right bell-pull. She was there in an instant, and I caught a glimpse of it as she half drew it out. When I cried out that it was a false alarm, she replaced it, glanced at the rocket, rushed from the room, and I have not seen her since. I rose, and, making my excuses, escaped from the house. I hesitated whether to attempt to secure the photograph at once; but the coachman had come in, and as he was watching me narrowly, it seemed safer to wait. A little over-precipitance may ruin all.'

'And now?' I asked.

'Our quest is practically finished. I shall call with the king tomorrow, and with you, if you care to come with us. We will be shown into the sitting-room to wait for the lady, but it is probable that when she comes she may find neither us nor the photograph. It might be a satisfaction to his majesty to regain it with his own hands.'

'And when will you call?'

'At eight in the morning. She will not be up, so that we shall have a clear field. Besides, we must be prompt, for this marriage may mean a complete change in her life and habits. I must wire to the king without delay.'

We had reached Baker Street and had stopped at the door. He was searching his pockets for the key when someone passing said: 'Good-night,

Mr Sherlock Holmes.'

There were several people on the pavement at the time, but the greeting appeared to come from a slim youth in an ulster who had hurried by.

'I've heard that voice before,' said Holmes, staring down the dimly lit street. 'Now, I wonder who the deuce that could have been.'

3

I slept at Baker Street that night, and we were engaged upon our toast and coffee in the morning when the King of Bohemia rushed into the room.

'You have really got it!' he cried, grasping Sherlock Holmes by either shoulder and looking eagerly into his face.

'Not yet.'

'But you have hopes?'

'I have hopes.'

'Then, come. I am all impatience to be gone.'

'We must have a cab.'

'No, my brougham is waiting.'

'Then that will simplify matters.' We descended and started off once more for Briony Lodge.

'Irene Adler is married,' remarked Holmes.

'Married! When?'

'Yesterday.'

'But to whom?'

'To an English lawyer named Norton.'

'But she could not love him.'

'I am in hopes that she does.'

'And why in hopes?'

'Because it would spare your majesty all fear of future annoyance. If the lady loves her husband, she does not love your majesty. If she does not love your majesty, there is no reason why she should interfere with your majesty's plan.'

'It is true. And yet — ! Well! I wish she had been of my own station! What a queen she would have made!' He relapsed into a moody silence, which was not broken until we drew up in Serpentine Avenue.

The door of Briony Lodge was open, and an elderly woman stood upon the steps. She watched us with a sardonic eye as we stepped from the brougham.

'Mr Sherlock Holmes, I believe?' said she.

'I am Mr Holmes,' answered my companion, looking at her with a questioning and rather startled gaze.

'Indeed! My mistress told me that you were likely to call. She left this morning with her husband by the five-fifteen train from Charing Cross for the Continent.'

'What!' Sherlock Holmes staggered back, white with chagrin and surprise. 'Do you mean that she has left England?'

'Never to return.'

'And the papers?' asked the king hoarsely. 'All is lost.'

'We shall see.' Holmes pushed past the servant and rushed into the drawing-room, followed by the king and myself. The furniture was scattered about in every direction, with dismantled shelves and open drawers, as if the lady had hurriedly ransacked them before her flight. Holmes rushed at the bell-pull, tore back a small sliding shutter and, plunging in his hand, pulled out a photograph and a letter. The photograph was of Irene Adler herself in evening dress, the letter was superscribed: 'To Sherlock Holmes, Esq. To be left till called for.' My friend tore it open, and we all three read it together. It was dated at midnight of the preceding night and ran in this way:

My dear Mr Sherlock Holmes – You really did it very well. You took me in completely. Until after the alarm of fire, I had not a suspicion. But then, when I found how I had betrayed myself, I began to think. I had been warned against you months ago. I had been told that, if the King employed an agent, it would certainly be you. And your address had been given me. Yet, with all this, you made me reveal what you wanted to know. Even after I became suspicious, I found it hard to think evil of such a dear, kind old clergyman. But, you know, I have been trained as an actress myself. Male costume is nothing new to me. I often take advantage of the freedom which it gives. I sent John, the coachman, to watch you, ran upstairs, got into my walking clothes, as I call them, and came down just as you departed.

Well, I followed you to your door, and so made sure that I was really an object of interest to the celebrated Mr Sherlock Holmes. Then I, rather imprudently, wished you good-night, and started for the Temple to see my husband.

We both thought the best resource was flight, when pursued by so formidable an antagonist; so you will find the nest empty when you call tomorrow. As to the photograph, your client may rest in peace. I love and am loved by a better man than he. The king may do what he will without hindrance from one whom he has cruelly wronged. I keep it only to safeguard myself, and to preserve a weapon which will always secure me from any steps which he might take in the future. I leave a photograph which he might care to possess; and I remain, dear Mr Sherlock Holmes,

Very truly yours,

IRENE NORTON, *née* ADLER

'What a woman – oh, what a woman!' cried the King of Bohemia, when we had all three read this epistle. 'Did I not tell you how quick and resolute she was? Would she not have made an admirable queen? Is it not a pity that she was not on my level?'

'From what I have seen of the lady, she seems, indeed, to be on a very different level from your majesty,' said Holmes coldly. 'I am sorry that I have not been able to bring your majesty's business to a more successful conclusion.'

'On the contrary, my dear sir,' cried the king; 'nothing could be more successful. I know that her word is inviolate. The photograph is now as safe as if it were in the fire.'

'I am glad to hear your majesty say so.'

'I am immensely indebted to you. Pray tell me in what way I can reward you. This ring — ' He slipped an emerald snake ring from his finger and held it out upon the palm of his hand.

'Your majesty has something which I should value even more highly,' said Holmes.

'You have but to name it.'

'This photograph!'

The king stared at him in amazement.

'Irene's photograph!' he cried. 'Certainly, if you wish it.'

'I thank your majesty. Then there is no more to be done in the matter. I have the honour to wish you a very good-morning.' He bowed, and, turning away without observing the hand which the king had stretched out to him, he set off in my company for his chambers.

And that was how a great scandal threatened to affect the kingdom of Bohemia, and how the best plans of Mr Sherlock Holmes were beaten by a woman's wit. He used to make merry over the cleverness of women, but I have not heard him do it of late. And when he speaks of Irene Adler, or when he refers to her photograph, it is always under the honourable title of *the* woman.

The Red-Headed League

I had called upon my friend Mr Sherlock Holmes one day in the autumn of last year and found him in deep conversation with a very stout, florid-faced, elderly gentleman with fiery red hair. With an apology for my intrusion, I was about to withdraw when Holmes pulled me abruptly into the room and closed the door behind me.

'You could not possibly have come at a better time, my dear Watson,' he said cordially.

'I was afraid that you were engaged.'

'So I am. Very much so.'

'Then I can wait in the next room.'

'Not at all. This gentleman, Mr Wilson, has been my partner and helper in many of my most successful cases, and I have no doubt that he will be of the utmost use to me in yours also.'

The stout gentleman half rose from his chair and gave a bob of greeting, with a quick little questioning glance from his small fat-encircled eyes.

'Try the settee,' said Holmes, relapsing into his armchair and putting his fingertips together, as was his custom when in judicial moods. 'I know, my dear Watson, that you share my love of all that is bizarre and outside the conventions and humdrum routine of everyday life. You have shown your relish for it by the enthusiasm which has prompted you to chronicle, and, if you will excuse my saying so, somewhat to embellish so many of my own little adventures.'

'Your cases have indeed been of the greatest interest to me,' I observed.

'You will remember that I remarked the other day, just before we went into the very simple problem presented by Miss Mary Sutherland, that for strange effects and extraordinary combinations we must go to life itself, which is always far more daring than any effort of the imagination.'

'A proposition which I took the liberty of doubting.'

'You did, doctor, but none the less you must come round to my view, for otherwise I shall keep on piling fact upon fact on you until your reason breaks down under them and acknowledges me to be right. Now, Mr Jabez

Wilson here has been good enough to call upon me this morning, and to begin a narrative which promises to be one of the most singular which I have listened to for some time. You have heard me remark that the strangest and most unique things are very often connected not with the larger but with the smaller crimes, where occasionally, indeed, there is room for doubt as to whether any positive crime has been committed. As far as I have heard, it is impossible for me to say whether the present case is an instance of crime or not, but the course of events is certainly among the most singular that I have ever listened to. Perhaps, Mr Wilson, you would have the great kindness to recommence your narrative. I ask you not merely because my friend Dr Watson has not heard the opening part but also because the peculiar nature of the story makes me anxious to have every possible detail from your lips. As a rule, when I have heard some slight indication of the course of events, I am able to guide myself by the thousands of other similar cases which occur to my memory. In the present instance I am forced to admit that the facts are, to the best of my belief, unique.'

The portly client puffed out his chest with an appearance of some little pride and pulled a dirty and wrinkled newspaper from the inside pocket of his greatcoat. As he glanced down the advertisement column, with his head thrust forward and the paper flattened out upon his knee, I took a good look at the man and endeavoured, after the fashion of my companion, to read the indications which might be presented by his dress or appearance.

I did not gain very much, however, by my inspection. Our visitor bore every mark of being an average commonplace British tradesman, obese, pompous and slow. He wore rather baggy grey shepherd's-check trousers, a not over-clean black frock-coat, unbuttoned in the front, and a drab waistcoat with a heavy brassy Albert chain and a square pierced bit of metal dangling down as an ornament. A frayed top-hat and a faded brown overcoat with a wrinkled velvet collar lay upon the chair beside him. Altogether, look as I would, there was nothing remarkable about the man save his blazing red head, and the expression of extreme chagrin and discontent upon his features.

Sherlock Holmes' quick eye took in my occupation, and he shook his head with a smile as he noticed my questioning glances. 'Beyond the obvious facts that he has at some time done manual labour, that he takes snuff, that he is a Freemason, that he has been in China and that he has done a considerable amount of writing lately, I can deduce nothing else.'

Mr Jabez Wilson started up in his chair, with his forefinger upon the paper, but his eyes upon my companion.

'How, in the name of good-fortune, did you know all that, Mr Holmes?' he asked. 'How did you know, for example, that I did manual labour. It's as true as gospel, for I began as a ship's carpenter.'

'Your hands, my dear sir. Your right hand is quite a size larger than your left. You have worked with it, and the muscles are more developed.'

'Well, the snuff, then, and the Freemasonry?'

'I won't insult your intelligence by telling you how I read that, especially as, rather against the strict rules of your order, you use an arc-and-compass breastpin.'

'Ah, of course, I forgot that. But the writing?'

'What else can be indicated by that right cuff so very shiny for five inches, and the left one with the smooth patch near the elbow where you rest it upon the desk?'

'Well, but China?'

'The fish that you have tattooed immediately above your right wrist could only have been done in China. I have made a small study of tattoo marks and have even contributed to the literature on the subject. That trick of staining the fishes' scales a delicate pink is quite peculiar to China. When, in addition, I see a Chinese coin hanging from your watch-chain, the matter becomes even more simple.'

Mr Jabez Wilson laughed heavily. 'Well, I never!' said he. 'I thought at first that you had done something clever, but I see that there was nothing in it after all.'

'I begin to think, Watson,' said Holmes, 'that I make a mistake in explaining. *Omne ignotum pro magnifico*, you know, and my poor little reputation, such as it is, will suffer shipwreck if I am so candid. Can you not find the advertisement, Mr Wilson?'

'Yes, I have got it now,' he answered with his thick red finger planted halfway down the column. 'Here it is. This is what began it all. You just read it for yourself, sir.'

I took the paper from him and read as follows:

To the Red-Headed League: On account of the bequest of the late Ezekiah Hopkins, of Lebanon, Pennsylvania, USA, there is now another vacancy open which entitles a member of the league to a salary of £4 a week for purely nominal services. All red-headed men who are sound in body and mind, and above the age of twenty-one years, are eligible. Apply in person on Monday, at eleven o'clock, to Duncan Ross, at the offices of the league, 7 Pope's Court, Fleet Street.

'What on earth does this mean?' I ejaculated after I had twice read over the extraordinary announcement.

Holmes chuckled and wriggled in his chair, as was his habit when in high spirits. 'It is a little off the beaten track, isn't it?' said he. 'And now, Mr Wilson, off you go at scratch and tell us all about yourself, your household, and the effect which this advertisement had upon your fortunes. You will first make a note, doctor, of the paper and the date.'

'It is the *Morning Chronicle* of 27 April 1890. Just two months ago.'

'Very good. Now, Mr Wilson?'

'Well, it is just as I have been telling you, Mr Sherlock Holmes,' said Jabez Wilson, mopping his forehead. 'I have a small pawnbroker's business at Coburg Square, near the City. It's not a very large affair, and of late years it has not done more than just give me a living. I used to be able to keep two assistants, but now I only keep one; and I would have a job to pay him but that he is willing to come for half wages so as to learn the business.'

'What is the name of this obliging youth?' asked Sherlock Holmes.

'His name is Vincent Spaulding, and he's not such a youth, either. It's hard to say his age. I should not wish a smarter assistant, Mr Holmes; and I know very well that he could better himself and earn twice what I am able to give him. But, after all, if he is satisfied, why should I put ideas in his head?'

'Why, indeed? You seem most fortunate in having an employee who comes under the full market price. It is not a common experience among employers in this age. I don't know that your assistant is not as remarkable as your advertisement.'

'Oh, he has his faults, too,' said Mr Wilson. 'Never was there such a fellow for photography. Snapping away with a camera when he ought to be improving his mind, and then diving down into the cellar like a rabbit into its hole to develop his pictures. That is his main fault, but on the whole he's a good worker. There's no vice in him.'

'He is still with you, I presume?'

'Yes, sir. He and a girl of fourteen, who does a bit of simple cooking and keeps the place clean – that's all I have in the house, for I am a widower and never had any family. We live very quietly, sir, the three of us; and we keep a roof over our heads and pay our debts, if we do nothing more.

'The first thing that put us out was that advertisement. Spaulding, he came down into the office just this day eight weeks, with this very paper in his hand, and he says, "I wish to the Lord, Mr Wilson, that I was a red-headed man."

' "Why is that?" I asks.

' "Why," says he, "here's another vacancy in the League of the Red-Headed Men. It's worth quite a little fortune to any man who gets it, and I understand that there are more vacancies than there are men, so that the trustees are at their wits' end what to do with the money. If my hair would only change colour, here's a nice little crib all ready for me to step into."

' "Why, what is it, then?" I asked. You see, Mr Holmes, I am a very stay-at-home man, and as my business came to me instead of my having to go to it, I was often weeks on end without putting my foot over the doormat. In that way I didn't know much of what was going on outside, and I was always glad of a bit of news.

' "Have you never heard of the League of the Red-Headed Men?" he asked with his eyes open.

' "Never."

' "Why, I wonder at that, for you are eligible yourself for one of the vacancies."

' "And what are they worth?" I asked.

' "Oh, merely a couple of hundred a year, but the work is slight, and it need not interfere very much with one's other occupations."

'Well, you can easily think that that made me prick up my ears, for the business has not been over good for some years, and an extra couple of hundred would have been very handy.

' "Tell me all about it," said I.

' "Well," said he, showing me the advertisement, "you can see for yourself that the league has a vacancy, and there is the address where you should apply for particulars. As far as I can make out, the league was founded by an American millionaire, Ezekiah Hopkins, who was very peculiar in his ways. He was himself red-headed, and he had a great sympathy for all red-headed men; so, when he died, it was found that he had left his enormous fortune in the hands of trustees, with instructions to apply the interest to the providing of easy berths to men whose hair is of that colour. From all I hear it is splendid pay and very little to do."

' "But," said I, "there would be millions of red-headed men who would apply."

' "Not so many as you might think," he answered. "You see it is really confined to Londoners, and to grown men. This American had started from London when he was young, and he wanted to do the old town a good turn. Then, again, I have heard it is no use your applying if your hair is light red, or dark red, or anything but real bright, blazing, fiery red. Now, if you cared to apply, Mr Wilson, you would just walk in; but perhaps it would hardly be worth your while to put yourself out of the way for the sake of a few hundred pounds."

'Now, it is a fact, gentlemen, as you may see for yourselves, that my hair is of a very full and rich tint, so that it seemed to me that if there was to be any competition in the matter I stood as good a chance as any man that I had ever met. Vincent Spaulding seemed to know so much about it that I thought he might prove useful, so I just ordered him to put up the shutters for the day and to come right away with me. He was very willing to have a holiday, so we shut the business up and started off for the address that was given us in the advertisement.

'I never hope to see such a sight as that again, Mr Holmes. From north, south, east and west, every man who had a shade of red in his hair had tramped into the city to answer the advertisement. Fleet Street was choked with red-headed folk, and Pope's Court looked like a coster's orange barrow. I should not have thought there were so many in the whole country as were brought together by that single advertisement. Every shade of colour they were – straw, lemon, orange, brick, Irish-setter, liver, clay; but, as Spaulding said, there were not many who had the real vivid flame-coloured tint. When I saw how many were waiting, I would have given it up in despair; but Spaulding would not hear of it. How he did it I could not imagine, but he pushed and pulled and butted until he got me through the crowd, and right up to the steps which led to the office. There was a double stream upon the stair, some going up in hope, and some coming back dejected; but we wedged in as well as we could and soon found ourselves in the office.'

'Your experience has been a most entertaining one,' remarked Holmes as his client paused and refreshed his memory with a huge pinch of snuff. 'Pray continue your very interesting statement.'

'There was nothing in the office but a couple of wooden chairs and a deal table, behind which sat a small man with a head that was even redder than mine. He said a few words to each candidate as he came up, and then he always managed to find some fault in them which would disqualify them. Getting a vacancy did not seem to be such a very easy matter, after all. However, when our turn came the little man was much more favourable to me than to any of the others, and he closed the door as we entered, so that he might have a private word with us.

' "This is Mr Jabez Wilson," said my assistant, "and he is willing to fill a vacancy in the league."

' "And he is admirably suited for it," the other answered. "He has every requirement. I cannot recall when I have seen anything so fine." He took a step backward, cocked his head on one side, and gazed at my hair until I felt quite bashful. Then suddenly he plunged forward, wrung my hand, and congratulated me warmly on my success.

' "It would be injustice to hesitate," said he. "You will, however, I am sure, excuse me for taking an obvious precaution." With that he seized my hair in both his hands, and tugged until I yelled with the pain. "There is water in your eyes," said he as he released me. "I perceive that all is as it should be. But we have to be careful, for we have twice been deceived by wigs and once by paint. I could tell you tales of cobbler's wax which would disgust you with human nature.' He stepped over to the window and shouted through it at the top of his voice that the vacancy was filled. A groan of disappointment came up from below, and the folk all trooped away in different directions until there was not a red-head to be seen except my own and that of the manager.

' "My name," said he, "is Mr Duncan Ross, and I am myself one of the pensioners upon the fund left by our noble benefactor. Are you a married man, Mr Wilson? Have you a family?"

'I answered that I had not.

'His face fell immediately.

' "Dear me!" he said gravely, "that is very serious indeed! I am sorry to hear you say that. The fund was, of course, for the propagation and spread of red-heads as well as for their maintenance. It is exceedingly unfortunate that you should be a bachelor."

'My face lengthened at this, Mr Holmes, for I thought that I was not to have the vacancy after all; but after thinking it over for a few minutes he said that it would be all right.

' "In the case of another," said he, "the objection might be fatal, but we must stretch a point in favour of a man with such a head of hair as yours. When shall you be able to enter upon your new duties?"

' "Well, it is a little awkward, for I have a business already," said I.

' "Oh, never mind about that, Mr Wilson!" said Vincent Spaulding. "I should be able to look after that for you."

' "What would be the hours?" I asked.

' "Ten to two."

'Now a pawnbroker's business is mostly done of an evening, Mr Holmes, especially Thursday and Friday evening, which is just before pay-day; so it would suit me very well to earn a little in the mornings. Besides, I knew that my assistant was a good man, and that he would see to anything that turned up.

' "That would suit me very well," said I. "And the pay?"

' "Is £4 a week."

' "And the work?"

' "Is purely nominal."

' "What do you call purely nominal?"

' "Well, you have to be in the office, or at least in the building, the whole time. If you leave, you forfeit your whole position for ever. The will is very clear upon that point. You don't comply with the conditions if you budge from the office during that time."

' "It's only four hours a day, and I should not think of leaving," said I.

' "No excuse will avail," said Mr Duncan Ross; "neither sickness nor business nor anything else. There you must stay, or you lose your billet."

' "And the work?"

' "Is to copy out the *Encyclopaedia Britannica*. There is the first volume of it in that press. You must find your own ink, pens and blotting-paper, but we provide this table and chair. Will you be ready tomorrow?"

' "Certainly," I answered.

' "Then, goodbye, Mr Jabez Wilson, and let me congratulate you once more on the important position which you have been fortunate enough to gain." He bowed me out of the room and I went home with my assistant, hardly knowing what to say or do, I was so pleased at my own good fortune.

'Well, I thought over the matter all day, and by evening I was in low spirits again; for I had quite persuaded myself that the whole affair must be some great hoax or fraud, though what its object might be I could not imagine. It seemed altogether past belief that anyone could make such a will, or that they would pay such a sum for doing anything so simple as copying out the *Encyclopaedia Britannica*. Vincent Spaulding did what he could to cheer me up, but by bedtime I had reasoned myself out of the whole thing. However, in the morning I determined to have a look at it anyhow, so I bought a penny bottle of ink, and with a quill-pen and seven sheets of foolscap paper, I started off for Pope's Court.

'Well, to my surprise and delight, everything was as right as possible. The table was set out ready for me, and Mr Duncan Ross was there to see that I got fairly to work. He started me off upon the letter A, and then he left me; but he would drop in from time to time to see that all was right with me. At two o'clock he bade me good-day, complimented me upon the amount that I had written, and locked the door of the office after me.

'This went on day after day, Mr Holmes, and on Saturday the manager came in and planked down four golden sovereigns for my week's work. It was the same next week, and the same the week after. Every morning I was there at ten, and every afternoon I left at two. By degrees Mr Duncan Ross took to coming in only once of a morning, and then, after a time, he did not come in at all. Still, of course, I never dared to leave the room for an instant, for I was not sure when he might come, and the billet was such a good one, and suited me so well, that I would not risk the loss of it.

'Eight weeks passed away like this, and I had written about Abbots and Archery and Armour and Architecture and Attica, and hoped with diligence that I might get on to the Bs before very long. It cost me something in foolscap, and I had pretty nearly filled a shelf with my writings. And then suddenly the whole business came to an end.'

'To an end?'

'Yes, sir. And no later than this morning. I went to my work as usual at ten o'clock, but the door was shut and locked, with a little square of cardboard hammered on to the middle of the panel with a tack. Here it is, and you can read for yourself.'

He held up a piece of white cardboard about the size of a sheet of notepaper. It read in this fashion:

THE RED-HEADED LEAGUE IS DISSOLVED
9 October 1890

Sherlock Holmes and I surveyed this curt announcement and the rueful face behind it, until the comical side of the affair so completely overtopped every other consideration that we both burst into a roar of laughter.

'I cannot see that there is anything very funny,' cried our client, flushing up to the roots of his flaming head. 'If you can do nothing better than laugh at me, I can go elsewhere.'

'No, no,' cried Holmes, shoving him back into the chair from which he had half risen. 'I really wouldn't miss your case for the world. It is most refreshingly unusual. But there is, if you will excuse my saying so, something just a little funny about it. Pray what steps did you take when you found the card upon the door?'

'I was staggered, sir. I did not know what to do. Then I called at the offices round, but none of them seemed to know anything about it. Finally, I went to the landlord, who is an accountant living on the ground floor, and I asked him if he could tell me what had become of the Red-Headed League. He said that he had never heard of any such body. Then I asked him who Mr Duncan Ross was. He answered that the name was new to him.

' "Well," said I, "the gentleman at No. 4."

' "What, the red-headed man?"

' "Yes."

' "Oh," said he, "his name was William Morris. He was a solicitor and was using my room as a temporary convenience until his new premises were ready. He moved out yesterday."

' "Where could I find him?"

' "Oh, at his new offices. He did tell me the address. Yes, 17 King Edward Street, near St Paul's.'

'I started off, Mr Holmes, but when I got to that address it was a manufactory of artificial kneecaps, and no one in it had ever heard of either Mr William Morris or Mr Duncan Ross.'

'And what did you do then?' asked Holmes.

'I went home to Saxe-Coburg Square, and I took the advice of my assistant. But he could not help me in any way. He could only say that if I waited I should hear by post. But that was not quite good enough, Mr Holmes. I did not wish to lose such a place without a struggle, so, as I had heard that you were good enough to give advice to poor folk who were in need of it, I came right away to you.'

'And you did very wisely,' said Holmes. 'Your case is an exceedingly remarkable one, and I shall be happy to look into it. From what you have told me I think that it is possible that graver issues hang from it than might at first sight appear.'

'Grave enough!' said Mr Jabez Wilson. 'Why, I have lost four pound a week.'

'As far as you are personally concerned,' remarked Holmes, 'I do not see that you have any grievance against this extraordinary league. On the contrary, you are, as I understand, richer by some thirty pounds, to say nothing of the minute knowledge which you have gained on every subject which comes under the letter A. You have lost nothing by them.'

'No, sir. But I want to find out about them, and who they are, and what their object was in playing this prank – if it was a prank – upon me. It was a pretty expensive joke for them, for it cost them two and thirty pounds.'

'We shall endeavour to clear up these points for you. And, first, one or two questions, Mr Wilson. This assistant of yours who first called your attention to the advertisement – how long had he been with you?'

'About a month then.'

'How did he come?'

'In answer to an advertisement.'

'Was he the only applicant?'

'No, I had a dozen.'

'Why did you pick him?'

'Because he was handy and would come cheap.'

'At half wages, in fact.'

'Yes.'

'What is he like, this Vincent Spaulding?'

'Small, stout-built, very quick in his ways, no hair on his face, though he's not short of thirty. Has a white splash of acid upon his forehead.'

Holmes sat up in his chair in considerable excitement. 'I thought as much,' said he. 'Have you ever observed that his ears are pierced for earrings?'

'Yes, sir. He told me that a gypsy had done it for him when he was a lad.'

'Hum!' said Holmes, sinking back in deep thought. 'He is still with you?'

'Oh, yes, sir; I have only just left him.'

'And has your business been attended to in your absence?'

'Nothing to complain of, sir. There's never very much to do of a morning.'

'That will do, Mr Wilson. I shall be happy to give you an opinion upon the subject in the course of a day or two. Today is Saturday, and I hope that by Monday we may come to a conclusion.'

'Well, Watson,' said Holmes when our visitor had left us, 'what do you make of it all?'

'I make nothing of it,' I answered frankly. 'It is a most mysterious business.'

'As a rule,' said Holmes, 'the more bizarre a thing is the less mysterious it proves to be. It is your commonplace, featureless crimes which are really puzzling, just as a commonplace face is the most difficult to identify. But I must be prompt over this matter.'

'What are you going to do, then?' I asked.

'To smoke,' he answered. 'It is quite a three-pipe problem, and I beg that you won't speak to me for fifty minutes.' He curled himself up in his chair, with his thin knees drawn up to his hawk-like nose, and there he sat with his eyes closed and his black clay pipe thrusting out like the bill of some strange bird. I had come to the conclusion that he had dropped asleep, and indeed was nodding myself, when he suddenly sprang out of his chair, with the gesture of a man who has made up his mind, and put his pipe down upon the mantelpiece.

'Sarasate plays at the St James's Hall this afternoon,' he remarked.

'What do you think, Watson? Could your patients spare you for a few hours?'

'I have nothing to do today. My practice is never very absorbing.'

'Then put on your hat and come. I am going through the City first, and we can have some lunch on the way. I observe that there is a good deal of German music on the programme, which is rather more to my taste than Italian or French. It is introspective, and I want to introspect. Come along!'

We travelled by the Underground as far as Aldersgate; and a short walk took us to Saxe-Coburg Square, the scene of the singular story which we had listened to in the morning. It was a poky little shabby-genteel place, where four lines of dingy two-storeyed brick houses looked out into a small railed-in enclosure, where a lawn of weedy grass and a few clumps of faded laurel bushes made a hard fight against a smoke-laden and uncongenial atmosphere. Three gilt balls and a brown board with Jabez Wilson in white letters upon a corner house announced the place where our red-headed client carried on his business. Sherlock Holmes stopped in front of it with his head on one side and looked it all over, with his eyes shining brightly between puckered lids. Then he walked slowly up the street, and then down again to the corner, still looking keenly at the houses. Finally he returned to the pawnbroker's, and, having thumped vigorously upon the pavement with his stick two or three times, he went up to the door and knocked. It was instantly opened by a bright-looking, clean-shaven young fellow, who asked him to step in.

'Thank you,' said Holmes, 'but I only wished to ask you how you would go from here to the Strand.'

'Third right, fourth left,' answered the assistant promptly, closing the door.

'Smart fellow, that,' observed Holmes as we walked away. 'He is, in my judgement, the fourth smartest man in London, and for daring I am not sure that he has not a claim to be the third. I have known something of him before.'

'Evidently,' said I, 'Mr Wilson's assistant counts for a good deal in this mystery of the Red-Headed League. I am sure that you enquired your way merely in order that you might see him.'

'Not him.'

'What then?'

'The knees of his trousers.'

'And what did you see?'

'What I expected to see.'

'Why did you beat the pavement?'

'My dear doctor, this is a time for observation, not for talk. We are spies in an enemy's country. We know something of Saxe-Coburg Square. Let us now explore the parts which lie behind it.'

The road in which we found ourselves as we turned round the corner from the retired Saxe-Coburg Square presented as great a contrast to it as the front of a picture does to the back. It was one of the main arteries which conveyed the traffic of the City to the north and west. The roadway was blocked with the immense stream of commerce flowing in a double tide inward and outward, while the footpaths were black with the hurrying swarm of pedestrians. It was difficult to realise as we looked at the line of fine shops and stately business premises that they really abutted on the other side upon the faded and stagnant square which we had just quitted.

'Let me see,' said Holmes, standing at the corner and glancing along the line. 'I should like just to remember the order of the houses here. It is a hobby of mine to have an exact knowledge of London. There is Mortimer's, the tobacconist, the little newspaper shop, the Coburg branch of the City and Suburban Bank, the Vegetarian Restaurant and McFarlane's carriage-building depot. That carries us right on to the other block. And now, doctor, we've done our work, so it's time we had some play. A sandwich and a cup of coffee, and then off to violin-land, where all is sweetness and delicacy and harmony, and there are no red-headed clients to vex us with their conundrums.'

My friend was an enthusiastic musician, being himself not only a very capable performer but a composer of no ordinary merit. All the afternoon he sat in the stalls wrapped in the most perfect happiness, gently waving his long, thin fingers in time to the music, while his gently smiling face and his languid, dreamy eyes were as unlike those of Holmes the sleuthhound, Holmes the relentless, keen-witted, ready-handed criminal agent, as it was possible to conceive. In his singular character the dual nature alternately asserted itself, and his extreme exactness and astuteness represented, as I have often thought, the reaction against the poetic and contemplative mood which occasionally predominated in him. The swing of his nature took him from extreme languor to devouring energy; and, as I knew well, he was never so truly formidable as when, for days on end, he had been lounging in his armchair amid his improvisations and his blackletter editions. Then it was that the lust of the chase would suddenly come upon him, and that his brilliant reasoning power would rise to the level of intuition, until those who were unacquainted with his methods would look askance at him as on a man whose knowledge was not that of other mortals. When I saw him that afternoon so enwrapped in the music at St James's Hall I felt that an evil time might be coming upon those whom he had set himself to hunt down.

'You want to go home, no doubt, doctor,' he remarked as we emerged.

'Yes, it would be as well.'

'And I have some business to do which will take some hours. This business at Coburg Square is serious.'

'Why serious?'

'A considerable crime is in contemplation. I have every reason to believe that we shall be in time to stop it. But today being Saturday rather complicates matters. I shall want your help tonight.'

'At what time?'

'Ten will be early enough.'

'I shall be at Baker Street at ten.'

'Very well. And, I say, doctor, there may be some little danger, so kindly put your army revolver in your pocket.' He waved his hand, turned on his heel, and disappeared in an instant among the crowd.

I trust that I am not more dense than my neighbours, but I was always oppressed with a sense of my own stupidity in my dealings with Sherlock Holmes. Here I had heard what he had heard, I had seen what he had seen, and yet from his words it was evident that he saw clearly not only what had happened but what was about to happen, while to me the whole business was still confused and grotesque. As I drove home to my house in Kensington I thought over it all, from the extraordinary story of the red-headed copier of the *Encyclopaedia* down to the visit to Saxe-Coburg Square and the ominous words with which he had parted from me. What was this nocturnal expedition, and why should I go armed? Where were we going, and what were we to do? I had the hint from Holmes that this smooth-faced pawnbroker's assistant was a formidable man – a man who might play a deep game. I tried to puzzle it out, but gave it up in despair and set the matter aside until night should bring an explanation.

It was a quarter past nine when I started from home and made my way across the park, and so through Oxford Street to Baker Street. Two hansoms were standing at the door, and as I entered the passage I heard the sound of voices from above. On entering his room, I found Holmes in animated conversation with two men, one of whom I recognised as Peter Jones, the official police agent, while the other was a long, thin, sad-faced man, with a very shiny hat and oppressively respectable frock-coat.

'Ha! Our party is complete,' said Holmes, buttoning up his pea-jacket and taking his heavy hunting crop from the rack. 'Watson, I think you know Mr Jones, of Scotland Yard? Let me introduce you to Mr Merry-weather, who is to be our companion in tonight's adventure.'

'We're hunting in couples again, doctor, you see,' said Jones in his consequential way. 'Our friend here is a wonderful man for starting a chase. All he wants is an old dog to help him to do the running down.'

'I hope a wild goose may not prove to be the end of our chase,' observed Mr Merryweather gloomily.

'You may place considerable confidence in Mr Holmes, sir,' said the police agent loftily. 'He has his own little methods, which are, if he won't mind my saying so, just a little too theoretical and fantastic, but he has the makings of a detective in him. It is not too much to say that once or twice, as in that business of the Sholto murder and the Agra treasure, he has been more nearly correct than the official force.'

'Oh, if you say so, Mr Jones, it is all right,' said the stranger with deference. 'Still, I confess that I miss my rubber. It is the first Saturday night for seven-and-twenty years that I have not had my rubber.'

'I think you will find,' said Sherlock Holmes, 'that you will play for a higher stake tonight than you have ever done yet, and that the play will be more exciting. For you, Mr Merryweather, the stake will be some thirty thousand pounds; and for you, Jones, it will be the man upon whom you wish to lay your hands.'

'John Clay, the murderer, thief, smasher and forger. He's a young man, Mr Merryweather, but he is at the head of his profession, and I would rather have my bracelets on him than on any criminal in London. He's a remarkable man, is young John Clay. His grandfather was a royal duke, and he himself has been to Eton and Oxford. His brain is as cunning as his fingers, and though we meet signs of him at every turn, we never know where to find the man himself. He'll crack a crib in Scotland one week, and be raising money to build an orphanage in Cornwall the next. I've been on his track for years and have never set eyes on him yet.'

'I hope that I may have the pleasure of introducing you tonight. I've had one or two little turns also with Mr John Clay, and I agree with you that he is at the head of his profession. It is past ten, however, and quite time that we started. If you two will take the first hansom, Watson and I will follow in the second.'

Sherlock Holmes was not very communicative during the long drive and lay back in the cab humming the tunes which he had heard in the afternoon. We rattled through an endless labyrinth of gaslit streets until we emerged into Farrington Street.

'We are close there now,' my friend remarked. 'This fellow Merryweather is a bank director, and personally interested in the matter. I thought it as well to have Jones with us also. He is not a bad fellow, though an absolute imbecile in his profession. He has one positive virtue. He is as brave as a bulldog and as tenacious as a lobster if he gets his claws upon anyone. Here we are, and they are waiting for us.'

We had reached the same crowded thoroughfare in which we had found ourselves in the morning. Our cabs were dismissed, and, following the guidance of Mr Merryweather, we passed down a narrow passage and through a side door, which he opened for us. Within there was a small corridor, which ended in a very massive iron gate. This also was opened, and led down a flight of winding stone steps, which terminated at another formidable gate. Mr Merryweather stopped to light a lantern, and then conducted us down a dark, earth-smelling passage, and so, after opening a third door, into a huge vault or cellar, which was piled all round with crates and massive boxes.

'You are not very vulnerable from above,' Holmes remarked as he held up the lantern and gazed about him.

'Nor from below,' said Mr Merryweather, striking his stick upon the flags which lined the floor. 'Why, dear me, it sounds quite hollow!' he remarked, looking up in surprise.

'I must really ask you to be a little more quiet!' said Holmes severely. 'You have already imperilled the whole success of our expedition. Might I beg that you would have the goodness to sit down upon one of those boxes, and not to interfere?'

The solemn Mr Merryweather perched himself upon a crate, with a very injured expression upon his face, while Holmes fell upon his knees upon the floor and, with the lantern and a magnifying lens, began to examine minutely the cracks between the stones. A few seconds sufficed to satisfy him, for he sprang to his feet again and put his glass in his pocket.

'We have at least an hour before us,' he remarked, 'for they can hardly take any steps until the good pawnbroker is safely in bed. Then they will not lose a minute, for the sooner they do their work the longer time they will have for their escape. We are at present, doctor – as no doubt you have divined – in the cellar of the City branch of one of the principal London banks. Mr Merryweather is the chairman of directors, and he will explain to you that there are reasons why the more daring criminals of London should take a considerable interest in this cellar at present.'

'It is our French gold,' whispered the director. 'We have had several warnings that an attempt might be made upon it.'

'Your French gold?'

'Yes. We had occasion some months ago to strengthen our resources and borrowed for that purpose thirty thousand napoleons from the Bank of France. It has become known that we have never had occasion to unpack the money, and that it is still lying in our cellar. The crate upon which I sit contains two thousand napoleons packed between layers of lead foil. Our reserve of bullion is much larger at present than is usually kept in a single branch office, and the directors have had misgivings upon the subject.'

'Which were very well justified,' observed Holmes. 'And now it is time that we arranged our little plans. I expect that within an hour matters will come to a head. In the meantime, Mr Merryweather, we must put the screen over that dark-lantern.'

'And sit in the dark?'

'I am afraid so. I had brought a pack of cards in my pocket, and I thought that, as we were a *partie carrée*, you might have your rubber after all. But I see that the enemy's preparations have gone so far that we cannot risk the presence of a light. And, first of all, we must choose our positions. These are daring men, and though we shall take them at a disadvantage, they may do us some harm unless we are careful. I shall stand behind this crate, and do you conceal yourselves behind those. Then, when I flash a light upon them, close in swiftly. If they fire, Watson, have no compunction about shooting them down.'

I placed my revolver, cocked, upon the top of the wooden case behind which I crouched. Holmes shot the slide across the front of his lantern and left us in pitch darkness – such an absolute darkness as I have never before experienced. The smell of hot metal remained to assure us that the light was still there, ready to flash out at a moment's notice. To me, with my nerves worked up to a pitch of expectancy, there was something depressing and subduing in the sudden gloom and in the cold dank air of the vault.

'They have but one retreat,' whispered Holmes. 'That is back through the house into Saxe-Coburg Square. I hope that you have done what I asked you, Jones?'

'I have an inspector and two officers waiting at the front door.'

'Then we have stopped all the holes. And now we must be silent and wait.'

What a time it seemed! From comparing notes afterwards it was but an hour and a quarter, yet it appeared to me that the night must have almost gone and the dawn be breaking above us. My limbs were weary and stiff, for I feared to change my position; yet my nerves were worked up to the highest pitch of tension, and my hearing was so acute that I could not only hear the gentle breathing of my companions, but I could distinguish the deeper, heavier in-breath of the bulky Jones from the thin, sighing note of the bank director. From my position I could look over the case in the direction of the floor. Suddenly my eyes caught the glint of a light.

At first it was but a lurid spark upon the stone pavement. Then it lengthened out until it became a yellow line, and then, without any warning or sound, a gash seemed to open and a hand appeared, a white, almost womanly hand, which felt about in the centre of the little area of light. For a minute or more the hand, with its writhing fingers, protruded out of the floor. Then it was withdrawn as suddenly as it appeared, and all was dark again save for the single lurid spark which marked a chink between the stones.

Its disappearance, however, was but momentary. With a rending, tearing sound, one of the broad, white stones turned over upon its side and left a square, gaping hole, through which streamed the light of a lantern. Over the edge there peeped a clean-cut, boyish face, which looked keenly about it, and then, with a hand on either side of the aperture, drew itself shoulder-high and waist-high, until one knee rested upon the edge. In another instant he stood at the side of the hole and was hauling after him a companion, lithe and small like himself, with a pale face and a shock of very red hair.

'It's all clear,' he whispered. 'Have you the chisel and the bags? – Great Scott! Jump, Archie, jump, and I'll swing for it!'

Sherlock Holmes had sprung out and seized the intruder by the collar. The other dived down the hole, and I heard the sound of rending cloth as Jones clutched at his skirts. The light flashed upon the barrel of a revolver, but Holmes's hunting-crop came down on the man's wrist and the pistol clinked upon the stone floor.

'It's no use, John Clay,' said Holmes blandly. 'You have no chance at all.'

'So I see,' the other answered with the utmost coolness. 'I fancy that my pal is all right, though I see you have got his coat-tails.'

'There are three men waiting for him at the door,' said Holmes.

'Oh, indeed! You seem to have done the thing very completely. I must compliment you.'

'And I you,' Holmes answered. 'Your red-headed idea was very new and effective.'

'You'll see your pal again presently,' said Jones. 'He's quicker at climbing down holes than I am. Just hold out while I fix the derbies.'

'I beg that you will not touch me with your filthy hands,' remarked our prisoner, as the handcuffs clattered upon his wrists. 'You may not be aware that I have royal blood in my veins. Have the goodness, also, when you address me always to say "sir" and "please".'

'All right,' said Jones, with a stare and a snigger. 'Well, would you please, sir, march upstairs, where we can get a cab to carry your highness to the police-station?'

'That is better,' said John Clay serenely. He made a sweeping bow to the three of us and walked quietly off in the custody of the detective.

'Really, Mr Holmes,' said Mr Merryweather as we followed them from the cellar, 'I do not know how the bank can thank you or repay you. There is no doubt that you have detected and defeated in the most complete manner one of the most determined attempts at bank robbery that have ever come within my experience.'

'I have had one or two little scores of my own to settle with Mr John Clay,' said Holmes. 'I have been at some small expense over this matter, which I shall expect the bank to refund, but beyond that I am amply repaid by having had an experience which is in many ways unique, and by hearing the very remarkable narrative of the Red-Headed League.'

'You see, Watson,' he explained in the early hours of the morning as we sat over a glass of whisky and soda in Baker Street, 'it was perfectly obvious from the first that the only possible object of this rather fantastic business of the advertisement of the league, and the copying of the *Encyclopaedia*, must be to get this not over-bright pawnbroker out of the way for a number of hours every day. It was a curious way of managing it but, really, it would be difficult to suggest a better. The method was no doubt suggested to Clay's ingenious mind by the colour of his accomplice's hair. The four pounds a week was a lure which must draw him, and what was it to them, who were playing for thousands? They put in the advertisement, one rogue has the temporary office, the other rogue incites the man to apply for it, and together they manage to secure his absence every morning in the week. From the time that I heard of the assistant having come for half wages, it was obvious to me that he had some strong motive for securing the situation.'

'But how could you guess what the motive was?'

'Had there been women in the house, I should have suspected a mere vulgar intrigue. That, however, was out of the question. The man's business was a small one, and there was nothing in his house which could account for such elaborate preparations, and such an expenditure as they were at. It must, then, be something out of the house. What could it be? I thought of the assistant's fondness for photography, and his trick of vanishing into the cellar. The cellar! There was the end of this tangled clue. Then I made enquiries as to this mysterious assistant and found that I had to deal with one of the coolest and most daring criminals in London. He was doing something in the cellar – something which took many hours a day for months on end. What could it be, once more? I could think of nothing save that he was running a tunnel to some other building.

'So far I had got when we went to visit the scene of action. I surprised you by beating upon the pavement with my stick. I was ascertaining whether the cellar stretched out in front or behind. It was not in front. Then I rang the bell and, as I hoped, the assistant answered it. We have had some skirmishes, but we had never set eyes upon each other before. I hardly looked at his face. His knees were what I wished to see. You must yourself have remarked how worn, wrinkled, and stained they were. They spoke of those hours of burrowing. The only remaining point was what they were burrowing for. I walked round the corner, saw the City and Suburban Bank abutted on our friend's premises, and felt that I had solved my problem. When you drove home after the concert I called upon Scotland Yard and upon the chairman of the bank directors, with the result that you have seen.'

'And how could you tell that they would make their attempt tonight?' I asked.

'Well, when they closed their league offices that was a sign that they cared no longer about Mr Jabez Wilson's presence – in other words, that they had completed their tunnel. But it was essential that they should use it soon, as it might be discovered, or the bullion might be removed. Saturday would suit them better than any other day, as it would give them two days for their escape. For all these reasons I expected them to come tonight.'

'You reasoned it out beautifully,' I exclaimed in unfeigned admiration. 'It is so long a chain, and yet every link rings true.'

'It saved me from ennui,' he answered, yawning. 'Alas! I already feel it closing in upon me. My life is spent in one long effort to escape from the commonplaces of existence. These little problems help me to do so.'

'And you are a benefactor of the race,' said I.

He shrugged his shoulders. 'Well, perhaps, after all, it is of some little use,' he remarked. '*L'homme c'est rien – l'oeuvre c'est tout*, as Gustave Flaubert wrote to George Sand.'

The Five Orange Pips

When I glance over my notes and records of the Sherlock Holmes cases between the years 1882 and 1890, I am faced by so many which present strange and interesting features that it is no easy matter to know which to choose and which to leave. Some, however, have already gained publicity through the papers, and others have not offered a field for those peculiar qualities which my friend possessed in so high a degree, and which it is the object of these papers to illustrate. Some, too, have baffled his analytical skill, and would be, as narratives, beginnings without an ending, while others have been but partially cleared up, and have their explanations founded rather upon conjecture and surmise than on that absolute logical proof which was so dear to him. There is, however, one of these last which was so remarkable in its details and so startling in its results that I am tempted to give some account of it in spite of the fact that there are points in connection with it which never have been, and probably never will be, entirely cleared up.

The year 1887 furnished us with a long series of cases of greater or less interest, of which I retain the records. Among my headings under this one twelve months, I find an account of the adventure of the Paradol Chamber, of the Amateur Mendicant Society, who held a luxurious club in the lower vault of a furniture warehouse, of the facts connected with the loss of the British barque *Sophy Anderson*, of the singular adventures of the Grice Patersons in the island of Uffa and, finally, of the Camberwell poisoning case. In the latter, as may be remembered, Sherlock Holmes was able, by winding up the dead man's watch, to prove that it had been wound up two hours before, and that therefore the deceased had gone to bed within that time – a deduction which was of the greatest importance in clearing up the case. All these I may sketch out at some future date, but none of them presents such singular features as the strange train of circumstances which I have now taken up my pen to describe.

It was in the latter days of September, and the equinoctial gales had set in with exceptional violence. All day the wind had screamed and the rain had beaten against the windows, so that even here in the heart of great, hand-made London we were forced to raise our minds for the instant from the routine of life and to recognise the presence of those great elemental forces which shriek at mankind through the bars of his civilisation, like untamed beasts in a cage. As evening drew in, the storm grew higher and louder, and the wind cried and sobbed like a child in the chimney. Sherlock Holmes sat moodily at one side of the fireplace cross-indexing his records of crime, while I at the other was so deep in one of Clark Russell's fine sea-stories that the howl of the gale from without seemed to blend with the text and the splash of the rain to lengthen out into the long swash of the sea waves. My wife was on a visit to her mother's, and for a few days I was a dweller once more in my old quarters at Baker Street.

'Why,' said I, glancing up at my companion, 'that was surely the bell. Who could come tonight? Some friend of yours, perhaps?'

'Except yourself I have none,' he answered. 'I do not encourage visitors.'

'A client, then?'

'If so, it is a serious case. Nothing less would bring a man out on such a day and at such an hour. But I take it that it is more likely to be some crony of the landlady's.'

Sherlock Holmes was wrong in his conjecture, however, for there came a step in the passage and a tapping at the door. He stretched out his long arm to turn the lamp away from himself and towards the vacant chair upon which a newcomer must sit.

'Come in!' said he.

The man who entered was young, some two-and-twenty at the outside, well-groomed and trimly clad, with something of refinement and delicacy in his bearing. The streaming umbrella which he held in his hand, and his long shining waterproof told of the fierce weather through which he had come. He looked about him anxiously in the glare of the lamp, and I could see that his face was pale and his eyes heavy, like those of a man who is weighed down with some great anxiety.

'I owe you an apology,' he said, raising his golden pince-nez to his eyes. 'I trust that I am not intruding. I fear that I have brought some traces of the storm and rain into your snug chamber.'

'Give me your coat and umbrella,' said Holmes. 'They may rest here on the hook and will be dry presently. You have come up from the southwest, I see.'

'Yes, from Horsham.'

'That clay and chalk mixture which I see upon your toe-caps is quite distinctive.'

'I have come for advice.'

'That is easily got.'

'And help.'

'That is not always so easy.'

'I have heard of you, Mr Holmes. I heard from Major Prendergast how you saved him in the Tankerville Club scandal.'

'Ah, of course. He was wrongfully accused of cheating at cards.'

'He said that you could solve anything.'

'He said too much.'

'That you are never beaten.'

'I have been beaten four times – three times by men, and once by a woman.'

'But what is that compared with the number of your successes?'

'It is true that I have been generally successful.'

'Then you may be so with me.'

'I beg that you will draw your chair up to the fire and favour me with some details as to your case.'

'It is no ordinary one.'

'None of those which come to me are. I am the last court of appeal.'

'And yet I question, sir, whether, in all your experience, you have ever listened to a more mysterious and inexplicable chain of events than those which have happened in my own family.'

'You fill me with interest,' said Holmes. 'Pray give us the essential facts from the commencement, and I can afterwards question you as to those details which seem to me to be the most important.'

The young man pulled his chair up and pushed his wet feet out towards the blaze.

'My name,' said he, 'is John Openshaw, but my own affairs have, as far as I can understand, little to do with this awful business. It is a hereditary matter; so in order to give you an idea of the facts, I must go back to the commencement of the affair.

'You must know that my grandfather had two sons – my uncle Elias and my father Joseph. My father had a small factory at Coventry, which he enlarged at the time of the invention of bicycling. He was a patentee of the Openshaw unbreakable tyre, and his business met with such success that he was able to sell it and to retire upon a handsome competence.

'My uncle Elias emigrated to America when he was a young man and became a planter in Florida, where he was reported to have done very well. At the time of the war he fought in Jackson's army, and afterwards under Hood, where he rose to be a colonel. When Lee laid down his arms, my uncle returned to his plantation, where he remained for three or four years. About 1869 or 1870 he came back to Europe and took a small estate in Sussex, near Horsham. He had made a very considerable fortune in the States, and his reason for leaving them was his aversion to the negroes and his dislike of the Republican policy in extending the franchise to them. He was a singular man, fierce and quick-tempered, very foul-mouthed when he was angry, and of a most retiring disposition. During all the years that he lived at Horsham, I doubt if he ever set foot in the town. He had a garden and two or three fields round his house, and there he would take his exercise, though very often for weeks on end he would never leave his room. He drank a great deal of brandy and smoked very heavily, but he would see no society and did not want any friends, not even his own brother.

'He didn't mind me; in fact, he took a fancy to me, for at the time when he saw me first I was a youngster of twelve or so. This would be in the year 1878, after he had been eight or nine years in England. He begged my father to let me live with him and he was very kind to me in his way. When he was sober he used to be fond of playing backgammon and draughts with me, and he would make me his representative both with the servants and with the tradespeople, so that by the time that I was sixteen I was quite master of the house. I kept all the keys and could go where I liked and do what I liked, so long as I did not disturb him in his privacy. There was one singular exception, however, for he had a single room, a lumber-room up among the attics, which was invariably locked, and which he would never permit either me or anyone else to enter. With a boy's curiosity I have peeped through the keyhole, but I was never able to see more than such a collection of old trunks and bundles as would be expected in such a room.

'One day – it was in March 1883 – a letter with a foreign stamp lay upon the table in front of the colonel's plate. It was not a common thing for him to receive letters, for his bills were all paid in ready money, and he had no friends of any sort. "From India!" said he as he took it up, "Pondicherry postmark! What can this be?" He opened it hurriedly and out there jumped five little dried orange pips, which pattered down upon his plate. I began to laugh at this, but the laugh was struck from my lips at the sight of his face. His lip had fallen, his eyes were protruding, his skin was the colour of putty and he glared at the envelope which he still held in his trembling hand. "KKK!" he shrieked, and then, "My God, my God, my sins have overtaken me!"

' "What is it, uncle?" I cried.

' "Death," said he, and rising from the table he retired to his room, leaving me palpitating with horror. I took up the envelope and saw scrawled in red ink upon the inner flap, just above the gum, the letter K three times repeated. There was nothing else save the five dried pips. What could be the reason for his overpowering terror? I left the breakfast-table, and as I ascended the stair I met him coming down with an old rusty key, which must have belonged to the attic, in one hand, and a small brass box, like a cashbox, in the other.

' "They may do what they like, but I'll checkmate them still," said he with an oath. "Tell Mary that I shall want a fire in my room today, and send down to Fordham, the Horsham lawyer."

'I did as he ordered, and when the lawyer arrived I was asked to step up to the room. The fire was burning brightly, and in the grate there was a mass of black, fluffy ash, as of burned paper, while the brass box stood open and empty beside it. As I glanced at the box I noticed, with a start, that upon the lid was printed the treble K which I had read in the morning upon the envelope.

' "I wish you, John," said my uncle, "to witness my will. I leave my estate, with all its advantages and all its disadvantages, to my brother, your father, whence it will, no doubt, descend to you. If you can enjoy it in peace, well and good! If you find you cannot, take my advice, my boy, and leave it to your deadliest enemy. I am sorry to give you such a two-edged thing, but I can't say what turn things are going to take. Kindly sign the paper where Mr Fordham shows you."

'I signed the paper as directed, and the lawyer took it away with him. The singular incident made, as you may think, the deepest impression upon me, and I pondered over it and turned it every way in my mind without being able to make anything of it. Yet I could not shake off the vague feeling of dread which it left behind, though the sensation grew less keen as the weeks passed and nothing happened to disturb the usual routine of our lives. I could see a change in my uncle, however. He drank more than ever, and he was less inclined for any sort of society. Most of his time he would spend in his room, with the door locked upon the inside, but sometimes he would emerge in a sort of drunken frenzy and would burst out of the house and tear about the garden with a revolver in his hand, screaming out that he was afraid of no man, and that he was not to be cooped up, like a sheep in a pen, by man or devil. When these hot fits were over, however, he would rush tumultuously in at the door and lock and bar it behind him, like a man who can brazen it out no longer against the terror which lies at the roots of his soul. At such times I have seen his face, even on a cold day, glisten with moisture, as though it were new raised from a basin.

'Well, to come to an end of the matter, Mr Holmes, and not to abuse your patience, there came a night when he made one of those drunken sallies but this time never came back. We found him, when we went to search for him, face downward in a little green-scummed pool, which lay at the foot of the garden. There was no sign of any violence, and the water was but two feet deep, so that the jury, having regard to his known eccentricity, brought in a verdict of suicide. But I, who knew how he winced at the very thought of death, had much ado to persuade myself that he had gone out of his way to meet it. The matter passed, however, and my father entered into possession of the estate, and of some fourteen thousand pounds, which lay to his credit at the bank.'

'One moment,' Holmes interposed, 'your statement is, I foresee, one of the most remarkable to which I have ever listened. Let me have the date of the reception by your uncle of the letter, and the date of his supposed suicide.'

'The letter arrived on the 10th March 1883. His death was seven weeks later, upon the night of May 2nd.'

'Thank you. Pray proceed.'

'When my father took over the Horsham property, he, at my request, made a careful examination of the attic, which had been always locked up. We found the brass box there, although its contents had been destroyed. On the inside of the lid was a paper label, with the initials of KKK repeated upon it, and "Letters, memoranda, receipts and a register" written beneath. This, we presumed, indicated the nature of the papers which had been destroyed by Colonel Openshaw. For the rest, there was nothing of much importance in the attic save a great many scattered papers and notebooks bearing upon my uncle's life in America. Some of them were of the wartime and showed that he had done his duty well and had borne the repute of a brave soldier. Others were of a date during the reconstruction of the Southern states, and were mostly concerned with politics, for he had evidently taken a strong part in opposing the carpetbag politicians who had been sent down from the North.

'Well, it was the beginning of 1884 when my father came to live at Horsham, and all went as well as possible with us until the January of 1885. On the fourth day after the New Year I heard my father give a sharp cry of surprise as we sat together at the breakfast-table. There he was, sitting with a newly opened envelope in one hand and five dried orange pips in the outstretched palm of the other one. He had always laughed at what he called my cock-and-bull story about the colonel, but he looked very scared and puzzled now that the same thing had come upon himself.

' "Why, what on earth does this mean, John?" he stammered.

'My heart had turned to lead. "It is KKK," said I.

'He looked inside the envelope. "So it is," he cried. "Here are the very letters. But what is this written above them?"

' "Put the papers on the sundial," I read, peeping over his shoulder.

' "What papers? What sundial?" he asked.

' "The sundial in the garden. There is no other," said I; "but the papers must be those that are destroyed."

' "Pooh!" said he, gripping hard at his courage. "We are in a civilised land here, and we can't have tomfoolery of this kind. Where does the thing come from?"

' "From Dundee," I answered, glancing at the postmark.

' "Some preposterous practical joke," said he. "What have I to do with sundials and papers? I shall take no notice of such nonsense."

' "I should certainly speak to the police," I said.

' "And be laughed at for my pains. Nothing of the sort."

' "Then let me do so."

' "No, I forbid you. I won't have a fuss made about such nonsense."

'It was in vain to argue with him, for he was a very obstinate man. I went about, however, with a heart which was full of forebodings.

'On the third day after the coming of the letter my father went from home to visit an old friend of his, Major Freebody, who is in command of one of the forts upon Portsdown Hill. I was glad that he should go, for it seemed to me that he was farther from danger when he was away from home. In that, however, I was in error. Upon the second day of his absence I received a telegram from the major, imploring me to come at once. My father had fallen into one of the deep chalk-pits which abound in the neighbourhood, and was lying senseless, with a shattered skull. I hurried to him, but he passed away without having ever recovered consciousness. He had, as it appears, been returning from Fareham in the twilight, and as the country was unknown to him, and the chalk-pit unfenced, the jury had no hesitation in bringing in a verdict of "death from accidental causes". Carefully as I examined every fact connected with his death, I was unable to find anything which could suggest the idea of murder. There were no signs of violence, no footmarks, no robbery, no record of strangers having been seen upon the roads. And yet I need not tell you that my mind was far from at ease, and that I was well-nigh certain that some foul plot had been woven round him.

'In this sinister way I came into my inheritance. You will ask me why I did not dispose of it? I answer, because I was well convinced that our troubles were in some way dependent upon an incident in my uncle's life, and that the danger would be as pressing in one house as in another.

'It was in January 1885 that my poor father met his end, and two years and eight months have elapsed since then. During that time I have lived happily at Horsham, and I had begun to hope that this curse had passed away from the family, and that it had ended with the last generation. I had begun to take comfort too soon, however; yesterday morning the blow fell in the very shape in which it had come upon my father.'

The young man took from his waistcoat a crumpled envelope and turning to the table he shook out upon it five little dried orange pips.

'This is the envelope,' he continued. 'The postmark is London – eastern division. Within are the very words which were upon my father's last message: "KKK"; and then, "Put the papers on the sundial." '

'What have you done?' asked Holmes.

'Nothing.'

'Nothing?'

'To tell the truth' – he sank his face into his thin, white hands – 'I have felt helpless. I have felt like one of those poor rabbits when the snake is writhing towards it. I seem to be in the grasp of some resistless, inexorable evil, which no foresight and no precautions can guard against.'

'Tut! tut!' cried Sherlock Holmes. 'You must act, man, or you are lost. Nothing but energy can save you. This is no time for despair.'

'I have seen the police.'

'Ah!'

'But they listened to my story with a smile. I am convinced that the inspector has formed the opinion that the letters are all practical jokes, and that the deaths of my relations were really accidents, as the jury stated, and were not to be connected with the warnings.'

Holmes shook his clenched hands in the air. 'Incredible imbecility!' he cried.

'They have, however, allowed me a policeman, who may remain in the house with me.'

'Has he come with you tonight?'

'No. His orders were to stay in the house.'

Again Holmes raved in the air.

'Why did you come to me,' he cried, 'and, above all, why did you not come at once?'

'I did not know. It was only today that I spoke to Major Prendergast about my troubles and was advised by him to come to you.'

'It is really two days since you had the letter. We should have acted before this. You have no further evidence, I suppose, than that which you have placed before us – no suggestive detail which might help us?'

'There is one thing,' said John Openshaw. He rummaged in his coat pocket, and, drawing out a piece of discoloured, blue-tinted paper, he laid it out upon the table. 'I have some remembrance,' said he, 'that on the day when my uncle burned the papers I observed that the small, unburned margins which lay amid the ashes were of this particular colour. I found this single sheet upon the floor of his room, and I am inclined to think that it may be one of the papers which had, perhaps, fluttered out from among the others, and in that way had escaped destruction. Beyond the mention of pips, I do not see that it helps us much. I think myself that it is a page from some private diary. The writing is undoubtedly my uncle's.'

Holmes moved the lamp, and we both bent over the sheet of paper, which showed by its ragged edge that it had indeed been torn from a book. It was headed, 'March 1869', and beneath were the following enigmatical notices:

4th   Hudson came. Same old platform.
7th   Set the pips on McCauley, Paramore and John Swain
       of St Augustine.
9th   McCauley cleared.
10th   John Swain cleared.
12th   Visited Paramore. All well.

'Thank you!' said Holmes, folding up the paper and returning it to our visitor. 'And now you must on no account lose another instant. We cannot spare time even to discuss what you have told me. You must get home instantly and act.'

'What shall I do?'

'There is but one thing to do. It must be done at once. You must put this piece of paper which you have shown us into the brass box which you have described. You must also put in a note to say that all the other papers were burned by your uncle and that this is the only one which remains. You must assert that in such words as will carry conviction with them. Having done this, you must at once put the box out upon the sundial, as directed. Do you understand?'

'Entirely.'

'Do not think of revenge, or anything of the sort, at present. I think that we may gain that by means of the law; but we have our web to weave, while theirs is already woven. The first consideration is to remove the pressing danger which threatens you. The second is to clear up the mystery and to punish the guilty parties.'

'I thank you,' said the young man, rising and pulling on his overcoat. 'You have given me fresh life and hope. I shall certainly do as you advise.'

'Do not lose an instant. And, above all, take care of yourself in the meanwhile, for I do not think that there can be a doubt that you are threatened by a very real and imminent danger. How do you go back?'

'By train from Waterloo.'

'It is not yet nine. The streets will be crowded, so I trust that you may be in safety. And yet you cannot guard yourself too closely.'

'I am armed.'

'That is well. Tomorrow I shall set to work upon your case.'

'I shall see you at Horsham, then?'

'No, your secret lies in London. It is there that I shall seek it.'

'Then I shall call upon you in a day, or in two days, with news as to the box and the papers. I shall take your advice in every particular.' He shook hands with us and took his leave. Outside the wind still screamed and the rain splashed and pattered against the windows. This strange, wild story seemed to have come to us from amid the mad elements – blown in upon us like a sheet of seaweed in a gale – and now to have been reabsorbed by them once more.

Sherlock Holmes sat for some time in silence, with his head sunk forward and his eyes bent upon the red glow of the fire. Then he lit his pipe, and leaning back in his chair he watched the blue smoke-rings as they chased each other up to the ceiling.

'I think, Watson,' he remarked at last, 'that of all our cases we have had none more fantastic than this.'

'Save, perhaps, the Sign of the Four.'

'Well, yes. Save, perhaps, that. And yet this John Openshaw seems to me to be walking amid even greater perils than did the Sholtos.'

'But have you,' I asked, 'formed any definite conception as to what these perils are?'

'There can be no question as to their nature,' he answered.

'Then what are they? Who is this KKK, and why does he pursue this unhappy family?'

Sherlock Holmes closed his eyes and placed his elbows upon the arms of his chair, with his fingertips together. 'The ideal reasoner,' he remarked, 'would, when he had once been shown a single fact in all its bearings, deduce from it not only all the chain of events which led up to it but also all the results which would follow from it. As Cuvier could correctly describe a whole animal by the contemplation of a single bone, so the observer who has thoroughly understood one link in a series of incidents should be able accurately to state all the other ones, both before and after. We have not yet grasped the results which the reason alone can attain to. Problems may be solved in the study which have baffled all those who have sought a solution by the aid of their senses. To carry the art, however, to its highest pitch, it is necessary that the reasoner should be able to utilise all the facts which have come to his knowledge; and this in itself implies, as you will readily see, a possession of all knowledge, which, even in these days of free education and encyclopaedias, is a somewhat rare accomplishment. It is not so impossible, however, that a man should possess all knowledge which is likely to be useful to him in his work, and this I have endeavoured in my case to do. If I remember rightly, you on one occasion, in the early days of our friendship, defined my limits in a very precise fashion.'

'Yes,' I answered, laughing. 'It was a singular document. Philosophy, astronomy and politics were marked at zero, I remember. Botany variable, geology profound as regards the mud-stains from any region within fifty miles of town, chemistry eccentric, anatomy unsystematic, library of sensational literature and crime records unique, violin-player, boxer, swordsman, lawyer and self-poisoner by cocaine and tobacco. Those, I think, were the main points of my analysis.'

Holmes grinned at the last item. 'Well,' he said, 'I say now, as I said then, that a man should keep his little brain-attic stocked with all the furniture that he is likely to use, and the rest he can put away in the lumber-room of his library, where he can get it if he wants it. Now, for such a case as the one which has been submitted to us tonight, we need certainly to muster all our resources. Kindly hand me down the letter K of the *American Encyclopaedia* which stands upon the shelf beside you. Thank you. Now let us consider the situation and see what may be deduced from it. In the first place, we may start with a strong presumption that Colonel Openshaw had some very strong reason for leaving America. Men at his time of life do not change all their habits and exchange willingly the charming climate of Florida for the lonely life of an English provincial town. His extreme love of solitude in England suggests the idea that he was in fear of someone or something, so we may assume as a working hypothesis that it was fear of someone or something which drove him from America. As to what it was he feared, we can only deduce that by considering the formidable letters which were received by himself and his successors. Did you remark the postmarks of those letters?'

'The first was from Pondicherry, the second from Dundee, and the third from London.'

'From East London. What do you deduce from that?'

'They are all seaports. That the writer was on board a ship.'

'Excellent. We have already a clue. There can be no doubt that the probability – the strong probability – is that the writer was on board a ship. And now let us consider another point. In the case of Pondicherry, seven weeks elapsed between the threat and its fulfilment, in Dundee it was only some three or four days. Does that suggest anything?'

'A greater distance to travel.'

'But the letter had also a greater distance to come.'

'Then I do not see the point.'

'There is at least a presumption that the vessel in which the man or men are is a sailing-ship. It looks as if they always send their singular warning or token before them when starting upon their mission. You see how quickly the deed followed the sign when it came from Dundee. If they had come from Pondicherry in a steamer they would have arrived almost as soon as their letter. But, as a matter of fact, seven weeks elapsed. I think that those seven weeks represented the difference between the mail-boat which brought the letter and the sailing vessel which brought the writer.'

'It is possible.'

'More than that. It is probable. And now you see the deadly urgency of this new case, and why I urged young Openshaw to caution. The blow has always fallen at the end of the time which it would take the senders to travel the distance. But this one comes from London, and therefore we cannot count upon delay.'

'Good God!' I cried. 'What can it mean, this relentless persecution?'

'The papers which Openshaw carried are obviously of vital importance to the person or persons in the sailing-ship. I think that it is quite clear that there must be more than one of them. A single man could not have carried out two deaths in such a way as to deceive a coroner's jury. There must have been several in it, and they must have been men of resource and determination. Their papers they mean to have, be the holder of them who it may. In this way you see KKK ceases to be the initials of an individual and becomes the badge of a society.'

'But of what society?'

'Have you never – ' said Sherlock Holmes, bending forward and sinking his voice – 'have you never heard of the Ku Klux Klan?'

'I never have.'

Holmes turned over the leaves of the book upon his knee. 'Here it is,' said he presently:

'Ku Klux Klan. A name derived from the fanciful resemblance to the sound produced by cocking a rifle. This terrible secret society was formed by some ex-Confederate soldiers in the Southern states after the Civil War, and it rapidly formed local branches in different parts of the country, notably in Tennessee, Louisiana, the Carolinas, Georgia and Florida. Its power was used for political purposes, principally for the terrorising of the negro voters and the murdering and driving from the country of those who were opposed to its views. Its outrages were usually preceded by a warning sent to the marked man in some fantastic but generally recognised shape – a sprig of oak-leaves in some parts, melon seeds or orange pips in others. On receiving this the victim might either openly abjure his former ways, or might fly from the country. If he braved the matter out, death would unfailingly come upon him, and usually in some strange and unforeseen manner. So perfect was the organisation of the society, and so systematic its methods, that there is hardly a case upon record where any man succeeded in braving it out with impunity or in which any of its outrages were traced home to the perpetrators. For some years the organisation flourished in spite of the efforts of the United States government and of the better classes of the community in the South. Eventually, in the year 1869, the movement rather suddenly collapsed, although there have been sporadic outbreaks of the same sort since that date.'

'You will observe,' said Holmes, laying down the volume, 'that the sudden breaking up of the society was coincident with the disappearance of Openshaw from America with their papers. It may well have been cause and effect. It is no wonder that he and his family have some of the more implacable spirits upon their track. You can understand that this register and diary may implicate some of the first men in the South, and that there may be many who will not sleep easy at night until it is recovered.'

'Then the page we have seen – '

'Is such as we might expect. It ran, if I remember right, "sent the pips to A, B and C" – that is, sent the society's warning to them. Then there are successive entries that A and B cleared, or left the country, and finally that C was visited, with, I fear, a sinister result for C. Well, I think, doctor, that we may let some light into this dark place, and I believe that the only chance young Openshaw has in the meantime is to do what I have told him. There is nothing more to be said or to be done tonight, so hand me over my violin and let us try to forget for half an hour the miserable weather and the still more miserable ways of our fellow men.'

It had cleared in the morning, and the sun was shining with a subdued brightness through the dim veil which hangs over the great city. Sherlock Holmes was already at breakfast when I came down.

'You will excuse me for not waiting for you,' said he; 'I have, I foresee, a very busy day before me in looking into this case of young Openshaw's.'

'What steps will you take?' I asked.

'It will very much depend upon the results of my first enquiries. I may have to go down to Horsham, after all.'

'You will not go there first?'

'No, I shall commence with the City. Just ring the bell and the maid will bring up your coffee.'

As I waited, I lifted the unopened newspaper from the table and glanced my eye over it. It rested upon a heading which sent a chill to my heart.

'Holmes,' I cried, 'you are too late.'

'Ah!' said he, laying down his cup, 'I feared as much. How was it done?' He spoke calmly, but I could see that he was deeply moved.

'My eye caught the name of Openshaw, and the heading "Tragedy Near Waterloo Bridge". Here is the account:

Between nine and ten last night Police-Constable Cook, of the H Division, on duty near Waterloo Bridge, heard a cry for help and a splash in the water. The night, however, was extremely dark and stormy, so that, in spite of the help of several passers-by, it was quite impossible to effect a rescue. The alarm, however, was given, and, by the aid of the water-police, the body was eventually recovered. It proved to be that of a young gentleman, whose name, as it appears from an envelope which was found in his pocket, was John Openshaw, and whose residence is near Horsham. It is conjectured that he may have been hurrying down to catch the last train from Waterloo Station and that in his haste and the extreme darkness he missed his path and walked over the edge of one of the small landing-places for river steamboats. The body exhibited no traces of violence, and there can be no doubt that the deceased had been the victim of an unfortunate accident, which should have the effect of calling the attention of the authorities to the condition of the riverside landing-stages.

We sat in silence for some minutes, Holmes more depressed and shaken than I had ever seen him.

'That hurts my pride, Watson,' he said at last. 'It is a petty feeling, no doubt, but it hurts my pride. It becomes a personal matter with me now, and, if God sends me health, I shall set my hand upon this gang. That he should come to me for help, and that I should send him away to his death — !' He sprang from his chair and paced about the room in uncontrollable agitation, with a flush upon his sallow cheeks and a nervous clasping and unclasping of his long thin hands.

'They must be cunning devils,' he exclaimed at last. 'How could they have decoyed him down there? The Embankment is not on the direct line to the station. The bridge, no doubt, was too crowded, even on such a night, for their purpose. Well, Watson, we shall see who will win in the long run. I am going out now!'

'To the police?'

'No; I shall be my own police. When I have spun the web they may take the flies, but not before.'

All day I was engaged in my professional work, and it was late in the evening before I returned to Baker Street. Sherlock Holmes had not yet come back. It was nearly ten o'clock before he entered, looking pale and worn. He walked up to the sideboard and tearing a piece from the loaf he devoured it voraciously, washing it down with a long draught of water.

'You are hungry,' I remarked.

'Starving. It had escaped my memory. I have had nothing since breakfast.'

'Nothing?'

'Not a bite. I had no time to think of it.'

'And how have you succeeded?'

'Well.'

'You have a clue?'

'I have them in the hollow of my hand. Young Openshaw shall not long remain unavenged. Why, Watson, let us put their own devilish trademark upon them. It is well thought of!'

'What do you mean?'

He took an orange from the cupboard, and tearing it to pieces he squeezed out the pips upon the table. Of these he took five and thrust them into an envelope. On the inside of the flap he wrote 'SH for JC'. Then he sealed it and addressed it to 'Captain James Calhoun, Barque *Lone Star*, Savannah, Georgia'.

'That will await him when he enters port,' said he, chuckling. 'It may give him a sleepless night. He will find it as sure a precursor of his fate as Openshaw did before him.'

'And who is this Captain Calhoun?'

'The leader of the gang. I shall have the others, but he first.'

'How did you trace it, then?'

He took a large sheet of paper from his pocket, all covered with dates and names.

'I have spent the whole day,' said he, 'over Lloyd's registers and files of the old papers, following the future career of every vessel which touched at Pondicherry in January and February in 1883. There were thirty-six ships of fair tonnage which were reported there during those months. Of these, one, the *Lone Star*, instantly attracted my attention, since, although it was reported as having cleared from London, the name is that which is given to one of the states of the Union.'

'Texas, I think.'

'I was not and am not sure which; but I knew that the ship must have an American origin.'

'What then?'

'I searched the Dundee records, and when I found that the barque *Lone Star* was there in January 1885, my suspicion became a certainty. I then enquired as to the vessels which lay at present in the port of London.'

'Yes?'

'The *Lone Star* had arrived here last week. I went down to the Albert Dock and found that she had been taken down the river by the early tide this morning, homeward bound to Savannah. I wired to Gravesend and learned that she had passed some time ago, and as the wind is easterly I have no doubt that she is now past the Goodwins and not very far from the Isle of Wight.'

'What will you do, then?'

'Oh, I have my hand upon him. He and the two mates are, as I learn, the only native-born Americans on the ship. The others are Finns and Germans. I know, also, that they were all three away from the ship last night. I had it from the stevedore who has been loading their cargo. By the time their sailing-ship reaches Savannah, the mail-boat will have carried this letter and the cable will have informed the police of Savannah that these three gentlemen are badly wanted here upon a charge of murder.'

There is ever a flaw, however, in the best laid of human plans, and the murderers of John Openshaw were never to receive the orange pips which would show them that another, as cunning and as resolute as themselves, was upon their track. Very long and very severe were the equinoctial gales that year. We waited long for news of the *Lone Star* of Savannah, but none ever reached us. We did at last hear that somewhere far out in the Atlantic a shattered stern-post of a boat was seen swinging in the trough of a wave, with the letters *LS* carved upon it, and that is all we shall ever know of the fate of the *Lone Star*.

The Man with the Twisted Lip

Isa Whitney, brother of the late Elias Whitney, DD, Principal of the Theological College of St George's, was much addicted to opium. The habit grew upon him, as I understand, from some foolish freak when he was at college; for having read De Quincey's description of his dreams and sensations, he had drenched his tobacco with laudanum in an attempt to produce the same effects. He found, as so many more have done, that the practice is easier to attain than to get rid of, and for many years he continued to be a slave to the drug, an object of mingled horror and pity to his friends and relatives. I can see him now, with yellow, pasty face, drooping lids and pinpoint pupils, all huddled in a chair, the wreck and ruin of a noble man.

One night – it was in June 1889 – there came a ring to my bell, about the hour when a man gives his first yawn and glances at the clock. I sat up in my chair, and my wife laid her needlework down in her lap and made a little face of disappointment.

'A patient!' said she. 'You'll have to go out.'

I groaned, for I was newly come back from a weary day.

We heard the door open, a few hurried words, and then quick steps upon the linoleum. Our own door flew open, and a lady, clad in some dark-coloured stuff, with a black veil, entered the room.

'You will excuse my calling so late,' she began, and then, suddenly losing her self-control, she ran forward, threw her arms about my wife's neck, and sobbed upon her shoulder. 'Oh, I'm in such trouble!' she cried; 'I do so want a little help.'

'Why,' said my wife, pulling up her veil, 'it is Kate Whitney. How you startled me, Kate! I had not an idea who you were when you came in.'

'I didn't know what to do, so I came straight to you.' That was always the way. Folk who were in grief came to my wife like birds to a lighthouse.

'It was very sweet of you to come. Now, you must have some wine and water, and sit here comfortably and tell us all about it. Or should you rather that I sent James off to bed?'

'Oh, no, no! I want the doctor's advice and help, too. It's about Isa. He has not been home for two days. I am so frightened about him!'

It was not the first time that she had spoken to us of her husband's trouble, to me as a doctor, to my wife as an old friend and school companion. We soothed and comforted her by such words as we could find. Did she know where her husband was? Was it possible that we could bring him back to her?

It seems that it was. She had the surest information that of late he had, when the fit was on him, made use of an opium den in the farthest east of the City. Hitherto his orgies had always been confined to one day, and he had come back, twitching and shattered, in the evening. But now the spell had been upon him eight-and-forty hours, and he lay there, doubtless among the dregs of the docks, breathing in the poison or sleeping off the effects. There he was to be found, she was sure of it, at the Bar of Gold in Upper Swandam Lane. But what was she to do? How could she, a young and timid woman, make her way into such a place and pluck her husband out from among the ruffians who surrounded him?

There was the case, and of course there was but one way out of it. Might I not escort her to this place? And then, as a second thought, why should she come at all? I was Isa Whitney's medical adviser, and as such I had influence over him. I could manage it better if I were alone. I promised her on my word that I would send him home in a cab within two hours if he were indeed at the address which she had given me. And so in ten minutes I had left my armchair and cheery sitting-room behind me, and was speeding eastward in a hansom on a strange errand, as it seemed to me at the time, though the future only could show how strange it was to be.

But there was no great difficulty in the first stage of my adventure. Upper Swandam Lane is a vile alley lurking behind the high wharves which line the north side of the river to the east of London Bridge. Between a slop-shop and a gin-shop, approached by a steep flight of steps leading down to a black gap like the mouth of a cave, I found the den of which I was in search. Ordering my cab to wait, I passed down the steps, worn hollow in the centre by the ceaseless tread of drunken feet, and by the light of a flickering oil-lamp above the door I found the latch and made my way into a long, low room, thick and heavy with the brown opium smoke and terraced with wooden berths, like the forecastle of an emigrant ship.

Through the gloom one could dimly catch a glimpse of bodies lying in strange fantastic poses, bowed shoulders, bent knees, heads thrown back, and chins pointing upward, with here and there a dark, lack-lustre eye turned upon the newcomer. Out of the black shadows there glimmered little red circles of light, now bright, now faint, as the burning poison waxed or waned in the bowls of the metal pipes. The most lay silent, but some muttered to themselves, and others talked together in strange, low, monotonous voices, their conversation coming in gushes and then suddenly tailing off into silence, each mumbling out his own thoughts and paying little heed to the words of his neighbour. At the farther end was a small brazier of burning charcoal, beside which on a three-legged wooden stool there sat a tall, thin old man, with his jaw resting upon his two fists and his elbows upon his knees, staring into the fire.

As I entered, a sallow Malay attendant had hurried up with a pipe for me and a supply of the drug, beckoning me to an empty berth.

'Thank you. I have not come to stay,' said I. 'There is a friend of mine here, Mr Isa Whitney, and I wish to speak with him.'

There was a movement and an exclamation from my right, and peering through the gloom, I saw Whitney, pale, haggard and unkempt, staring out at me.

'My God! It's Watson,' said he. He was in a pitiable state of reaction, with every nerve in a twitter. 'I say, Watson, what o'clock is it?'

'Nearly eleven.'

'Of what day?'

'Of Friday, June 19th.'

'Good heavens! I thought it was Wednesday. It *is* Wednesday. What d'you want to frighten a chap for?' He sank his face on to his arms and began to sob in a high treble key.

'I tell you that it is Friday, man. Your wife has been waiting these two days for you. You should be ashamed of yourself!'

'So I am. But you've got mixed, Watson, for I have only been here a few hours, three pipes, four pipes – I forget how many. But I'll go home with you. I wouldn't frighten Kate – poor little Kate. Give me your hand! Have you a cab?'

'Yes, I have one waiting.'

'Then I shall go in it. But I must owe something. Find what I owe, Watson. I am all off colour. I can do nothing for myself.'

I walked down the narrow passage between the double row of sleepers, holding my breath to keep out the vile, stupefying fumes of the drug, and looking about for the manager. As I passed the tall man who sat by the brazier I felt a sudden pluck at my skirt, and a low voice whispered, 'Walk past me, and then look back at me.' The words fell quite distinctly upon my ear. I glanced down. They could only have come from the old man at my side, and yet he sat now as absorbed as ever, very thin, very wrinkled, bent with age, an opium pipe dangling down from between his knees, as though it had dropped in sheer lassitude from his fingers. I took two steps forward and looked back. It took all my self-control to prevent me from breaking out into a cry of astonishment. He had turned his back so that none could see him but I. His form had filled out, his wrinkles were gone, the dull eyes had regained their fire, and there, sitting by the fire and grinning at my surprise, was none other than Sherlock Holmes. He made a slight motion to me to approach him, and instantly, as he turned his face half round to the company once more, subsided into a doddering, loose-lipped senility.

'Holmes!' I whispered, 'what on earth are you doing in this den?'

'As low as you can,' he answered; 'I have excellent ears. If you would have the great kindness to get rid of that sottish friend of yours, I should be exceedingly glad to have a little talk with you.'

'I have a cab outside.'

'Then pray send him home in it. You may safely trust him, for he appears to be too limp to get into any mischief. I should recommend you also to send a note by the cabman to your wife to say that you have thrown in your lot with me. If you will wait outside, I shall be with you in five minutes.'

It was difficult to refuse any of Sherlock Holmes's requests, for they were always so exceedingly definite and put forward with such a quiet air of mastery. I felt, however, that when Whitney was once confined in the cab my mission was practically accomplished; and for the rest, I could not wish anything better than to be associated with my friend in one of those singular adventures which were the normal condition of his existence. In a few minutes I had written my note, paid Whitney's bill, led him out to the cab and seen him driven through the darkness. In a very short time a decrepit figure had emerged from the opium den and I was walking down the street with Sherlock Holmes. For two streets he shuffled along with a bent back and an uncertain foot. Then, glancing quickly round, he straightened himself out and burst into a hearty fit of laughter.

'I suppose, Watson,' said he, 'that you imagine that I have added opium-smoking to cocaine injections and all the other little weaknesses on which you have favoured me with your medical views.'

'I was certainly surprised to find you there.'

'But not more so than I to find you.'

'I came to find a friend.'

'And I to find an enemy.'

'An enemy?'

'Yes; one of my natural enemies, or, shall I say, my natural prey.

Briefly, Watson, I am in the midst of a very remarkable inquiry, and I had hoped to find a clue in the incoherent ramblings of these sots, as I have done before now. Had I been recognised in that den my life would not have been worth an hour's purchase, for I have used it before now for my own purposes, and the rascally Lascar who runs it has sworn to have vengeance upon me. There is a trap-door at the back of that building, near the corner of Paul's Wharf, which could tell some strange tales of what has passed through it upon moonless nights.'

'What! You do not mean bodies?'

'Ay, bodies, Watson. We should be rich men if we had a thousand pounds for every poor devil who has been done to death in that den. It is the vilest murder-trap on the whole riverside, and I fear that Neville St Clair has entered it never to leave it more. But our trap should be here.' He put his two forefingers between his teeth and whistled shrilly – a signal which was answered by a similar whistle from the distance, followed shortly by the rattle of wheels and the clink of horses' hoofs.

'Now, Watson,' said Holmes, as a tall dogcart dashed up through the gloom, throwing out two golden tunnels of yellow light from its side lanterns, 'you'll come with me, won't you?'

'If I can be of use.'

'Oh, a trusty comrade is always of use; and a chronicler still more so. My room at The Cedars is a double-bedded one.'

'The Cedars?'

'Yes; that is Mr St Clair's house. I am staying there while I conduct the inquiry.'

'Where is it, then?'

'Near Lee, in Kent. We have a seven-mile drive before us.'

'But I am all in the dark.'

'Of course you are. You'll know all about it presently. Jump up here. All right, John; we shall not need you. Here's half a crown. Look out for me tomorrow, about eleven. Give her her head. So long, then!'

He flicked the horse with his whip, and we dashed away through the endless succession of sombre and deserted streets which widened gradually until we were flying across a broad balustraded bridge, with the murky river flowing sluggishly beneath us. Beyond lay another dull wilderness of bricks and mortar, its silence broken only by the heavy, regular footfall of the policeman or the songs and shouts of some belated party of revellers. A dull wrack was drifting slowly across the sky, and a star or two twinkled dimly here and there through the rifts of the clouds. Holmes drove in silence, with his head sunk upon his breast, and the air of a man who is lost in thought, while I sat beside him, curious to learn what this new quest might be which seemed to tax his powers so sorely and yet afraid to break in upon the current of his thoughts. We had driven several miles, and were beginning to get to the fringe of the belt of suburban villas, when he shook himself, shrugged his shoulders and lit up his pipe with the air of a man who has satisfied himself that he is acting for the best.

'You have a grand gift of silence, Watson,' said he. 'It makes you quite invaluable as a companion. 'Pon my word, it is a great thing for me to have someone to talk to, for my own thoughts are not over-pleasant. I was wondering what I should say to this dear little woman tonight when she meets me at the door.'

'You forget that I know nothing about it.'

'I shall just have time to tell you the facts of the case before we get to Lee. It seems absurdly simple, and yet somehow I can get nothing to go upon. There's plenty of thread, no doubt, but I can't get the end of it in my hand. Now, I'll state the case clearly and concisely to you, Watson, and maybe you can see a spark where all is dark to me.'

'Proceed, then.'

'Some years ago – to be definite, in May 1884 – there came to Lee a gentleman, Neville St Clair by name, who appeared to have plenty of money. He took a large villa, laid out the grounds very nicely, and lived generally in good style. By degrees he made friends in the neighbourhood, and in 1887 he married the daughter of a local brewer, by whom he now has two children. He had no occupation, but was interested in several companies and went into town as a rule in the morning, returning by the 5.14 from Cannon Street every night. Mr St Clair, who is now thirty-seven years of age, is a man of temperate habits, a good husband, a very affectionate father and a man who is popular with all who know him. I may add that his whole debts at the present moment, as far as we have been able to ascertain, amount to £88 10s., while he has £220 standing to his credit in the Capital and Counties Bank. There is no reason, therefore, to think that money troubles have been weighing upon his mind.

'Last Monday, Mr Neville St Clair went into town rather earlier than usual, remarking before he started that he had two important commissions to perform, and that he would bring his little boy home a box of bricks. Now, by the merest chance, his wife received a telegram upon this same Monday, very shortly after his departure, to the effect that a small parcel of considerable value which she had been expecting was waiting for her at the offices of the Aberdeen Shipping Company. Now, if you are well up in your London, you will know that the office of the company is in Fresno Street, which branches out of Upper Swandam Lane, where you found me tonight. Mrs St Clair had her lunch, started for the City, did some shopping, proceeded to the company's office, got her packet, and found herself at exactly 4.35 walking through Swandam Lane on her way back to the station. Have you followed me so far?'

'It is very clear.'

'If you remember, Monday was an exceedingly hot day, and Mrs St Clair walked slowly, glancing about in the hope of seeing a cab, as she did not like the neighbourhood in which she found herself. While she was walking in this way down Swandam Lane, she suddenly heard an ejaculation or cry, and was struck cold to see her husband looking down at her and, as it seemed to her, beckoning to her from a second-floor window. The window was open, and she distinctly saw his face, which she describes as being terribly agitated. He waved his hands frantically to her, and then vanished from the window so suddenly that it seemed to her that he had been plucked back by some irresistible force from behind. One singular point which struck her quick feminine eye was that although he wore some dark coat, such as he had started to town in, he had on neither collar nor necktie.

'Convinced that something was amiss with him, she rushed down the steps – for the house was none other than the opium den in which you found me tonight – and running through the front room she attempted to ascend the stairs which led to the first floor. At the foot of the stairs, however, she met this Lascar scoundrel of whom I have spoken, who thrust her back and, aided by a Dane, who acts as assistant there, pushed her out into the street. Filled with the most maddening doubts and fears, she rushed down the lane and, by rare good-fortune, met in Fresno Street a number of constables with an inspector, all on their way to their beat. The inspector and two men accompanied her back, and in spite of the continued resistance of the proprietor, they made their way to the room in which Mr St Clair had last been seen. There was no sign of him there. In fact, in the whole of that floor there was no one to be found save a crippled wretch of hideous aspect, who, it seems, made his home there. Both he and the Lascar stoutly swore that no one else had been in the front room during the afternoon. So determined was their denial that the inspector was staggered, and had almost come to believe that Mrs St Clair had been deluded when, with a cry, she sprang at a small deal box which lay upon the table and tore the lid from it. Out there fell a cascade of children's bricks. It was the toy which he had promised to bring home.

'This discovery, and the evident confusion which the cripple showed, made the inspector realise that the matter was serious. The rooms were carefully examined, and results all pointed to an abominable crime. The front room was plainly furnished as a sitting-room, and led into a small bedroom, which looked out upon the back of one of the wharves. Between the wharf and the bedroom window is a narrow strip, which is dry at low tide but is covered at high tide with at least four and a half feet of water. The bedroom window was a broad one and opened from below. On examination traces of blood were to be seen upon the windowsill, and several scattered drops were visible upon the wooden floor of the bedroom. Thrust away behind a curtain in the front room were all the clothes of Mr Neville St Clair, with the exception of his coat. His boots, his socks, his hat, and his watch – all were there. There were no signs of violence upon any of these garments, and there were no other traces of Mr Neville St Clair. Out of the window he must apparently have gone for no other exit could be discovered, and the ominous bloodstains upon the sill gave little promise that he could save himself by swimming, for the tide was at its very highest at the moment of the tragedy.

'And now as to the villains who seemed to be immediately implicated in the matter. The Lascar was known to be a man of the vilest antecedents, but as, by Mrs St Clair's story, he was known to have been at the foot of the stairs within a very few seconds of her husband's appearance at the window, he could hardly have been more than an accessory to the crime. His defence was one of absolute ignorance, and he protested that he had no knowledge as to the doings of Hugh Boone, his lodger, and that he could not account in any way for the presence of the missing gentleman's clothes.

'So much for the Lascar manager. Now for the sinister cripple who lives upon the second floor of the opium den, and who was certainly the last human being whose eyes rested upon Neville St Clair. His name is Hugh Boone, and his hideous face is one which is familiar to every man who goes much to the City. He is a professional beggar, though in order to avoid the police regulations he pretends to a small trade in wax vestas. Some little distance down Threadneedle Street, upon the left-hand side, there is, as you may have remarked, a small angle in the wall. Here it is that this creature takes his daily seat, cross-legged with his tiny stock of matches on his lap, and as he is a piteous spectacle a small rain of charity descends into the greasy leather cap which lies upon the pavement beside him. I have watched the fellow more than once before ever I thought of making his professional acquaintance, and I have been surprised at the harvest which he has reaped in a short time. His appearance, you see, is so remarkable that no one can pass him without observing him. A shock of orange hair, a pale face disfigured by a horrible scar, which, by its contraction, has turned up the outer edge of his upper lip, a bulldog chin and a pair of very penetrating dark eyes, which present a singular contrast to the colour of his hair, all mark him out from amid the common crowd of mendicants and so, too, does his wit, for he is ever ready with a reply to any piece of chaff which may be thrown at him by the passers-by. This is the man whom we now learn to have been the lodger at the opium den and to have been the last man to see the gentleman of whom we are in quest.'

'But a cripple!' said I. 'What could he have done single-handed against a man in the prime of life?'

'He is a cripple in the sense that he walks with a limp; but in other respects he appears to be a powerful and well-nurtured man. Surely your medical experience would tell you, Watson, that weakness in one limb is often compensated for by exceptional strength in the others.'

'Pray continue your narrative.'

'Mrs St Clair had fainted at the sight of the blood upon the window, and she was escorted home in a cab by the police, as her presence could be of no help to them in their investigations. Inspector Barton, who had charge of the case, made a very careful examination of the premises, but without finding anything which threw any light upon the matter. One mistake had been made in not arresting Boone instantly, as he was allowed some few minutes during which he might have communicated with his friend the Lascar, but this fault was soon remedied, and he was seized and searched, without anything being found which could incriminate him. There were, it is true, some blood-stains upon his right shirt-sleeve, but he pointed to his ring-finger, which had been cut near the nail, and explained that the bleeding came from there, adding that he had been to the window not long before, and that the stains which had been observed there came doubtless from the same source. He denied strenuously having ever seen Mr Neville St Clair and swore that the presence of the clothes in his room was as much a mystery to him as to the police. As to Mrs St Clair's assertion that she had actually seen her husband at the window, he declared that she must have been either mad or dreaming. He was removed, loudly protesting, to the police-station, while the inspector remained upon the premises in the hope that the ebbing tide might afford some fresh clue.

'And it did, though they hardly found upon the mudbank what they had feared to find. It was Neville St Clair's coat, and not Neville St Clair, which lay uncovered as the tide receded. And what do you think they found in the pockets?'

'I cannot imagine.'

'No, I don't think you would guess. Every pocket was stuffed with pennies and halfpennies – four hundred and twenty-one pennies and two hundred and seventy halfpennies. It was no wonder that it had not been swept away by the tide. But a human body is a different matter. There is a fierce eddy between the wharf and the house. It seemed likely enough that the weighted coat had remained when the stripped body had been sucked away into the river.'

'But I understand that all the other clothes were found in the room. Would the body be dressed in a coat alone?'

'No, sir, but the facts might be met speciously enough. Suppose that this man Boone had thrust Neville St Clair through the window, there is no human eye which could have seen the deed. What would he do then? It would of course instantly strike him that he must get rid of the tell-tale garments. He would seize the coat, then, and be in the act of throwing it out, when it would occur to him that it would swim and not sink. He has little time, for he has heard the scuffle downstairs when the wife tried to force her way up, and perhaps he has already heard from his Lascar confederate that the police are hurrying up the street. There is not an instant to be lost. He rushes to some secret hoard, where he has accumulated the fruits of his beggary, and he stuffs all the coins upon which he can lay his hands into the pockets to make sure of the coat's sinking. He throws it out, and would have done the same with the other garments had he not heard the rush of steps below and only just had time to close the window when the police appeared.'

'It certainly sounds feasible.'

'Well, we will take it as a working hypothesis for want of a better. Boone, as I have told you, was arrested and taken to the station, but it could not be shown that there had ever before been anything against him. He had for years been known as a professional beggar, but his life appeared to have been a very quiet and innocent one. There the matter stands at present, and the questions which have to be solved – what Neville St Clair was doing in the opium den, what happened to him when there, where is he now, and what Hugh Boone had to do with his disappearance – are all as far from a solution as ever. I confess that I cannot recall any case within my experience which looked at the first glance so simple and yet which presented such difficulties.'

While Sherlock Holmes had been detailing this singular series of events we had been whirling through the outskirts of the great town until the last straggling houses had been left behind and we rattled along with a country hedge upon either side of us. Just as he finished, however, we drove through two scattered villages, where a few lights still glimmered in the windows.

'We are on the outskirts of Lee,' said my companion. 'We have touched on three English counties in our short drive, starting in Middlesex, passing over an angle of Surrey and ending in Kent. See that light among the trees? That is The Cedars, and beside that lamp sits a woman whose anxious ears have already, I have little doubt, caught the clink of our horse's feet.'

'But why are you not conducting the case from Baker Street?' I asked.

'Because there are many enquiries which must be made out here. Mrs St Clair has most kindly put two rooms at my disposal, and you may rest assured that she will have nothing but a welcome for my friend and colleague. I hate to meet her, Watson, when I have no news of her husband. Here we are. Whoa, there, whoa!'

We had pulled up in front of a large villa which stood within its own grounds. A stable-boy had run out to the horse's head, and springing down, I followed Holmes up the small, winding gravel drive which led to the house. As we approached, the door flew open, and a little blonde woman stood in the opening, clad in some sort of light *mousseline-de-soie*, with a touch of fluffy pink chiffon at her neck and wrists. She stood with her figure outlined against the flood of light, one hand upon the door, one half-raised in her eagerness, her body slightly bent, her head and face protruded, with eager eyes and parted lips, a standing question mark.

'Well?' she cried, 'well?' And then, seeing that there were two of us, she gave a cry of hope which sank into a groan as she saw that my companion shook his head and shrugged his shoulders.

'No good news?'

'None.'

'No bad?'

'No.'

'Thank God for that. But come in. You must be weary, for you have had a long day.'

'This is my friend, Dr Watson. He has been of most vital use to me in several of my cases, and a lucky chance has made it possible for me to bring him out and associate him with this investigation.'

'I am delighted to see you,' said she, pressing my hand warmly. 'You will, I am sure, forgive anything that may be wanting in our arrangements when you consider the blow which has come so suddenly upon us.'

'My dear madam,' said I, 'I am an old campaigner, and if I were not I can very well see that no apology is needed. If I can be of any assistance, either to you or to my friend here, I shall be indeed happy.'

'Now, Mr Sherlock Holmes,' said the lady as we entered a well-lit dining-room, upon the table of which a cold supper had been laid out, 'I should very much like to ask you one or two plain questions, to which I beg that you will give a plain answer.'

'Certainly, madam.'

'Do not trouble about my feelings. I am not hysterical, nor given to fainting. I simply wish to hear your real, real opinion.'

'Upon what point?'

'In your heart of hearts, do you think that Neville is alive?'

Sherlock Holmes seemed to be embarrassed by the question.

'Frankly, now!' she repeated, standing upon the rug and looking keenly down at him as he leaned back in a basket-chair.

'Frankly, then, madam, I do not.'

'You think that he is dead?'

'I do.'

'Murdered?'

'I don't say that. Perhaps.'

'And on what day did he meet his death?'

'On Monday.'

'Then perhaps, Mr Holmes, you will be good enough to explain how it is that I have received a letter from him today.'

Sherlock Holmes sprang out of his chair as if he had been galvanised.

'What!' he roared.

'Yes, today.' She stood smiling, holding up a little slip of paper in the air.

'May I see it?'

'Certainly.'

He snatched it from her in his eagerness, and smoothing it out upon the table he drew over the lamp and examined it intently. I had left my chair and was gazing at it over his shoulder. The envelope was a very coarse one and was stamped with the Gravesend postmark and with the date of that very day, or rather of the day before, for it was considerably after midnight.

'Coarse writing,' murmured Holmes. 'Surely this is not your husband's writing, madam.'

'No, but the enclosure is.'

'I perceive also that whoever addressed the envelope had to go and enquire as to the address.'

'How can you tell that?'

'The name, you see, is in perfectly black ink, which has dried itself. The rest is of the greyish colour which shows that blotting-paper has been used. If it had been written straight off, and then blotted, none would be of a deep black shade. This man has written the name, and there has then been a pause before he has written the address, which can only mean that he was not familiar with it. It is, of course, a trifle, but there is nothing so important as trifles. Let us now see the letter. Ha! there has been an enclosure here!'

'Yes, there was a ring. His signet-ring.'

'And you are sure that this is your husband's hand?'

'One of his hands.'

'One?'

'His hand when he wrote hurriedly. It is very unlike his usual writing, and yet I know it well.'

' "Dearest, do not be frightened. All will come well. There is a huge error which it may take some little time to rectify. Wait in patience – Neville." Written in pencil upon the flyleaf of a book, octavo size, no water-mark. Hum! Posted today in Gravesend by a man with a dirty thumb. Ha! And the flap has been gummed, if I am not very much in error, by a person who had been chewing tobacco. And you have no doubt that it is your husband's hand, madam?'

'None. Neville wrote those words.'

'And they were posted today at Gravesend. Well, Mrs St Clair, the clouds lighten, though I should not venture to say that the danger is over.'

'But he must be alive, Mr Holmes.'

'Unless this is a clever forgery to put us on the wrong scent. The ring, after all, proves nothing. It may have been taken from him.'

'No, no; it is, it is his very own writing!'

'Very well. It may, however, have been written on Monday and only posted today.'

'That is possible.'

'If so, much may have happened between.'

'Oh, you must not discourage me, Mr Holmes. I know that all is well with him. There is so keen a sympathy between us that I should know if evil came upon him. On the very day that I saw him last he cut himself in the bedroom, and yet I in the dining-room rushed upstairs instantly with the utmost certainty that something had happened. Do you think that I would respond to such a trifle and yet be ignorant of his death?'

'I have seen too much not to know that the impression of a woman may be more valuable than the conclusion of an analytical reasoner. And in this letter you certainly have a very strong piece of evidence to corroborate your view. But if your husband is alive and able to write letters, why should he remain away from you?'

'I cannot imagine. It is unthinkable.'

'And on Monday he made no remarks before leaving you?'

'No.'

'And you were surprised to see him in Swandam Lane?'

'Very much so.'

'Was the window open?'

'Yes.'

'Then he might have called to you?'

'He might.'

'He only, as I understand, gave an inarticulate cry?'

'Yes.'

'A call for help, you thought?'

'Yes. He waved his hands.'

'But it might have been a cry of surprise. Astonishment at the unexpected sight of you might have caused him to throw up his hands?'

'It is possible.'

'And you thought he was pulled back?'

'He disappeared so suddenly.'

'He might have leaped back. You did not see anyone else in the room?'

'No, but this horrible man confessed to having been there, and the Lascar was at the foot of the stairs.'

'Quite so. Your husband, as far as you could see, had his ordinary clothes on?'

'But without his collar or tie. I distinctly saw his bare throat.'

'Had he ever spoken of Swandam Lane?'

'Never.'

'Had he ever shown any signs of having taken opium?'

'Never.'

'Thank you, Mrs St Clair. Those are the principal points about which I wished to be absolutely clear. We shall now have a little supper and then retire, for we may have a very busy day tomorrow.'

A large and comfortable double-bedded room had been placed at our disposal, and I was quickly between the sheets, for I was weary after my night of adventure. Sherlock Holmes was a man, however, who, when he had an unsolved problem upon his mind, would go for days, and even for a week, without rest, turning it over, rearranging his facts, looking at it from every point of view until he had either fathomed it or convinced himself that his data were insufficient. It was soon evident to me that he was now preparing for an all-night sitting. He took off his coat and waistcoat, put on a large blue dressing-gown, and then wandered about the room collecting pillows from the bed and cushions from the sofa and armchairs. With these he constructed a sort of Eastern divan, upon which he perched himself cross-legged, with an ounce of shag tobacco and a box of matches laid out in front of him. In the dim light of the lamp I saw him sitting there, an old briar pipe between his lips, his eyes fixed vacantly upon the corner of the ceiling, the blue smoke curling up from him, silent, motionless, with the light shining upon his strong-set aquiline features. So he sat as I dropped off to sleep, and so he sat when a sudden ejaculation caused me to wake up and I found the summer sun shining into the apartment. The pipe was still between his lips, the smoke still curled upwards, and the room was full of a dense tobacco haze, but nothing remained of the heap of shag which I had seen upon the previous night.

'Awake, Watson?' he asked.

'Yes.'

'Game for a morning drive?'

'Certainly.'

'Then dress. No one is stirring yet, but I know where the stable-boy sleeps, and we shall soon have the trap out.' He chuckled to himself as he spoke, his eyes twinkled, and he seemed a different man from the sombre thinker of the previous night.

As I dressed I glanced at my watch. It was no wonder that no one was stirring. It was twenty-five minutes past four. I had hardly finished when Holmes returned with the news that the boy was putting in the horse.

'I want to test a little theory of mine,' said he, pulling on his boots. 'I think, Watson, that you are now standing in the presence of one of the most absolute fools in Europe. I deserve to be kicked from here to Charing Cross. But I think I have the key of the affair now.'

'And where is it?' I asked, smiling.

'It was in the bathroom,' he answered. 'Oh, yes, I am not joking,' he continued, seeing my look of incredulity. 'I have just been there, and I have taken it out, and I have got it in this Gladstone bag. Come on, my boy, and we shall see whether it will not fit the lock.'

We made our way downstairs as quietly as possible and out into the bright morning sunshine. In the road stood our horse and trap, with the half-clad stable-boy waiting at the head. We both sprang in, and away we dashed down the London Road. A few country carts were stirring, bearing in vegetables to the metropolis, but the lines of villas on either side were as silent and lifeless as some city in a dream.

'It has been in some points a singular case,' said Holmes, flicking the horse on into a gallop. 'I confess that I have been as blind as a mole, but it is better to learn wisdom late than never to learn it at all.'

In town the earliest risers were just beginning to look sleepily from their windows as we drove through the streets of the Surrey side. Passing down the Waterloo Bridge Road we crossed over the river, and dashing up Wellington Street wheeled sharply to the right and found ourselves in Bow Street. Sherlock Holmes was well known to the force, and the two constables at the door saluted him. One of them held the horse's head while the other led us in.

'Who is on duty?' asked Holmes.

'Inspector Bradstreet, sir.'

'Ah, Bradstreet, how are you?' A tall, stout official, in a peaked cap and frogged jacket, had come down the stone-flagged passage. 'I wish to have a quiet word with you, Bradstreet.'

'Certainly, Mr Holmes. Step into my room here.' It was a small, office-like room, with a huge ledger upon the table and a telephone projecting from the wall. The inspector sat down at his desk. 'What can I do for you, Mr Holmes?'

'I called about that beggarman, Boone – the one who was charged with being concerned in the disappearance of Mr Neville St Clair of Lee.'

'Yes. He was brought up and remanded for further enquiries.'

'So I heard. You have him here?'

'In the cells.'

'Is he quiet?'

'Oh, he gives no trouble. But he is a dirty scoundrel.'

'Dirty?'

'Yes, it is all we can do to make him wash his hands, and his face is as black as a tinker's. Well, when once his case has been settled, he will have a regular prison bath; and I think, if you saw him, you would agree with me that he needed it.'

'I should like to see him very much.'

'Would you? That is easily done. Come this way. You can leave your bag.'

'No, I think that I'll take it.'

'Very good. Come this way, if you please.' He led us down a passage, opened a barred door, passed down a winding stair and brought us to a whitewashed corridor with a line of doors on each side.

'The third on the right is his,' said the inspector. 'Here it is!' He quietly shot back a panel in the upper part of the door and glanced through.

'He is asleep,' said he. 'You can see him very well.'

We both put our eyes to the grating. The prisoner lay with his face towards us in a very deep sleep, breathing slowly and heavily. He was a middle-sized man, coarsely clad as became his calling, with a coloured shirt protruding through the rent in his tattered coat. He was, as the inspector had said, extremely dirty, but the grime which covered his face could not conceal its repulsive ugliness. A broad wheal from an old scar ran right across it from eye to chin, and by its contraction had turned up one side of the upper lip, so that three teeth were exposed in a perpetual snarl. A shock of very bright red hair grew low over his eyes and forehead.

'He's a beauty, isn't he?' said the inspector.

'He certainly needs a wash,' remarked Holmes. 'I had an idea that he might, and I took the liberty of bringing the tools with me.' He opened the Gladstone bag as he spoke, and took out, to my astonishment, a very large bath-sponge.

'He! he! You are a funny one,' chuckled the inspector.

'Now, if you will have the great goodness to open that door very quietly, we will soon make him cut a much more respectable figure.'

'Well, I don't know why not,' said the inspector. 'He doesn't look a credit to the Bow Street cells, does he?' He slipped his key into the lock, and we all very quietly entered the cell. The sleeper half turned, and then settled down once more into a deep slumber. Holmes stooped to the water-jug, moistened his sponge, and then rubbed it twice vigorously across and down the prisoner's face.

'Let me introduce you,' he shouted, 'to Mr Neville St Clair, of Lee, in the county of Kent.'

Never in my life have I seen such a sight. The man's face peeled off under the sponge like the bark from a tree. Gone was the coarse brown tint! Gone, too, was the horrid scar which had seamed it across and the twisted lip which had given the repulsive sneer to the face! A twitch brought away the tangled red hair, and there, sitting up in his bed, was a pale, sad-faced, refined-looking man, black-haired and smooth-skinned, rubbing his eyes and staring about him with sleepy bewilderment. Then suddenly realising the exposure, he broke into a scream and threw himself down with his face to the pillow.

'Great heavens!' cried the inspector, 'it is, indeed, the missing man. I know him from the photograph.'

The prisoner turned with the reckless air of a man who abandons himself to his destiny. 'Be it so,' said he. 'And pray what am I charged with?'

'With making away with Mr Neville St – Oh, come, you can't be charged with that unless they make a case of attempted suicide of it,' said the inspector with a grin. 'Well, I have been twenty-seven years in the force, but this really takes the cake.'

'If I am Mr Neville St Clair, then it is obvious that no crime has been committed, and that, therefore, I am illegally detained.'

'No crime, but a very great error has been committed,' said Holmes. 'You would have done better to have trusted your wife.'

'It was not my wife, it was the children,' groaned the prisoner. 'God help me, I would not have them ashamed of their father. My God! What an exposure! What can I do?'

Sherlock Holmes sat down beside him on the couch and patted him kindly on the shoulder.

'If you leave it to a court of law to clear the matter up,' said he, 'of course you can hardly avoid publicity. On the other hand, if you convince the police authorities that there is no possible case against you, I do not know that there is any reason that the details should find their way into the papers. Inspector Bradstreet would, I am sure, make notes upon anything you might tell us and submit them to the proper authorities. The case would then never go into court at all.'

'God bless you!' cried the prisoner passionately. 'I would have endured imprisonment, ay, even execution, rather than have left my miserable secret as a family blot to my children.

'You are the first who have ever heard my story. My father was a schoolmaster in Chesterfield, where I received an excellent education. I travelled in my youth, took to the stage, and finally became a reporter on an evening paper in London. One day my editor wished to have a series of articles upon begging in the metropolis, and I volunteered to supply them. There was the point from which all my adventures started. It was only by trying begging as an amateur that I could get the facts upon which to base my articles. When an actor I had, of course, learned all the secrets of making up, and had been famous in the green-room for my skill. I took advantage now of my attainments. I painted my face, and to make myself as pitiable as possible I made a good scar and fixed one side of my lip in a twist by the aid of a small slip of flesh-coloured plaster. Then with a red head of hair, and an appropriate dress, I took my station in the business part of the city, ostensibly as a matchseller but really as a beggar. For seven hours I plied my trade, and when I returned home in the evening I found to my surprise that I had received no less than twenty-six shillings and fourpence.

'I wrote my articles and thought little more of the matter until, some time later, I backed a bill for a friend and had a writ served upon me for twenty-five pounds. I was at my wit's end where to get the money, but a sudden idea came to me. I begged a fortnight's grace from the creditor, asked for a holiday from my employers, and spent the time in begging in the City under my disguise. In ten days I had the money and had paid the debt.

'Well, you can imagine how hard it was to settle down to arduous work at two pounds a week when I knew that I could earn as much in a day by smearing my face with a little paint, laying my cap on the ground and sitting still. It was a long fight between my pride and the money, but the dollars won at last, and I threw up reporting and sat day after day in the corner which I had first chosen, inspiring pity by my ghastly face and filling my pockets with coppers. Only one man knew my secret. He was the keeper of a low den in which I used to lodge in Swandam Lane; every morning I could emerge as a squalid beggar and in the evening return to transform myself into a well-dressed man about town. This fellow, a Lascar, was well paid by me for his rooms, so that I knew that my secret was safe in his possession.

'Well, very soon I found that I was saving considerable sums of money. I do not mean that any beggar in the streets of London could earn £700 a year – which is less than my average takings – but I had exceptional advantages in my power of making up, and also in a facility of repartee, which improved by practice and made me quite a recognised character in the City. All day a stream of pennies, varied by silver, poured in upon me, and it was a very bad day in which I failed to take two pounds.

'As I grew richer I grew more ambitious, took a house in the country, and eventually married, without anyone having a suspicion as to my real occupation. My dear wife knew that I had business in the City. She little knew what.

'Last Monday I had finished for the day and was dressing in my room above the opium den when I looked out of my window and saw, to my horror and astonishment, that my wife was standing in the street with her eyes fixed full upon me. I gave a cry of surprise, threw up my arms to cover my face, and, rushing to my confidant, the Lascar, entreated him to prevent anyone from coming up to me. I heard her voice downstairs, but I knew that she could not ascend. Swiftly I threw off my clothes, pulled on those of a beggar and put on my pigments and wig. Even a wife's eyes could not pierce so complete a disguise. But then it occurred to me that there might be a search in the room, and that the clothes might betray me. I threw open the window, reopening by my violence a small cut which I had inflicted upon myself in the bedroom that morning. Then I seized my coat, which was weighted by the coppers which I had just transferred to it from the leather bag in which I carried my takings. I hurled it out of the window, and it disappeared into the Thames. The other clothes would have followed, but at that moment there was a rush of constables up the stairs, and a few minutes after I found, rather, I confess, to my relief, that instead of being identified as Mr Neville St Clair, I was arrested as his murderer.

'I do not know that there is anything else for me to explain. I was determined to preserve my disguise as long as possible, and hence my preference for a dirty face. Knowing that my wife would be terribly anxious, I slipped off my ring and confided it to the Lascar at a moment when no constable was watching me, together with a hurried scrawl telling her that she had no cause to fear.'

'That note only reached her yesterday,' said Holmes.

'Good God! What a week she must have spent!'

'The police have watched this Lascar,' said Inspector Bradstreet, 'and I can quite understand that he might find it difficult to post a letter unobserved. Probably he handed it to some sailor customer of his, who forgot all about it for some days.'

'That was it,' said Holmes, nodding approvingly; 'I have no doubt of it. But have you never been prosecuted for begging?'

'Many times; but what was a fine to me?'

'It must stop here, however,' said Bradstreet. 'If the police are to hush this thing up, there must be no more of Hugh Boone.'

'I have sworn it by the most solemn oaths which a man can take.'

'In that case I think that it is probable that no further steps may be taken. But if you are found again, then all must come out. I am sure, Mr Holmes, that we are very much indebted to you for having cleared the matter up. I wish I knew how you reach your results.'

'I reached this one,' said my friend, 'by sitting upon five pillows and consuming an ounce of shag. I think, Watson, that if we drive to Baker Street we shall just be in time for breakfast.'

The Blue Carbuncle

I had called upon my friend Sherlock Holmes on the second morning after Christmas, with the intention of wishing him the compliments of the season. He was lounging upon the sofa in a purple dressing-gown, a pipe-rack within his reach upon the right and a pile of crumpled morning papers, evidently newly studied, near at hand. Beside the couch was a wooden chair, and on the angle of the back hung a very seedy and disreputable hard felt hat, much the worse for wear and cracked in several places. A lens and a forceps lying upon the seat of the chair suggested that the hat had been suspended in this manner for the purpose of examination.

'You are engaged,' said I; 'perhaps I interrupt you.'

'Not at all. I am glad to have a friend with whom I can discuss my results. The matter is a perfectly trivial one' – he jerked his thumb in the direction of the old hat – 'but there are points in connection with it which are not entirely devoid of interest and even of instruction.'

I seated myself in his armchair and warmed my hands before his crackling fire, for a sharp frost had set in and the windows were thick with the ice crystals. 'I suppose,' I remarked, 'that, homely as it looks, this thing has some deadly story linked on to it – that it is the clue which will guide you in the solution of some mystery and the punishment of some crime.'

'No, no. No crime,' said Sherlock Holmes, laughing. 'Only one of those whimsical little incidents which will happen when you have four million human beings all jostling each other within the space of a few square miles. Amid the action and reaction of so dense a swarm of humanity, every possible combination of events may be expected to take place, and many a little problem will be presented which may be striking and bizarre without being criminal. We have already had experience of such.'

'So much so,' I remarked, 'that of the last six cases which I have added to my notes, three have been entirely free of any legal crime.'

'Precisely. You allude to my attempt to recover the Irene Adler papers, to the singular case of Miss Mary Sutherland and to the adventure of the man with the twisted lip. Well, I have no doubt that this small matter will fall into the same innocent category. You know Peterson, the commissionaire?'

'Yes.'

'It is to him that this trophy belongs.'

'It is his hat.'

'No, no, he found it. Its owner is unknown. I beg that you will look upon it not as a battered billycock but as an intellectual problem. And, first, as to how it came here. It arrived upon Christmas morning, in company with a good fat goose, which is, I have no doubt, roasting at this moment in front of Peter- son's fire. The facts are these: about four o'clock on Christmas morning, Peterson, who, as you know, is a very honest fellow, was returning from some small jollification and was making his way homeward down Tottenham Court Road. In front of him he saw, in the gaslight, a tallish man, walking with a slight stagger and carrying a white goose slung over his shoulder. As he reached the corner of Goodge Street, a row broke out between this stranger and a little knot of roughs. One of the latter knocked off the man's hat, on which he raised his stick to defend himself, and, swinging it over his head, smashed the shop window behind him. Peterson had rushed forward to protect the stranger from his assailants; but the man, shocked at having broken the window and seeing an official-looking person in uniform rushing towards him, dropped his goose, took to his heels and vanished amid the labyrinth of small streets which lie at the back of Tottenham Court Road. The roughs had also fled at the appearance of Peterson, so that he was left in possession of the field of battle, and also of the spoils of victory in the shape of this battered hat and a most unimpeachable Christmas goose.'

'Which surely he restored to their owner?'

'My dear fellow, there lies the problem. It is true that "For Mrs Henry Baker" was printed upon a small card which was tied to the bird's left leg, and it is also true that the initials "H.B." are legible upon the lining of this hat, but as there are some thousands of Bakers, and some hundreds of Henry Bakers in this city of ours, it is not easy to restore lost property to any one of them.'

'What, then, did Peterson do?'

'He brought round both hat and goose to me on Christmas morning, knowing that even the smallest problems are of interest to me. The goose we retained until this morning, when there were signs that, in spite of the slight frost, it would be well that it should be eaten without unnecessary delay. Its finder has carried it off, therefore, to fulfil the ultimate destiny of a goose, while I continue to retain the hat of the unknown gentleman who lost his Christmas dinner.'

'Did he not advertise?'

'No.'

'Then what clue could you have as to his identity?'

'Only as much as we can deduce.'

'From his hat?'

'Precisely.'

'But you are joking. What can you gather from this old battered felt?'

'Here is my lens. You know my methods. What can you gather your-self as to the individuality of the man who has worn this article?'

I took the tattered object in my hands and turned it over rather ruefully. It was a very ordinary black hat of the usual round shape, hard and much the worse for wear. The lining had been of red silk, but was a good deal discoloured. There was no maker's name; but, as Holmes had remarked, the initials 'H.B.' were scrawled upon one side. It was pierced in the brim for a hat-securer, but the elastic was missing. For the rest, it was cracked, exceedingly dusty and spotted in several places, although there seemed to have been some attempt to hide the discoloured patches by smearing them with ink.

'I can see nothing,' said I, handing it back to my friend.

'On the contrary, Watson, you can see everything. You fail, however, to reason from what you see. You are too timid in drawing your inferences.'

'Then, pray tell me what is it that you can infer from this hat?'

He picked it up and gazed at it in the peculiar introspective fashion which was characteristic of him. 'It is perhaps less suggestive than it might have been,' he remarked, 'and yet there are a few inferences which are very distinct and a few others which represent at least a strong balance of probability. That the man was highly intellectual is of course obvious upon the face of it, and also that he was fairly well-to-do within the last three years, although he has now fallen upon evil days. He had foresight, but has less now than formerly, pointing to a moral retrogression, which, when taken with the decline of his fortunes, seems to indicate some evil influence, probably drink, at work upon him. This may account also for the obvious fact that his wife has ceased to love him.'

'My dear Holmes!'

'He has, however, retained some degree of self-respect,' he continued, disregarding my remonstrance. 'He is a man who leads a sedentary life, goes out little, is out of training entirely, is middle-aged, has grizzled hair which he has had cut within the last few days and which he anoints with lime-cream. These are the more patent facts which are to be deduced from his hat. Also, by the way, it is extremely improbable that he has gas laid on in his house.'

'You are certainly joking, Holmes.'

'Not in the least. Is it possible that even now, when I give you these results, you are unable to see how they are attained?'

'I have no doubt that I am very stupid, but I must confess that I am unable to follow you. For example, how did you deduce that this man was intellectual?'

For answer Holmes clapped the hat upon his head. It came right over the forehead and settled upon the bridge of his nose. 'It is a question of cubic capacity,' said he; 'a man with so large a brain must have something in it.'

'The decline of his fortunes, then?'

'This hat is three years old. These flat brims curled at the edge came in then. It is a hat of the very best quality. Look at the band of ribbed silk and the excellent lining. If this man could afford to buy so expensive a hat three years ago, and has had no hat since, then he has assuredly gone down in the world.'

'Well, that is clear enough, certainly. But how about the foresight and the moral retrogression?'

Sherlock Holmes laughed. 'Here is the foresight,' said he putting his finger upon the little disc and loop of the hat-securer. 'They are never sold upon hats. If this man ordered one, it is a sign of a certain amount of foresight, since he went out of his way to take this precaution against the wind. But since we see that he has broken the elastic and has not troubled to replace it, it is obvious that he has less foresight now than formerly, which is a distinct proof of a weakening nature. On the other hand, he has endeavoured to conceal some of these stains upon the felt by daubing them with ink, which is a sign that he has not entirely lost his self-respect.'

'Your reasoning is certainly plausible.'

'The further points, that he is middle-aged, that his hair is grizzled, that it has been recently cut and that he uses lime-cream, are all to be gathered from a close examination of the lower part of the lining. The lens discloses a large number of hair-ends, clean cut by the scissors of the barber. They all appear to be adhesive, and there is a distinct odour of lime-cream. This dust, you will observe, is not the gritty, grey dust of the street but the fluffy brown dust of the house, showing that it has been hung up indoors most of the time, while the marks of moisture upon the inside are proof positive that the wearer perspired very freely, and could, therefore, hardly be in the best of training.'

'But his wife – you said that she had ceased to love him.'

'This hat has not been brushed for weeks. When I see you, my dear Watson, with a week's accumulation of dust upon your hat, and when your wife allows you to go out in such a state, I shall fear that you also have been unfortunate enough to lose your wife's affection.'

'But he might be a bachelor.'

'Nay, he was bringing home the goose as a peace-offering to his wife. Remember the card upon the bird's leg.'

'You have an answer to everything. But how on earth do you deduce that the gas is not laid on in his house?'

'One tallow stain, or even two, might come by chance; but when I see no less than five, I think that there can be little doubt that the individual must be brought into frequent contact with burning tallow – walks upstairs at night probably with his hat in one hand and a guttering candle in the other. Anyhow, he never got tallow-stains from a gas-jet. Are you satisfied?'

'Well, it is very ingenious,' said I, laughing; 'but since, as you said just now, there has been no crime committed, and no harm done save the loss of a goose, all this seems to be rather a waste of energy.'

Sherlock Holmes had opened his mouth to reply, when the door flew open, and Peterson, the commissionaire, rushed into the apartment with flushed cheeks and the face of a man who is dazed with astonishment.

'The goose, Mr Holmes! The goose, sir!' he gasped.

'Eh? What of it, then? Has it returned to life and flapped off through the kitchen window?' Holmes twisted himself round upon the sofa to get a fairer view of the man's excited face.

'See here, sir! See what my wife found in its crop!' He held out his hand and displayed upon the centre of the palm a brilliantly scintillating blue stone, rather smaller than a bean in size, but of such purity and radiance that it twinkled like an electric point in the dark hollow of his hand.

Sherlock Holmes sat up with a whistle. 'By Jove, Peterson,' said he, 'this is treasure trove indeed! I suppose you know what you have got?'

'A diamond, sir? A precious stone. It cuts into glass as though it were putty.'

'It's more than a precious stone. It is *the* precious stone.'

'Not the Countess of Morcar's blue carbuncle!' I ejaculated.

'Precisely so. I ought to know its size and shape, seeing that I have read the advertisement about it in *The Times* every day lately. It is absolutely unique, and its value can only be conjectured, but the reward offered of a thousand ponds is certainly not within a twentieth part of the market price.'

'A thousand pounds! Great Lord of mercy!' The commissionaire plumped down into a chair and stared from one to the other of us.

'That is the reward, and I have reason to know that there are sentimental considerations in the back- ground which would induce the countess to part with half her fortune if she could but recover the gem.'

'It was lost, if I remember aright, at the Hotel Cosmopolitan,' I remarked.

'Precisely so, on December 22nd, just five days ago. John Horner, a plumber, was accused of having abstracted it from the lady's jewel-case. The evidence against him was so strong that the case has been referred to the Assizes. I have some account of the matter here, I believe.' He rummaged amid his newspapers, glancing over the dates, until at last he smoothed one out, doubled it over, and read the following paragraph:

'Hotel Cosmopolitan Jewel Robbery. John Horner, 26, plumber, was brought up upon the charge of having, upon the 22nd inst., abstracted from the jewel-case of the Countess of Morcar the valuable gem known as the blue carbuncle. James Ryder, upper-attendant at the hotel, gave his evidence to the effect that he had shown Horner up to the dressing-room of the Countess of Morcar upon the day of the robbery in order that he might solder the second bar of the grate, which was loose. He had remained with Horner some little time, but had finally been called away. On returning, he found that Horner had disappeared, that the bureau had been forced open and that the small morocco casket in which, as it afterwards transpired, the countess was accustomed to keep her jewel, was lying empty upon the dressing-table. Ryder instantly gave the alarm, and Horner was arrested the same evening; but the stone could not be found either upon his person or in his rooms. Catherine Cusack, maid to the countess, deposed to having heard Ryder's cry of dismay on discovering the robbery, and to having rushed into the room, where she found matters as described by the last witness. Inspector Bradstreet, B division, gave evidence as to the arrest of Horner, who struggled frantically and protested his innocence in the strongest terms. Evidence of a previous conviction for robbery having been given against the prisoner, the magistrate refused to deal summarily with the offence, but referred it to the Assizes. Horner, who had shown signs of intense emotion during the proceedings, fainted away at the conclusion and was carried out of court.'

'Hum! So much for the police-court,' said Holmes thoughtfully, tossing aside the paper. 'The question for us now to solve is the sequence of events leading from a rifled jewel-case at one end to the crop of a goose in Tottenham Court Road at the other. You see, Watson, our little deductions have suddenly assumed a much more important and less innocent aspect. Here is the stone; the stone came from the goose, and the goose came from Mr Henry Baker, the gentleman with the bad hat and all the other characteristics with which I have bored you. So now we must set ourselves very seriously to finding this gentleman and ascertaining what part he has played in this little mystery. To do this, we must try the simplest means first, and these lie undoubtedly in an advertisement in all the evening papers. If this fail, I shall have recourse to other methods.'

'What will you say?'

'Give me a pencil and that slip of paper. Now, then: "Found at the corner of Goodge Street, a goose and a black felt hat. Mr Henry Baker can have the same by applying at 6:30 this evening at 221b Baker Street." That is clear and concise.'

'Very. But will he see it?'

'Well, he is sure to keep an eye on the papers, since, to a poor man, the loss was a heavy one. He was clearly so scared by his mischance in breaking the window and by the approach of Peterson that he thought of nothing but flight, but since then he must have bitterly regretted the impulse which caused him to drop his bird. Then, again, the introduction of his name will cause him to see it, for everyone who knows him will direct his attention to it. Here you are, Peterson, run down to the advertising agency and have this put in the evening papers.'

'In which, sir?'

'Oh, in the *Globe, Star, Pall Mall, St James's Gazette, Evening News, Standard, Echo* and any others that occur to you.'

'Very well, sir. And this stone?'

'Ah, yes, I shall keep the stone. Thank you. And, I say, Peterson, just buy a goose on your way back and leave it here with me, for we must have one to give to this gentleman in place of the one which your family is now devouring.'

When the commissionaire had gone, Holmes took up the stone and held it against the light. 'It's a bonny thing,' said he. 'Just see how it glints and sparkles. Of course it is a nucleus and focus of crime. Every good stone is. They are the devil's pet baits. In the larger and older jewels every facet may stand for a bloody deed. This stone is not yet twenty years old. It was found in the banks of the Amoy River in southern China and is remarkable in having every characteristic of the carbuncle save that it is blue in shade instead of ruby red. In spite of its youth, it has already a sinister history. There have been two murders, a vitriol-throwing, a suicide and several robberies brought about for the sake of this forty-grain weight of crystallised charcoal. Who would think that so pretty a toy would be a purveyor to the gallows and the prison? I'll lock it up in my strong box now and drop a line to the countess to say that we have it.'

'Do you think that this man Horner is innocent?'

'I cannot tell.'

'Well, then, do you imagine that this other one, Henry Baker, had anything to do with the matter?'

'It is, I think, much more likely that Henry Baker is an absolutely innocent man, who had no idea that the bird which he was carrying was of considerably more value than if it were made of solid gold. That, however, I shall determine by a very simple test if we have an answer to our advertisement.'

'And you can do nothing until then?'

'Nothing.'

'In that case I shall continue my professional round. But I shall come back this evening at the hour you have mentioned, for I should like to see the solution of so tangled a business.'

'Very glad to see you. I dine at seven. There is a woodcock, I believe. By the way, in view of recent occurrences, perhaps I ought to ask Mrs Hudson to examine its crop.'

I had been delayed at a case, and it was a little after half-past six when I found myself in Baker Street once more. As I approached the house I saw a tall man in a Scotch bonnet and a coat which was buttoned up to his chin waiting outside in the bright semi-circle which was thrown from the fanlight. Just as I arrived, the door was opened, and we were shown up together to Holmes's room.

'Mr Henry Baker, I believe,' said he, rising from his armchair and greeting his visitor with the easy air of geniality which he could so readily assume. 'Pray take this chair by the fire, Mr Baker. It is a cold night, and I observe that your circulation is more adapted for summer than for winter. Ah, Watson, you have just come at the right time. Is that your hat, Mr Baker?'

'Yes, sir, that is undoubtedly my hat.'

He was a large man with rounded shoulders, a massive head and a broad, intelligent face sloping down to a pointed beard of grizzled brown. A touch of red in nose and cheeks, with a slight tremor of his extended hand, recalled Holmes's surmise as to his habits. His rusty black frock-coat was buttoned right up in front, with the collar turned up, and his lank wrists protruded from his sleeves without a sign of cuff or shirt. He spoke in a slow staccato fashion, choosing his words with care, and gave the impression generally of a man of learning and letters who had had ill-usage at the hands of fortune.

'We have retained these things for some days,' said Holmes, 'because we expected to see an advertisement from you giving your address. I am at a loss to know now why you did not advertise.'

Our visitor gave a rather shamefaced laugh. 'Shillings have not been so plentiful with me as they once were,' he remarked. 'I had no doubt that the gang of roughs who assaulted me had carried off both my hat and the bird. I did not care to spend more money in a hopeless attempt at recovering them.'

'Very naturally. By the way, about the bird, we were compelled to eat it.'

'To eat it!' Our visitor half rose from his chair in his excitement.

'Yes, it would have been of no use to anyone had we not done so. But I presume that this other goose upon the sideboard, which is about the same weight and perfectly fresh, will answer your purpose equally well?'

'Oh, certainly, certainly,' answered Mr Baker with a sigh of relief.

'Of course, we still have the feathers, legs, crop and so on of your own bird, so if you wish — '

The man burst into a hearty laugh. 'They might be useful to me as relics of my adventure,' said he, 'but beyond that I can hardly see what use the *disjecta membra* of my late acquaintance are going to be to me. No, sir, I think that, with your permission, I will confine my attentions to the excellent bird which I perceive upon the sideboard.'

Sherlock Holmes glanced sharply across at me with a slight shrug of his shoulders.

'There is your hat, then, and there your bird,' said he. 'By the way, would it bore you to tell me where you got the other one from? I am somewhat of a fowl fancier, and I have seldom seen a better grown goose.'

'Certainly, sir,' said Baker, who had risen and tucked his newly gained property under his arm. 'There are a few of us who frequent the Alpha Inn, near the Museum – we are to be found in the Museum itself during the day, you understand. This year our good host, Windigate by name, instituted a goose club, by which, on consideration of some few pence every week, we were each to receive a bird at Christmas. My pence were duly paid, and the rest is familiar to you. I am much indebted to you, sir, for a Scotch bonnet is fitted neither to my years nor my gravity.' With a comical pomposity of manner he bowed solemnly to both of us and strode off upon his way.

'So much for Mr Henry Baker,' said Holmes when he had closed the door behind him. 'It is quite certain that he knows nothing whatever about the matter. Are you hungry, Watson?'

'Not particularly.'

'Then I suggest that we turn our dinner into a supper and follow up this clue while it is still hot.'

'By all means.'

It was a bitter night, so we drew on our ulsters and wrapped cravats about our throats. Outside, the stars were shining coldly in a cloudless sky, and the breath of the passers-by blew out into smoke like so many pistol shots. Our footfalls rang out crisply and loudly as we swung through the doctors' quarter, Wimpole Street and Harley Street, and so through Wigmore Street into Oxford Street. In a quarter of an hour we were in Bloomsbury at the Alpha Inn, which is a small public-house at the corner of one of the streets which runs down into Holborn. Holmes pushed open the door of the private bar and ordered two glasses of beer from the ruddy-faced, white-aproned landlord.

'Your beer should be excellent if it is as good as your geese,' said he.

'My geese!' The man seemed surprised.

'Yes. I was speaking only half an hour ago to Mr Henry Baker, who was a member of your goose club.'

'Ah! yes, I see. But you see, sir, them's not *our* geese.'

'Indeed! Whose, then?'

'Well, I got the two dozen from a salesman in Covent Garden.'

'Indeed? I know some of them. Which was it?'

'Breckinridge is his name.'

'Ah! I don't know him. Well, here's your good health, landlord, and prosperity to your house. Good-night.'

'Now for Mr Breckinridge,' he continued, buttoning up his coat as we came out into the frosty air. 'Remember, Watson, that though we have so homely a thing as a goose at one end of this chain, we have at the other a man who will certainly get seven years' penal servitude unless we can establish his innocence. It is possible that our inquiry may but confirm his guilt; but, in any case, we have a line of investigation which has been missed by the police, and which a singular chance has placed in our hands. Let us follow it out to the bitter end. Faces to the south, then, and quick march!'

We passed across Holborn, down Endell Street, and so through a zigzag of slums to Covent Garden Market. One of the largest stalls bore the name of Breckinridge upon it, and the proprietor, a horsey-looking man, with a sharp face and trim side-whiskers, was helping a boy to put up the shutters.

'Good-evening. It's a cold night,' said Holmes.

The salesman nodded and shot a questioning glance at my companion.

'Sold out of geese, I see,' continued Holmes, pointing at the bare slabs of marble.

'Let you have five hundred tomorrow morning.'

'That's no good.'

'Well, there are some on the stall with the gas-flare.'

'Ah, but I was recommended to you.'

'Who by?'

'The landlord of the Alpha.'

'Oh, yes; I sent him a couple of dozen.'

'Fine birds they were, too. Now where did you get them from?'

To my surprise the question provoked a burst of anger from the salesman.

'Now, then, mister,' said he, with his head cocked and his arms akimbo, 'what are you driving at? Let's have it straight, now.'

'It is straight enough. I should like to know who sold you the geese which you supplied to the Alpha.'

'Well, then, I shan't tell you. So now!'

'Oh, it is a matter of no importance; but I don't know why you should be so warm over such a trifle.'

'Warm! You'd be as warm, maybe, if you were as pestered as I am. When I pay good money for a good article there should be an end of the business; but it's, "Where are the geese?" and, "Who did you sell the geese to?" and, "What will you take for the geese?" One would think they were the only geese in the world, to hear the fuss that is made over them.'

'Well, I have no connection with any other people who have been making enquiries,' said Holmes carelessly. 'If you won't tell us the bet is off, that is all. But I'm always ready to back my opinion on a matter of fowls, and I have a fiver on it that the bird I ate is country bred.'

'Well, then, you've lost your fiver, for it's town bred,' snapped the salesman.

'It's nothing of the kind.'

'I say it is.'

'I don't believe it.'

'D'you think you know more about fowls than I, who have handled them ever since I was a nipper? I tell you, all those birds that went to the Alpha were town bred.'

'You'll never persuade me to believe that.'

'Will you bet, then?'

'It's merely taking your money, for I know that I am right. But I'll have a sovereign on with you, just to teach you not to be obstinate.'

The salesman chuckled grimly. 'Bring me the books, Bill,' said he.

The small boy brought round a small thin volume and a great greasy-backed one, laying them out together beneath the hanging lamp.

'Now then, Mr Cocksure,' said the salesman, 'I thought that I was out of geese, but before I finish you'll find that there is still one left in my shop. You see this little book?'

'Well?'

'That's the list of the folk from whom I buy. D'you see? Well, then, here on this page are the country folk, and the numbers after their names are where their accounts are in the big ledger. Now, then! You see this other page in red ink? Well, that is a list of my town suppliers. Now, look at that third name. Just read it out to me.'

'Mrs Oakshott, 117 Brixton Road – 249,' read Holmes.

'Quite so. Now turn that up in the ledger.'

Holmes turned to the page indicated. 'Here you are, "Mrs Oakshott, 117 Brixton Road, egg and poultry supplier".'

'Now, then, what's the last entry?'

' "December 22nd. Twenty-four geese at 7s. 6d." '

'Quite so. There you are. And underneath?'

' "Sold to Mr Windigate of the Alpha, at 12s." '

'What have you to say now?'

Sherlock Holmes looked deeply chagrined. He drew a sovereign from his pocket and threw it down upon the slab, turning away with the air of a man whose disgust is too deep for words. A few yards off he stopped under a lamp-post and laughed in the hearty, noiseless fashion which was peculiar to him.

'When you see a man with whiskers of that cut and the "pink 'un" protruding out of his pocket, you can always draw him by a bet,' said he. 'I dare say that if I had put a hundred pounds down in front of him, that man would not have given me such complete information as was drawn from him by the idea that he was doing me on a wager. Well, Watson, we are, I fancy, nearing the end of our quest, and the only point which remains to be determined is whether we should go on to this Mrs Oakshott tonight, or whether we should reserve it for tomorrow. It is clear from what that surly fellow said that there are others besides ourselves who are anxious about the matter, and I should — '

His remarks were suddenly cut short by a loud hubbub which broke out from the stall which we had just left. Turning round we saw a little rat-faced fellow standing in the centre of the circle of yellow light which was thrown by the swinging lamp, while Breckinridge, the salesman, framed in the door of his stall, was shaking his fists fiercely at the cringing figure.

'I've had enough of you and your geese,' he shouted. 'I wish you were all at the devil together. If you come pestering me any more with your silly talk, I'll set the dog at you. You bring Mrs Oakshott here and I'll answer her, but what have you to do with it? Did I buy the geese off you?'

'No; but one of them was mine all the same,' whined the little man.

'Well, then, ask Mrs Oakshott for it.'

'She told me to ask you.'

'Well, you can ask the King of Proosia, for all I care. I've had enough of it. Get out of this!' He rushed fiercely forward, and the enquirer flitted away into the darkness.

'Ha! this may save us a visit to Brixton Road,' whispered Holmes. 'Come with me, and we will see what is to be made of this fellow.' Striding through the scattered knots of people who lounged round the flaring stalls, my companion speedily overtook the little man and touched him upon the shoulder. He sprang round, and I could see in the gaslight that every vestige of colour had been driven from his face.

'Who are you, then? What do you want?' he asked in a quavering voice.

'You will excuse me,' said Holmes blandly, 'but I could not help over-hearing the questions which you put to the salesman just now. I think that I could be of assistance to you.'

'You? Who are you? How could you know anything of the matter?'

'My name is Sherlock Holmes. It is my business to know what other people don't know.'

'But you can know nothing of this!'

'Excuse me, I know everything of it. You are endeavouring to trace some geese which were sold by Mrs Oakshott of Brixton Road to a salesman named Breckinridge, by him in turn to Mr Windigate of the Alpha, and by him to his club, of which Mr Henry Baker is a member.'

'Oh, sir, you are the very man whom I have longed to meet,' cried the little fellow, with outstretched hands and quivering fingers. 'I can hardly explain to you how interested I am in this matter.'

Sherlock Holmes hailed a four-wheeler which was passing. 'In that case we had better discuss it in a cosy room rather than in this windswept market-place,' said he. 'But pray tell me, before we go farther, who it is that I have the pleasure of assisting.'

The man hesitated for an instant. 'My name is John Robinson,' he answered with a sidelong glance.

'No, no; the real name,' said Holmes sweetly. 'It is always awkward doing business with an alias.'

A flush sprang to the white cheeks of the stranger. 'Well then,' said he, 'my real name is James Ryder.'

'Precisely so. Head attendant at the Hotel Cosmopolitan. Pray step into the cab, and I shall soon be able to tell you everything which you would wish to know.'

The little man stood glancing from one to the other of us with half-frightened, half-hopeful eyes, as one who is not sure whether he is on the verge of a windfall or of a catastrophe. Then he stepped into the cab, and in half an hour we were back in the sitting-room at Baker Street. Nothing had been said during our drive, but the high, thin breathing of our new companion, and the claspings and unclaspings of his hands, spoke of the nervous tension within him.

'Here we are!' said Holmes cheerily as we filed into the room. 'The fire looks very seasonable in this weather. You look cold, Mr Ryder. Pray take the basket-chair. I will just put on my slippers before we settle this little matter of yours. Now, then! You want to know what became of those geese?'

'Yes, sir.'

'Or rather, I fancy, of that goose. It was one bird, I imagine, in which you were interested – white, with a black bar across the tail.'

Ryder quivered with emotion. 'Oh, sir,' he cried, 'can you tell me where it went to?'

'It came here.'

'Here?'

'Yes, and a most remarkable bird it proved. I don't wonder that you should take an interest in it. It laid an egg after it was dead – the bonniest, brightest little blue egg that ever was seen. I have it here in my museum.'

Our visitor staggered to his feet and clutched the mantelpiece with his right hand. Holmes unlocked his strong-box and held up the blue carbuncle, which shone out like a star with a cold, brilliant, many-pointed radiance. Ryder stood glaring with a drawn face, uncertain whether to claim or to disown it.

'The game's up, Ryder,' said Holmes quietly. 'Hold up, man, or you'll be into the fire! Give him an arm back into his chair, Watson. He's not got blood enough to go in for felony with impunity. Give him a dash of brandy. So! Now he looks a little more human. What a shrimp it is, to be sure!'

For a moment he had staggered and nearly fallen, but the brandy brought a tinge of colour into his cheeks, and he sat staring with frightened eyes at his accuser.

'I have almost every link in my hands, and all the proofs which I could possibly need, so there is little which you need tell me. Still, that little may as well be cleared up to make the case complete. You had heard, Ryder, of this blue stone of the Countess of Morcar's?'

'It was Catherine Cusack who told me of it,' said he, in a crackling voice.

'I see – her ladyship's waiting-maid. Well, the temptation of sudden wealth so easily acquired was too much for you, as it has been for better men before you; but you were not very scrupulous in the means you used. It seems to me, Ryder, that there is the making of a very pretty villain in you. You knew that this man Horner, the plumber, had been concerned in some such matter before, and that suspicion would rest the more readily upon him. What did you do, then? You made some small job in my lady's room – you and your confederate Cusack – and you managed that he should be the man sent for. Then, when he had left, you rifled the jewel-case, raised the alarm, and had this unfortunate man arrested. You then — '

Ryder threw himself down suddenly upon the rug and clutched at my companion's knees. 'For God's sake, have mercy!' he shrieked. 'Think of my father! Of my mother! It would break their hearts. I never went wrong before! I never will again. I swear it. I'll swear it on a Bible. Oh, don't bring it into court! For Christ's sake, don't!'

'Get back into your chair!' said Holmes sternly. 'It is very well to cringe and crawl now, but you thought little enough of this poor Horner in the dock for a crime of which he knew nothing.'

'I will fly, Mr Holmes. I will leave the country, sir. Then the charge against him will break down.'

'Hum! We will talk about that. And now let us hear a true account of the next act. How came the stone into the goose, and how came the goose into the open market? Tell us the truth, for there lies your only hope of safety.'

Ryder passed his tongue over his parched lips. 'I will tell you it just as it happened, sir,' said he. 'When Horner had been arrested, it seemed to me that it would be best for me to get away with the stone at once, for I did not know at what moment the police might not take it into their heads to search me and my room. There was no place about the hotel where it would be safe. I went out, as if on some commission, and I made for my sister's house. She had married a man named Oakshott, and lived in Brixton Road, where she fattened fowls for the market. All the way there every man I met seemed to me to be a policeman or a detective; and, for all that it was a cold night, the sweat was pouring down my face before I came to the Brixton Road. My sister asked me what was the matter, and why I was so pale; but I told her that I had been upset by the jewel robbery at the hotel. Then I went into the back-yard and smoked a pipe and wondered what it would be best to do.

'I had a friend once called Maudsley, who went to the bad, and has just been serving his time in Pentonville. One day he had met me, and fell into talk about the ways of thieves, and how they could get rid of what they stole. I knew that he would be true to me, for I knew one or two things about him, so I made up my mind to go right on to Kilburn, where he lived, and take him into my confidence. He would show me how to turn the stone into money. But how to get to him in safety? I thought of the agonies I had gone through in coming from the hotel. I might at any moment be seized and searched, and there would be the stone in my waistcoat pocket. I was leaning against the wall at the time and looking at the geese which were waddling about round my feet, and suddenly an idea came into my head which showed me how I could beat the best detective that ever lived.

'My sister had told me some weeks before that I might have the pick of her geese for a Christmas present, and I knew that she was always as good as her word. I would take my goose now, and in it I would carry my stone to Kilburn. There was a little shed in the yard, and behind this I drove one of the birds – a fine big one, white, with a barred tail. I caught it, and prising its bill open, I thrust the stone down its throat as far as my finger could reach. The bird gave a gulp, and I felt the stone pass along its gullet and down into its crop. But the creature flapped and struggled, and out came my sister to know what was the matter. As I turned to speak to her the brute broke loose and fluttered off among the others.

' "Whatever were you doing with that bird, Jem?" says she.

' "Well," said I, "you said you'd give me one for Christmas, and I was feeling which was the fattest."

' "Oh," says she, "we've set yours aside for you – Jem's bird, we call it. It's the big white one over yonder. There's twenty-six of them, which makes one for you, and one for us, and two dozen for the market."

' "Thank you, Maggie," says I; "but if it is all the same to you, I'd rather have that one I was handling just now."

' "The other is a good three pound heavier," said she, "and we fattened it expressly for you."

' "Never mind. I'll have the other, and I'll take it now," said I.

' "Oh, just as you like," said she, a little huffed. "Which is it you want, then?"

' "That white one with the barred tail, right in the middle of the flock."

' "Oh, very well. Kill it and take it with you."

'Well, I did what she said, Mr Holmes, and I carried the bird all the way to Kilburn. I told my pal what I had done, for he was a man that it was easy to tell a thing like that to. He laughed until he choked, and we got a knife and opened the goose. My heart turned to water, for there was no sign of the stone, and I knew that some terrible mistake had occurred. I left the bird, rushed back to my sister's, and hurried into the back-yard. There was not a bird to be seen there.

' "Where are they all, Maggie?" I cried.

' "Gone to the dealer's, Jem."

' "Which dealer's?"

' "Breckinridge, of Covent Garden."

' "But was there another with a barred tail?" I asked, "the same as the one I chose?"

' "Yes, Jem; there were two barred-tailed ones, and I could never tell them apart."

'Well, then, of course I saw it all, and I ran off as hard as my feet would carry me to this man Breckinridge; but he had sold the lot at once, and not one word would he tell me as to where they had gone. You heard him yourselves tonight. Well, he has always answered me like that. My sister thinks that I am going mad. Sometimes I think that I am myself. And now – and now I am myself a branded thief, without ever having touched the wealth for which I sold my character. God help me! God help me!' He burst into convulsive sobbing, with his face buried in his hands.

There was a long silence, broken only by his heavy breathing and by the measured tapping of Sherlock Holmes's fingertips upon the edge of the table. Then my friend rose and threw open the door.

'Get out!' said he.

'What, sir! Oh, heaven bless you!'

'No more words. Get out!'

And no more words were needed. There was a rush, a clatter upon the stairs, the bang of a door and the crisp rattle of running footfalls from the street.

'After all, Watson,' said Holmes, reaching up his hand for his clay pipe, 'I am not retained by the police to supply their deficiencies. If Horner were in danger it would be another thing; but this fellow will not appear against him, and the case must collapse. I suppose that I am commuting a felony, but it is just possible that I am saving a soul. This fellow will not go wrong again; he is too terribly frightened. Send him to gaol now, and you make him a gaolbird for life. Besides, it is the season of forgiveness. Chance has put in our way a most singular and whimsical problem, and its solution is its own reward. If you will have the goodness to touch the bell, doctor, we will begin another investigation, in which also a bird will be the chief feature.'

Silver Blaze

'I am afraid, Watson, that I shall have to go,' said Holmes, as we sat down together to our breakfast one morning.

'Go! Where to?'

'To Dartmoor; to King's Pyland.'

I was not surprised. Indeed, my only wonder was that he had not already been mixed up in this extraordinary case, which was the one topic of conversation through the length and breadth of England. For a whole day my companion had rambled about the room with his chin upon his chest and his brows knitted, charging and recharging his pipe with the strongest black tobacco, and absolutely deaf to any of my questions or remarks. Fresh editions of every paper had been sent up by our newsagent, only to be glanced over and tossed down into a corner. Yet, silent as he was, I knew perfectly well what it was over which he was brooding. There was but one problem before the public which could challenge his powers of analysis, and that was the singular disappearance of the favourite for the Wessex Cup, and the tragic murder of its trainer. When, therefore, he suddenly announced his intention of setting out for the scene of the drama it was only what I had both expected and hoped for.

'I should be most happy to go down with you if I should not be in the way,' said I.

'My dear Watson, you would confer a great favour upon me by coming. And I think that your time will not be misspent, for there are points about the case which promise to make it an absolutely unique one. We have, I think, just time to catch our train at Paddington, and I will go further into the matter upon our journey. You would oblige me by bringing with you your very excellent field-glass.'

And so it happened that an hour or so later I found myself in the corner of a first-class carriage flying along en route for Exeter, while Sherlock Holmes, with his sharp, eager face framed in his ear-flapped travelling-cap, dipped rapidly into the bundle of fresh papers which he had procured at Paddington. We had left Reading far behind us before he thrust the last one of them under the seat, and offered me his cigar-case.

'We are going well,' said he, looking out of the window and glancing at his watch. 'Our rate at present is fifty-three and a half miles an hour.'

'I have not observed the quarter-mile posts,' said I.

'Nor have I. But the telegraph posts upon this line are sixty yards apart, and the calculation is a simple one. I presume that you have looked into this matter of the murder of John Straker and the disappearance of Silver Blaze?'

'I have seen what the *Telegraph* and the *Chronicle* have to say.'

'It is one of those cases where the art of the reasoner should be used rather for the sifting of details than for the acquiring of fresh evidence. The tragedy has been so uncommon, so complete and of such personal importance to so many people, that we are suffering from a plethora of surmise, conjecture, and hypothesis. The difficulty is to detach the framework of fact – of absolute undeniable fact – from the embellishments of theorists and reporters. Then, having established ourselves upon this sound basis, it is our duty to see what inferences may be drawn and what are the special points upon which the whole mystery turns. On Tuesday evening I received telegrams from both Colonel Ross, the owner of the horse, and from Inspector Gregory, who is looking after the case, inviting my co-operation.'

'Tuesday evening!' I exclaimed. 'And this is Thursday morning. Why didn't you go down yesterday?'

'Because I made a blunder, my dear Watson – which is, I am afraid, a more common occurrence than anyone would think who only knew me through your memoirs. The fact is that I could not believe it possible that the most remarkable horse in England could long remain concealed, especially in so sparsely inhabited a place as the north of Dartmoor. From hour to hour yesterday I expected to hear that he had been found, and that his abductor was the murderer of John Straker. When, however, another morning had come, and I found that beyond the arrest of young Fitzroy Simpson nothing had been done, I felt that it was time for me to take action. Yet in some ways I feel that yesterday has not been wasted.'

'You have formed a theory, then?'

'At least I have got a grip of the essential facts of the case. I shall enumerate them to you, for nothing clears up a case so much as stating it to another person, and I can hardly expect your co-operation if I do not show you the position from which we start.'

I lay back against the cushions, puffing at my cigar, while Holmes, leaning forward, with his long, thin forefinger checking off the points upon the palm of his left hand, gave me a sketch of the events which had led to our journey.

'Silver Blaze,' said he, 'is from the Isonomy stock, and holds as brilliant a record as his famous ancestor. He is now in his fifth year, and has brought in turn each of the prizes of the turf to Colonel Ross, his fortunate owner. Up to the time of the catastrophe he was the first favourite for the Wessex Cup, the betting being three to one on him. He has always, however, been a prime favourite with the racing public, and has never yet disappointed them, so that even at those odds enormous sums of money have been laid upon him. It is obvious, therefore, that there were many people who had the strongest interest in preventing Silver Blaze from being there at the fall of the flag next Tuesday.

'The fact was, of course, appreciated at King's Pyland, where the colonel's training-stable is situated. Every precaution was taken to guard the favourite. The trainer, John Straker, is a retired jockey who rode in Colonel Ross's colours before he became too heavy for the weighing-chair. He has served the colonel for five years as jockey and for seven as trainer, and has always shown himself to be a zealous and honest servant. Under him were three lads; for the establishment was a small one, containing only four horses in all. One of these lads sat up each night in the stable, while the others slept in the loft. All three bore excellent characters. John Straker, who is a married man, lived in a small villa about two hundred yards from the stables. He has no children, keeps one maidservant, and is comfortably off. The country round is very lonely, but about half a mile to the north there is a small cluster of villas which have been built by a Tavistock contractor for the use of invalids and others who may wish to enjoy the pure Dartmoor air. Tavistock itself lies two miles to the west, while across the moor, also about two miles distant, is the larger training establishment of Capleton, which belongs to Lord Backwater, and is managed by Silas Brown. In every other direction the moor is a complete wilderness, inhabited only by a few roaming gypsies. Such was the general situation last Monday night when the catastrophe occurred.

'On that evening the horses had been exercised and watered as usual, and the stables were locked up at nine o'clock. Two of the lads walked up to the trainer's house, where they had supper in the kitchen, while the third, Ned Hunter, remained on guard. At a few minutes after nine the maid, Edith Baxter, carried down to the stables his supper, which consisted of a dish of curried mutton. She took no liquid, as there was a water-tap in the stables, and it was the rule that the lad on duty should drink nothing else. The maid carried a lantern with her, as it was very dark and the path ran across the open moor.

'Edith Baxter was within thirty yards of the stables, when a man appeared out of the darkness and called to her to stop. As he stepped into the circle of yellow light thrown by the lantern she saw that he was a person of gentlemanly bearing, dressed in a grey suit of tweeds, with a cloth cap. He wore gaiters, and carried a heavy stick with a knob to it. She was most impressed, however, by the extreme pallor of his face and by the nervousness of his manner. His age, she thought, would be rather over thirty than under it.

' "Can you tell me where I am?" he asked. "I had almost made up my mind to sleep on the moor, when I saw the light of your lantern."

' "You are close to the King's Pyland training-stables," said she.

' "Oh, indeed! What a stroke of luck!" he cried. "I understand that a stable-boy sleeps there alone every night. Perhaps that is his supper which you are carrying to him. Now I am sure that you would not be too proud to earn the price of a new dress, would you?" He took a piece of white paper folded up out of his waistcoat pocket. "See that the boy has this tonight, and you shall have the prettiest frock that money can buy."

'She was frightened by the earnestness of his manner, and ran past him to the window through which she was accustomed to hand the meals. It was already opened, and Hunter was seated at the small table inside. She had begun to tell him of what had happened, when the stranger came up again.

' "Good-evening," said he, looking through the window. "I wanted to have a word with you." The girl has sworn that as he spoke she noticed the corner of the little paper packet protruding from his closed hand.

' "What business have you here?" asked the lad.

' "It's business that may put something into your pocket," said the other. "You've two horses in for the Wessex Cup – Silver Blaze and Bayard. Let me have the straight tip and you won't be a loser. Is it a fact that at the weights Bayard could give the other a hundred yards in five furlongs, and that the stable have put their money on him?"

' "So, you're one of those damned touts!" cried the lad. "I'll show you how we serve them in King's Pyland." He sprang up and rushed across the stable to unloose the dog. The girl fled away to the house, but as she ran she looked back and saw that the stranger was leaning through the window. A minute later, however, when Hunter rushed out with the hound he was gone, and though he ran all round the buildings he failed to find any trace of him.'

'One moment,' I asked. 'Did the stable-boy, when he ran out with the dog, leave the door unlocked behind him?'

'Excellent, Watson, excellent!' murmured my companion. 'The importance of the point struck me so forcibly that I sent a special wire to Dartmoor yesterday to clear the matter up. The boy locked the door before he left it. The window, I may add, was not large enough for a man to get through.

'Hunter waited until his fellow-grooms had returned, when he sent a message to the trainer and told him what had occurred. Straker was excited at hearing the account, although he does not seem to have quite realised its true significance. It left him, however, vaguely uneasy, and Mrs Straker, waking at one in the morning, found that he was dressing. In reply to her enquiries, he said that he could not sleep on account of his anxiety about the horses, and that he intended to walk down to the stables to see that all was well. She begged him to remain at home, as she could hear the rain pattering against the window, but in spite of her entreaties he pulled on his large mackintosh and left the house.

'Mrs Straker awoke at seven in the morning, to find that her husband had not yet returned. She dressed herself hastily, called the maid, and set off for the stables. The door was open; inside, huddled together upon a chair, Hunter was sunk in a state of absolute stupor, the favourite's stall was empty, and there were no signs of his trainer.

'The two lads who slept in the chaff-cutting loft above the harness-room were quickly roused. They had heard nothing during the night, for they are both sound sleepers. Hunter was obviously under the influence of some powerful drug, and as no sense could be got out of him, he was left to sleep it off while the two lads and the two women ran out in search of the absentees. They still had hopes that the trainer had for some reason taken out the horse for early exercise, but on ascending the knoll near the house, from which all the neighbouring moors were visible, they not only could see no signs of the missing favourite, but they perceived something which warned them that they were in the presence of a tragedy.

'About a quarter of a mile from the stables John Straker's overcoat was flapping from a furze bush. Immediately beyond there was a bowl-shaped depression in the moor, and at the bottom of this was found the dead body of the unfortunate trainer. His head had been shattered by a savage blow from some heavy weapon, and he was wounded on the thigh, where there was a long, clean cut, inflicted evidently by some very sharp instrument. It was clear, however, that Straker had defended himself vigorously against his assailants, for in his right hand he held a small knife, which was clotted with blood up to the handle, while in his left he clasped a red and black silk cravat, which was recognised by the maid as having been worn on the preceding evening by the stranger who had visited the stables. Hunter, on recovering from his stupor, was also quite positive as to the ownership of the cravat. He was equally certain that the same stranger had, while standing at the window, drugged his curried mutton, and so deprived the stables of their watchman. As to the missing horse, there were abundant proofs in the mud which lay at the bottom of the fatal hollow that he had been there at the time of the struggle. But from that morning he has disappeared, and although a large reward has been offered, and all the gypsies of Dartmoor are on the alert, no news has come of him. Finally, an analysis has shown that the remains of his supper left by the stable-lad contain an appreciable quantity of powdered opium, while the people at the house partook of the same dish on the same night without any ill effect.

'Those are the main facts of the case, stripped of all surmise, and stated as baldly as possible. I shall now recapitulate what the police have done in the matter.

'Inspector Gregory, to whom the case has been committed, is an extremely competent officer. Were he but gifted with imagination he might rise to great heights in his profession. On his arrival he promptly found and arrested the man upon whom suspicion naturally rested. There was little difficulty in finding him, for he inhabited one of those villas which I have mentioned. His name, it appears, was Fitzroy Simpson. He was a man of excellent birth and education, who had squandered a fortune upon the turf, and who lived now by doing a little quiet and genteel book-making in the sporting clubs of London. An examination of his betting-book shows that bets to the amount of five thousand pounds had been registered by him against the favourite. On being arrested he volunteered the statement that he had come down to Dartmoor in the hope of getting some information about the King's Pyland horses, and also about Desborough, the second favourite, which was in charge of Silas Brown at the Capleton stables. He did not attempt to deny that he had acted as described upon the evening before, but declared that he had no sinister designs, and had simply wished to obtain first-hand information. When confronted with his cravat, he turned very pale, and was utterly unable to account for its presence in the hand of the murdered man. His wet clothing showed that he had been out in the storm of the night before, and his stick, which was a Penang-lawyer weighted with lead, was just such a weapon as might, by repeated blows, have inflicted the terrible injuries to which the trainer had succumbed. On the other hand, there was no wound upon his person, while the state of Straker's knife would show that one at least of his assailants must bear his mark upon him. There you have it all in a nutshell, Watson, and if you can give me any light I shall be infinitely obliged to you.'

I had listened with the greatest interest to the statement which Holmes, with characteristic clearness, had laid before me. Though most of the facts were familiar to me, I had not sufficiently appreciated their relative importance, nor their connection to each other.

'Is it not possible,' I suggested, 'that the incised wound upon Straker may have been caused by his own knife in the convulsive struggles which follow any brain injury?'

'It is more than possible; it is probable,' said Holmes. 'In that case one of the main points in favour of the accused disappears.'

'And yet,' said I, 'even now I fail to understand what the theory of the police can be.'

'I am afraid that whatever theory we state has very grave objections to it,' returned my companion. 'The police imagine, I take it, that this Fitzroy Simpson, having drugged the lad, and having in some way obtained a duplicate key, opened the stable door and took out the horse, with the intention, apparently, of kidnapping him altogether. His bridle is missing, so that Simpson must have put this on. Then, having left the door open behind him, he was leading the horse away over the moor, when he was either met or overtaken by the trainer. A row naturally ensued. Simpson beat out the trainer's brains with his heavy stick without receiving any injury from the small knife which Straker used in self-defence, and then the thief either led the horse on to some secret hiding-place, or else it may have bolted during the struggle, and be now wandering out on the moors. That is the case as it appears to the police, and improbable as it is, all other explanations are more improbable still. However, I shall very quickly test the matter when I am once upon the spot, and until then I cannot really see how we can get much further than our present position.'

It was evening before we reached the little town of Tavistock, which lies, like the boss of a shield, in the middle of the huge circle of Dartmoor. Two gentlemen were awaiting us at the station – the one a tall, fair man with lion-like hair and beard and curiously penetrating light blue eyes; the other a small, alert person, very neat and dapper, in a frock-coat and gaiters, with trim little side-whiskers and an eyeglass. The latter was Colonel Ross, the well-known sportsman; the other, Inspector Gregory, a man who was rapidly making his name in the English detective service.

'I am delighted that you have come down, Mr Holmes,' said the colonel. 'The inspector here has done all that could possibly be suggested, but I wish to leave no stone unturned in trying to avenge poor Straker and in recovering my horse.'

'Have there been any fresh developments?' asked Holmes.

'I am sorry to say that we have made very little progress,' said the inspector. 'We have an open carriage outside, and as you would no doubt like to see the place before the light fails, we might talk it over as we drive.'

A minute later we were all seated in a comfortable landau, and were rattling through the quaint old Devonshire town. Inspector Gregory was full of his case, and poured out a

stream of remarks, while Holmes threw in an occasional question or interjection. Colonel Ross leaned back with his arms folded and his hat tilted over his eyes, while I listened with interest to the dialogue of the two detectives. Gregory was formulating his theory, which was almost exactly what Holmes had foretold in the train.

'The net is drawn pretty close round Fitzroy Simpson,' he remarked, 'and I believe myself that he is our man. At the same time I recognise that the evidence is purely circumstantial, and that some new development may upset it.'

'How about Straker's knife?'

'We have quite come to the conclusion that he wounded himself in his fall.'

'My friend Dr Watson made that suggestion to me as we came down. If so, it would tell against this man Simpson.'

'Undoubtedly. He has neither a knife nor any sign of a wound. The evidence against him is certainly very strong. He had a great interest in the disappearance of the favourite. He lies under suspicion of having poisoned the stable-boy, he was undoubtedly out in the storm, he was armed with a heavy stick, and his cravat was found in the dead man's hand. I really think we have enough to go before a jury.'

Holmes shook his head. 'A clever counsel would tear it all to rags,' said he. 'Why should he take the horse out of the stable? If he wished to injure it why could he not do it there? Has a duplicate key been found in his possession? What chemist sold him the powdered opium? Above all, where could he, a stranger to the district, hide a horse, and such a horse as this? What is his own explanation as to the paper which he wished the maid to give to the stable-boy?'

'He says that it was a ten-pound note. One was found in his purse. But your other difficulties are not so formidable as they seem. He is not a stranger to the district. He has twice lodged at Tavistock in the summer. The opium was probably brought from London. The key, having served its purpose, would be hurled away. The horse may be at the bottom of one of the pits or old mines upon the moor.'

'What does he say about the cravat?'

'He acknowledges that it is his, and declares that he had lost it. But a new element has been introduced into the case which may account for his leading the horse from the stable.'

Holmes pricked up his ears.

'We have found traces which show that a party of gypsies encamped on Monday night within a mile of the spot where the murder took place. On Tuesday they were gone. Now, presuming that there was some understanding between Simpson and these gypsies, might he not have been leading the horse to them when he was overtaken, and may they not have him now?'

'It is certainly possible.'

'The moor is being scoured for these gypsies. I have also examined every stable and outhouse in Tavistock, and for a radius of ten miles.'

'There is another training-stable quite close, I understand?'

'Yes, and that is a factor which we must certainly not neglect. As Desborough, their horse, was second in the betting, they had an interest in the disappearance of the favourite. Silas Brown, the trainer, is known to have had large bets upon the event, and he was no friend to poor Straker. We have, however, examined the stables, and there is nothing to connect him with the affair.'

'And nothing to connect this man Simpson with the interests of the Capleton stable?'

'Nothing at all.'

Holmes leaned back in the carriage, and the conversation ceased. A few minutes later our driver pulled up at a neat little redbrick villa with overhanging eaves, which stood by the road. Some distance off, across a paddock, lay a long grey-tiled outbuilding. In every other direction the low curves of the moor, bronze-coloured from the fading ferns, stretched away to the skyline, broken only by the steeples of Tavistock, and by a cluster of houses away to the westward which marked the Capleton stables. We all sprang out with the exception of Holmes, who continued to lean back with his eyes fixed upon the sky in front of him, entirely absorbed in his own thoughts. It was only when I touched his arm that he roused himself with a violent start and stepped out of the carriage.

'Excuse me,' said he, turning to Colonel Ross, who had looked at him in some surprise. 'I was daydreaming.' There was a gleam in his eyes and a suppressed excitement in his manner which convinced me, used as I was to his ways, that his hand was upon a clue, though I could not imagine where he had found it.

'Perhaps you would prefer at once to go on to the scene of the crime, Mr Holmes?' said Gregory.

'I think that I should prefer to stay here a little and go into one or two questions of detail. Straker was brought back here, I presume?'

'Yes; he lies upstairs. The inquest is tomorrow.'

'He has been in your service some years, Colonel Ross?'

'I have always found him an excellent servant.'

'I presume that you made an inventory of what he had in his pockets at the time of his death, inspector?'

'I have the things themselves in the sitting-room, if you would care to see them.'

'I should be very glad.'

We all filed into the front room and sat round the central table while the inspector unlocked a square tin box and laid a small heap of things before us. There was a box of vestas, two inches of tallow candle, an A. D. P. brier-root pipe, a pouch of sealskin with half an ounce of long-cut Cavendish, a silver watch with a gold chain, five sovereigns in gold, an aluminium pencil-case, a few papers, and an ivory-handled knife with a very delicate, inflexible blade marked Weiss & Co., London.

'This is a very singular knife,' said Holmes, lifting it up and examining it minutely. 'I presume, as I see bloodstains upon it, that it is the one which was found in the dead man's grasp. Watson, this knife is surely in your line?'

'It is what we call a cataract knife,' said I.

'I thought so. A very delicate blade devised for very delicate work. A strange thing for a man to carry with him upon a rough expedition, especially as it would not shut in his pocket.'

'The tip was guarded by a disc of cork which we found beside his body,' said the inspector. 'His wife tells us that the knife had lain upon the dressing-table, and that he had picked it up as he left the room. It was a poor weapon, but perhaps the best that he could lay his hands on at the moment.'

'Very possible. How about these papers?'

'Three of them are receipted hay-dealers' accounts. One of them is a letter of instructions from Colonel Ross. This other is a milliner's account for thirty-seven pounds fifteen made out by Madame Lesurier, of Bond Street, to William Derbyshire. Mrs Straker tells us that Derbyshire was a friend of her husband's and that occasionally his letters were addressed here.'

'Madame Derbyshire had somewhat expensive tastes,' remarked Holmes, glancing down the account. 'Twenty-two guineas is rather heavy for a single costume. However there appears to be nothing more to learn, and we may now go down to the scene of the crime.'

As we emerged from the sitting-room a woman, who had been waiting in the passage, took a step forward and laid her hand upon the inspector's sleeve. Her face was haggard and thin and eager, stamped with the print of a recent horror.

'Have you got them? Have you found them?' she panted.

'No, Mrs Straker. But Mr Holmes here has come from London to help us, and we shall do all that is possible.'

'Surely I met you in Plymouth at a garden-party some little time ago, Mrs Straker?' said Holmes.

'No, sir; you are mistaken.'

'Dear me! Why, I could have sworn to it.

You wore a costume of dove-coloured silk with ostrich-feather trimming.'

'I never had such a dress, sir,' answered the lady.

'Ah, that quite settles it,' said Holmes. And with an apology he followed the inspector outside. A short walk across the moor took us to the hollow in which the body had been found. At the brink of it was the furze bush upon which the coat had been hung.

'There was no wind that night, I understand,' said Holmes.

'None; but very heavy rain.'

'In that case the overcoat was not blown against the furze bush, but placed there.'

'Yes, it was laid across the bush.'

'You fill me with interest, I perceive that the ground has been tram-pled up a good deal. No doubt many feet have been here since Monday night.'

'A piece of matting has been laid here at the side, and we have all stood upon that.'

'Excellent.'

'In this bag I have one of the boots which Straker wore, one of Fitzroy Simpson's shoes, and a cast horseshoe of Silver Blaze.'

'My dear inspector, you surpass yourself!' Holmes took the bag, and, descending into the hollow, he pushed the matting into a more central position. Then stretching himself upon his face and leaning his chin upon his hands, he made a careful study of the trampled mud in front of him.

'Hullo!' said he, suddenly. 'What's this?'

It was a wax vesta, half burned, which was so coated with mud that it looked at first like a little chip of wood.

'I cannot think how I came to overlook it,' said the inspector, with an expression of annoyance.

'It was invisible, buried in the mud. I only saw it because I was looking for it.'

'What! You expected to find it?'

'I thought it not unlikely.'

He took the boots from the bag, and compared the impressions of each of them with marks upon the ground. Then he clambered up to the rim of the hollow, and crawled about among the ferns and bushes.

'I am afraid that there are no more tracks,' said the inspector. 'I have examined the ground very carefully for a hundred yards in each direction.'

'Indeed!' said Holmes, rising. 'I should not have the impertinence to do it again after what you say. But I should like to take a little walk over the moor before it grows dark, that I may know my ground tomorrow, and I think that I shall put this horseshoe into my pocket for luck.'

Colonel Ross, who had shown some signs of impatience at my companion's quiet and systematic method of work, glanced at his watch.

'I wish you would come back with me, inspector,' said he. 'There are several points on which I should like your advice, and especially as to whether we do not owe it to the public to remove our horse's name from the entries for the Cup.'

'Certainly not,' cried Holmes, with decision. 'I should let the name stand.'

The colonel bowed. 'I am very glad to have had your opinion, sir,' said he. 'You will find us at poor Straker's house when you have finished your walk, and we can drive together into Tavistock.'

He turned back with the inspector, while Holmes and I walked slowly across the moor. The sun was beginning to sink behind the stables of Capleton, and the long, sloping plain in front of us was tinged with gold, deepening into rich, ruddy browns where the faded ferns and brambles caught the evening light. But the glories of the landscape were all wasted upon my companion, who was sunk in the deepest thought.

'It's this way, Watson,' said he at last. 'We may leave the question of who killed John Straker for the instant, and confine ourselves to finding out what has become of the horse. Now, supposing that he broke away during or after the tragedy, where could he have gone to? The horse is a very gregarious creature. If left to himself his instincts would have been either to return to King's Pyland or go over to Capleton. Why should he run wild upon the moor? He would surely have been seen by now. And why should gypsies kidnap him? These people always clear out when they hear of trouble, for they do not wish to be pestered by the police. They could not hope to sell such a horse. They would run a great risk and gain nothing by taking him. Surely that is clear.'

'Where is he, then?'

'I have already said that he must have gone to King's Pyland or to Capleton. He is not at King's Pyland. Therefore he is at Capleton. Let us take that as a working hypothesis and see what it leads us to. This part of the moor, as the inspector remarked, is very hard and dry. But it falls away towards Capleton, and you can see from here that there is a long hollow over yonder, which must have been very wet on Monday night. If our supposition is correct, then the horse must have crossed that, and there is the point where we should look for his tracks.'

We had been walking briskly during this conversation, and a few more minutes brought us to the hollow in question. At Holmes's request I walked down the bank to the right, and he to the left, but I had not taken fifty paces before I heard him give a shout, and saw him waving his hand to me. The track of a horse was plainly outlined in the soft earth in front of him, and the shoe which he took from his pocket exactly fitted the impression.

'See the value of imagination,' said Holmes. 'It is the one quality which Gregory lacks. We imagined what might have happened, acted upon the supposition, and find ourselves justified. Let us proceed.'

We crossed the marshy bottom and passed over a quarter of a mile of dry, hard turf. Again the ground sloped, and again we came on the tracks. Then we lost them for half a mile, but only to pick them up once more quite close to Capleton. It was Holmes who saw them first, and he stood pointing with a look of triumph upon his face. A man's track was visible beside the horse's.

'The horse was alone before,' I cried.

'Quite so. It was alone before. Hullo, what is this?'

The double track turned sharp off and took the direction of King's Pyland. Holmes whistled, and we both followed along after it. His eyes were on the trail, but I happened to look a little to one side, and saw to my surprise the same tracks coming back again in the opposite direction.

'One for you, Watson,' said Holmes, when I pointed it out. 'You have saved us a long walk, which would have brought us back on our own traces. Let us follow the return track.'

We had not to go far. It ended at the paving of asphalt which led up to the gates of the Capleton stables. As we approached, a groom ran out from them.

'We don't want any loiterers about here,' said he.

'I only wished to ask a question,' said Holmes, with his finger and thumb in his waistcoat pocket. 'Should I be too early to see your master, Mr Silas Brown, if I were to call at five o'clock tomorrow morning?'

'Bless you, sir, if anyone is about he will be, for he is always the first stirring. But here he is, sir, to answer your questions for himself. No, sir, no; it is as much as my place is worth to let him see me touch your money. Afterwards, if you like.'

As Sherlock Holmes replaced the half-crown which he had drawn from his pocket, a fierce-looking elderly man strode out from the gate with a hunting-crop swinging in his hand.

'What's this, Dawson!' he cried. 'No gossiping! Go about your business! And you, what the devil do you want here?'

'Ten minutes' talk with you, my good sir,' said Holmes in the sweetest of voices.

'I've no time to talk to every gadabout. We want no stranger here. Be off, or you may find a dog at your heels.'

Holmes leaned forward and whispered something in the trainer's ear. He started violently and flushed to the temples.

'It's a lie!' he shouted, 'an infernal lie!'

'Very good. Shall we argue about it here in public or talk it over in your parlour?'

'Oh, come in if you wish to.'

Holmes smiled. 'I shall not keep you more than a few minutes, Watson,' said he. 'Now, Mr Brown, I am quite at your disposal.'

It was twenty minutes, and the reds had all faded into greys before Holmes and the trainer reappeared. Never have I seen such a change as had been brought about in Silas Brown in that short time. His face was ashy pale, beads of perspiration shone upon his brow, and his hands shook until the hunting-crop wagged like a branch in the wind. His bullying, overbearing manner was all gone too, and he cringed along at my companion's side like a dog with its master.

'You instructions will be done. It shall all be done,' said he.

'There must be no mistake,' said Holmes, looking round at him. The other winced as he read the menace in his eyes.

'Oh no, there shall be no mistake. It shall be there. Should I change it first or not?'

Holmes thought a little and then burst out laughing. 'No, don't,' said he; 'I shall write to you about it. No tricks, now, or — '

'Oh, you can trust me, you can trust me!'

'Yes, I think I can. Well, you shall hear from me tomorrow.' He turned upon his heel, disregarding the trembling hand which the other held out to him, and we set off for King's Pyland.

'A more perfect compound of the bully, coward, and sneak than Master Silas Brown I have seldom met with,' remarked Holmes as we trudged along together.

'He has the horse, then?'

'He tried to bluster out of it, but I described to him so exactly what his actions had been upon that morning that he is convinced that I was watching him. Of course you observed the peculiarly square toes in the impressions, and that his own boots exactly corresponded to them. Again, of course no subordinate would have dared to do such a thing. I described to him how, when according to his custom he was the first down, he perceived a strange horse wandering over the moor. How he went out to it, and his astonishment at recognising, from the white forehead which has given the favourite its name, that chance had put in his power the only horse which could beat the one upon which he had put his money. Then I described how his first impulse had been to lead him back to King's Pyland, and how the devil had shown him how he could hide the horse until the race was over, and how he had led it back and concealed it at Capleton. When I told him every detail he gave it up and thought only of saving his own skin.'

'But his stables had been searched?'

'Oh, an old horse-faker like him has many a dodge.'

'But are you not afraid to leave the horse in his power now, since he has every interest in injuring it?'

'My dear fellow, he will guard it as the apple of his eye. He knows that his only hope of mercy is to produce it safe.'

'Colonel Ross did not impress me as a man who would be likely to show much mercy in any case.'

'The matter does not rest with Colonel Ross. I follow my own methods, and tell as much or as little as I choose. That is the advantage of being unofficial. I don't know whether you observed it, Watson, but the colonel's manner has been just a trifle cavalier to me. I am inclined now to have a little amusement at his expense. Say nothing to him about the horse.'

'Certainly not, without your permission.'

'And of course this is all quite a minor point compared to the question of who killed John Straker.'

'And you will devote yourself to that?'

'On the contrary, we both go back to London by the night train.'

I was thunderstruck by my friend's words. We had only been a few hours in Devonshire, and that he should give up an investigation which he had begun so brilliantly was quite incomprehensible to me. Not a word more could I draw from him until we were back at the trainer's house. The colonel and the inspector were awaiting us in the parlour.

'My friend and I return to town by the midnight express,' said Holmes. 'We have had a charming little breath of your beautiful Dartmoor air.'

The inspector opened his eyes, and the colonel's lip curled in a sneer.

'So you despair of arresting the murderer of poor Straker,' said he.

Holmes shrugged his shoulders. 'There are certainly grave difficulties in the way,' said he. 'I have every hope, however, that your horse will start upon Tuesday, and I beg that you will have your jockey in readiness. Might I ask for a photograph of Mr John Straker?'

The inspector took one from an envelope and handed it to him.

'My dear Gregory, you anticipate all my wants. If I might ask you to wait here for an instant, I have a question which I should like to put to the maid.'

'I must say that I am rather disappointed in our London consultant,' said Colonel Ross, bluntly, as my friend left the room. 'I do not see that we are any further than when he came.'

'At least you have his assurance that your horse will run,' said I.

'Yes, I have his assurance,' said the colonel, with a shrug of his shoulders. 'I should prefer to have the horse.'

I was about to make some reply in defence of my friend when he entered the room again.

'Now, gentlemen,' said he, 'I am quite ready for Tavistock.'

As we stepped into the carriage one of the stable-lads held the door open for us. A sudden idea seemed to occur to Holmes, for he leaned forward and touched the lad upon the sleeve.

'You have a few sheep in the paddock,' he said. 'Who attends to them?'

'I do, sir.'

'Have you noticed anything amiss with them of late?'

'Well, sir, not of much account; but three of them have gone lame, sir.'

I could see that Holmes was extremely pleased, for he chuckled and rubbed his hands together.

'A long shot, Watson; a very long shot,' said he, pinching my arm. 'Gregory, let me recommend to your attention this singular epidemic among the sheep. Drive on, coachman!'

Colonel Ross still wore an expression which showed the poor opinion which he had formed of my companion's ability, but I saw by the inspector's face that his attention had been keenly aroused.

'You consider that to be important?' he asked.

'Exceedingly so.'

'Is there any point to which you would wish to draw my attention?'

'To the curious incident of the dog in the night-time.'

'The dog did nothing in the night-time.'

'That was the curious incident,' remarked Sherlock Holmes.

Four days later Holmes and I were again in the train, bound for Winchester to see the race for the Wessex Cup. Colonel Ross met us by appointment outside the station, and we drove in his drag to the course beyond the town. His face was grave, and his manner was cold in the extreme.

'I have seen nothing of my horse,' said he.

'I suppose you would know him if you saw him.' asked Holmes.

The colonel was very angry. 'I have been on the turf for twenty years, and never was asked such a question as that before,' said he. 'A child would know Silver Blaze, with his white forehead and his mottled off-foreleg.'

'How is the betting?'

'Well, that is the curious part of it. You could have got fifteen to one yesterday, but the price has become shorter and shorter, until you can hardly get three to one now.'

'Hum!' said Holmes. 'Somebody knows something, that is clear.'

As the drag drew up in the enclosure near the grandstand, I glanced at the card to see the entries.

Wessex Plate [it ran] 50 sovs each h ft with 1,000 sovs added for four and five year olds. Second, £300. Third, £200. New course (one mile and five furlongs). Mr Heath Newton's The Negro. Red cap. Cinnamon jacket. Colonel Wardlaw's Pugilist. Pink cap. Blue and black jacket. Lord Backwater's Desborough. Yellow cap and sleeves. Colonel Ross's Silver Blaze. Black cap. Red jacket. Duke of Balmoral's Iris. Yellow and black stripes. Lord Singleford's Rasper. Purple cap. Black sleeves.

'We scratched our other one, and put all hopes on your word,' said the colonel. 'Why, what is that? Silver Blaze favourite?'

'Five to four against Silver Blaze!' roared the ring. 'Five to four against Silver Blaze! Fifteen to five against Desborough! Five to four on the field!'

'There are the numbers up,' I cried. 'They are all six there.'

'All six there? Then my horse is running,' cried the colonel in great agitation. 'But I don't see him. My colours have not passed.'

'Only five have passed. This must be he.'

As I spoke a powerful bay horse swept out from the weighing-enclosure and cantered past us, bearing on its back the well-known black and red of the colonel.

'That's not my horse,' cried the owner. 'That beast has not a white hair upon its body. What is this that you have done, Mr Holmes?'

'Well, well, let us see how he gets on,' said my friend, imperturbably. For a few minutes he gazed through my field-glass. 'Capital! An excellent start!' he cried suddenly. 'There they are, coming round the curve!'

From our drag we had a superb view as they came up the straight. The six horses were so close together that a carpet could have covered them, but halfway up the yellow of the Capleton stable showed to the front. Before they reached us, however, Desborough's bolt was shot, and the colonel's horse, coming away with a rush, passed the post a good six lengths before its rival, the Duke of Balmoral's Iris making a bad third.

'It's my race, anyhow,' gasped the colonel, passing his hand over his eyes. 'I confess that I can make neither head nor tail of it. Don't you think that you have kept up your mystery long enough, Mr Holmes?'

'Certainly, colonel, you shall know everything. Let us all go round and have a look at the horse together. Here he is,' he continued, as we made our way into the weighing-enclosure, where only owners and their friends find admittance. 'You have only to wash his face and his leg in spirits of wine, and you will find that he is the same old Silver Blaze as ever.'

'You take my breath away!'

'I found him in the hands of a faker, and took the liberty of running him just as he was sent over.'

'My dear sir, you have done wonders. The horse looks very fit and well. It never went better in its life. I owe you a thousand apologies for having doubted your ability. You have done me a great service by recovering my horse. You would do me a greater still if you could lay your hands on the murderer of John Straker.'

'I have done so,' said Holmes quietly.

The colonel and I stared at him in amazement. 'You have got him! Where is he, then?'

'He is here.'

'Here! Where?'

'In my company at the present moment.'

The colonel flushed angrily. 'I quite recognise that I am under obligations to you, Mr Holmes,' said he, 'but I must regard what you have just said as either a very bad joke or an insult.'

Sherlock Holmes laughed. 'I assure you that I have not associated you with the crime, colonel,' said he. 'The real murderer is standing immediately behind you.' He stepped past and laid his hand upon the glossy neck of the thoroughbred.

'The horse!' cried both the colonel and myself.

'Yes, the horse. And it may lessen his guilt if I say that it was done in self-defence, and that John Straker was a man who was entirely unworthy of your confidence. But there goes the bell, and as I stand to win a little on this next race, I shall defer a lengthy explanation until a more fitting time.'

We had the corner of a Pullman car to ourselves that evening as we whirled back to London, and I fancy that the journey was a short one to Colonel Ross as well as to myself, as we listened to our companion's narrative of the events which had occurred at the Dartmoor training-stables upon the Monday night, and the means by which he had unravelled them.

'I confess,' said he, 'that any theories which I had formed from the newspaper reports were entirely erroneous. And yet there were indications there, had they not been overlaid by other details which concealed their true import. I went to Devonshire with the conviction that Fitzroy Simpson was the true culprit, although, of course, I saw that the evidence against him was by no means complete. It was while I was in the carriage, just as we reached the trainer's house, that the immense significance of the curried mutton occurred to me. You may remember that I was distrait, and remained sitting after you had all alighted. I was marvelling in my own mind how I could possibly have overlooked so obvious a clue.'

'I confess,' said the colonel, 'that even now I cannot see how it helps us.'

'It was the first link in my chain of reasoning. Powdered opium is by no means tasteless. The flavour is not disagreeable, but it is perceptible. Were it mixed with any ordinary dish the eater would undoubtedly detect it, and would probably eat no more. A curry was exactly the medium which would disguise this taste. By no possible supposition could this stranger, Fitzroy Simpson, have caused curry to be served in the trainer's family that night, and it is surely too monstrous a coincidence to suppose that he happened to come along with powdered opium upon the very night when a dish happened to be served which would disguise the flavour. That is unthinkable. Therefore Simpson becomes eliminated from the case, and our attention centres upon Straker and his wife, the only two people who could have chosen curried mutton for supper that night. The opium was added after the dish was set aside for the stable-boy, for the others had the same for supper with no ill effects. Which of them, then, had access to that dish without the maid seeing them?

'Before deciding that question I had grasped the significance of the silence of the dog, for one true inference invariably suggests others. The Simpson incident had shown me that a dog was kept in the stables, and yet, though someone had been in and had fetched out a horse, he had not barked enough to arouse the two lads in the loft. Obviously the midnight visitor was someone whom the dog knew well.

'I was already convinced, or almost convinced, that John Straker went down to the stables in the dead of the night and took out Silver Blaze. For what purpose? For a dishonest one, obviously, or why should he drug his own stable-boy? And yet I was at a loss to know why. There have been cases before now where trainers have made sure of great sums of money by laying against their own horses, through agents, and then preventing them from winning by fraud. Sometimes it is a pulling jockey. Sometimes it is some surer and subtler means. What was it here? I hoped that the contents of his pockets might help me to form a conclusion.

'And they did so. You cannot have forgotten the singular knife which was found in the dead man's hand, a knife which certainly no sane man would choose for a weapon. It was, as Dr Watson told us, a form of knife which is used for the most delicate operations known in surgery. And it was to be used for a delicate operation that night. You must know, with your wide experience of turf matters, Colonel Ross, that it is possible to make a slight nick upon the tendons of a horse's ham, and to do it subcutaneously, so as to leave absolutely no trace. A horse so treated would develop a slight lameness, which would be put down to a strain in exercise or a touch of rheumatism, but never to foul play.'

'Villain! Scoundrel!' cried the colonel.

'We have here the explanation of why John Straker wished to take the horse out on to the moor. So spirited a creature would have certainly roused the soundest of sleepers when it felt the prick of the knife. It was absolutely necessary to do it in the open air.'

'I have been blind!' cried the colonel. 'Of course that was why he needed the candle, and struck the match.'

'Undoubtedly. But in examining his belongings I was fortunate enough to discover not only the method of the crime, but even its motives.

343

As a man of the world, colonel, you know that men do not carry other people's bills about in their pockets. We have most of us quite enough to do to settle our own. I at once concluded that Straker was leading a double life, and keeping a second establishment. The nature of the bill showed that there was a lady in the case, and one who had expensive tastes. Liberal as you are with your servants, one can hardly expect that they can buy twenty-guinea walking dresses for their ladies. I questioned Mrs Straker as to the dress without her knowing it, and having satisfied myself that it had never reached her, I made a note of the milliner's address, and felt that by calling there with Straker's photograph I could easily dispose of the mythical Derbyshire.

'From that time on all was plain. Straker had led out the horse to a hollow where his light would be invisible. Simpson in his flight had dropped his cravat, and Straker had picked it up – with some idea, perhaps, that he might use it in securing the horse's leg. Once in the hollow, he had got behind the horse and had struck a light; but the creature, frightened at the sudden glare, and with the strange instinct of animals feeling that some mischief was intended, had lashed out, and the steel shoe had struck Straker full on the forehead. He had already, in spite of the rain, taken off his overcoat in order to do his delicate task, and so, as he fell, his knife gashed his thigh. Do I make it clear?'

'Wonderful!' cried the colonel. 'Wonderful! You might have been there!'

'My final shot was, I confess, a very long one. It struck me that so astute a man as Straker would not undertake this delicate tendon-nicking without a little practice. What could he practise on? My eyes fell upon the sheep, and I asked a question which, rather to my surprise, showed that my surmise was correct.

'When I returned to London I called upon the milliner, who had recognised Straker as an excellent customer of the name of Derbyshire, who had a very dashing wife, with a strong partiality for expensive dresses. I have no doubt that this woman had plunged him over head and ears in debt, and so led him into this miserable plot.'

'You have explained all but one thing,' cried the colonel. 'Where was the horse?'

'Ah, it bolted, and was cared for by one of your neighbours. We must have an amnesty in that direction, I think. This is Clapham Junction, if I am not mistaken, and we shall be in Victoria in less than ten minutes. If you care to smoke a cigar in our rooms, colonel, I shall be happy to give you any other details which might interest you.'